THE ANATALIAN THRONE

REBECCA MIKKELSON

AUTHORS 4 AUTHORS PUBLISHING
Marysville, WA, USA

Published by Authors 4 Authors Publishing
1214 6th St
Marysville, WA 98270
www.authors4authorspublishing.com

Library of Congress Control Number: 2022950406

E-book ISBN: 978-1-64477-157-0
Hardcover ISBN: 978-1-64477-159-4
Paperback ISBN: 978-1-64477-158-7
Audiobook ISBN: 978-1-64477-160-0

Edited by Renee Frey
Copyedited by Brandi Spencer

Cover design ©2022 Brandi Spencer. All rights reserved.
Interior design and map of Aratia by Brandi Spencer.

Authors 4 Authors Publishing branding is set in Bavire. Titles and headings are set in Beguns and Goudy Twenty. Correspondence is set in IM Fell and Gothic Ultra. All other text is set in Garamond.

THE ANATALIAN THRONE

REBECCA MIKKELSON

Authors 4 Authors Content Rating

This title has been rated S, appropriate adults, and contains:

- intense sex
- intense sexual violence
- rape
- domestic abuse
- strong language
- frequent alcohol use
- child death

Please, keep the following in mind when using our rating system:

1. A content rating is not a measure of quality.

Great stories can be found for every audience. One book with many content warnings and another with none at all may be of equal depth and sophistication. Our ratings can work both ways: to avoid content or to find it.

2. Ratings are merely a tool.

For our young adult (YA) and children's titles, age ratings are generalized suggestions. For parents, our descriptive ratings can help you make informed decisions, but at the end of the day, only you know what kinds of content are appropriate for your individual child. This is why we provide details in addition to the general age rating.

For more information on our rating system, please, visit our Content Guide at: www.authors4authorspublishing.com/books/ratings

DEDICATION

For Paige,

Your face, it's face pale face.

Thank you for being my very first reader
and finding all my funny errors with me.

WORKS BY REBECCA MIKKELSON

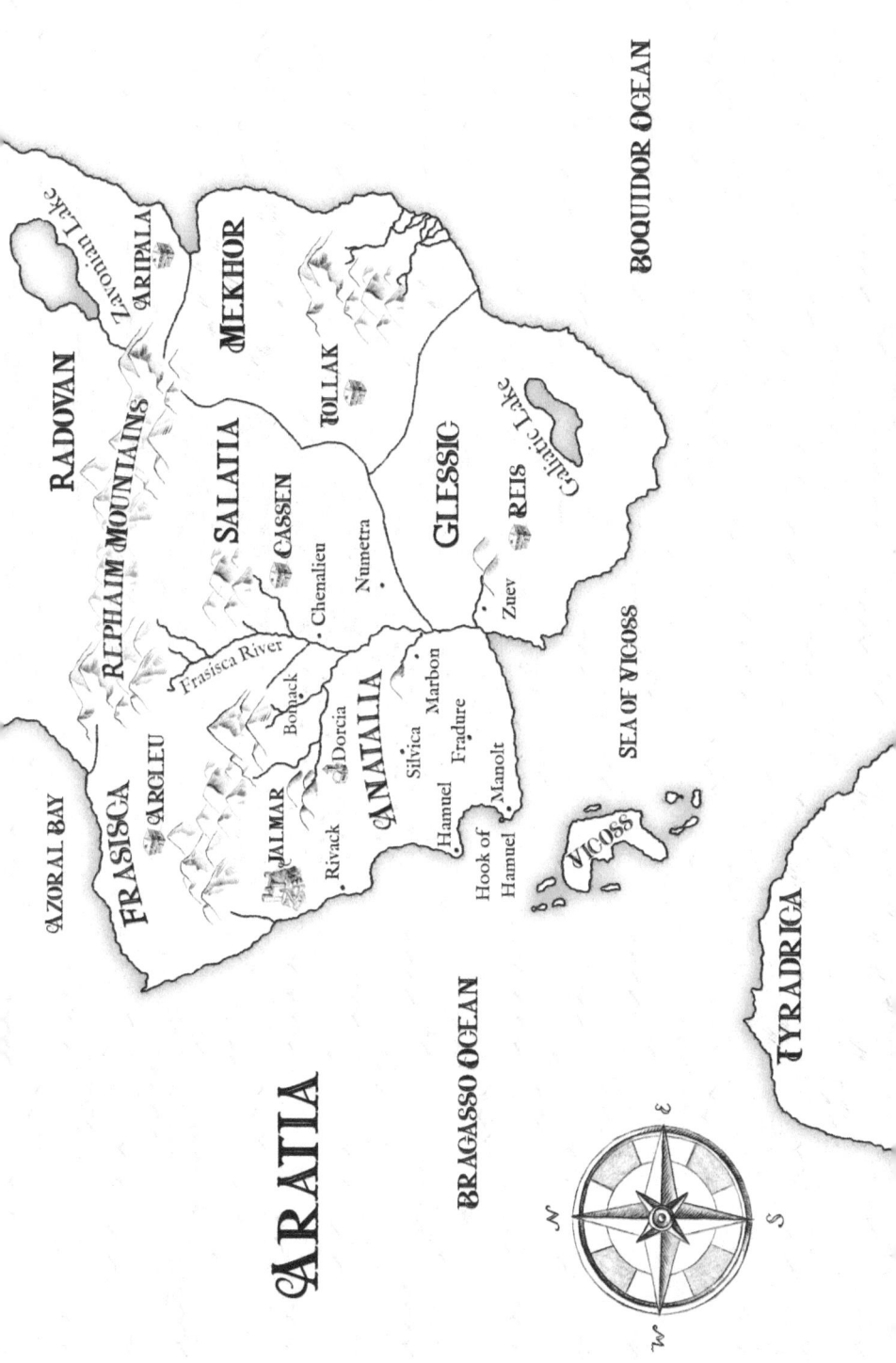

TABLE OF CONTENTS

 **1**

y king, she's here."

Sorren pulled himself from the window, looking back to his spymaster, Sir Germain Wouverman. "The Lady Margaret?"

Wouverman nodded. "She was spotted outside the city walls last night, Majesty."

Irritation quelled his excitement. "Then why are you only now telling me?" Sorren demanded.

"We waited for certainty," Wouverman said, not waiting for permission to approach the king. "What is it you would like us to do with her?"

"Nothing—for now." Sorren waved a dismissive hand at Wouverman, waiting until he was gone before turning back to the window. He held his chin, forefinger curled against his mouth as he watched dark clouds leisurely saunter toward the palace.

It had been nearly a year since Lord Nicholas Oliphant had returned to the capital with the news of Lady Margaret's betrayal before he died in the infirmary. She had helped the traitor and escaped prisoner, Liam Fulton, the simple foot soldier who had almost cost Sorren the war with Salatia. She'd thrown caution to the wind and helped the bastard—even fled with him to Theotes knew where— leaving Jerone, Sorren's good friend and her father, to die.

He knew she would not be able to avoid returning—with her father gone, she would need his permission to claim the title of countess to the lands her father had cultivated. All the while, Sorren waited patiently, mulling over the infinite possibilities for her punishment.

When rain began pattering against the thick glass of the window, Sorren poured himself a brandy. There was one punishment that he would enjoy more than all others.

A slow grin slid across his face.

Yes, he would enjoy it very much.

 **2**

iam could barely keep his eyes open as he rode Ashka into a small village three days' ride past the Salatian border. They had been traveling the entirety of the day, Liam regularly switching from riding to walking so as to not overburden his horse. They rested every few hours, stopping to eat or drink. It was well after dark when Liam finally dismounted in the village.

Rain pattered lightly on his shoulders, dampening the cotton of his cloak. Despite the late hour, there were still people about. The squelching of mud surrounded him as he ventured further into the town. Liam led Ashka, looking at the faces of the people who passed.

"Excuse me," he called, holding an arm out toward a man who passed.

The man kept his head down, ignoring Liam.

"Excuse me," he tried again and was similarly ignored. A woman dressed in blue homespun, her hem in tatters, was passing him when he finally got to the heart of it. "What is the name of this place?" Liam demanded.

"Numetra," she called over her shoulder when she passed him, continuing on her way.

Liam looked around. It seemed innocuous enough. There were few buildings on either side of the muddied road where people could purchase wares or eat— the focus would primarily be on the farmland surrounding them. It wasn't a place he had been before, but he would have to wander Aratia for several lifetimes to visit every single village.

He sought out the first place with a stable for Ashka. It was a tavern, the sign in front naming it the Frothing Wench. A stable boy was throwing down fresh hay when Liam entered. Only one other horse occupied one of the four stalls. The sweet smell of hay enticed Ashka, the bay's ears pointing forward. He let out a chuff, shaking his head.

"Excuse me, boy?" Liam called out, getting the child's attention. "How much for the night?"

The boy didn't look up from his work. "Six coppers."

"Rather steep, no?" Liam raised his brow.

"No." The boy glanced up at him, steely-eyed.

Sighing, Liam dug out the copper strals, placing them in the child's outstretched hand. "Are there rooms to rent here?"

"Inside." The boy went back to ignoring Liam, unsaddling Ashka and rubbing the horse down.

Liam shook his head, grabbing his saddle bag before entering the Frothing Wench. The tavern was surprisingly full, the roar of voices almost deafening. He searched the crowd for someone with a ring of keys on their belt. Such a man descended the back stairs—Liam assumed it led to rooms—and sat behind a small bar to the side of the establishment.

Liam went to the man. "Are you who I speak to in regards to a room?"

"Yes," the man said simply.

Liam quirked his brow.The stable boy must be his son. They certainly had the same penchant for monosyllabic answers.

"Are there any rooms available for the week?" he asked.

"There are."

"May I have one, and how much for the week?" Liam was already digging for money.

"The room is two gold and six copper strals," the man with the keys said.

Liam blanched. "Are there any cheaper rooms?"

"No." The man shook his head. "The price includes meals and drinks."

Breathing a sigh of relief, Liam set down the money. "Then I'll take the room, please."

The man quickly snatched the coins up, handing him a key with a number on it. "You'll find your room upstairs."

"Are the stables also included in the price?" Liam asked.

"Yes."

"Please tell the stable boy to return my six coppers before the end of my stay," Liam instructed, waiting until the proprietor nodded before he went to his new room.

It was sparse, holding only a bed and a night table. That was enough, he supposed. Liam hoped he would not be staying long at the Frothing Wench. Once Liam found work in Numetra, he would rent a room and bide his time to check on Margaret. No one knew him here—it would be safe enough.

He was sad to have left Margaret's company so soon after they had been reunited. She gave him hope again—her love of life and desire to make the people around her better never wavering with anything that happened to her. Even in the unthinkable.

His blood still boiled thinking about her attack. It had been so callous—so pointless. If only he had arrived the day before. If only he hadn't let Lord Stelios and Lady Adelena keep him rooted in place for so long. He could have protected her completely from the scars the rebel soldier inflicted—both physical and emotional. He had thought of many *if onlys* after he parted Margaret's company— they would only ever do her any good in his thoughts.

3

Liam slept uneasily, his night plagued with dreams. He bounced from place to place, never staying anywhere long in his dream world. He started awake when he heard his mother's screams in his sleep, heart thudding as he scanned his surroundings. Liam sighed in relief when he saw his sparse room and sank back into the bed.

Soon after closing his eyes, he found himself in front of a wooden cottage. Smoke poured out of the chimney, snow glistening in the sunlight. Liam turned his head sharply when snow crunched under several pairs of feet.

"Papa, papa!" one of the children running toward him yelled—there were six, all told.

Liam looked behind him for their father, letting out a surprised yell when he was knocked over by their small bodies. They were all giggling, throwing fistfuls of snow at him.

"Papa, play with us!" the oldest girl squealed.

Apparently, the children were his.

They looked like they couldn't have been more than a year apart from each other in age. His heart swelled at the sight of them—six children of his own. Could he ever hope for so much? He let out a laugh and sat up, children tumbling into the snow, all fits of giggles. Liam stood, pelted with snow, and snatched two of the children in his arms. He jogged from the brook next to the cottage, twirling with the children in his arms when he went far enough away.

"Me next!" one cried when the two were set down.

Liam grinned, prepared to lift the child, when the bell on the front of the cottage rang with three hard beats. He looked toward the home and saw a woman in blue homespun, a stark white apron over it.

"Dinner!" she summoned loudly.

Liam picked up the children he could, one in each arm and one hanging about his shoulders, going to the home. He stopped short of the door when he saw it was Margaret in the blue homespun.

Margaret gave him a strange look. "Is there something wrong?"

"Nothing at all." He set down the children and grinned, pulling her into his arms. "I couldn't be happier."

Margaret smiled up at him, her hands on his chest. "I'm pleased to hear it."

Liam kissed her soundly before going inside. The table was laden with food, steam rising from the roast at the center.

He closed his eyes to give thanks to Theotes before they ate. When he opened them again, he found himself in bed next to Margaret. She was already sleeping, her back turned to him. Her hair fell out of her loose braid, shift falling off her shoulder. He sighed happily, his arm tucked behind his head as he watched her.

Liam heard a bang on the side of the cottage. Unease washed over him as he dressed to investigate the noise.

He circled the house once, then again before he saw the flame crawling over the dining table. Liam ran to the front door and tried to yank it open. It wouldn't budge, no matter how hard he pulled. Liam tried the back door to the same result. He beat on the windows, trying to wake his family. The heat of the fire radiated under his palms.

"Margaret," he bellowed, beating on the window in their bedroom. "Margaret, wake up! Grab the children!"

She came to the window, her face swollen and bruised on one side. Her eye was bruised purple, blood dripping from the cut under it. Her lip was split and puffed to twice its usual size.

Liam jumped back from the window; her face had been perfect when he left their bed. "Margaret!" he yelled. "Margaret, grab the children!"

She stared at him hopelessly. "Why didn't you help me?"

"Grab the children, Margaret!" he screamed once more before taking a bucket to the brook, filling it with water. He tried to douse the fire licking up the wall, but the water only worked to spread it faster.

"Maggie, get out of there!" Liam desperately cried. "Grab the children, and come to me!"

"Why didn't you help me?" she wailed as the fire overtook her.

Liam gasped, waking instantly. He put a hand to his chest, his heart thundering under his palm. Light shone through the wooden shutters. Liam lay back, breathing heavily. He was relieved his dreams were over, his chest slowly starting to loosen.

He rose and splashed water on his face to clear his mind—he could still see the accusing look on Margaret's battered face. He wanted free of the vapors left by his dream before he went downstairs.

Liam nodded to the bartender when he hit the final step, sitting at the near-empty bar. "Barkeep."

The man came to him. "Yes, sir?"

"What is there in the way of work here?"

"There's always work to be had in the fields," the bartender told him, "and there's a smithy across the way that's looking for an assistant."

Liam nodded again as he stood. "My thanks," he said before leaving.

Liam looked around the village he would be making a temporary life in. He could easily fit in with the people there, surrounded by miles of farmlands. Men were already at work in the fields, plowing them for the next planting season.

THE ANATALIAN THRONE

There was always work in the fields, as the bartender had said, but Liam thought he would take his chances with the blacksmith.

3

"What time is it?" Margaret groaned, turning her face away from the light spilling in through the opening of the tent.

Sarah pulled aside the blankets for Margaret to sit up. "Just after dawn, my lady."

"Can't we sleep for a little while longer?" Margaret tried to pull the blanket back up, squinting at her maid.

The blankets were firmly snatched away. "No."

Margaret groaned again, pushing her head back into the pillow as she irritably stared at the ceiling of the tent. She regretted telling Sarah she didn't care what time she had to get up; she was going to look presentable going into the city with her entourage.

"Up, my lady," Sarah commanded, clapping her hands as though she were dealing with an unruly child. "Your hair needs to be washed."

"Taskmaster," Margaret grumbled before leaving her bed.

After her hair was washed, Sarah scrubbed Margaret's skin until it shone pink. Sarah handed Margaret a soft cloth to wipe away the excess moisture while she wrung her hair free of water.

"What dress would you like to wear today?" Sarah asked, slipping Margaret's shift over her head.

"I should think one of the blue ones." Margaret tied the strings loosely on the front of her shift. "It's one of my best colors."

"A very good color on you, my lady," Sarah agreed. She dug through the chests and found one of the more conservative dresses, laying it out to settle, fluffing out the fabric to rid it of any wrinkles.

Margaret held up a looking glass, scrutinizing her face. The bruising had faded before they reached the capital, but the scar had turned an ugly maroon she hoped would eventually fade into white. "Do you really think you'll be able to cover this?"

Sarah smiled at her reassuringly. "It will not be flawless, but no one will notice unless they are close enough to kiss you."

Margaret gave an amused snort. "I doubt that will happen any time soon."

"Mr. Liam seemed to rather like being that close before he left," Sarah commented, her mouth twitching in amusement.

Margaret choked in surprise, coughing as her cheeks heated. "I won't see him for a very long time, I think."

Sarah simply shrugged. "Would you like to eat before we put on your gown?"

"I'm not sure I can eat anything," Margaret confided, hand on her stomach. "My stomach is in knots."

"Why, my lady?" Sarah picked up the boar bristle brush for Margaret's hair.

Margaret closed her eyes, enjoying the maid's ministrations. "Helping Liam was a treasonable offense, Sarah. If anyone found out somehow and turned me into the king before I could explain myself, I would be executed or imprisoned."

"You think you'll be seized at the gates?"

Margaret shook her head. "No. Nothing would happen until I've seen the king, at least. There would be too many questions asked."

"Then rest easy—we don't know when you'll be able to see the king yet," Sarah said.

Sarah was putting the finishing touches on Margaret's face when a throat cleared from the doorway of the tent. They could only see a ramrod stiff back and a sprinkling of white hair.

"Are you dressed, your ladyship?" Captain Marius Vojvo asked gruffly.

Margaret turned away from the door, bunching her shift at her neck. "No Captain, I am not. What is it I can do for you?"

"There is a question of when the supplies will be moved into the city and to where," Vojvo told her.

"Have the servants had their breakfast yet?"

"Not yet, my lady," the captain admitted.

"Then we can think of the dismantling of camp after everyone has eaten," Margaret told him. "Will there be anything else?"

There was a long silence. "No, my lady. Nothing else."

Margaret waited until he left to unclench her hand on her shift. "Perhaps before we begin my hair, we should put the gown on."

Margaret stared at the gate to the city, watching the rest of her party go through. Her stomach cramped viciously. She feared she would throw up over the side of her horse.

"My lady?"

Her eyes wide, Margaret looked to the side at her captain.

"Are you all right?" Concern wrinkled his brow.

"Yes," she said breathlessly, turning her eyes back to the gate. "I'll be all right once I'm inside the city—once I know what is to happen."

"You have to move to get through the gate, my lady."

"Yes," Margaret agreed, "I suppose I do."

"Would you like for me to lead your horse?" Captain Vojvo asked, preparing to dismount.

"No, no." She held her hand up to stop him. "I can do it on my own."

Vojvo nodded, waiting for her to move ahead of him. He cleared his throat after a few moments when she had yet to move.

Margaret shot him a look, urging Duchess forward. Her chest tightened, the closer she came to the guards. She felt a trickle of sweat run down her neck and knew it was not from the oppressive humidity. Maybe she should have gone with Liam like he wanted.

The guards were focused on the other people going through, checking for any contraband. The guard to her left noticed her first, bowing to her at the waist. "Lady Margaret, welcome back to Jalmar," he said, holding his hand out for her papers.

She handed him her identification papers, a pleasant smile on her face. Inside, her stomach twisted. How had he even recognized her? She had not been to the capital in seven years. Would this mean that the king had people watching for her? Had her fears been realized?

"You may go through, my lady." He handed them back, barely glancing at them.

"Thank you, sir," Margaret said. "A pleasant day to you."

"Theotes bless you, your ladyship."

On the way to the inn, Margaret caught sight of a familiar face. She let out a breath when she saw him, all thoughts of Liam vanishing. Charles was just how she remembered him. A little older, of course, but she found him no less attractive for it.

Margaret watched as Charles walked through the crowd. He had an uncommon shade of reddish-blond hair that was just starting to recede. He had grown a beard since the last time she had seen him. She found it a very becoming feature on him. Once he disappeared again in the crowd, Margaret sighed. She would have to call on him sooner rather than later.

Margaret instructed one of her servants to travel ahead of their party to the inn of the Flying Horse to alert the proprietor of their arrival. She looked around her. It was odd being back—everything looked the same, but different as well. She swallowed hard. She didn't anticipate the feelings the city would bring—coming back without her father. Her mother was Theotes knows where. They had never heard a word since she abandoned them all those years ago.

Upon riding up to the inn, the proprietor was waiting for them. "My Lady Margaret," he greeted as he bowed over her hands. "I am pleased you have made it safely."

"As am I, Mr. Wabeight," Margaret smiled at him when he offered his arm to escort her to her rooms. "Captain Vojvo, will you supervise the stabling of the horses and the unloading of our goods?"

"Shall I bring them upstairs?" Vojvo asked.

She turned a questioning eye on Mr. Wabeight. "Will there be room enough?"

"Plenty, your ladyship," assured the proprietor. "Each guest is given a suite of three joining chambers for themselves, their servants, and whatever supplies they're traveling with."

"I will have your things brought to your chambers promptly." Vojvo bowed his head to her before commanding the rest of the servants to follow him to the stables behind the Flying Horse.

"Sarah, come with me, please," Margaret said over her shoulder.

Mr. Wabeight led Margaret to the second floor. The corridors were paneled with dark wood, the candles in the wall sconces barely lighting the passageway. "Each room has its own entrance from the hallway, and also connects in the inside," the proprietor explained.

Margaret nodded along as he spoke, inspecting the cleanliness. "Are there any meals provided for the servants?"

Mr. Wabeight nodded emphatically. "Breakfast, lunch, and dinner are provided in the downstairs for the servants, and breakfast is provided for the guests in their rooms. Lunch is a buffet whenever you wish between midday and two o'clock. Dinner is served in the dining room at seven."

He used the key on his belt to open the door to the middle of the three rooms. "This is your room, my lady," he said as he opened the room. "Will there be anything else I can do for you?"

"No, thank you, that will be all, Mr. Wabeight." Margaret smiled at him.

She looked around the room upon entering. It was more spacious than she'd expected, boasting its own facilities, a four poster bed, and a sitting area at first glance. Sarah closed the door behind them, revealing a small vanity with a stool in front of it.

"Will you let down my hair, Sarah?" Margaret asked, sitting at the vanity.

"Right away, my lady." Sarah set down her things and went to her mistress. "How long will we be staying here?"

Margaret sighed as the pins were taken out of her hair, the tight pull released. She massaged the sides of her head briefly. It had been years since she'd had her hair styled instead of leaving it loose. There had been no one to impress until now. "Not long, I hope. I will arrange to have a private audience with the king and hope he will either invite me to stay at court, or give me my title and allow me to return to Dorcia."

She turned her eyes to the mirror, starting slightly when she caught sight of the scar under her eye—she must have sweated off the makeup Sarah had covered it with. Margaret was happy Mr. Wabeight hadn't brought attention to it at least. She sighed, touching it lightly with the tips of her fingers.

Even for all the trouble it brought her, she never regretted helping Liam when he stumbled upon her cottage—at least, not for more than a few moments. Margaret had believed his innocence from the day of the trial all those years ago, and she believed it now. Sometimes doing the right thing was the hardest of all, with the most consequences, but she didn't know if she could do otherwise.

One day, when she had power of her own, she would help him live a life not as a traitor, but a free man.

Margaret hoped she could make a reasonable case to King Sorren for that power in the form of her title and freedom. She hoped she would be able to stay on her own, but she doubted the king would allow her such a privilege. She would more than likely be put with another count or a duke until a suitable marriage could be made for her. Margaret frowned at the idea that her plans to marry Charles could be thwarted.

4

Liam found the smithy, the Heated Forge, not far from the Frothing Wench as the bartender had said. The heat from the forge hit him a few paces outside the door, the smell of smoke and molten metal hanging thick in the air. Liam saw the blacksmith bending a horseshoe over the horn before hammering the imperfections out on top of the anvil while the metal still glowed. The metal sang loudly as the smith struck it with his hammer.

Sweat quickly started to gather on his back. Liam cleared his throat. "Master Smith?"

The smith grunted, continuing to strike the hot metal.

"I'm looking for work, and I hear that you are in need of help." He looked around the small shop. There were horseshoes and swords alike on the wall.

"Aye," the smith said. "I am."

Liam felt awkward with the short answer. "I would like to work for you."

"Would ye now?" The smith grunted in amusement. "Have ye ever done any metalwork?"

"Only a day here and there for coin, but I'm a quick study," Liam told him hurriedly, as if his answer would go unheard otherwise. "I'm a hard worker and in desperate need of work."

"I need someone who can do the work without me havin' to stop an' teach 'im," the smith said.

"Smith, what is your name?"

"Jossnon Thorkelin."

"Master Thorkelin, I need this job," Liam pleaded. "I have some knowledge of what you do here, and I promise I won't slow you down."

The smith picked up his hammer, spinning it in thought before extending it toward Liam. "I've had an order fer four decorative nails—diamond heads. Can ye make 'em?"

Liam hesitated. It was a deceptively simple task. He'd only made a few before, and it had not gone well. But he couldn't miss his opportunity for work. "If you'll direct me to your iron," he said as he grabbed the hammer.

"O'er there, lad." Jossnon pointed to the wall across from the forge.

Liam grabbed a smaller bar of iron, putting it into the coals of the forge. It should be enough to give him double the nails he needed to make if he ruined some. Once the bar burned bright orange, he took it from the coals and hit it with the hammer on the anvil.

With each finished nail, he dumped them into the bucket of water next to the anvil. They hissed in turn, the water briefly bubbling behind them. After a few moments, the smith took the nails from the bucket with tongs. Liam's work was serviceable but sloppy.

The smith looked them over critically. "I'll give ye one week, an' tha's it, lad," Thorkelin conceded. "If ye canna keep pace, ye'll be let go."

Liam nodded. "You won't regret it, Master Thorkelin."

The week came and went as Liam learned better how to bend, draw, punch, and forge. He watched the smith as much as he could, trying to be the quick study he promised, and often went to his temporary home at the Frothing Wench with a face blackened by smoke. His muscles were sore from the hammering, the constant striking slowly making his arms stronger. Liam looked across the room at Thorkelin—the man was too quiet for his comfort.

"Are ye settlin' in well, lad?" Thorkelin asked when he caught Liam looking at him.

"Well enough. The tavern is feeling a bit small for me now, though I don't know where I can rent a flat for myself." He had hardly talked to anyone in Numetra other than Elias at the Frothing Wench and his new employer. "And I'll need to find a more permanent stable for my horse."

Thorkelin nodded along as Liam spoke. "I can help ye find those now that ye'll be stayin' in my employ."

Liam flashed him a grin. "That would be helpful, thank you."

Thorkelin let out a grunt, falling silent again. "Do ye have a lady, lad?" he asked after a while.

Liam stared at him, dumbfounded. The smith had shown little interest in anything but the work he was producing, much less the matters of Liam's heart. "No, not really," he said hesitantly.

Margaret, despite how much he would have liked for her to be his lady, as the smith put it, would never be his. He was a wanted criminal, and she was too ambitious to give up her life for him.

Jossnon raised a brow at Liam. "Ye sure that there's no one special to ye?"

"There's a woman, but she would never agree to be my special one, Master Thorkelin," Liam said before going back to his hammering.

"Why not?" he demanded. "Ye're an attractive lad, well-spoken an' such."

Liam let out a small bark of a laugh. "Are you trying to compliment me, Master Thorkelin?"

Jossnon gave him a look, his mouth turned in a grimace. "Ye ken what I mean."

"She's too ambitious to settle for a man of my standing," Liam told him, striking the sword in hand particularly hard with his hammer. "I asked her to come away with me, and she refused my offer."

"Sorry, lad." Jossnon shoved his sword back into the coals to reheat.

Liam shrugged, taking his frustration out on the glowing metal. "I'll see her again one day."

"Good man." Jossnon clapped him on the shoulder. "Sup with me tonight an' ye can tell me all about this lady of yers an' her ambitions."

The two men worked for the rest of the afternoon in silence and made no more mention of Margaret. Liam was thankful that no new customers came in that day. Liam was not prepared for the extra workload they would bring. While he was decent at his new craft, it would be years before he learned all Master Thorkelin thought he should know.

If he even stayed that long. He hadn't thought past a quiet place to stay until Margaret needed him again.

"C'mon, lad." Jossnon put away the last of his tools. "It'll be a simple supper."

"Any supper not in a tavern is a welcome reprieve," Liam told him, resting a hand on Jossnon's shoulder.

Thorkelin led Liam to a humble home at the end of a winding road not far from the forge. It was small with wooden floors and plain walls. There was no hint of a woman's touch, despite the fact the blacksmith wore a wedding band. The smith had a pot already hanging over a fire that he must have put on early in the day.

"A lovely home, Jossnon," Liam told him.

"Thank ye, lad." Jossnon poured Liam a mug of ale, setting it in front of him before sitting opposite him. "Now tell me about this lady of yers."

Liam looked into the mug. "She's very strongheaded."

Jossnon chuckled. "I haven't met a woman who isn't."

Liam licked his dry lips before continuing. "Maggie is one of those people you want to be around no matter how much she irritates you," he said with a fond smile. "And she is so generous with other people. She'll help anyone in need— even if it will get her into trouble."

"She sounds wonderful, lad. Bein' generous—truly generous—is a rare thing t' find," Jossnon told him. "Where is this Maggie of yers now?"

"She's on her way back to the capital," Liam said with a dark look on his face. "I wish she would have stayed where she was until she recovered."

"Is she sick?" The smith asked, taking a long drink of his ale.

"She was attacked by Sa—" Liam paused to correct himself. Anatalians were not welcome in Salatia and he was not about to reveal to his employer that he was a forbidden. "A soldier while she was out for a walk. I was lucky enough to catch him, and I will murder anyone else who tries to hurt her again."

"That's good that ye have a loyalty like that," Thorkelin told him. "She's a lucky lady, even if she does'na ken it."

Liam woke at dawn, sweat coating his chest. The day was already hot and muggy, and he was happy he did not have to work in the smithy today. It was unseasonably hot for Semonat, the temperature being the hottest he could remember for the season in Aratia. It felt as though it were still Jumonat in the height of summer.

He slipped out of bed, padding his way with bare feet to his table where he filled a glass with water. Liam looked around the room. His newly rented home was a sparse one-room flat. Liam was unsure of what to do with himself. It was the first day he had taken off since starting work with Thorkelin three weeks ago. Liam wanted to meet more of the townspeople. Liam dressed in light clothing and left his rented home. He didn't know where he was going, but he could not stay in the room all day. It was sufficient for his needs, though lonely.

Lonelier than he expected, having never before minded being on his own. At least, not until Margaret had come into his life and reminded him what it was like to want a family to come home to every day—to confide in one special person and be able to rely upon them for anything.

The town was starting to wake; shopkeepers opening their windows and setting out wares to sell—most were poorly handcrafted items. The humidity weighed heavily against Liam, his shirt clinging to him after his short walk to the main street. He saw children turned out of the shops, outfitted in homespun garments filled with holes. They immediately ran toward the fields to play in the high cornstalks. The smell of frying meat wafted toward him, making Liam's stomach growl.

He followed his nose until he came to a small eating house, The Smiling Fox, that had few people within, despite the delightful smell. Liam decided to dine there, sitting at one of the tables.

A waif-thin woman came to his table within moments, dark bags under her eyes. "What'll ye have?" she asked blandly.

"What is there?"

"Eggs, bacon, an' biscuits."

It was a short reply that made Liam uncomfortable. "I'll have all of that, please."

She rolled her eyes at him before going to her other customers, a much friendlier conversation exchanged between them.

Liam raised his brows, irritation swelling in his chest. There were not many customers, the two patrons looking better fed than the hostess herself. He had to wait until after the other two patrons were served before his food arrived, the bacon limp, the grease starting to solidify from sitting too long.

He frowned at his food. "Excuse me," he called out to her.

"What?"

"My food is cold," Liam complained.

"And?"

"Do you have a problem, ma'am?"

She scowled at him. "Ye are'na from around here."

"I wasn't aware that was an issue." Liam's face darkened at the implication he wasn't welcome. If he wasn't, Thorkelin surely wouldn't have hired him.

"We don't like people who aren't from around here," she told him coldly.

"No one else here has a problem with my money but you," he informed her. "And I would appreciate you showing me the same kindness you show everyone else."

She only looked at him blankly before walking away.

Liam threw down the money, no longer hungry for the inadequate food. He walked away to find another eatery, but not before seeing the woman swoop in to take his food, shoving a piece of bacon whole into her mouth. Liam wondered if she had goaded him away on purpose to have something to eat for that morning.

He could find nowhere else serving breakfast, deciding instead to go to the smithy and speak with Master Thorkelin.

Thorkelin was just starting to open the forge when Liam walked up. "What are ye doing here, lad? Ye've got the day off."

"I don't know what to do with my free day," Liam admitted.

"Ye can do anything ye want. What d'ye normally do?"

Liam shrugged. "I'm usually on the road, looking for work or somewhere to sleep."

Thorkelin's lips flattened as he thought. "You can go explore Castenra," he suggested.

"How far away is it?"

"Only an hour's walk at a good pace," Thorkelin said, still pondering. "They have much more there for a single man to do."

Liam wondered if Thorkelin meant that there was a brothel there and that he thought Liam would like to partake in those activities. He supposed he wouldn't complain if he did happen across such an establishment.

"Is there any hunting to do in the area?" Liam asked.

"Plenty, lad." The blacksmith rubbed his chin. "If you go out on the western side, there are plenty of deer to choose from."

"And to sell?" Liam knew there was not a need for him to keep a full deer to himself.

Jossnon shrugged. "Anywhere you find space, the people will flock to ye."

Liam nodded as he thought.

Jossnon went about starting the fire in the forge and gathering the materials for the day.

"Do you have any arrowheads?" Liam asked, going into the smithy.

Liam waited patiently in the near-silent woods, a mile away from Numetra. He could hear the shuffling in the fallen leaves; a herd of deer were snuffling the layer of leaves for grass. He could hear the excited chomping on an acorn and was happy the wind was blowing his scent away from the herd. He slowly drew back his bow to aim. A deer would come between the two trees on either side of him soon.

Liam breathed slow and deep. He lowered his head to look down the length of the arrow as he waited. All the muscles in his right arm burned. A buck, nose to the ground, came into sight. Liam waited long enough to aim where the arrow would hit the lung—or better, the heart. He took a deep breath and held it as he released the arrow.

The arrow struck the buck behind his foreleg, lodging deep in his chest cavity. Liam swallowed hard when the buck let out an echoing bleat as he fell to the forest floor.

Hearing it, the remainder of the herd scattered. Liam pressed himself against the tree to avoid their sharp hooves. When they were gone, Liam could hear the spasmodic kicks as the buck vainly tried to escape his fate. He went to the fallen beast, resting a hand on his neck.

"Thank you for your sacrifice," Liam murmured as he slid his dagger from its sheath. "Thank you, Theotes, for providing."

He slit the buck's throat, stroking his side until there was no more life in his eyes. Liam removed the organs to lighten his burden. He constructed a litter for the large animal, using the bit of rope he brought to tie to the front of the craft. Grunting, he rolled the buck onto it.

By the time Liam made the mile trek back to Numetra, it was growing dark. His clothes clung to his sweat-drenched body as he dragged his kill to the eatery he had been at that morning, panting.

"Hello!" he called out loudly, hands still clutching tightly to the rope. When there was no answer, he called again, "Hello! Is anyone there?"

The shutters on the second floor burst open, the woman from that morning poking her head out. "What d'ye think ye're doin', disruptin' the peace?"

"I have a deer for you," Liam told her, jerking his head back to the buck, "if you'll have it."

"If I'll have it…" The woman pulled her head from the window, quickly popping it back out. "I'll be down presently."

Liam let out a snort, waiting for her to reach him.

She was down as quickly as she had said, squatting to examine the beast. She disdainfully examined the slit belly. "Ye dinna leave the organs, I see," she muttered before standing. "How much d'ye want fer 'im?"

"For you?" Liam asked. "Today he is free."

Surprise blossomed across her face. "Free?"

Liam nodded. "Free," he confirmed, "but I expect to be treated kindly when I come for breakfast tomorrow. Nothing like this morning."

She grudgingly nodded. "Help me get 'im inside, then."

Liam dragged the deer where she instructed.

"Cut off his head, please," she said, dragging a cauldron over. She grimaced, putting a hand to her back when she stood.

"What?" Liam looked at her, surprised.

"We can use whatever's left of the blood for blood pudding" She pointed to the cauldron. "'Tis a fine head someone would pay for, to say they killed it instead. I dinna want t' take the time to clean the blood from his chin."

Liam curled his lip, disgusted at the thought, but did as he was bid. He strung the deer on a beam, letting the remaining blood drip into the container.

"What's your name?" Liam finally thought to ask.

"Gretta," she answered, checking all the knots to make sure the deer would not fall.

"Liam," he gave his name, though she didn't ask for it.

"Mama?" a cracking voice asked from the doorway.

Gretta turned and gathered the young boy in her arms. "What is it, child? Why are ye no sleepin'?"

The young boy rubbed his bleary eyes. "I had a nightmare…about Da."

Gretta held him tighter, kissing the top of his pale blond head. "Dinna worry," she murmured against his hair. "He's with Olam now, ne'er to be in pain again."

He nodded, clutching her tightly.

Liam pulled his eyes away from the private scene, starting to skin the deer.

"Back to bed with ye, lad," Gretta commanded, kissing his forehead. "Grab a cup o' milk on yer way."

Liam waited until the boy was back inside before speaking. "What happened to his father?"

"A hunting accident," she said coldly. "Or, at least, that's what I tell them."

He paused his ministrations, holding tightly to the skin. "What really happened?"

"Murdered by a band o' rebels."

"I'm sorry to hear that," he told her sincerely. "How many children do you have?"

"Three boys," Gretta told him. "The one ye saw and two that work in the fields to provide what I canna."

Liam fell silent as he finished his task. He washed his hands free of blood with the water Gretta provided.

"I'll see you in the morning, Gretta," he told her by way of goodbye.

"Thank ye, Liam," she said him from the doorway.

5

argaret looked at the home her carriage pulled up to. It was modest for what Charles earned running her father's business as their executor. She found the yellow color of it charming, the white molding stood out boldly against its brightness. She sent a calling card ahead of her to alert the Luthers she would be visiting later that day. She imagined Charles would be surprised to see her back in Jalmar.

She sat nervously in her coach—what if Charlotte was still there? Margaret had been told upon her inquiries that Charlotte had yet to give Charles any children. No one had told her if they were still married, however. The king had passed a law that a man could set aside his wife without any repercussion if she could not produce a son. A man needed an heir to carry on his legacy, after all.

Margaret was let in by a butler and led to the parlor. She looked around the room and saw that, like the outside of the house, it was modestly decorated. In front of a pink couch was a woman with hair like spun gold.

The woman gave Margaret the barest of curtsies. "You honor my house with your visit, my lady."

"You are Mrs. Luther, I presume?" Margaret hoped her dismay did not show on her face.

"I am, Lady Margaret." Charlotte looked her over as she inclined her head. "Please, call me Charlotte."

Margaret ignored the attempt at familiarity. "Where is Mr. Luther?" She glanced around the room again. Margaret had made sure that her appearance was as close to perfection as possible.

Charlotte frowned. "I'm afraid he's in a meeting."

"I need to speak with him about the business." Margaret looked at the older woman pointedly. "Surely, he can make time for me."

"Is there something wrong, my lady?" Charlotte furrowed her brow.

"That is for Mr. Luther to hear. If he decides to tell you, then I won't stop him." Margaret was pleased to see the look of irritation on Charlotte's face. "I would like to speak with him privately, Mrs. Luther."

"If you would wait here," Charlotte said before she disappeared.

Margaret furrowed her brow. Why not have a servant fetch him, if not to dissuade Charles from seeing her? She went to the far wall where a glass-door cabinet rested. It displayed several different knickknacks, a few of which she recognized from Dorcia. She smiled, wishing she could go back there. One day she would. Tears welled in her eyes, and she hastily wiped them away.

"Lady Margaret?"

Margaret turned around, and she heard him take in a small breath.

Charles looked her over slowly before closing the gap between them. He took her face gently in his hands when she looked up at him. "Lady Margaret, what has happened to your face?"

She must have wiped away the makeup Sarah had put on her scar. Margaret pursed her lips as she debated telling him. "There were rebels in the town that I was staying in." Tears jumped unbidden to her eyes. Even months later, the memory was still too fresh for her.

"Lady Margaret, please, tell me that they didn't..."

Margaret wiped her eyes. "He was stopped before he could." As much as she enjoyed having him close to her, she moved away from him. "But that isn't what I came here to talk to you about."

Charles guided her to the couch. "Please, sit."

"Charles, I have some terrible news." Margaret sat gracefully on the couch with a sweep of her skirts.

"What is it, my dear?"

Margaret clenched her hands on her lap. She had admitted it to herself a long time ago—had been told of its certainty by Liam—but it still hurt to bring it up. Liam had told the Gollacks for her, and she had never had to say anything more about it. They had made her comfortable with what had happened, never mentioning it or looking at her with pitying glances as most people would have done.

"Papa is dead."

The color drained from Charles' face. "He's what?"

"He was killed by Lord Nicholas Oliphant in our home a year ago. He intruded when I—" Margaret looked down at her hands.

Charles raised his brows. "When you what?"

"When I let a criminal into our home," she admitted. She had rehearsed a fabricated story to tell him, but looking him in the face had washed away the plan like a crashing wave.

"Theotes!" Charles stood abruptly, an angry look on his face. "You did *what?*"

Margaret looked up at him tearfully. "I let Liam Fulton into our home to bathe and eat, and soldiers followed him. We had to leave right after Nicholas stabbed Papa. He died alone because of me. He died scared and alone, all because I was stupid," Margaret said with her voice trembling. "How could I do that to him?"

Charles gently grabbed her hands, kneeling in front of her. "Why would you let him in, Margaret?"

"I don't know!" Margaret took her hands from his and wiped her face clean of the tears. Standing, she went to the window. "I've asked myself that same question for months, and I still have no answers."

"What are you going to do now?"

"I will have an audience with the king to request that I legally become the Countess of Dorcia so I can keep my lands until I marry." She hoped the king would grant her request instead of setting her up with a guardian and finding a husband for her.

"What will you say to the king?" Charles frowned at her. "You can't tell him what you told me. You'll lose everything your father worked so hard for."

Margaret pulled her bottom lip between her teeth. "I don't know." She wasn't even able to lie to Charles—what would she do with the King of Anatalia? He was far more intimidating than her father's executor.

"Theotes, Margaret!" Charles looked at her, incredulous. "Think of all the people—your people!—who will be lost without you."

Margaret looked to her lap. "They're all I think of, Charles. They're the reason I'm here to beg for my title like a common whore."

Charles grabbed her hand, cupping it within his other. "It should be yours—it should have been yours a year ago."

She squeezed his hand, nodding silently.

"You know that's what your father wanted. He petitioned the king several times to make you the heir to the title."

"Thank you, Charles." Margaret gave him a small smile. "I'll remind His Majesty of that when I petition him."

Selecting a light plate of fruit for her lunch, Margaret sat in the dining hall of The Flying Horse. She had been in Jalmar just over a week, and she had yet to receive a response from the king's secretary in regards to her audience. She was starting to worry that the king would refuse her request. As she picked a grape and popped it in her mouth, one of the maids came to her side.

The maid bobbed a quick curtsy. "Begging your pardon, my lady, this just arrived for you."

Margaret saw the royal seal, a circle of wax with an eagle wearing a crown, and immediately opened it.

Lady Margaret Doremis,
Your presence is requested on the fifteenth day of Semonat, in the year
of our Lord Theotes two thousand two hundred and eighty-two, at two
o'clock in the afternoon.
His Majesty, King Sorren of Anatalia, has granted your request for
a private audience.

"Thank you." Margaret ripped her eyes away from the summons to dismiss the maid. "You may go now."

Margaret leaned against the high-backed chair, resting a hand on her flipping stomach. The audience was scheduled for tomorrow, not much time to mentally prepare herself. She finished her lunch before she went to find Sarah. The lady's maid was in her own room. Captain Vojvo and Sarah each had pushed two of the beds together on opposite sides of the room to give them larger beds. Sarah was lying on hers.

"Sarah?" Margaret tentatively called.

Sarah shot from her recline. "Yes, my lady?"

"I have an audience with the king tomorrow," Margaret told her. "I was wondering if you might help me select a dress?"

"Of course, my lady," gushed Sarah.

Margaret nervously waited in the king's antechamber for her audience. She smoothed the front of her dress, trying to make every detail perfect. She paced the room, heart pounding. Margaret sat heavily, sighing to try to release her anxiety. It seemed like she was waiting for hours.

Margaret stood abruptly when she heard the door open.

"My lady, if you please." The servant moved to let her pass.

She smoothed her skirts once more as she passed through the door. She curtsied deeply to King Sorren. "Your Majesty," she breathed.

"My dear Lady Margaret, it has been too long!" King Sorren went to her, lifting her out of her curtsy. He looked her over slowly. "How have you and your father been faring in the country?"

Margaret's face fell at the mention of her father. "My king, I have very unfortunate news." She took a deep breath before continuing, "Papa is dead."

The king looked at her in disbelief, returning to his chair as he brought a hand to his mouth. "When?"

"A year ago." Margaret looked down at the fists she clenched in her skirts. "He was murdered by one of your soldiers."

Since receiving the summons, she had debated long and hard on whether or not to tell the king about how her father had died. Margaret would not, of course, make any mention of Liam's name in her tale. She would tell the king as much as she could without incriminating herself.

The king's face fell into a mask she could not read. It made Margaret uneasy. "I beg your pardon?"

"The soldier claimed to have seen a criminal come into my home and refused to take me at my word that no such person had come to my door. Lord Nicholas Oliphant recognized me and, out of spite and anger, killed my father where he lay in his bed." Margaret looked at him desperately. "He then turned on me, and I had to defend myself. I don't know if he died there or if his fellow soldiers helped him in time. I fled to a nearby town, and an elderly couple took pity on me and allowed me to stay for the winter to commission new clothing and recuperate whatever I had lost."

Her lie came more easily than she thought it would. After her confession to Charles, she didn't know if she could tell the lie she had prepared. She had repeatedly stumbled over the story when she rehearsed it with Sarah.

King Sorren's face held a frosty expression as he rose and paced in front of his chair. "Have you gone back to find out what happened to your father and home?"

"I sent inquiries, Majesty." Margaret unconsciously chewed on her lip when he looked at her, wincing when it split open. "Someone was kind enough to bury my father under an old oak tree behind our home."

King Sorren remained quiet as he once again sat, an unreadable mask returning to his face.

Margaret did not want to dwell on her father—even a year later, it was still too fresh for her. "Your Majesty, it would please me greatly if you would make me the Countess of Dorcia in my father's stead so that I might be able to keep his legacy and business growing, as he had so wished." Margaret steeled herself to whatever answer she might receive. "And there is also the question of whether I will require a guardian or if I will be allowed to live on my own until a suitable husband is found for me."

"I must think on the matter for a time." The king ran a hand over his face. "Until I have made a decision, you will be granted rooms in the palace and become my ward."

"Thank you, Majesty." She curtsied again and left the room when she was dismissed. The meeting had gone better than she expected, though she still had no answers that helped her.

To her surprise, the king personally accompanied Margaret to assist in picking her new rooms. He kept her hand on his arm the entirety of the lengthy expedition. Captain Vojvo trailed behind them at a discrete distance, an unpleasant look on his face.

King Sorren stopped at a room, waving his hand impatiently for a servant to open the door. "Will this one be to your liking?"

He escorted Margaret into the open room and smiled when she gasped. The floor was a light-colored hardwood, partially covered by a rug imported from Radovan—a highly coveted prize—filled with blues and reds mixed with creams. The ceiling was high, and the edges were gilded with golden leaves. The walls were a grayish blue, each in paneled sections, edged with gold, and painted with a piece from each province in Anatalia.

At the far end of the room was an alcove with three floor-length windows and a table of white granite and two chairs with plush white cushions. Under a crystalline chandelier in the center of the room were a pair of plush white chairs and a long white high-backed couch and another white granite table in front of the set. On the wall facing the furniture was a large fireplace with gold-painted molding, topped with gilded scrollwork. The fire was not lit, but would have been a magnificent sight to see had it been.

"Your Majesty, this is extraordinary!" Margaret let go of his arm to go farther into the room. She could hardly take it all in—there was so much to look at.

The king smiled at her. "You should see the bedchambers."

Margaret smiled at him with bright eyes. "May I?"

He raised his arm in the direction of the bedroom. "After you, my lady."

Margaret squealed with girlish enthusiasm before going to the entrance to the bedchamber, throwing the double doors open. She gasped again, walking into the room. She spun slowly in a circle, her eyes devouring everything in sight. The ceiling had a raised look with another chandelier. At the side of the room was a

25

wall of windows covered by white gossamer drapery, corniced light blue drapes lined with gold tassels atop them. Another set of the blue drapes were at the ends of the windows to pull forward to block out the light.

The bed was in the center of the wall of windows, a small canopy at the head of the bed; drapes flowing down each side of the large frame. The mattress, covered with blue-and-white bedding, looking as if it was stuffed to capacity. On the opposite side was an inner parlor that would allow a small private audience with close companions to meet in secret, the same coloring and flooring that were in the parlor and bedroom, as well as the white furniture and imported rugs, flowed into the smaller side chamber.

"These are far too rich for me, Your Majesty," Margaret said, wistfully looking around the room again.

The king smiled at her. "As my ward, you have a right to any rooms in the palace, my dear. These will be your apartments, if you so desire."

Margaret curtsied low to him "You are most gracious, Majesty."

"Anything for you, my dear." The king looked her over. "You look just like your mother," he said, cupping her cheek. "I still think of her from time to time."

Margaret smiled at him. "Thank you, Your Majesty."

The king grabbed her hand, gently kissing her knuckles. "I'll leave you to become acquainted with your new rooms."

Margaret curtsied low again as King Sorren left the room. She watched as Captain Vojvo entered the room with a scowl.

"Something wrong, Captain?" she asked.

Vojvo looked around the room slowly. "I don't like the way His Majesty is looking at you."

"And how is that, Vojvo?"

"Like a prize, my lady." He looked at Margaret pointedly. "And he wants to win."

"I think you are imagining things, Captain. You don't like how anyone looks at me. The king loved my father like a brother, and he would never be interested in me in such a way," she said before sitting on her bed with a relaxed sigh. "Will you arrange the transport of my chests here? Don't forget yours and Sarah's things."

"As you wish, my lady." Vojvo bowed, mouth tight, before he left.

Margaret sighed contentedly. These rooms were far better than she had ever hoped for. She inhaled deeply, smelling the fresh linens that she lay on. She would be very happy in her new rooms.

Margaret settled in for a week before she went to see Charles again. She was just as nervous as the first time. She once again waited in the parlor with Charlotte for Charles to have a spare moment. It was awkwardly silent in the room, Charlotte looking at Margaret with barely veiled contempt. She was glad when Charles walked into the room.

"Lady Margaret, it's good to see you again," he told her.

Margaret stood, smiling pleasantly. "Charles, thank you for seeing me."

"Of course, Lady Margaret. What can I do for you?"

"I have a few things I want to discuss about the business," Margaret said. "I would like to learn more about how my enterprise is run."

Charles raised his eyebrows, coming to stand next to his wife. "Oh? What would you like to know?"

"Everything that I can." Margaret's smile was a broad one. "I want to do my father proud."

It was Charlotte's turn to raise her eyebrows. "That could take months, and my husband is a very busy man. He is running the business just fine on his own."

"Ah, yes. But Mrs. Luther, it is *my* business," Margaret said matter-of-factly.

Charles put his hand on Charlotte's shoulder as she inhaled deeply. "Lady Margaret is right, my dear. It is her business."

Margaret smiled smugly. "When can we get started, Charles?"

"We can start whenever you'd like," Charles said.

"I'd like to start now."

Charles raised his eyebrows again. "If you'd like to join me in my study, we can start with keeping track of accounts."

"Lead the way."

Margaret sighed contentedly as she walked through the market. This was the first day she had taken for herself since arriving the month prior. She had spent almost every day of Semonat with Charles, learning the inner workings of her father's business. She had no idea how much actually went into the running of a massive industry. They were rich in their own right but still required investors to make the enterprise her father built run smoothly and continuously.

The accounting portion of her tutelage had particularly made her head spin— the referencing and the cross-referencing of sales, product amount, and investors had been a maddening process. Margaret was glad that Charles was running her business; he had a knack for the inner workings of the job. He was like a well-trained healer, knowing how to fix the problem with a single glance.

Sarah was her companion for the trip to the market, their arms linked so they wouldn't get separated. The captain insisted he trail behind them at a distance so they could gossip, or whatever it was women did. His Majesty wanted to have Margaret in his queen's ladies-in-waiting, and that required having dresses made in the same cut and fashion as the queen's own wardrobe. This time, her mother would not ruin things for her by insulting the queen. Margaret would need to establish herself as an asset to the queen. She ran her hands over the fabrics with a sigh.

"They're all so beautiful, Sarah." Margaret would also need to dress Sarah appropriately for life at the capital.

Sarah's eyes looked this way and that, bright excitement radiating from her. "Yes, my lady. You would look splendid in all of them." She would have never seen such a spectacle before, from the small amount Sarah had told Margaret.

"We're not just here for me, Sarah." Margaret smiled at her. "We're going to be getting some clothes for you as well."

Sarah's eyes widened. "For me, my lady?" She could not hide the delight from her face.

Margaret nodded. "Anything you want, Sarah. I am to provide for you, and I want you to have the best."

"My lady, I don't know what to say." Sarah disentangled herself to curtsy to her. "Thank you."

"Of course. Why don't you take a look at some of the bolts? And remember, money isn't an object."

Sarah nodded, wandering only a short distance from Margaret. She seemed to be particularly engrossed in the bazaar, looking as if she was trying to see everything at once. Margaret smiled to herself. It was sweet to see her looking so amazed.

To her great surprise, a man came up to Sarah.

"Hello, lamb," the new man said.

Sarah looked surprised he had spoken to her. "Hello," she responded timidly.

Margaret raised her eyebrows. He must have thought that Sarah was here by herself. Margaret did not plan on changing his impression. She was surprised the captain hadn't come between them to stop any conversation. Looking around, she didn't see Captain Vojvo anywhere.

"What's a pretty girl like yourself doing here without an escort?"

Sarah blushed prettily at him. "My lady is here to purchase fabrics."

"And where is your lady, my lamb?" the young man asked flirtatiously.

Sarah bit her bottom lip, looking around. "I must have wandered farther away than I thought…"

The young man held his arm out to her. "Then allow me to help you reunite with your lady."

Margaret looked him over. He was not the most handsome of men, but he seemed charming at least. He was lanky, with a thin, almost gaunt face. It was slightly pock marked on his cheeks, and he had rusty hair tumbling in tight curls. The young man had bright green eyes that held a childlike enthusiasm in them.

Sarah looked at the young man skeptically. "What's your name?"

The lanky boy bowed to her with a flourish. "George, my lamb."

Sarah couldn't help but smile. "My name is—"

"Sarah, is this young man bothering you?" Vojvo took the opportunity to intervene.

Sarah gave him a hard look. "No, Captain, he's not."

George looked between the two. "Captain?"

To Margaret's amusement, Vojvo stood a little straighter. "I am the Captain of the Countess of Dorcia's guard, and you are fraternizing with her lady's maid." He looked over the lanky man critically. "And it looks to me as if you should be anywhere but here."

The boy's brow wrinkled in consternation. He looked at Sarah with softened eyes. "You can find me here any time, my lamb."

Margaret walked up to the captain and Sarah as George left. "Is everything all right?"

Sarah cast an accusing eye on Vojvo. "Yes, my lady."

Vojvo bowed his head to her. "Of course, my lady."

At some point, Margaret would have to talk to the captain about allowing Sarah to find her own adventures, but this was not the time.

 **6**

ojvo went to Lady Margaret's chambers at her request. He had barely seen her since the day at the market. Now that she was back among her kind, she seemed almost not to need him anymore. He wondered if she was summoning him for a dismissal. He twitched uncomfortably as he waited in her sitting room, impatient to find out why he had been brought here.

Lady Margaret entered the sitting room from her bedchambers, freshly changed for the evening meal. "Captain," she said as if she were surprised to see him.

Vojvo stood quickly and bowed. "My lady, you look lovely this evening."

She smiled at him charmingly, her eyes glittering. She was in her element. "Thank you, Captain. That's very kind of you to say."

"What is it that you wished to speak with me about?" he asked when an awkward silence fell between them.

"Oh, yes!" Another dazzling smile came to her face. "I would like to make a request of you."

"Anything, my lady," he said with ease, but he was hesitant about what she could possibly need from him.

"I wondered if…" Lady Margaret trailed off slowly, chewing on her bottom lip. "If you might stay closer than you have been, Captain. I know you were thinking of returning to Marbon since there is not much for you to do here."

Marius remained silent as he waited for Lady Margaret to continue. He had learned long ago to wait until anyone who had command over him was finished so that he wouldn't put his foot in his mouth.

"I know that I call myself a countess, though, until His Majesty grants me my father's title or I find myself a husband to take the title, I am not. I would like to have another person in my confidence to help guide me so I can ensure I am not chosen just for my lands and fortune." She looked at him, trying to keep the worry from her face. "I need someone to protect me from my own ambitions, as Liam would say."

"My lady, I'm honored that you would consider me for such a duty," he told her politely. In truth, he *was* honored, but he was also wary of the chance he would be taking. He could easily say something she would not like and be dismissed from her service.

A cry of excitement escaped from her. "Wonderful! I am very happy to hear it, Captain."

"Is there anything else I can do for you, my lady?"

"No, that will be all for now," Lady Margaret said with a smile.

"I will be back in the morning to discuss my duties," Marius told her before bowing out of her chambers.

In the morning, Vojvo returned to his mistress's chambers, earlier than she had anticipated, he thought, based on the sour look she gave him while they waited for their tea.

Sarah looked between them awkwardly as she set their cups in front of them.

"Thank you, Sarah," Vojvo said with a nod.

"Yes, thank you, Sarah," Lady Margaret echoed before she brought her cup to her mouth. "Now that we have our tea, you may proceed, Captain."

He was amused she needed her morning tea to function. "As you wish, my lady. I would like to detail what duties you are actually expecting of me."

Lady Margaret's face pinched, one side more than the other, as she thought deeply. It was not unlike disgust showing on her face at the prospect of having to think so early in the morning. Vojvo waited, almost impatiently, for her orders.

"I suppose you could consider it being my personal guard, where you're with me at all times, save for decency?"

It was obvious Lady Margaret did not know what it was she wanted him to do. He would have to figure out himself what exactly she needed—he was no noble himself, but he had worked with and for plenty of them over his years. She was like none other that he knew. Was it because she'd spent so little time at court or that she didn't have anyone to guide her, with her mother abandoning her and her father being too ill? Or was it just her one-track mind that wanted to accomplish every thought that came into it?

Vojvo took a sip of his tea as he looked over her unsure face. Either way, he would do his best for her. She had won him over on their journey to the capital, and he wanted nothing but her success. "Shall we just say that you will leave it to my discretion, my lady?"

She gave him a smile that she commonly used in order to charm or to show that a person had guessed her wishes correctly. "Yes, yes, of course, Captain. You would certainly know much more in these types of matters."

THE ANATALIAN THRONE

"You will learn what you like and don't like in time." Vojvo set down his cup and clasped his hands in front of him. "And just remember, my lady: I cannot read your mind. You must tell me what you would like changed."

Lady Margaret nodded silently, sipping on her tea thoughtfully. "And when will this start?"

"It already has."

 7

Lord General Crompton pulled up with a start when he saw Lady Margaret seated next to the king at the table in his private dining room. No one else was supposed to be there so they could discuss matters of state. "Cousin—I thought it was to just be us today."

"We can talk business later." Sorren waved his hand. "I wanted to hear all about what's happened since Lady Margaret left us."

Lady Margaret smiled timidly at his side. "There isn't much to tell, Majesty."

"Sit." Sorren gestured to the chair across from them. "Tell me what is happening, Cousin."

Crompton sat and inhaled deeply. "The Duchess is well. She's looking forward to our latest vintage being delivered."

"What will you call this one?"

"Amarantha." Crompton sighed through his nose and smiled briefly. "It's time."

Lady Margaret looked at him with furrowed brow. "Time?"

"For my daughter, Lady Margaret."

She glanced between him and the king, looking even more confused. "I didn't know you had a daughter, Your Grace."

"She passed before you ever came to court, my lady."

"Oh, I'm sor—"

"We don't speak of her." Sorren squeezed her hand. "Let's move on to happier subjects. You were going to tell me about your life in Silvica."

Lady Margaret smiled at him. "I loved it there—it was so peaceful. I learned how to do so many things I never would have as a lady of the court."

Crompton raised his brows. "What would that be? The ladies here are very well educated."

Lady Margaret turned almost shy. "My servants left to start their own lives only a few years into moving to our home in Silvica. I was entirely self-sufficient and could cook and clean for myself, and I was starting to learn some herbology from the healers so I could better help Papa—I even had my own garden I tended."

The king looked as impressed as Crompton felt. A lot of the ladies would benefit from having their hands in the dirt. "That is quite impressive, Lady Margaret."

"I agree," the king said, raising his glass to her. "I would be honored if you would one day share your gifts with me."

Crompton looked at Sorren sharply. The king was leering over her. Crompton's stomach twisted—he had seen that look many times before from his cousin.

"It would be my pleasure, Your Majesty," Lady Margaret said with a smile.

Theotes. She did not know what she was saying to the king. Had she never had someone express explicit interest in her, or was she genuinely this naive? Crompton cleared his throat. "When is it that luncheon is to be served?"

Sorren beckoned a servant forward. "His Grace is hungry."

After they had eaten, Crompton stood. "Lady Margaret, may I escort you back to your chambers to rest before afternoon tea?"

She looked to the king, and once he nodded, stood. "Thank you, Your Grace."

He led to her chambers, walking in silence and nodding to the other nobles they passed. He waited until the hallways were free of people before speaking again. "I see that you are developing a close relationship with the king." Crompton played it as an off-handed comment.

"My family has always been close with His Majesty," she said with a confused look, "and he has made me his ward."

"You are far too old to be a ward, Lady Margaret," Crompton reminded her.

"Feel free to take issue with His Majesty, Your Grace," came her tight reply.

Crompton shrugged. "That is an issue between you and Sorren. What is between you and me is your safety." He hoped he would be able to convince her to be wary of Sorren. He'd seen too many times what could happen when someone wasn't.

Lady Margaret stopped, pulling her arm from his. "I beg your pardon?"

"You cannot stay in the company of the king for long without harm coming to you." Crompton pivoted to look at her directly, his face turning serious.

Her brows raised, doubt clouding her face. "The king has no ill will toward me."

"That is not the harm I speak of, my lady," Crompton stated. "You need to be careful."

"Then you have no basis for your fear-mongering, Your Grace." Lady Margaret huffed, turning from him. "Good day to you."

Crompton watched the young woman walk away from him with a stiff back. He hoped that, even though she dismissed him now, his words would stay with her.

8

Margaret anxiously awaited the arrival of her childhood friends. She had not seen them since she had left court with her father to care for him in Silvica. They had all returned to court for the season with their husbands, staying within the palace and elsewhere to attend the upcoming feasts of celebration. She stood in front of the mirror, wearing the same dress she had worn to first see Charles. It wonderfully accentuated her features, and Margaret had Sarah curl her hair becomingly.

Sarah appeared behind her and placed a string of pearls around her neck. "You look beautiful, my lady."

"Thank you." Margaret smiled timidly.

"How long has it been since you've seen these women?"

"Almost eight years now." Her reply came with a nervous sigh.

Sarah smiled comfortingly at her. "You'll have no trouble today, I'm sure."

Margaret squeezed Sarah's arm before she went to her sitting room to wait for the women to arrive.

Clairissa Beauchamp, or rather Clairissa Boumonte after her marriage, was the first of her old friends to arrive. Clairissa had her hand resting protectively over her slightly distended stomach.

"Margaret," she said, her eyes alight in her excitement. "Have you returned?"

Margaret smiled, holding a hand out for her to take. "I've returned."

Clairissa smiled brightly at her. "Good," she said, "we've missed having our little Margaret around."

After a few moments, the remainder of the women arrived. Ingrid Adrienn, Elise Magdala, and Annalise Loreto completed the group that Margaret knew so intimately—or had, rather. Now Margaret did not even know the names of their husbands. As Margaret stood, she felt awkward with the line of thought. She was once again the odd one out in the group, having no husband or children.

"Ladies, thank you all for coming here today." She smiled at all of them. "I am so excited to see you all again. There is nothing I would delight in more than hearing all about what has happened here and to all of you since I left for the country."

"Not much has changed about you, still indefatigable as always," Ingrid piped, making the rest of the women giggle.

Margaret blushed, sitting. "Tea will be served shortly."

"Oh, don't let your feelings get hurt," Annalise told Margaret, laying a hand on her arm. "Ingrid is just being Ingrid. We couldn't wait to see you when we heard you were back."

"First, tell us what has happened with you," Elise commanded. "We want to know what happened in the country."

"Well," Margaret started slowly. "Papa and I settled in the country until about a year ago when he died, and then I went to the other side of the country to live with a couple who housed me until I could hire servants and commission a wardrobe for court, and now here I am."

"Well that's bland," Ingrid said with a bored look. "Typical of you, I suppose."

"Ingrid!" Clairissa snapped. "Don't be rude!"

Ingrid rolled her eyes as Margaret looked at her lap. "Sorry, Margaret."

"Her pregnancy is making her irritable," Annalise tried to comfort Margaret. "Don't pay any attention to her."

Margaret was starting to wonder why she had invited them—despite aging, they had not matured much. She had expected some of the vapidity to go away at least.

Elise smiled timidly at Margaret. "As you know, we've all married since last we saw you. Clairissa has two children, with another on the way; Ingrid is on her second child, and Annalise and I both have one child each."

"And trying for more," Annalise said with a warm smile. "Do you have any prospective husbands, Margaret?"

"Not yet." Margaret's cheeks heated at the thought of Liam having asked her on several occasions to go away with him and start a new life. It was the closest she had come to receiving a marriage proposal since she had turned Lord Nicholas down. "I don't know if I'm ready anyway."

"It doesn't matter if you're ready," Ingrid said. "You're reaching a point in your life where you'll be doomed to spinsterhood."

"There are plenty of women who marry past my age," Margaret defended. "I'm only twenty-five."

"Yes," Ingrid countered, "for their second marriage."

"My ladies," Sarah interrupted with a small curtsy. "Lady Margaret, His Majesty is here to see you."

The ladies all stood and curtsied deeply as King Sorren entered and pulled up short at the sight of the crowded room. "Lady Margaret, I wasn't aware you had company."

Margaret smiled at him. "Just reminiscing with old friends, Your Majesty."

"I won't keep you," King Sorren told her, an odd look on his face. "I wanted to let you know that I have requested Her Majesty to take you into her ladies."

"You honor me greatly, Your Majesty," Margaret said with her head bowed demurely. She wasn't sure why he was telling her this—he had told she would be joining the queen's retinue not long after their first meeting. Was there something to Crompton's warning the other day? No, the king had likely forgotten with everything else he must have to keep track of.

"I'll leave you to your entertaining," the king said, looking at the other women closely. "Ladies. Lady Margaret."

The women quietly curtsied again as the king left Margaret's chambers.

"You're on close speaking terms with the king?" Ingrid demanded as they returned to their seats.

"He's made me his ward," Margaret told them offhandedly. "When there are no feasts, I have dinners with the royal family."

"You must get us invited to their private dinners!" Elise commanded, her eyes calculating.

"It is really up to His Majesty who dines with him."

"But you can suggest it to the king," Ingrid told her, suddenly looking more pleasant. "Surely, you would do this for your oldest and best of friends."

"Well…" Margaret looked at her wide-eyed. Ingrid had never much liked her, and Ingrid calling herself Margaret's best friend made her wary. "I suppose…"

The old friends pulled in a collective gasp and all tried to speak at once, sheepishly giggling at each other.

"We've missed you, Margaret," Annalise told her.

The remainder of the afternoon was spent learning of the goings-on of court that Margaret had missed in the time she had been gone. Nothing particularly scandalous happened, only the usual affairs and illegitimate children born and passed off as their husband's offspring. Margaret was almost disappointed she had missed so little.

Margaret walked through the markets with Ingrid to shop for a new dress for Ingrid's upcoming birthday. Sarah dutifully trailed behind with Captain Vojvo, holding any fabric Margaret bought. There were vendors as far as the eye could see, no possible way for someone to see them all in one day. It had grown considerably since Margaret left years ago, though she was surprised to see so many in the late autumn month.

Margaret stopped and ran her hand over one of the silks that caught her eye.

"These are beautiful," Margaret said kindly to the older woman who sat behind the booth.

She gave Margaret a toothless grin. "Thank ye, milady." Her voice whistled through the gaps in her teeth, breath showing in the cold.

Margaret smiled at her, looking through the rest of the fabrics.

"D'ye see annithin' ye like, milady?" the vendor asked, hovering close to Margaret, accidentally running into Ingrid.

"Get your filth off me!" Ingrid snapped.

The vendor flushed deeply and tried to apologize when Ingrid shoved past her, causing her to fall.

Margaret gasped, kneeling next to the older woman. "Are you all right?" she asked worriedly, helping her to sit up. Tears stood in the older woman's eyes, making Margaret's face flush in anger. "What is wrong with you?" Margaret snapped at Ingrid.

"What's wrong with me? What's wrong with you? Why are you touching that thing?" Ingrid yelled at her, drawing a crowd.

Margaret made sure the old woman could sit up on her own and stood to confront Ingrid. "I am helping a person you wrongfully harmed, Ingrid!" She balled her gloved hands into fists to restrain herself. "You need to leave now."

"I need to leave?" Ingrid demanded of her, face shocked, a hand resting on her fur-covered chest.

"Yes, you need to leave, Ingrid," Margaret said quietly, "before I help this woman press charges against you."

"They would never believe that thing in rags!" Ingrid sounded disgusted as she looked at the old woman.

"No, but they would believe me." The look on Margaret's face dared Ingrid to contradict her. "And you can forget any notion of me helping you get a dinner with the king after this."

"Margaret!" Ingrid gasped. "You wouldn't do that to your best friend, would you?"

"Leave, Ingrid," Margaret said coldly. She could see Vojvo coming in closer to her in case she needed assistance. "Now."

Ingrid glared at her, turning with an indignant huff.

Margaret stooped once more to help the older woman up, leading her to her stool. Margaret knelt in front of her so that the older woman wouldn't have to strain her neck to look her in the face. "Are you hurt?" she asked, concerned.

"M'all right, milady," the older woman said. "You shouldna be kneelin' in the dirt like tha'. Ye'll be ruinin' yer dress on my account."

Margaret smiled. "It'll wash."

The older woman squeezed her hands tightly, her gnarled fingers holding Margaret's with surprising strength, an appreciative look on her face.

The captain came to help Margaret stand, handing a coin to the crone before he escorted Lady Margaret away. "Are you all right, my lady?" Vojvo asked, his brow furrowed.

Margaret nodded, even though her hand trembled on his arm. "I have never in my life done something like that—stood my ground against one of those ladies," she said more to herself than to him.

"You did well, my lady," Vojvo said, "It was a very honorable thing to do, something that only you could have done in that situation. You must remember you are worth more than friends who would use you for your connections."

"Thank you, Captain." Margaret gave him a tired smile. He was right. The only reason Ingrid had started to spend time with her was because Margaret was the king's ward. It reminded her very much of her mother, and Margaret couldn't say she'd miss Ingrid after this.

Vojvo gently squeezed her hand on his arm. "Would you like to go back to the palace, my lady?"

"No," Margaret said quietly. "No, there are things that need to be done today before Mr. Luther comes to visit tomorrow."

The captain bowed his head to her. "As you wish, my lady."

They returned to the palace several hours later, a light layer of snow on their shoulders. Margaret went into her chambers, leaving the door open for Vojvo to follow.

Vojvo shut the door behind him. "May I speak frankly, my lady?"

"Of course, Captain," she said, sitting on the white couch facing the fireplace. "Please, sit."

Vojvo sat with a relaxed sigh. "I'm very proud of you, my lady," he told her in a fatherly manner. "You were very honorable in your actions today."

"Thank you, Captain. That means the world coming from you."

"I want you to always remember to treat people kindly, whether they be peasant or royalty, my lady. They are people all the same; you will be a better person for it," Vojvo advised her. "But never allow anyone to treat you less than what you deserve—even if they're your friend."

Margaret nodded. "Very apt advice, Captain, and I will try to follow it."

Margaret was pleased to find she was able to get her dresses finished much faster in the capital than she had anywhere else. She watched as Sarah laced up one of her newest arrivals. It was a midnight blue gown that had a high back and a sweetheart neckline. The surcoat buttoned in the front, stopping at her waistline, and ended in two triangles that rested on her thighs, the back trailing behind her on the floor. The edges were embroidered in gold thread. Tightly fitted sleeves went all the way down to her wrists, from her elbows to wrists was an intricately sewn pattern in gold beads.

"Do you think Mr. Luther will like it, Sarah?" she asked, examining herself in the looking glass.

"I think any man would be a fool not to, my lady," Sarah said as she fluffed Margaret's skirts.

Margaret smiled at that. "Is everything ready for Mr. Luther's arrival?"

Margaret had requested Charles come to her in her apartments. She was tired of Charlotte giving her disparaging looks while she waited for Charles to join them in the drawing room. Having Charles come to her would work to her advantage. He would be able to see her in a setting without having his wife there to give him gentle touches and murmur in his ear.

"Everything is as you asked it to be, my lady. Once Mr. Luther has arrived, I will go to the kitchens to fetch your refreshments."

"Wonderful, Sarah, thank you." Margaret was thrilled everything was going smoothly for Charles' first visit.

Margaret went to wait in the small alcove in her drawing room.

"My lady," the captain said to make his presence known.

"Good morning, Captain," Margaret said pleasantly. "Have you been here long?"

"Only a few moments, your ladyship." Vojvo pulled his pocket watch from his waistcoat, snapping it shut when he was done looking at it. "Mr. Luther should be arriving shortly. Do you wish for me to stay?"

Margaret nodded. It wouldn't be proper for her to be alone in her chambers with a man without someone else there. "I think that would be wise."

"As you wish, my lady." Vojvo bowed his head before he settled himself at the other side of the room to give her enough privacy.

Margaret picked up the needlework she was practicing with in anticipation for her time with the queen. She sighed as she waited; she wanted to look occupied when Charles entered the room. Looking out the window, she could see tiny flecks of snow lazily falling to the ground.

Luckily she did not have to wait long before Sarah came to her side, saying, "My lady, Mr. Luther is here."

"Bring him in, Sarah, and then get the wine."

Charles looked around the room in awe. It was a spectacular sight to see the brightly colored room for the first time—it still was to her, and she had been living in them almost three months. He went to Margaret sitting in the niche at the far end of the room with a smile.

"These are quite impressive rooms you have, Lady Margaret."

Margaret tore her eyes away from the delicate work in her hands, smiling at him. "Thank you—" She cut off when she saw the flowers he had in his hand. "What are those?"

Charles handed her the flowers. "For you. They're the same as the bouquet I got you when we first met."

Margaret smiled brightly, burying her face in the blooms and inhaling deeply. She felt just like a child again, discovering a new kind of affection.

"I remember, thank you, Charles." Margaret smiled. "How did you ever find them in Demonat?"

"I know a gentleman who grows them indoors." Charles sat across from her, watching her smell the flowers. "I suppose being the king's ward has its benefits," he said, gesturing to the room.

Margaret looked around the room. "I suppose it does. I feel these are a little excessive, but His Majesty insisted nothing was too lavish for me."

"They're beautiful." Charles took another look around the room, eyes staying on Captain Vojvo for a few long moments.

Margaret set aside the blossoms—she would have Sarah find something to put them in when she returned. Her attention moved back to Charles. "What shall you teach me today?"

"You're going to tell me what you've learned about our investors," Charles said, his face turning serious.

"My father primarily preferred silent investors because he had his own way of doing things and did not want others giving their input." Margaret looked at him, brow furrowed.

"Correct, but tell me about the investors," Charles instructed.

Margaret threw him a mildly exasperated look. This was one of her least favorite portions of her education. She went over the information she could remember of their four biggest investors, though she found it difficult to remember why they had invested when her father had just been starting out.

"Excellent, Lady Margaret. Now tell me what their return is."

"Each investor gets three percent above what they put in. Even after doling out their portions, the business is making over twenty thousand gold tals a year."

Margaret furrowed her brow in concentration. "After salaries for workers and the king's percentage, I'm personally earning around eleven thousand gold tals a year."

"If only your bookkeeping were as good as your knowledge of our investors," Charles commented, an amused look on his face.

Margaret looked chagrined but laughed nonetheless. Margaret was atrocious at bookkeeping. "And now what?"

Sarah took this opportunity to set bread and cheese with cold meats in front of them. "Wine, my lady, sir?"

"Yes, thank you." Margaret smiled at Charles. "I guess we're having a small lunch next."

"I suppose so," Charles commented, taking a drink from his wine glass.

"How is Charlotte doing?" Margaret asked, a hint of disinterest in her voice. She knew it was expected of her to ask after his wife.

Charles made a face. "She's none too happy that we'll now be having your instruction here."

Margaret raised her brows. She would be lying if she said she was disappointed that Charlotte was upset over the arrangement. "Why is that?"

Charles shrugged. "She thinks that it's improper. She wants to have a chaperone around, particularly herself."

"There is nothing improper about the owner of a business and her executor meeting," Margaret said irritably. "We'll be working closely for a very long time. She'll need to get used to the idea. Besides, Captain Vojvo is here."

Charles conceded to the fact. "I'm sure Charlotte would feel more comfortable if she were allowed to come along."

Margaret felt her hackles starting to raise. She wasn't fond of Charlotte, and Charlotte felt much the same. "I have no doubt that she would, but I will not have your wife looking at me as if I'm a pariah."

"She's not looking at you like a pariah, Lady Margaret," Charles said. "Charlotte thinks that you're taking the business away from me."

"How can I take the business away from you?" Margaret demanded. "It's not even yours to begin with."

"I know, Margaret." Charles' mouth hardened as he rested his hand on hers to calm her. "That's just the way she sees it."

Margaret quickly gathered her composure after she saw the stern look the captain gave her. "I just feel like I can learn much better with Charlotte in her own home."

"Then I will tell her she needs to stay at home and tend to her work," Charles said to her. "Will that make you feel better?"

"Much," Margaret said, smug.

Charles sighed. "I wish that you and Charlotte could get along. Like you said, we will be working together for a long while."

Margaret avoided answering his wish. It was her hope that she could plant the seed in his mind of setting aside Charlotte and picking up a more capable wife.

"Perhaps we should return to your lessons?" Charles said after a long moment of silence.

Margaret nodded with a charming smile. "Let the master instruct me fully."

Charles quirked his eyebrow but went to lecture her on how a field should be prepared for tobacco, rotations, and how to tell when the leaves were perfect for cultivating.

Her father had taught Charles in much the same way when he had been hired. They had traveled from Jalmar to Dorcia many times during his instruction to show Charles the stages of the leaves over the months and to get his hands dirty. Having grown up near the fields, Margaret mostly knew what the plants looked like and how to cultivate them, though it had been a long time since she had been there.

Once their lesson was through, Captain Vojvo waited patiently in the corner for Charles to leave before he peeled himself off the wall. "That seemed to be a productive meeting, my lady," Vojvo commented blandly.

"If you can call it that," Margaret said, aggravated.

"Might I make a suggestion?"

Margaret raised a single brow, motioning for him to continue.

"I think it would be wise not to ostracize Mr. Luther's wife. It will make him more reluctant to continue on with your instruction," Vojvo told her. "You need to be on good terms with the man running your business."

"We are on good terms, Captain," she defended.

"For now," he countered. "Until you push him too far, and then you will have an executor who resents you and is unwilling to tell you what is going on—good or bad."

Margaret remained silent, staring at him stubbornly.

"My lady," —Vojvo sounded strained— "please don't take this as a criticism on your person. I have more experience in dealing with subordinates."

"I will take your comments under advisement, Captain Vojvo," Margaret said quietly. "If you will excuse me, I need to change for dinner."

Vojvo bowed to her. "Yes, my lady," he said before he left her chambers.

9

Liam grunted as he hoisted a small doe on his shoulders, electing not to remove the organs and have blood drip down his back as he returned to Numetra. Sweat fell down his face, despite the snow that covered the ground. The first snowfall of the season had come the night before, creating a white void in the forest. He carried the deer the two miles back to town before coming to a stop.

He lowered the animal by the legs, heaving a relieved sigh as the weight was lifted from his shoulders.

"Hello!" he called out to anyone who would listen. The town had been awake before he left, so he felt no guilt in calling loudly.

Gretta poked her head out of the window of her eatery, face puckered, ready to yell at the person disturbing the peace. Her expression lightened when she saw who was yelling and came to his side. "Only one today?" She looked at the animal, seeming disappointed.

"She's big enough to feed you for a week!" Liam protested, gesturing at how fat she was. "You *and* those sons of yours!"

Gretta waved a dismissive hand at him, squatting for a closer look. "Kept the organs this time?"

"Just for you," Liam assured her.

"Good." She grinned. "The liver is the best."

"I'll take your word for it, Gretta." Liam sounded unconvinced.

"Help me get her inside," she commanded as she stood.

Liam grunted again as he lifted the doe by the feet, waddling to the back of the eatery where Gretta would butcher the deer. He strung up the deer by her feet before washing his hands.

"There's food on the hearth for ye," Gretta told him. "I saved it for ye when ye didna show up fer breakfast. Go on an' eat, an' then come back to help."

"Yes ma'am." Liam grinned at her before going inside.

Her youngest, Eli, was sitting at the table, eating already.

"Your brothers working?"

Eli nodded, his mouth full with bread.

Liam smiled, picking up his plate. It was heaped with eggs, bacon, and sausage. Smile morphing into a wide grin, he sat across from Eli to dig into the feast. He could get used to this.

Liam wiped his brow, the heat from the forge sweltering, despite the winter chill of Demonat blowing through the door. It was near the end of the work day, and Liam looked forward to going home to sleep.

"Ahem," came the feminine interruption from the doorway.

Thorkelin looked up, nudging Liam. "I think it's for ye, lad."

Liam turned, seeing Gretta there, Eli's hand in hers. "Gretta, what are you doing here?"

"I thought ye might would like to join us all for dinner?" she asked, almost shyly as she fidgeted with the nails on her free hand.

Liam smiled at her. "I'll be over once I'm done here in about an hour if that is all right?"

Gretta nodded, pulling Eli out of the smithy.

"That lass is soft on ye, lad," Jossnon told him, amusement lighting his eyes.

"Gretta?" Liam was surprised Thorkelin would say such a thing.

"Did ye no see her?" Jossnon shoved the metal he was hammering back into the hot forge. "Her hair was done, an' that dress looked fair new."

Liam paused, realizing Jossnon was correct in his assessment. "What should I do?"

"That, lad, is somethin' only ye can decide." Jossnon rubbed the back of his neck, giving Liam a look of sympathy. "I dinna envy ye."

Liam didn't envy himself, either. "Do you think I could go early?"

Thorkelin raised his brows, looking him over. "Aye, if ye'd like, I can handle the rest of it."

"Thanks."

Liam put his tools away before he went to his flat. He filled a pitcher with water from the well outside the building. After rooting around for the soap, he scrubbed himself until his skin shone red. After washing his hair and rinsing it out, Liam dumped the rest of the water over himself. Rivulets ran down his nude form, cleansing his skin of the harsh soap.

Drying himself, Liam searched for the clothes he had purchased—or been given, rather—in Zuev. They still fit, if a little more snugly than before. He grabbed his small mirror, scraping away the stubble that had returned during the day. When he was finished, he sat quietly for a moment.

What would happen if he allowed Gretta to get the wrong impression? Did he want her to continue to have the wrong impression? *Was* it the wrong impression? What would happen if she found out who he was? Could he even tell her? How would he explain Margaret? Did he even want to get involved with someone when Margaret could need him at any moment? What if someone found out who he was and he had to run again?

Liam sighed heavily as the thoughts swirled around his head. He would go with an open mind, and he would deal with what came. Sighing again, he made his way to Gretta's, going around the back to the family entrance.

His knock was answered quickly by Gretta's oldest son, Jamie. His face lit when he saw Liam. "Ye're early!"

He grinned at Jamie, putting an arm around the teen's shoulder. "I wanted to surprise your Ma."

"She will be," assured Jamie as they walked into the kitchen. "Ma!"

Gretta turned away from the hearth, beaming when she saw him. "Liam, ye're early!"

"I hope it's not a problem?" Liam asked.

"Not at all!" Gretta gushed. "Not at all! Please, sit." She led him toward their table, hands on his shoulders.

He sat, looking up at her when she let her hands rest on his shoulders longer than was necessary. Liam couldn't say he disliked the feeling.

"Would ye like something to drink?" She did not take her hands away while she asked.

Liam nodded. "Anything you have on hand would be fine."

Squeezing his shoulders, she then poked her head through the doorway. "Simon, bring Liam a drink!"

When the drinks were served, all three boys joined him at the table. They, too, cleaned themselves for dinner. The boys were looking at him, barely veiled excitement growing on their faces.

Liam turned his eye on Jamie. "What is it you're doing for work?"

"Simon an' myself are set to choppin' wood out in the forest to sell for winter," Jamie told him proudly.

"Do you have your own axes?" Liam took a sip of the sweet mead Gretta had brewed.

"Aye," Jamie hesitantly answered. The excitement was gone from his face.

Liam raised a brow at his change of demeanor. "Is there something wrong with them?"

"They dinna chop well," Simon answered for his brother. "An' they're verra old."

"Bring them to me tomorrow, and I'll fix them for you," Liam said.

"Ye dinna have to do that," Gretta interjected.

"I'm happy to," he answered. "A man should have proper working tools."

Jamie's excitement returned as his mother thanked Liam. A dinner of roast venison with potatoes and carrots was served shortly thereafter. He looked around the table, a contented sigh escaping his lips. He could get used to dinners like this, the family of four taking away the sting of being alone in a country that wasn't his own.

Liam sat back when he was finished, hands on his full stomach. "That was the most wonderful thing I have ever eaten."

Gretta smiled, her cheeks coloring with pleasure. "I'm verra happy to hear it." She turned her eyes to her children. "Go an' wash before bed, aye?"

Liam felt his stomach clench at their dismissal. He didn't want to get too attached, just in case. "I should go too."

"Wait a moment," she told him.

She kissed each of her sons goodnight before she turned her gaze on Liam. She, too, was nervous. Gretta came to sit next to him, the light of the fire softening her features.

"Thank you again," Liam said quickly, wanting to break the silence, "for having me for dinner."

Gretta waved her hand dismissively. "I was wonderin' if I could ask a favor of ye, Liam."

His stomach clenched tighter. "Anything."

She grabbed his hand, not looking at him. "Ye ken the boys dinna have a father to teach 'em certain things a mother canna teach."

Liam began to relax, squeezing her hand. This wasn't a romantic request as Thorkelin had eluded to. "And you want me to teach them these things?"

She looked up, her eyes hopeful. "Would ye be willin', Liam?"

"I would be." Liam smiled at her.

Gretta let out a relieved sigh. "Thank ye, Liam."

"Of course, Gretta." Liam smiled again, standing. "I really should be going now."

She walked him to the door. "I'll bid ye a goodnight, then."

"Goodnight," Liam returned. "Remind Jamie to bring me those axes tomorrow."

Gretta looked over Liam's face before grabbing it and pulling him toward her. She kissed him soundly, slowly pulling away from him. "I will."

Nodding silently, Liam left her home. He touched his lips, still tingling from her kiss.

10

Margaret clasped her hands nervously in front of her. She waited in the corridor outside the queen's chambers. "What time is it?"

Captain Vojvo sighed, pulling out his pocket watch. "Five 'til, my lady."

She started to pace. She couldn't show up early, and she could not be late either. Margaret had to make a good impression with the queen, especially after her mother's slight years ago.

Vojvo held a hand out to stop her pacing. "My lady, you will do fine."

Clenching her hands tighter, she looked up at him anxiously. She had waited years for this position after her mother had ruined it for her—she couldn't bear to lose it again. "But what if I don't?"

"I will be right there with you," the captain assured her. "You'll do fine."

Margaret sighed, trying to loosen the tension from the middle of her back. "What time is it?"

He pulled out his watch again. "It's time."

Margaret hurried to the door, knocking. When they opened, she said, "Lady Margaret for the queen."

The herald announced her, and she entered the chamber with Vojvo following behind. When she was in front of the queen, she curtsied deeply. "Your Majesty."

The queen looked her over with cold eyes. "Lady Margaret, you certainly are prompt."

Margaret rose. "I did not want to keep Your Majesty waiting."

"Very considerate of you, Lady Margaret," Queen Lillian told her boredly.

Margaret frowned. "Have I done something to offend, Your Majesty?"

"You have circumvented my authority as to whom I choose to be in my private company by having your guardian order you to be in my ladies," she said with her voice raised.

"Your Majesty," Margaret said with a look of surprise, "I did not ask His Majesty to procure me a position within your ladies. He told me on his own that he had requested of you to take me into your company."

The queen furrowed her brow at Margaret. Clearly, she didn't believe her. "Either way, you are to be among my ladies, and that requires a certain level of decorum. In public, you are to act as a representative of me, and that entails always speaking gently to others and avoiding putting yourself in compromising positions. I do not want to hear any rumors of misconduct on your part, and I do not want to catch you in any trysts. Do you understand?"

"Yes, Majesty," Margaret said. "I would never disrespect you in such a way."

The queen grabbed the Book of Books from a side table. "Swear it on Theotes."

Margaret looked around the room. All the women were looking at her expectantly, several of whom she recognized from evening meals or entertaining with her parents. She rested her hand on the book. "I swear on the holy word of Theotes that I will not bring shame to you or to myself."

"Good." The queen nodded. "I'll expect you here in the morning to help ready me with the rest of my ladies."

Margaret curtsied deeply again and turned to leave.

"Oh, and Lady Margaret?" the queen called when she had reached the door. She turned, eagerly looking at the queen. "Yes, Your Majesty?"

"Leave your dog at home tomorrow," Lillian said harshly, staring pointedly at Captain Vojvo.

Margaret cast a brief glance at Vojvo. "As you wish, Your Majesty."

Margaret arrived early to the queen's chambers. She wore one of her recent commissions in the style of the queen's ladies. Margaret knocked on the door, waiting impatiently for it to open.

The knock went unanswered.

Margaret knocked again, more firmly this time. Her knocking remained unanswered. She frowned, knocking for a third time. Frown deepening, Margaret crossed her arms over her chest.

"Hello?" she called, knocking on the door again.

With no answer, Margaret let herself into the chambers. She saw the queen already being dressed by Duchess Cecily and Lady Victoria.

"You're late," Queen Lillian growled at her.

Margaret curtsied low to her. "My apologies, Your Majesty."

The queen waved a hand at her before tightening her grip on her bed post. "Tighter!" she commanded.

Margaret frowned. Had no one told the queen that she shouldn't tight-lace? She looked around for the next clothing item to put on, grabbing the first petticoat she saw. She spread the strings to make it easier for the queen to step into.

Lady Victoria snatched it from Margaret's hands, glaring icily at her. "Don't touch anything."

"But—"

"You don't touch anything of the queen's!" Lady Victoria snapped.

"I am a lady in waiting for Her Majesty," Margaret fumed, standing taller. "It is my duty to touch the queen's things."

"You are a maid of honor, Lady Margaret," Queen Lillian irritably corrected her. "The only reason you are here is for you to be introduced to my ladies of the bedchamber and, after I'm finished being dressed, the ladies of the privy chamber."

"Why was I not told this yesterday?" Margaret's face fell. "I thought—"

"You thought wrong, Lady Margaret," Cecily, Duchess of Rivack, interrupted. "Now go into the privy chamber and wait. You are disturbing the queen and interrupting our work."

"But—"

"Get out, Lady Margaret!" Queen Lillian commanded.

Margaret flushed. "Yes, Your Majesty," she said, bobbing a quick curtsy before fleeing from the queen's bedchamber.

She almost ran into Lady Elizabeth in the privy chambers when she turned around, letting out a gasp. The other woman glared at her, pushing Margaret aside. She looked around helplessly, unsure of where she should be.

Margaret clenched her hands in her skirts. How could she have so easily gone from being promised she would be waiting on the queen to a glorified room decoration as a maid of honor in the span of a day?

The queen emerged from her bedchamber after a few tense moments. She looked at Margaret blandly, her two ladies of the bedchamber flanking her. "Lady Margaret, may I present Duchess Cecily and Lady Victoria, Ladies of the Bedchamber," —Lillian motioned to each woman in turn— "and the Ladies Elizabeth, Aurora, and Marsaille of the Privy Chamber."

Margaret nodded to each of them. "The honor is mine," she said.

"Lady Margaret, you are a maid of honor within my ladies, meaning you are only here to raise your standing and find a husband."

Margaret frowned, looking around the room. None of the other women looked happy she was there. "I am honored nonetheless, Your Majesty."

Margaret waited for Charles in her sitting room, her back to the fire. The winter chill seeped through the windows, and Margaret didn't dare sit next to them. She pulled her shawl tighter around her shoulders, as if the motion would banish the chill even from outside.

With her duties with the queen, she had not seen him since the Demonat two months prior and missed being able to send a new year's letter to the workers, as had been her father's custom, with his guidance.

The door opened abruptly, making Margaret jump. Charles stood in the open space, snow coating his shoulders. She stood, dropping her shawl.

"Sarah, get Mr. Luther's cloak and bring a blanket for his lap," she commanded.

Sarah swarmed Charles, taking his cloak and shaking it in the hallway.

Charles went immediately to the fire, sticking his hands as close to the flames as he could. "It's colder than Apollyon's soul out there," he complained.

Margaret brought him a hot cup of tea. "Drink this," she commanded. "It will warm you."

He took it without a word, tossing it to the back of his throat. Charles let out a hiss after he swallowed. "Hot," he said simply.

Margaret raised her brow, taking the cup from his hand. "Come sit. Sarah has a blanket to warm you."

Charles followed her to the sofa, sitting close to her. Margaret helped Sarah tuck the blanket to warm him.

"Did you walk here?" Margaret grabbed his cold hands and rubbed them between hers.

"Yes," he confirmed, "the carriages were having trouble in the snow."

Margaret made a sympathetic noise in her throat, moving closer to him. "You should have sent word. We could have canceled."

"I wanted to come," Charles assured her, leaving his hand in hers.

Delighting in the gesture, Margaret felt her cheeks warm. He had never shown her any physical affection, and now he held her hand firmly and he was pressed against her side. She did not have long to delight in the closeness before he spoke.

"Is your man not here today?" Charles asked, looking in the corners for Vojvo.

Margaret looked around the room herself. "He should be here already. Perhaps he did not remember the time?"

Charles raised a single brow. "I should not complain to having you without eyes boring holes in the back of my head."

She lowered her lashes. "What is it you would like to teach me today?"

"Plenty."

Margaret's stomach tingled. Perhaps she had done well enough at hinting her attraction to him.

Margaret sighed as she sat in the garden. Now that the weather was starting to warm as Amonat dawned, the queen wanted fresh air and chose a shaded area in the royal gardens to sojourn. Margaret found that most of the queen's ladies were undyingly loyal. They remembered her mother's insulting behavior toward the monarch and did not bother to veil their dislike since Margaret's first week of service to the queen. Margaret sat off to the side from the women but still within sight.

Surprise ran through the ladies when the king made an appearance. Margaret stood and curtsied with the rest of them. He looked tired, his brow permanently wrinkled from the weight of office. King Sorren's closely cropped beard and mustache seemed to grow whiter by the day, despite not being much older than her father would have been had he still lived. The king towered over the advisors he had surrounding him, standing at well over six feet.

The queen smiled at him. "My love, this is a pleasant surprise."

King Sorren kissed her knuckles. "I'm afraid that I am not here solely for a visit, my dear." The king looked at his queen's entourage, spotting Margaret in the back. "I need to speak with Lady Margaret."

The queen and her ladies turned a suspicious eye toward her. "Why do you need to speak with her?" she asked, an accusing tone in her voice.

"I need her opinion on the funeral that we will be holding for her father, Lillian. We are moving him from a pauper's grave to the one he deserves," Sorren told her tartly.

Surprise ran through Margaret. This was the first time she was hearing of her father being moved back to Dorcia. She was pleased that he would be—she was sure Liam had done a well enough job burying him in Silvica, but he deserved to be among his own people and the legacy he had built.

Queen Lillian had the grace to look chagrined. "Yes, my lord. Lady Margaret, you may go." She dismissed her with an absentminded wave of her hand.

Margaret curtsied low to the queen. "Thank you, Your Majesty," she said diminutively before going to the king's side.

King Sorren offered his arm to Margaret. "My lady." He escorted Margaret past the queen without a second look.

"You are also having a funeral for my father?" Margaret asked as she walked by his side.

The king nodded. "He deserves something better than just a reburial in Dorcia," he said quietly. "Will you travel to Silvica and then make the pilgrimage to Dorcia from there?"

"Yes," she vehemently told him. "I should be by his side this time." Margaret's eyes began to water, ashamed that she had not stayed with her father.

The king remained silent.

Margaret looked at him, worried. Since her arrival, he had not brought up her father or commented on her story of having to leave to save herself from being wrongly accused. She still didn't know for sure whether he believed her.

She cleared her throat after a moment of silence. "You wanted to discuss the details of the funeral, Majesty?"

"Yes," he said simply.

Margaret had a sinking feeling in her stomach. His face had become rigid at the mention of her leaving her father alone on his deathbed. "Papa would have loved for there to be music. Lots of music. It was his favorite thing about being at court with you."

The king smiled. Her father would always stay as close to the music as possible, saying that as a child he had never been able to hear anything like it. "Yes it was, and he will have endless music."

Margaret smiled at the king brightly. "Thank you, Your Majesty."

They continued to walk for a while, his hand occasionally resting on top of hers when he was making a point. It was not long before they were back in sight of the queen and her ladies, but the king did not release her from his company, instead keeping her on his arm as they walked past the queen into the palace.

"Is there something wrong, Majesty?" Margaret looked back at the queen.

He followed her eyes. "Her Majesty does not like that I spend any time alone with another woman. Her sister was set aside for another woman by the king in Mekhor, and she fears I will do the same to her." The wrinkles on his forehead deepened as he frowned.

"Will you?" Margaret asked quietly.

"No, and even so, a king has whom he wants—marriage or not."

The answer surprised Margaret. She did not think the king was capable of infidelity. He had always been incredibly loving and affectionate toward his wife. She remained quiet on the matter, not wanting to speak out of place.

He led her back to her apartments, stopping at the door. "You may return if you'd like, but I hope that you will take the rest of the day to think of any other plans that would suit your father."

"I will, Majesty." Margaret tried to smile but failed. "I'll make sure to have it for you by this evening."

He nodded. "Very good," he said before walking away.

11

Months passed as Liam earned his way with Master Thorkelin. He enjoyed walking about the town without the fear of being arrested and executed or bringing harm to the innocents living in the area. Liam found that the longer he worked for the smith, the more he opened up. Jossnon had managed to coax all he could about Margaret out of Liam. His advice was to stay as far away from her as possible if she was unwilling to take Liam as he was.

That would be easier said than done. Liam thought about Margaret often while he worked, wondering how she was faring in the capital. He hadn't heard from her, despite sending letters to the Gollacks to pass along to her to check on her health. At least he hadn't heard of any executions of a noblewoman, so he knew she had not suffered that fate when she arrived.

Thorkelin thought Gretta and her boys were much better suited for him, and Liam wasn't inclined to disagree. If anyone would be able to get him to forget Margaret, it would be Gretta. She had everything he wanted to offer—a permanent home, children, a living he could help build up. If it weren't for Margaret and his duty to her, Liam could very easily see himself never leaving.

"Master Thorkelin, why won't you tell me anything of yourself?" Liam still knew nothing of substance about the man he was working with. He was weary of Jossnon avoiding any questions that Liam asked of his own life.

"'Tis a sad story, lad," came his simple reply.

Liam was going to persist this time. "I'd still like to hear it."

"Would ye now?"

"Yes," Liam said with a stubborn look. "I would."

Jossnon Thorkelin sighed heavily. After a long moment, he finally spoke, "I was once married long ago, prob'ly before ye were born, to a woman much like yer Maggie." Jossnon lifted his hand to stem Liam's protest about labeling Margaret his. "She was the daughter of a baron an' she was married when we met."

Thorkelin's face looked softer as he talked about this woman. "She was the most beautiful woman I had ever seen in my life, an' I still think that she is. My Cora came in here to have a sword made fer 'er husband fer an anniversary gift an' it was an attraction like no other, lad."

Thorkelin fell silent for a moment, looking down at his tools. Liam wasn't sure if he would continue.

"She was so uninterested in what she was sayin' that he wanted. Cora came in every day fer two weeks to check on the progress of the blade before our affair began. This lasted months before her husband found out. He came to my shop with Cora in tow and an' confronted the both of us."

Jossnon's eyes grew haunted. "Her husband didna leave my shop that day. Later that year, we were married an' started a family of our own. My Cora gave me three beautiful babies, an' only one survived into boyhood."

"I'm sorry," Liam said quietly. He wasn't about to interrupt to ask if he had gone to jail for killing another man. If Jossnon wanted to provide that information, he would.

Thorkelin nodded. "He was thirteen when the war between Salatia an' Anatalia broke out. We were both considered to be able bodied an' were sent off to the fightin'. My son—Robert his name was—was killed in Chenalieu on the front lines. I was workin' in the smith's tent at the time, mendin' broken swords and makin' new ones from the ruined. I was allowed to return to my wife to tell her the news an' to gather more smithin' supplies.

"Cora was devastated, she was, and blamed me fer his death, sayin' that had she still been married to 'er first husband, she ne'er would have lost 'er son. Ne'er woulda known what the effects of war truly were." The haunted look on Jossnon's face turned tormented. "She told me she wished I had been killed in his place. I wished fer the same—honestly, I did. Cora divorced me an' begged fer 'er father to find 'er another suitable marriage. She no longer wished to dwell among us common folk."

Liam swallowed hard. It was no wonder Jossnon had not wanted to tell him this story.

"My Cora was married again by the time I had returned from war; 'er father had arranged a marriage to another baron twenty years 'er senior. Baron Voldure was a cruel man. He beat my Cora, and I found out one day that he had killed 'er when she defied his orders."

Master Thorkelin remained quiet after that, and Liam could not blame him. The smith had not lied to him when he said it was a sad tale. Liam regretted insisting on being told.

He didn't think Margaret would have done something like that to him. Margaret had known what it was like to live in an area below her station, and she had flourished. She had made everyone around her flourish too.

Liam quietly returned to his work, the only noise in the shop the hammering of the smith and his worker.

After the work day was done, Liam went to the Smiling Fox to see Gretta. He hoped she would be able to dispel the clouds Jossnon's story had brought over the day. It was no wonder Jossnon had been so invested in whether he had a special one in his life. Liam suspected the smith didn't want him to suffer anything like the same fate.

"I dinna ken ye were comin' today." A smile lit Gretta's face as she walked toward him. "Ye ken ye can go straight into the house fer food—ye've provided enough to earn a free meal."

Liam squeezed her hand when she offered it. "Will you meet me back there for a drink?"

"Aye, I'll join ye in a minute."

Liam went to the private kitchen where the family ate their meals and poured himself a cup of beer. It only took Gretta a few minutes to join him, a tea towel over her shoulder.

"I didna expect you until tomorrow at least," she said, sitting across from him. Liam poured her a cup of her own. "I wanted to ask you something."

She sat forward a little, her eyes suddenly intense. "Aye?"

"Do you know anything about the blacksmith?" He took a long drink, sighing when he put his cup down. "He told me about his late wife today."

"Oh, aye." Gretta's face fell. "He's a sad story, keeps mostly to himself these days."

Liam fidgeted with his cup. "I didn't think he had it in him to kill a man. Did he ever face any consequences?"

Gretta shook her head. "His wife told the authorities her husband attacked her at the forge an' Jossnon was only protecting her, an' she wouldna be pressin' charges against him."

That explained why Jossnon was able to move on to a marriage so quickly. Sighing over his cup, Liam said, "It's a sad thing to be sure."

"Why dinna ye stay, and I'll do my best to cheer ye up?" Gretta suggested. Liam nodded. He would like that.

Liam visited Gretta's eatery before going to the Heated Forge. He sat at a table, inhaling deeply, the tantalizing scent of bacon wafting from the kitchen. Liam smiled when he saw Gretta carrying a plate of food out of the kitchen.

She dropped the dish unceremoniously in front of the patron when she caught sight of Liam. "Ye ken ye dinna have to eat out here," she said when she reached him, "Ye always have a place at our table. The boys love it when ye eat with them."

"They do?" Liam felt an unfamiliar swell in his chest at the knowledge.

"Ye're all they talk about for a week after ye take them out," she went on.

Liam grinned at her. "I'll make sure to spend more time with them, then."

"I would like that." Gretta rested a hand on his arm. "Why dinna ye come for dinner tonight?"

He covered her hand, squeezing it gently. "I'll be sure to be in at a decent hour."

"We look forward to it," she told him with lowered lashes. "I'll be right out with yer breakfast."

When she set down his meal, she touched his shoulder. "Come see me in the back when ye're finished, aye?"

Liam smiled at her. "I will."

He savored his meal, eating slowly. As promised, when he finished, Liam found Gretta in the family kitchen. She was sitting at the table with Jamie and Simon as they ate before work as he did. Liam rested a hand on each of the boy's shoulders. They turned with delighted faces.

"Good morning, boys."

"Are ye here for breakfast, Liam?" Jamie asked.

"I've already had some in the main room," Liam told them. "I'm here to say goodbye to your Ma before going to the smithy."

"Can ye no stay a while?" Simon whined.

"I'll be back to have dinner with you tonight," Liam assured him, "and you two can tell me all about your days."

"I'll walk ye to the door," Gretta said, standing.

Liam squeezed the boys' shoulders before following Gretta to the door, and then further outside when she beckoned him more.

She closed the door and turned to him. "Ye ken ye're welcome here for as long as ye want," she reminded him, adding almost shyly, "whenever ye want."

"I appreciate that, Gretta. I really do," Liam sincerely told her.

"May I kiss ye goodbye, Liam?" Gretta looked up at him, her cheeks rosy.

"You may," Liam said, his own cheeks heating.

She stepped closer to him, resting one hand on his chest, snaking the other behind his neck. Liam's arms naturally went around her waist, pulling her against him. Gretta watched his mouth until she met his lips with hers.

Liam pulled her closer to him, feeling her hand grip his neck tighter. He almost regretted it when she broke their embrace.

"I'll see ye tonight," she said huskily, disappearing into her home.

Liam went to the smith, his expression bemused.

Thorkelin caught sight of him. "What's wrong wi' ye, lad?"

"Hmm?" Liam turned to look at him.

"Ye look like a man who just saw his first woman," Jossnon explained.

"I think Gretta is trying to court me," Liam said, sounding dazed.

"Is there annithin' wrong with that?" Thorkelin asked.

"I'm not sure," Liam admitted.

Thorkelin raised a brow. "Ye dinna ken?"

Liam shrugged with one shoulder. "I've always pictured myself a lifelong bachelor... Only Margaret made me think any different."

"An' now she's out o' yer reach," Jossnon said the unspoken.

Liam nodded, getting out his unfinished work.

"What will ye do?"

"I really don't know," Liam told him. "I'm fond of her—I'm especially fond of her boys."

Thorkelin shrugged and paused for a moment before speaking. "I think ye should see where this takes ye."

Liam still looked hesitant.

"If ye are thinkin' of that Maggie," Jossnon went on sternly, "she'll have been livin' with her kind of people, an' she willna be thinkin' of ye as a suitor."

He sighed heavily. "You're right, she will be living her own life, with her own kind of people." Jossnon was more right than he knew—he'd yet to hear from Margaret in the year since they'd parted ways, despite him sending several letters to her.

Thorkelin clapped him on the back. "Good lad. When d'ye see Gretta again?"

"Tonight—for dinner," Liam told him. "The boys are very excited about it."

"Ye'll do her a lot o' good, an' she'll do ye a lot o' good too," the smith told him.

Liam knocked on Gretta's door. It took longer than usual to answer, Gretta's face red and damp with perspiration.

Liam furrowed his brow, concerned. "Are you all right, Gretta?"

"Oh, aye," assured Gretta, "just standin' too close to the hearth. It's been a hot day, aye?"

Liam nodded. "It has been," he agreed.

She waved him inside. "Come in an' get yerself somethin' to drink then."

Liam did as he was bid, sitting at the table with a mug of ale. "Are the boys home from work?"

"No just yet," Gretta said over her shoulder, stirring the stew she had been making. "Eli hasna been feelin' well, so he's been sent to bed with a bit o' bread an' some milk."

"I'm sorry to hear he isn't feeling well." Liam's brow wrinkled again. "Does he need to see a healer?"

"Oh, no," —Gretta waved her hand— "nothin' but a belly ache."

Liam sat back, taking a deep gulp of his ale, assured by her confidence. The room was comfortably warm—compared to the smithy at least. Gretta's neck was slick with sweat, wisps of hair clinging to her. He watched her stir and taste, add spice and repeat until she was satisfied. It reminded him of being in his own mother's kitchen when he was a boy.

"Why don't you cool yourself off?" He went to her, taking the ladle from her hand. "I can stir it."

Gretta flashed him a bright smile. "Are ye certain?"

"Of course," assured Liam, shooing her away from the fire.

After a time, Gretta returned. She had changed her clothes to clean ones and had pinned her black hair up. She came to Liam's side, resting an affectionate hand on his back.

"Are ye hungry, Liam?" She asked, her voice husky.

Liam turned to look at her, a brow raised. "Should we not wait for the boys?"

She wet her lips. "They won't be here for a few hours yet."

"Gretta—"

She put both hands on his chest. "I'm very alone, Liam... Will ye come no upstairs wi' me?"

"Yes," Liam answered hoarsely.

12

I t took the traveling party almost the entire month of Mamonat to make the journey to Silvica. Many of the nobles wanted to have the king see that they were supporting the love he bore his friend, though Margaret had only ever seen them talking to her father once or twice before they left court. She didn't even know who most of them were. The king grew progressively more melancholy as they neared Silvica.

Margaret was allowed her own small entourage as it was her father this procession was for. She had the youngest daughter of Duke Bishop, Lady Jane, and the oldest daughter of a knight, Lady Annabel, as her entourage.

Margaret liked Lady Annabel much better than she did Lady Jane. Lady Jane looked as if she had been sucking on a lemon since the day the traveling party set out. Margaret knew that Lady Jane thought the task of waiting on her was beneath the daughter of a duke. Lady Annabel was more than happy to do what she asked and got on well with Sarah.

Both girls could not have been more than eighteen, and Margaret knew they would not gain any advantage in her entourage. She wasn't even sure where she stood in the nobility. Without a male heir, all that her father had was now hers, but women did not inherit titles without the blessing of the king.

Margaret rode at the front of the train of people behind the king and queen and their respective entourages. She watched as the queen laughed with her ladies and the king remained in his silent melancholy. Margaret found it grating that Queen Lillian did not care that her husband silently mourned, or even why they were traveling. She was glad to not be in the queen's entourage for this trip. Only the king and Margaret wore full morning attire, the rest of the travelers opting for gray armbands.

When the pilgrimage ended in Silvica, only the king and Margaret went to the country home where her father had perished, along with servants to remove the body and carry away any remaining valuables from the house. Margaret hesitated at the front door as she looked at its condition. She could see that her garden was completely dead, no new life coming from her years of hard work in the patch of earth. The king stood by her side patiently as she looked. After a few moments, she finally went in.

The home looked just the same to her. Dust gathered in the corners, the air musky. Everything sat in its place. She knew her jewels would not be there—Liam had given them to her when she had loaded the wagons to return to the capital.

The thought of Liam made her shoulders heavy. He had been the one to bury her father a year ago, not that she could tell the king that. Margaret looked around and could see each spot Liam had been in the home.

"Lady Margaret, your presence is requested in the back for the recovery of your father," one of the servants gently prodded her.

She pulled her eyes away from the doorway of her father's room. "Yes, of course," she said hastily. "I'm sorry for making you wait."

It was clear where her father had been laid to rest. Grass had overtaken the mound, growing a deeper green than the rest, and there was the simple six-pointed star Liam had fastened at the head of the grave. Margaret's heart dropped as she looked at the resting place.

"Shall we begin, my lady?" the same servant asked.

Margaret nodded silently, looking away from the grave.

King Sorren rested his hand on the base of her spine. "Are you all right, my dear?"

She nodded again, turning into him. "Yes, Your Majesty. I…I just can't bear to watch."

The king wrapped his arm around Margaret as he watched the servants uncover the grave. Once the recovery was finished, her father would be placed in a coffin that held a gilded depiction of tobacco fields. On the sides, ornate scrollwork accented the dark wood. The king was sparing no cost for the funeral.

The traveling court only stayed one night at Silvica before making the journey to Dorcia. Margaret spent most of the afternoon with Sarah, going through her home to see what was left of it, reliving childhood memories with her father still happy and healthy.

It was a bittersweet time for Margaret. She knew that her father was no longer locked in the internal prison of his disease, but he was no longer with her. The months that she had spent in Marbon with the Gollacks could not take away the empty pang she felt when she had entered the house again.

Margaret stopped at the portrait of her once happy family that hung in the hallway between her room and her father's. He was able to see it from his room when resting if he looked out the door, and he liked to stare at the painting often to remember the happiness that they had once had. Margaret covered her mouth as tears came to her eyes looking at the painting.

Sarah put a comforting hand on her shoulder. "My lady, you must be strong for him," Sarah said quietly.

Margaret nodded silently, her face reddening from her effort to keep her cries quiet. "I know," she said, voice heavy with emotion. "I know."

"Is there anything you'd like to take from here, my lady?" Sarah asked, gently rubbing her back.

Margaret shook her head. "Once we reach Dorcia, I'll arrange for servants to pack up the cottage and return it to our family home. There's nothing here I want to bring back to the palace with me."

It was early in the morning that the traveling court left Silvica to make their way up to Dorcia. Margaret brooded silently as they traveled, horrified at the aftermath of the decision she had made to run away with Liam rather than stay behind and face the consequences of helping a fugitive. She rode silently next to Sarah and Lady Annabel, lost in thought, and the two knew not to disturb her.

With all the stops their party made, it took until the end of Junmonat to reach her father's lands. Margaret wished Liam was her traveling companion rather than her new ladies and the other nobility. He would have remained respectfully quiet with her instead of merrily moving along with the rest of the group.

Margaret looked around the familiar grounds of Dorcia. She could hardly remember the last time she was here—fifteen years, at least. How she wished she could settle here and never return. But she wouldn't be able to leave the palace until she had ensured her title and ability to care for the people of Dorcia.

She inhaled deeply, smelling the wet dirt and the sweet smell of the tobacco plants. The leaves were still a dark green. It would be a while yet before they would be mature enough to harvest. She smiled when she saw the plants, remembering running through the fields as a child with her hands outstretched to feel the floppy leaves bouncing under her hands. Margaret sighed, longing to go back to those simple days.

Her father was buried at the center of his lands on the third day of Jumonat, three days after the court had arrived in the province. Margaret wore a simple gray dress made of silk. The sleeves opened at the wrists and pooled on the ground, creating a small train when she walked. To finish her look of mourning, Margaret wore a sheer gray veil that covered her face and extended out into a long train behind her. There was a single red rose in her hand as she stood beside the coffin, the prelate of Dorcia blessing the ground and praying for her father's soul to be delivered safely to Theotes.

She could barely hear what he was saying, thoughts thundering through her mind on what life should have been without her mistakes.

Margaret searched for Charles in the crowd. Before she left the capital, he had promised her that he would at least come to Dorcia to see her father buried. Margaret saw him near the back, along with his golden-haired wife. A small frown graced Margaret's face when she saw Charlotte's glowing face against her own gray gown.

Margaret waited in the receiving line for hours while the noblemen and women gave her their empty words of condolence.

Finally Charles was at her side. He grabbed her hands and kissed them gently. "Lady Margaret, this was a beautiful funeral."

"His Majesty has spared no expense for Papa." Margaret smiled only slightly. "I'm happy he was finally laid to rest properly."

"As are we." Charles wrapped his arm around his wife.

"There will be a feast in his honor in a few hours," Margaret told them. "Will you be attending?"

"Of course," Charlotte chirped. "We wouldn't miss honoring him."

Margaret looked the older woman over unpleasantly. Charlotte was looking particularly smug.

"I'm very pleased you're both here," Margaret said, trying to keep the displeasure from her face.

The feast lasted for hours, a total of twenty courses served. Margaret sat at the head table with the royal family next to the prince. Gareth had not joined them for the funeral, only arriving shortly before the feast began. Only practiced reserve had saved Gareth from being belittled in front of the traveling court. The king's displeasure was evident on his face when his son had arrived outrageously late.

Margaret would have preferred not to be placed next to the future monarch when there was wine to be had. He would make lewd gestures while he was speaking, and the drink made him overly fond of unwanted touches. She only half listened to the prince ramble on about his journey to Dorcia and how he looked forward to getting back to his current courtesan. She cast her eyes out on the hall to look at the people who had attended the funeral. The majority of the courtiers had still opted to wear the gray bands on their arms. Only the people who had close relationships with her father wore full mourning attire. Margaret took a long drink from her goblet before departing from the table in the middle of Gareth's sentence.

She caught Charles's eye as she went outside, a sour look on her face. Margaret wanted to have some fresh air. She felt like she was being suffocated in the great hall of her own home. The hall was filled with smells of alcohol, meats, and sweat that she wanted to escape from.

It was not long before Margaret heard footsteps behind her.

"Lady Margaret?"

Margaret turned around to see a concerned-looking Charles.

"Are you all right?" he asked, stepping closer.

"It's oppressively hot in there," she excused lamely, her voice clouded with emotions.

"Margaret." Charles gave her a look.

Margaret looked at him, chagrined. "Everyone is so happy in there. It's like it doesn't even matter that Papa was buried just a few hours ago."

"They've had time to accept the fact he's gone." Charles rested a hand on her arm, gently stroking her overly warm flesh with his thumb. "This is now a celebration of his life."

Margaret looked over his face, wishing for more comfort. She stepped up to him quickly and kissed him while she had the opportunity, her arms wrapping around his neck. His mouth was hard against hers, and his beard scraped her cheeks. She felt Charles put his hands on her waist.

It was not a long kiss, Charles pulling away from her quickly. Even so, there was no tingle as there had been with Liam, no electrifying feeling that slithered down her back and made her stomach flutter.

"Lady Margaret!" Charles looked at her with his mouth agape.

Margaret stepped back, feeling disappointed, her cheeks coloring a bright red. She had expected more of a spark, having loved the man in front of her since childhood.

"I'm sorry, Charles," she said quietly. "I must have had too much to drink."

Charles looked at her uncomfortably. "I'm married, Lady Margaret."

"Charles…"

Charles left her standing alone outside, not looking back at the young woman.

"Lady Margaret," Vojvo barked. "What are you doing?"

Margaret jumped, putting a hand to her chest. "Captain, I didn't see you there."

"Apparently not," he said with his brows raised. "I followed you just in case— His Majesty has ensured the wine will not run dry, and I didn't want you out here alone. It seems I didn't have to worry about that."

"You forget yourself, Captain," Margaret said tartly even as shame colored her cheeks.

"No, my lady, you forget yourself," he countered. "What are you doing out here, kissing a married man?"

"That's none of your business."

"It is my business, Lady Margaret!" Vojvo barely contained his anger to a loud whisper. "You asked me to save you from yourself, your ambitions, and that's what I'm trying to do. Mr. Luther is a married man, and he isn't married to you!"

"He should be!" Margaret cried. "My father should have proposed to him that we be married so Charles could inherit his title and the business and I wouldn't be alone for the rest of my life!"

Captain Vojvo moved closer to her and took her hands gently. "My lady, you won't be alone for the rest of your life," he told her quietly. "And you don't need to steal someone else's husband to accomplish that."

"There are no other options for me, Captain," Margaret said despondently, pulling her hands out of his. She extended her arms out, gesturing toward her home and lands. "Even with all of this, even with my fortune, no suitors come calling. If not Charles, who else?"

"You're not a trollop, Lady Margaret. Stop acting like one!" Captain Vojvo snapped exasperatedly.

"Would you speak to your daughter that way, Captain?" Margaret demanded, her eyes flashing dangerously.

"I would," Vojvo said quietly. "Had she lived to be your age, I would have told her the exact same thing I'm telling you now."

Margaret stepped back, feeling ashamed of herself. "I'm sorry, Captain, I shouldn't have said that."

"You should go back inside, my lady," he commanded, stepping aside to clear her way. "You'll catch a chill out here."

Margaret sighed, berating herself for her behavior. She should not have spoken to Vojvo that way. She shouldn't have kissed Charles; if all her flirting and insinuating during her lessons hadn't worked, why did she think it would now? Besides that, her father's funeral was certainly not the place to convince him to see her in a more romantic light.

And now she had ruined everything.

Margaret sat in the queen's apartments with the rest of the ladies in her service, their fans flapping in sync. The Aumonat day was too hot to be outside, the inside not much better. She sat off to the side, only offering her opinion when directly asked. She glanced at the book in her hand as she listened to the court gossip. The queen's closest friend, Duchess Cecily Crompton, the wife of Lord General Tobias Crompton, Duke of Rivack, had the juiciest snippets of court gossip of all the women. It was like a game to them, seeing who could find the most scandalous gossip to share.

Margaret could barely look at the woman whose husband had betrayed his country and set the blame on Liam.

They were currently listening to Duchess Cecily tell the queen about an affair one of the baronesses was having with a scullery boy. The baroness, it seemed, had a taste for men much younger than herself. "She's made her husband a cuckold, and he refuses to do anything about it," the duchess said, loudly laughing.

Queen Lillian chortled. "She is the head of the family now. Perhaps we should invite him here to learn embroidery!"

The rest of the ladies giggled alongside the queen, while Margaret only frowned.

Duchess Cecily took notice. "You do not find our musings funny, Lady Margaret?"

"No, Your Grace. I don't find it funny to laugh at a man who is being publicly humiliated by his wife," Margaret said heatedly. It upset her that these women couldn't care less about how the affair was affecting the baron.

The queen raised her eyebrows. "He's choosing to allow her to continue her behavior."

"He's not the king, Your Majesty. The baron cannot execute anyone his wife is having an affair with," Margaret said pointedly. "The only option he has is to threaten a divorce, and she would still go along with her trysts in the kitchen as she has already given him three sons."

There was a collective drawing back of the women, aghast Margaret spoke so frankly with their queen. As awkward looks exchanged between some of the more knowledgeable women, Margaret's stomach tightened. Not many knew that the queen had allegedly had an affair with the man she had formerly been engaged to marry in her first year of marriage to the king. King Sorren had him executed on charges of treason and that was the last it had been mentioned.

Queen Lillian glared daggers at Margaret. She had adamantly denied the affair had ever happened. "A man should be able to control his wife, whether he is a king or a peasant," she told Margaret.

The note of finality in her voice made Margaret keep quiet. It would do her no good to completely ostracize herself from the queen. Endearing herself to

Queen Lillian had not worked for her. After a long silence, the women began to slowly talk among themselves again.

As Margaret looked at the words on the page of the book she had been reading, the thought of kissing Charles sprang to her mind. While it had been short, it had turned their relationship upside down. She had ruined everything between them, even their friendship.

Charles had not spoken to her since her father's funeral in Jumonat, despite her attempt to send him a summons to teach her more about the business or call on him in his own home. Charlotte had turned Margaret away at the door, a scowl on her face. Margaret knew it could only be so long before Charles had to speak to her, and she would bide her time until that happened. At this point, she did not have much say in the running of the business anyway. Margaret sighed to herself, turning her attention back to the women in the room.

She started when she saw the queen looked at her like a cat that just caught a bird.

"Lady Margaret," the queen purred.

Margaret swallowed hard. "Yes, Your Majesty?"

"I find that my sitting room is lacking in brightness." Queen Lillian tilted her head, looking at Margaret through hooded eyes. "Would you clean the windows?"

"Your Majesty, surely, a servant would be better suited for this task?" Margaret looked at the other women failing to hide their smirks behind their fans.

"Surely not," corrected the queen. "We've all been told how eager you were to learn from your servants how to clean and care for your father—may Theotes keep his soul at rest—and you took to the work as though you were born to it."

Margaret's cheeks burned when Lady Aurora was unable to contain her giggle. "When would Your Majesty like me to clean the windows?"

"Now, if you would." Queen Lillian smirked. "The dreariness of the room is depressing me."

Margaret reluctantly rose and curtsied to the queen and her ladies. It was easy enough to find the supplies in the servant's hall but more difficult to convince the servant she asked them from that Margaret was the one to clean it.

"Are you certain, your ladyship?" The servant squinted at Margaret suspiciously. "You will be cleaning?"

"Yes," Margaret answered for the umpteenth time. "And I will not say that I asked you and you told me to do it myself because it was not your job, all right?"

The servant loosened her grip on the cleaning supplies only slightly. "If you promise that you will not…"

"I promise upon Theotes' silver star," came her emphatic reply before Margaret snatched the supplies from the woman's relaxed hands. "Good day to you." Margaret did not wait for a reply before turning on her heels and returned to the queen's chambers.

"And you've returned so quickly, Lady Margaret!" the queen praised. "Don't let us get in the way of your work."

Margaret almost cringed when the queen waved a dismissive hand. She laid a sheet in front of the first window she came to, setting the sudsy water on top of it. She washed each window carefully, drying it from the top to the bottom.

"Don't leave any streaks, Lady Margaret!" commanded Queen Lillian. "You wouldn't want to have to wash it again, would you?"

"Of course, Your Majesty," Margaret replied over a chorus of giggles.

When Margaret finished, she wiped her pruned hands clean of suds. She made a move to sit but was stopped by Queen Lillian clearing her throat.

"Yes, Your Majesty?" Margaret asked, trying to keep the irritation from her voice. All she wanted to do was sit. There were so many windows in the queen's quarters. Her back ached from all the work.

"Are you not going to return the supplies to the servants?" The queen asked innocently. "Surely they will need them—you've deprived them of a job, after all."

Margaret's mouth flattened. "Of course, Your Majesty. I don't know where my head went."

"Be sure to return when you have finished your errand, Lady Margaret!" Queen Lillian called when Margaret was almost out the door.

Margaret returned as quickly as she could, sweat breaking out on her forehead. She was looking forward to sitting with her fan and keeping her mouth shut until one of the ladies addressed her. Margaret regretted more than ever opening her mouth when speaking of the baroness. She was barely able to sit before the queen addressed her again.

"The room still looks dreary, Lady Margaret. Don't you think so?" the queen asked. "What is it we can do to brighten it?"

"Perhaps some flowers?" Margaret hesitantly suggested.

"What a splendid idea, Lady Margaret!" Queen Lillian praised. "Will you go and get some for me?"

Of course she would have to get them. She tried to keep a smile on her face, but it fell when the ladies in the room couldn't keep their amused smirks from their faces. Margaret slowly stood. "What kind of flowers would you like, Your Majesty?"

"Peonies, I think," Lillian told her. "They are just so beautiful this time of year."

Margaret curtsied to her, preparing to leave. "As you wish, Your Majesty."

"Lady Margaret?" Queen Lillian stopped her before she reached the door.

Margaret warily eyed the queen. "Yes, Your Majesty?"

"Don't come back until you have found them," she said lightly, though her eyes were gelid. "And I would like them before I change for the evening meal."

Margaret felt ice slide down her spine. "I will do my best, Your Majesty."

Sighing when the door was closed, Margaret went in search of Sarah. She found her dining with the other servants in their dining hall. Sarah rose first, the other servants following suit.

"What is it I can do for you, my lady?" Sarah asked.

Margaret waved her hand at the servants. "Please sit; don't let me interrupt your meal," she said to them before turning her attention on Sarah. "I need your help on an errand."

Sarah stepped away from the table. "Shall we go now, my lady?"

"I think that might be best," Margaret said with a sigh. "I'll wait for you in my chambers with Captain Vojvo."

Sarah bobbed a quick curtsy to her before grabbing her plate to bring to the kitchens.

Margaret left her there, seeking out Captain Vojvo in his chambers. She knocked lightly on the door, pleased when the door was answered promptly.

"Lady Margaret," he said, surprised. "Are you finished with the queen?"

"Not exactly," Margaret said bitterly. "Will you meet me in my chambers when you are ready? Sarah is coming from the servant's hall."

"Of course, Lady Margaret," he said. "I'll be there presently."

Margaret nodded to him before going to her chambers. She closed her eyes a moment when she saw she was alone in her sitting room. She hoped the task would be easier and far less embarrassing than the washing of the queen's windows.

Sarah knocked briefly before entering with the captain. Margaret stood, going to them.

"Shall we go?" Margaret asked.

Where are we going, my lady?" Vojvo asked.

"The queen has tasked me with retrieving her a bouquet of peonies." Margaret's mouth pinched in a pout. "We are going to the gardens."

Vojvo raised a brow. "Begging your pardon, my lady, but if you are only going to the gardens do you need me?"

"You, my good captain," Margaret said, patting his arm, "are coming in case we must go into the city so we do not waste any time coming to get you."

Vojvo sighed. "Shall we go, then?"

Margaret smiled at him. "It will be fun, Captain," she said before leaving her chambers.

Even with thorough searching, the garden held no peonies. Vojvo went ahead of them, arranging a carriage to the city. They arrived at the market shortly, the driver going as far as he could with the vehicle. The captain jumped down, helping the two women out.

"Will you wait for us?" Margaret asked the driver.

"O' course, milady," the driver nodded.

"Do you know where the flower market is?" Margaret asked, looking between Sarah and the captain.

"I can lead the way, my lady," Sarah told her, making her way through the crowd.

Margaret followed closely behind, the captain behind her. She looked around in amazement when they reached the flower section, it going as far as she could see.

"They must have them here," she commented excitedly.

"My lady," Vojvo said cautiously. "I would not get overexcited."

Margaret simply looked at him before delving into the market. She saw several flowers that looked like peonies, but were not. Her excitement was nearly gone when she came to the end of the flower section. Margaret felt her breath catch when she saw them. Blush pink peonies were tucked in among the roses. She found the vendor, holding the entirety of the peonies in her arms.

"I want these," Margaret said, clutching them protectively. "How much?"

The vendor looked over her shrewdly, his bottom lip pushed out with his heavy jowls. "Cost ya, milady," he said, voice gravely.

"I don't care," Margaret said hurriedly. "I need them."

"You're lucky you even found 'em, milady," the vendor went on, "they rarely bloom this late."

Margaret stared at him blankly, realization dawning on her. It was an impossible errand the queen wanted her to fail doing.

"How much are they?" Margaret asked again.

The vendor shrugged. "Five tholar for all of 'em."

"Captain, would you give him a tal for his trouble?" she asked as she gathered the flowers.

The vendor bowed reverently, not straightening until Vojvo gave him his money. Likely it was not often he was tipped the same amount his flowers cost.

Upon returning to the palace, Margaret followed Sarah in their search of finding a vase. She arranged them to the best of her ability, though she doubted it would be enough for the queen.

"Good enough," she said to herself before returning to the queen's chambers.

Margaret knocked briefly on the queen's door, unable to open it with the heavy vase. Lady Aurora answered, looking surprised when she saw the flowers in Margaret's arms. She impatiently pushed past Lady Aurora, nodding deeply to the queen.

Queen Lillian let out a sympathetic noise. "My apologies, Lady Margaret. I meant to tell you ranunculus."

"But I…"

"Did no one come and find you?" the queen continued, her face a mask of pity.

"No, Your Majesty," she said a little tartly. "No one found me."

Queen Lillian let out another hum of sympathy. "I will dismiss you for tonight, then, for your trouble. You may go, Lady Margaret, and rest well."

Margaret made to set down the base of peonies before leaving.

"Take those with you, Lady Margaret," commanded the queen. "They would look much better in your chambers."

Margaret gave the queen a tight smile. "Thank you, my queen. That is kind of you."

The queen waved a dismissive hand, turning her attention back to the ladies in her chambers.

She left, tempted to throw the vase to the floor. Being in the queen's service was not the honor it was made out to be—at least, not for those the monarch didn't like.

13

iam grunted while he filed down the tip of a nail, careful not to let his grip slip. He straightened to wipe the sweat from his brow as Thorkelin finished a sale. Jossnon shot him a happy grin, holding up several silver strals. Liam returned his excitement, a grin on his own face as he turned his attention back to his work.

Thorkelin came to Liam's side, bringing a lantern over to closely examine his work. "Good, lad. Verra good." He clapped Liam on the shoulder. "After yer done wi' that, I'd like fer ye to start workin' on inlayin' the swords. We'll be takin' 'em to the fair in Castenra day after next."

Liam looked at Jossnon sharply, a panicked expression pinching his face. "Master Thorkelin, I'm not ready to do the inlay."

"Ye'll do fine, lad. Ye've practiced on enough scrap," assured the smith. "Hurry up now."

"But—" Liam protested.

"Ye dinna have to forge the sword, lad," Jossnon interrupted almost irritably, "ye just have to put somethin' nice on it."

Liam frowned, picking out a sword to work with. He sat with it in front of him, his brow furrowed in concentration. His mind drew a blank, staring at the marbled steel as though it would etch itself a pattern.

Thorkelin watched him struggle for a few moments before shoving his own sword back into the forge to heat. "It doesna need to be annithin' fancy, Liam."

"I don't know what to do," he complained. "I am better at shoes and nails."

"Ye are," Thorkelin conceded, "but ye need to learn how to do this too."

Liam sighed, picking up a sharp blade to sketch a design near the hilt of the sword. He pursed his lips as he scratched the steel, eventually drawing out Theotes's six-pointed star. There weren't many who practiced the religion of Anatalia in Salatia, but there were some. He wasn't familiar enough with Olam's symbols to draw them with any certainty. Liam took one of the wooden handled gravers and carved out the star, frequently blowing away the scraps of steel. He caught Thorkelin's eye, raising his eyebrow at the older man.

Thorkelin looked intently at the star, mouth turning down. "Why would ye do that symbol?"

Liam looked down at Theotes' star. "What's wrong with it?"

"'Tis an Anatalian symbol." Thorkelin spat on the ground, shaking his head. "An' ye ken how I feel about them."

He didn't, but he could guess by the tone it wasn't anything good. Dread started to weigh down his shoulders. "Frasisca and Tyradrica also worship Theotes—and some people here too."

"Lamentable that mark is," Thorkelin said. "I dinna want to see it again after this."

"I promise." Liam wasn't particularly religious, so it wouldn't be an issue, but he would need to make sure he didn't let more of his Anatalian heritage slip.

"Good." Thorkelin quickly looked away, going back to his work.

Liam grabbed three different colored wires—silver, bronze, and gold—only twisting two of the wires together at a time. He twisted two sets of bronze and silver wires together, and also one silver and gold, and a bronze and gold. Liam laid them out to where no one color repeated, cutting the ends so they came to a point. He did this for each of the six lines.

He started to lay out the wire to be pounded in when another interruption came. "Dinna forget to undercut the design."

Liam sighed, picking up a flat graver, holding it straight as he prepared to hammer in the extra divots.

"Hold it at an angle, lad," Thorkelin instructed, coming to his side. He adjusted the angle of the graver for Liam before walking away.

Liam tried not to let the constant interruptions irritate him, reminding himself that it was just like when Aram taught him to build the shelters they constructed together. Thorkelin was only trying to help Liam succeed. He finished the undercut and relaid the wires.

Liam used a flat punch, hammering only a small amount in at a time. The wires flattened over the carved edges, making it look like a child had taken dough and flattened it out to make a malformed letter. Disappointment started to fill Liam as he hammered down the last bit of wire. A hole was left at one of the points where the edges were supposed to meet. Liam let out a groan when he saw he could not hammer the wire to meet the others.

"What is it?" Thorkelin asked, looking over at him. "What's the matter?"

Liam grabbed pliers to pull up the wiring. "I did it wrong."

Jossnon stayed Liam's hand. "Ye can always find yerself a jewel to fit in there and wrap it with the gold or silver wire."

"Do we have any?" Liam asked, putting down the pliers.

"Aye." Thorkelin went to a small safe in the other room, grabbing a small bag of jewels. He handed it to Liam upon his return.

"Where did you get all of these?" Liam looked at Jossnon, his brows raised high.

Thorkelin shrugged with one shoulder. "Cora left them behind."

"I see," Liam said slowly, picking six gems of the same color.

"File down the excess metal an' polish it before ye put them in," Jossnon said, seeming to be lost in thought as he took away the bag of assorted jewels.

Liam did as he was bid, polishing the blade and the inlay until it showed his reflection. He cut just enough of the inlay to tightly fit the gems and gold wrapping. He held the sword at a distance, proud of his work.

"Master Thorkelin," Liam called out, holding up the sword by the hilt. "I've finished."

Jossnon came to examine the work, eyeing it critically. When he found no fault, he stood straight. "Verra nice, Liam."

Liam grinned, pride welling with the smith's approval.

Liam wiped his brow clean of sweat when he set down the last of the goods he and Thorkelin brought to sell at the fair in Castenra. There were several vendors that sold anything from livestock to fabric. As far as Liam could see, they were the only ones selling forged items. He and Jossnon brought mostly horseshoes and other everyday items. They only brought a few blades along with him—his inlaid blade included.

"Do you sell here often, Master Thorkelin?" Liam curiously asked.

"Ev'ry once in a while." Jossnon shrugged, shading his eyes from the sun as he surveyed the crowd. "Sometimes we get a few lords to buy a blade an' they ask fer more."

The crowd was starting to pick up as they laid out the items in a pleasant arrangement. "Do they host the fair every month?"

"The locals gather once a week," the smith informed, "an' the outsiders come once a month."

Liam didn't have time to ask any more questions. A surge of customers approached asking for building supplies. Luckily, Liam had been making hundreds of nails since starting work with Thorkelin in Semonat almost a year ago. Their building supplies sold quickly, and the few swords they brought even quicker.

Liam shifted on his feet, looking out at the other vendors in the market. "Jossnon," he called out, sounding somewhere between hesitant and embarrassed.

Thorkelin raised a brow at him. "What is it, lad?"

"I was wondering if before we leave I might look through the market?" Liam's cheeks colored as he continued, "To find a gift for Gretta."

"Ye're at the point of gifts?" Thorkelin asked.

Liam colored deeper. "I think it would be nice..."

Jossnon nodded. "Help me pack up, an' we'll go together."

They finished in short order, then ventured into the market. Liam looked around helplessly.

"D'ye ken what she likes?" Thorkelin asked, seeing his lost look.

Liam shrugged. "She likes her children."

Thorkelin suppressed a laugh. "Have ye ever bought a gift for a lass?"

"No." Liam's cheeks flushed again, spreading to the tips of his ears.

Thorkelin laughed openly at him this time, wrapping an affectionate arm around Liam's shoulders. "Ye only need to ken one thing, laddy, and that's the lassies like somethin' pretty."

"I've never seen her wear any jewelry," Liam commented.

"She prob'ly doesna have any," Thorkelin told him. "If ye find somethin' ye like, I'd be happy to front ye the money."

Liam paused uncertainly in front of the jeweler's table, the items glittering in the light. None of them looked like Gretta. He could picture any one of them adorning Margaret's pale form, but not Gretta. Her dark features were not suited for any of these.

"Can I help ye?" the jeweler asked.

Liam ran his eyes over the array of jewels again before speaking. "Do you have anything...simpler?"

The jeweler nodded, pulling out a silk pouch. He laid it out, displaying pearl necklaces, bracelets, and ear bobs. Those, he could see on Gretta. He picked up a string of creamy pearls.

"How much are these?" Liam asked, still holding the pearls, each one slightly misshapen.

"One gold and two silver strals," the jeweler said dispassionately.

"One gold and—" Liam started.

"He'll take it," Thorkelin said beside him, setting down the money.

"Jossnon, I can't—"

"Dinna worry yerself over it," Jossnon interrupted him again. "Ye can pay me back when ye can."

"I cannot thank you enough, Master Thorkelin," Liam emphatically told him.

Liam lay in bed next to Gretta, his arm wrapped loosely around her waist. She sighed contentedly, her eyes closed. Liam kissed her shoulders until she looked at him.

"I have something for you," he said, trying to keep the excited grin off his face.

"Do ye now?" Gretta asked, raising a single brow.

"Sit up and close your eyes," Liam instructed, standing.

"I'm not fallin' for that one again," she snapped, eyeing him warily.

Liam laughed. "Close your eyes," he said, eyes alight with mirth. "You'll enjoy the surprise."

"That's what ye said last time." She snorted but closed her eyes nonetheless.

He slipped the cool pearls around her neck, latching it in place. Her eyes flew open, hand going to her neck.

"What is this?" she demanded.

"Why don't you go and take a look in the looking glass?" Liam suggested.

Gretta scurried to her mirror, gasping when she saw the lustrous gems. "Liam..."

He turned almost shy. "I thought you deserved something frivolous, just to make you feel pretty."

Gretta flung her arms around him, kissing Liam soundly.

14

"There, Lady Margaret," Queen Lillian commanded, pointing to the spot next to her vanity.

Margaret hesitated, squinting at the queen suspiciously. "Are you certain, Your Majesty?"

"Yes, I am certain, Lady Margaret," she snapped, her finger still pointing to the spot.

Margaret moved to the appointed spot, still suspicious of the queen's motives.

"Kneel," the queen commanded, Duchess Cecily barely concealing her smirk behind the monarch.

"Kneel?" Margaret burst, incredulous.

"Are you disobeying your queen?" Queen Lillian's eyebrows raised severely, daring Margaret to question her orders again.

Margaret's face soured, slowly lowering herself to her knees. How long was she to be punished for speaking out of turn to the queen?

"Now hold these." Queen Lillian shoved jewels into her hands, turning away from her.

"For how long?" Margaret was uncomfortable, pain already shooting through her knees.

"You will hold them until Her Majesty tells you otherwise." Duchess Cecily leveled Margaret with a glare. "It is a great honor to hold the queen's jewels, Lady Margaret."

Flattening her lips into a frown, Margaret remained silent for the two hours the queen took to be readied for the evening meal, the jewels still in hand.

"Your Majesty?" Margaret called out quietly.

"Yes, Lady Margaret?" The queen turned to look at her.

"Will you be needing...?" Margaret wilted with a sigh, seeing the queen was already wearing jewels.

"Yes?"

Margaret swallowed. "Will you be needing your jewels, Your Majesty?"

Queen Lillian wrinkled her nose at them, waving her hand in dismissal. "No. Put them away before you leave," she called over her shoulder as she left the room with her attendants.

Margaret arrived late for dinner in the hall, looking around the dining hall as she entered. Her cheeks colored as many turned to look at her. It was one of many ways the queen exacted her revenge on Margaret. Queen Lillian had no power to publicly punish anyone without the king's permission. The only way to make her displeasure known was through pettiness.

There had been a place set for her at one of the tables near the head table where the royals and honored guests sat. She sat quietly, nodding to the other men and women at her table. Margaret looked up at the head table to see the queen looking smug and the king already buried deeply in his drink. Either that would make him boisterous, or it would be a miserable night for everyone in the hall. The music soon picked up in the background to soothe moods as people ate.

No courses were sent directly to her table as a sign of respect that night. Margaret knew it was another way that the queen could show she was displeased with her newest lady. She regretted ever bringing up the queen's past to make a point. Unlike the king, Queen Lillian would draw out her retribution rather than make it swift. Margaret looked up at the head table once more to see the king glowering at her.

Margaret was shocked to see him so dour. She had always received a pleasant smile and a kind word. She smiled at him timidly only to have him turn his face away. Her stomach sank. Had the queen told him about her dredging up the past? She excused herself from dinner early and returned to her apartments. Margaret found Sarah turning down the bedcovers when she arrived.

"My lady, are you feeling all right?" Sarah frowned, her brows knitted together. It was unusual for Margaret to return this early.

"A little unwell," Margaret admitted. "I think it will be an early night for me."

"Yes, my lady." Sarah continued her work, and Margaret readied herself for bed until there was a knock on the door.

"Who is it, Sarah?" Margaret called from her bedroom.

"A message for you." Sarah handed her the note.

Margaret reluctantly broke the seal on the note when she saw that it was written in the king's handwriting.

Lady Margaret,
I have important matters to discuss with you. Immediately.

S

Margaret pursed her lips, an uneasy feeling settling over her. "Sarah, make sure I'm presentable. The king has requested my presence."

Margaret closed her eyes tightly as the king stepped closer to her. She couldn't help but feel she was in trouble, but for what, she didn't know.

"Do you know why you're here, Lady Margaret?" King Sorren asked her, his words slurred by drink.

"No, Your Majesty." Margaret looked at him with worry clear on her face.

"You lied to me when I made you my ward last Semonat." Sorren pointed at her with a drink in his hand, sloshing when it was haphazardly jostled. "You have been lying to me for eleven months."

"Majesty, I would never lie to you!" Margaret's stomach clenched at the fury on his face.

"Nicholas Oliphant died here in Jalmar of an infection in his wound." The king slammed his drink on the table carelessly, sitting down and swinging his arm over the back of the couch. "You lied to me about why Jerone is dead."

Margaret sank to her knees in front of him, tears gathering in her eyes. "My king, I did so to protect myself. Nicholas would have told you anything he could to have me executed for humiliating him."

The king grabbed her chin roughly. "So it is true, then. You did help the traitor."

"I let him bathe and gave him new clothes to wear, and Nicholas came before I could send him away." Margaret winced as the king tightened his grip on her chin. "That was all I did for him, I swear."

It was not exactly another lie. The rest of the time she and Liam were together, he had been the one helping her. She had been clueless on what to do during their journey.

King Sorren let go of her chin and leaned against the back of the couch. "You get your tenderheartedness from your father." He looked her over slowly. "You'll have to repay me for not bringing charges against you."

"Anything you ask, Your Majesty," Margaret said breathlessly. "Anything at all."

The king slid a finger from her collar bone to the flesh breaking from the top of her bodice. "I'm sure I can find something."

Margaret stood quickly, pulling her shawl tightly around her as though it would ward away any further touches. "Your Majesty!"

Sorren stood as well, wrapping an arm around her waist, pulling her to him. "Your mother was willing enough when she needed forgiveness." His fingers dug into her side as he tightened his grip on her. "Or when she wanted something."

"She would never do that!" Margaret protested.

"She did, and so will you," Sorren threatened. "I will come to your chambers tonight."

"Your Majesty, you mustn't." Margaret looked at his lecherous smirk. No wonder his son Gareth behaved the way he did. He'd learned it directly from the king. "I'm still chaste."

The king ran a finger down her cheek. "All the sweeter for me."

Margaret flinched, trying to pull away from him. "Your Majesty!"

King Sorren kept Margaret against him. "It's either this or an execution, Margaret."

Her breath caught in her throat, her body stilling. The steel in his eyes frightened her. What choice did she have? "As you wish, Your Majesty."

"Now, go wait for me." The king released his hold on her and dismissed her with a wave.

Margaret was shaking when she returned to her chambers. "Sarah?"

"My lady, you're as white as a sheet!" Sarah rushed to her side. "What happened to you?"

Vojvo came to stand next to her, a worried look on his face. "My lady?"

"The king has found me out." Margaret raised a shaking hand to her mouth. "And is coming to my chambers tonight to take payment for not executing me."

"No!" Vojvo's face grew red, his eyes flashing dangerously. "He can't do that to you!"

"He can do what he likes, Captain. He is the *king*," Margaret snapped. "It was either this or an execution—and I personally like living."

Sarah covered her mouth. "Oh, my lady!"

"There must be another option," Vojvo persisted.

"There is no other option," Margaret told him, her voice catching.

"We can leave. Sarah, pack Her Ladyship only the lightest dressed," Vojvo commanded, his hand going to the knife at his belt. "My lady—"

"No, Captain," Margaret cut him off. "I have no other choice. Now, I suggest that you return to your chambers so that you don't have to listen."

"Lady—"

"Captain—"

"You are not in your right mind." He shook his head. "I cannot let you do this."

"Let me?" Margaret laughed, her face pinched incredulously. "None of us have a choice in this, Captain."

Vojvo pulled himself up to his full height, pointing a finger in Margaret's direction. "You listen here, young lady. I will not let you—"

Margaret clenched her fists. "Go, Captain!" Margaret commanded. "Or I will dismiss you, and you will be no help to anyone."

Captain Vojvo retreated from the room without another word, slamming the door behind him.

Margaret jumped, closing her eyes tightly. "Sarah, you must help me prepare for his visit," Margaret said shakily. "And quickly."

Sarah helped her undress silently, resting her hands on Margaret's shoulders whenever she would start shaking. Sarah pinched Margaret's cheeks to bring the appropriate amount of blush to her face before leading her to the bed.

"Thank you," Margaret said, still trembling.

Sarah arranged her hair on the pillows as Margaret lay on the bed. "Is there no other way, my lady?"

Margaret looked at her lady's maid woefully. "He is taking this as payment, and I fear this is only the first installment."

Sarah gently moved some hair out of Margaret's face. "To survive the soldier only to be taken by the king."

Margaret gave her maid a withering look. "Thank you, Sarah. Why don't you go wait by the door?"

Sarah curtsied before leaving the room.

Margaret closed her eyes and inhaled deeply, her stomach tightening with fear when she heard his knock. She did not want to be executed, but she also did not want to lose her chances of a good marriage—even if she was mistress to a king.

"My lady, His Majesty is here."

"Thank you, Sarah." Margaret saw the king standing behind her lady's maid. "Leave us."

Sarah hesitated at the door, her eyes filled with worry. When Margaret nodded to her, Sarah looked at her sympathetically and finally left the room.

Margaret watched as the king stripped to his nightshirt and stood in front of her bed. He grabbed the sheets, ripping them back to expose her. She had undressed beforehand to avoid having his hands on her longer than necessary. He removed his nightshirt, exposing the rest of himself to her. Margaret looked away when she saw that he was ready. She closed her eyes tightly when the king climbed atop her, placing himself between her thighs. The weight of him brought back the memories of the day by the river, and she felt her breath quicken, panic rising in her throat, struggling under him.

"No!" Margaret yelled out as he put his hands on her waist. The only thing she could see was the soldier's vicious grin as he tried to take her, the hair on the back of her neck standing up.

"Quiet!" Sorren commanded as he buried his face in her neck, making her panic even more.

"Please don't do this to me!" Margaret hoarsely cried the familiar words as she pushed her hands against his shoulders.

The king snaked his hand behind her head, fisting it in her long locks, before forcing his way into her. Margaret cried out, digging her nails into his shoulders.

"You were telling the truth about being a maid." Sorren buried his face in her neck and let out a groan.

Tears fell down her face and into her hair. There was a searing pain in her lower abdomen that she could not bear. Pushing her hands against his shoulders as he moved inside her, she let out another pained cry.

Her cries quieted to sobs as he cried out his finish.

After he left, Margaret rolled onto her stomach and buried her face in the pillow. She had agreed to this arrangement, not knowing the pain he was capable of inflicting.

The shame she would feel.

Sarah quietly came into the room. "My lady?"

"Go away, Sarah!" Margaret's voice, muffled in the pillows, was thick with tears. Crompton's warning came back to her that she couldn't stay in the company of the king without harm coming to her.

She wished that Liam had been there to save her again. She should have gone with him. She curled into a ball, wishing Liam were there to comfort her as he had in Marbon.

15

aptain Vojvo stormed down the halls of the palace with his hands clenched tightly at his sides. He was more furious than he had ever been in his life. Vojvo stopped and rammed his first into the wall next to a portrait of the king.

Theotes damn him.

He shook his hand out, flexing it with a low growl in his throat. It was too bad it wasn't the actual king. How dare the king do something like this to his mistress?

Vojvo turned around to go back to her several times, stopping short before he actually reached her corridor. A war raged in his mind: do as he was commanded, or go back and risk the possibility of being arrested for trying to stop the king from doing what he wants? It brought a small amount of light to the decision that Lady Margaret had to make.

Vojvo had gotten almost to his room when he had changed his mind again. How could he allow her to put herself in this position? Vojvo shook his head. He had to go back and force her to leave before anything could happen to her.

Consequences be damned, he would not allow Lady Margaret to be so callously defiled.

Heart pounding, he ran back to Lady Margaret's chambers as quickly as he could. By the time he entered the drawing room, he could hear her pained cries. His mouth went dry, his stomach sick. He was too late.

Sarah was sitting on the plush couch, hugging herself to keep her trembling at bay, her face pale. She must have stayed in the chambers to see if their mistress would need anything once her ordeal was done.

His gaze was torn from the trembling lady's maid when the door to Lady Margaret's bedchambers flew open. The king swept through without a second glance to Sarah or himself. Paralyzed, Vojvo watched as Sarah immediately went into the bedroom.

"My lady?" he heard Sarah's timid call.

"Go away, Sarah!"

Hearing his mistress brought Vojvo out of his stupor. He came into the room to stand next to Sarah, seeing Lady Margaret with her face buried in her pillows, her whole body racking with sobs. Sarah was standing to the side, unsure what to do, looking at him pleadingly.

Vojvo knelt next to the bed and gently stroked back her hair. "My lady, please, let Sarah help you. You'll start to feel better once you are clean."

Lady Margaret looked up at him, eyes filled with fat tears, her face red. There was a hesitation on her face.

Vojvo tenderly cupped her cheek, speaking gently. "Lady Margaret, please, you must let us help you. I will wait in the drawing room until Sarah has settled you."

Nodding, Lady Margaret slowly sat up, the sheet pulled tightly against her with trembling fingers.

Vojvo gave a nod to Sarah, who immediately swooped in. He retreated from the room to give them privacy. He sat on one of the sofas, head in his hands. He'd seen her scared before, but not broken.

Broken, his heart couldn't stand.

Vojvo waited until Sarah came for him over an hour later.

"Captain?" Sarah said from the doorway of the bedroom. "Lady Margaret wishes to see you."

He stood and immediately went into her bedchamber. She was sitting in the middle of her bed, a white nightdress on. Her face had been washed, and there were no tearstains left, though her eyes were still red from crying.

"Lady Margaret?"

She looked at him, a haunted look in her eyes. "Captain, thank you for coming back."

"Tell me what I can do for you, my lady."

"I-I—" she started before tears welled in her eyes and spilled over.

Vojvo quickly sat on the edge of her bed and pulled her into his arms. He held her tightly as she wept on his shoulder. It was familiar, the way he had done for his own daughter when she was alive. Vojvo could feel her tightly digging her fingers into his back as she clung to him.

"Shh," he soothed, "I'm right here for you."

Vojvo gently rubbed her back. His heart ached for her. The suffering she endured—would endure—was coming to the surface. He rested his cheek on the top of her head, holding her close to him.

Starting to hiccup, her sobs slowed to a stop. She pulled away from him, wiping her eyes. "I'm sorry, Captain."

Vojvo shook his head. "You have no need to apologize, my lady."

"Sarah said you came back looking like a crazed murderer," Lady Margaret said with a small laugh.

Vojvo flushed, a nervous laugh escaping him. "I had hoped to return before the king came, my lady."

"Margaret."

"My Lady Margaret," Vojvo corrected himself.

"No—just Margaret." She gripped his hand tightly.

"I can't call you by your given name, my lady."

"Yes you can, Marius," Margaret told him. "I want you to."

"I won't call you Margaret in public," Vojvo said.

"Of course," she agreed, giving him a small smile.

"Will you be needing anything else?"

Margaret chewed on her lip, debating on her answer. "Will you stay with me until I fall asleep?"

He stood and held up her sheets for her to slide down. "Of course, my— Margaret."

Margaret slid down into the bed with a sigh, watching him closely.

Vojvo pulled a plush chair next to her bed and sat in it. He thought he would ease the awkwardness by quietly telling her stories of his childhood living in Marbon. He gently took her hand when she extended it, he thought for comfort, and was glad that he could offer it to her. It did not take long for Margaret to fall asleep—he assumed the long cry she had had had worn her out.

He leaned back in his chair. He would stay a little while longer in case she needed him.

16

Margaret inhaled deeply as she woke. There was a warm presence in her hand that confused her. She turned to look at what it was and let out a small cry as her stomach cramped unforgivingly.

"What happened? What's wrong?" Captain Vojvo asked groggily, squeezing her hand.

"Have you been here all night?" Margaret asked, not pulling her hand away from his.

Vojvo ran his other hand over his face and inhaled deeply. "Is it morning already?"

"Yes, it is," Margaret told him, finally taking her small hand from his. She rested it on her cramping stomach, a wave of queasiness passing through her throat.

"I must have fallen asleep while I was waiting," he said. "I wanted to make sure you didn't wake up with any nightmares and find yourself alone."

"That was very kind of you." Margaret was touched that he was so concerned.

"Do you need me to fetch Sarah?"

Margaret shook her head and tried to sit up, letting out another groan.

The captain shot to his feet, concern etched on his face, gently helping her up. "My lady, you should rest today."

His hands were more gentle in their movements than Margaret would have expected based on his generally rigid exterior. "I need to ready myself to go to…to the queen's chambers this morning."

He examined her critically. "I do not think you should be straining yourself, Margaret."

"I have no a choice," she said, a little irritably. "I am expected, o-ordeal or not." Margaret took a moment to steel herself. "I just want to put this behind me and pretend it never happened, all right?"

"At least take your time being readied, my lady." Vojvo sighed. "I will be back in enough time to escort you around the palace today."

"I don't think that is necessary," Margaret told him, starting to get out of the bed.

"This is not up for discussion."

Margaret could loudly hear the omitted "young lady." She chewed on her bottom lip. "Very well. Send for Sarah on your way out."

"Yes, my lady," he said with an ironic bow.

When he left, Margaret could hear muffled talking. Was Sarah already there? When the maid entered, she was wearing the same clothes as yesterday, wrinkles all down her front. She must have stayed there last night, the same as the captain. Margaret should have ordered them both to leave last night so that they could have gotten more sleep.

"My lady?"

Margaret gave her a hesitant smile. "Good morning, Sarah."

"Are you all right, my lady?" Sarah asked as she helped her out of the bed.

"I'll be fine," Margaret said, swallowing hard. "This will pass."

"My lady, will you not allow me to take your apologies of illness to the queen's chambers?" Sarah pleaded.

"Enough, Sarah," Margaret snapped. "Please help me dress. The captain will be back soon."

The look on Sarah's face screamed the desire to contradict Margaret, but she wasn't as bold as the captain. "Yes, my lady," she murmured.

Margaret sat at her vanity and brushed out her hair as she waited for her maid to return. She looked in the mirror and quickly turned away. Her face was pale, and her eyes rimmed red from her long cry. Luckily, Sarah returned before Margaret could dwell for long.

She did not want to even think of the previous night's events.

Sarah helped her dress in a light day dress appropriate for being in the queen's presence. By the time they were finished, a light knock sounded on the door to her private chambers.

"Enter," Margaret called as Sarah hooked a bracelet on her wrist.

"Are you certain we cannot convince you to stay here for the day?" Vojvo asked, uncertainty clouding his face.

"I have responsibilities, Captain, as you know," Margaret sternly told him.

Vojvo sighed, offering her his arm. "My lady?"

Margaret took his arm, hesitating at the door as they passed. She wanted to stay but knew that she could not. She took a deep breath before continuing on. They followed the corridor slowly, Vojvo making sure Margaret did not exert herself. They came across a group of workers patching a hole in the wall next to the king's portrait.

Vojvo's face colored when they stopped to examine the damage. When he tried to continue, Margaret stayed rooted in place. He looked over at her. "My lady?"

Margaret couldn't pull her eyes away from the portrait. All she could see was him and think of what he had done to her. She didn't know if she was even breathing.

"Lady Margaret?" Vojvo came to stand in front of her, his brows furrowed. The alarm in his voice woke Margaret from her stupor. "Take me back."

"My lady?" Vojvo looked at her confused.

"Take me back!" she commanded, her voice raised. Margaret started to back away from the portrait. She didn't want the king's eyes on her, even ones that were painted.

Captain Vojvo wrapped his arm around her back, taking her hurriedly back to her chambers.

Margaret was shaking by the time they reached her rooms. She should have listened to both Vojvo and Sarah and stayed there.

"My lady, what are you doing back?" Sarah asked, coming to her side.

She shook her head, her voice thick when she finally spoke. "I couldn't do it."

Sarah hesitated, looking between Margaret and the captain. "His Majesty has had something delivered for you."

Her stomach quivered. "What is it?"

Sarah cleared her throat, looking even more nervous. "It's…it's a tea for you in the morning and evening. To, um, prevent any children."

Margaret wanted to relieve her stomach. She hadn't even thought of that consequence.

"Would you like to get back in bed, and I'll pour you a cup to have while I get you breakfast?"

"No, I'll take it in here." Margaret certainly didn't want to get back in bed and think about what the tea she was drinking was meant for. "Captain Vojvo will stay with me. Please get him and yourself breakfast to take with me as well."

"Are you certain, my lady?" Vojvo asked. "We can leave you on your own to relax if you wish."

Margaret nodded, sitting with a heavy sigh. She quickly wrote a note to the queen to let her know that she was ill. "I am. And would you deliver this to the queen on your way?"

"Very good, my lady," Sarah said, taking the note before pouring the tea and putting it on a side table next to Margaret. "I'll be back shortly."

Once Sarah left, Vojvo sat on the sofa across from Margaret. "Is there anything you'd like to talk about?"

Margaret scoffed. "What would that be? How I brought this on myself by helping a traitor and lying to the king about it? How this was better than being murdered for taking pity on Liam?"

"My lady," he said quietly. "No matter what you've done in your past, I hope you know that you didn't bring this on yourself."

Sighing, Margaret slumped back against the sofa. "Didn't I, though?" She eyed the tea at her side. She might as well get it over with. Margaret drank the tea quickly, though she was pleasantly surprised that it tasted of raspberry.

When Sarah returned, her tray was laden with food. "I wasn't sure what you would be in the mood to eat, my lady, so I overindulged from the kitchens."

Margaret smiled. "Thank you, Sarah."

Sarah held out a sealed letter to Margaret. "You also have a letter from Lady Annabel."

Margaret furrowed her brow. She didn't expect to hear another word from the young lady who had helped her during her father's funeral. She opened it, quickly reading it over. "She wants to know if she could join my household and show her more of what court life is like."

"Will you be allowed?"

"I'll ask the queen if she would be opposed to me helping Lady Annabel instead of attending Her Majesty." Margaret's lips twisted into a wry smile. "I don't doubt that she'll allow me to pull back. She isn't happy I'm there in the first place."

Sarah smiled. "It will be nice to see her again."

"I agree—I think she'll be a welcome addition." And perhaps if Annabel was there under her charge, the king would leave Margaret alone.

17

Liam sleepily descended the stairs, rubbing his growling stomach with both hands. He could smell the tantalizing scent of fresh bread. "Gretta, I hope you've made something hearty," he said as he turned the corner. "I've worked up a mighty—"

Liam stopped short, seeing Simon and Jamie staring at him from the table. Simon's eyebrows were raised, Jamie's cheeks coloring brightly.

Gretta turned from the hearth, laughing at the awkwardness between the three of them. "Ye three look like ye've messed yer clouts," she chortled.

Liam gave her a look, and she stopped laughing. "What is there to eat?"

"Ye can have porridge an' toast." She set down a full bowl, pouring a bit of honey over it.

"There's no sausage left?" Liam's mouth watered from the lingering smell, adding to his disappointment.

"Served the last of it this mornin'." Gretta patted his shoulder in mock sympathy.

"I'll have to go hunting, then."

"I expect ye will," Gretta confirmed. "Will ye no take Jamie an' wee Simon with ye?"

Liam looked at the hopeful faces of her two older boys. "Do they know how to hunt?"

"No yet," Gretta turned shy. "Would ye be willin' to teach 'em, Liam? Without their da, they have no one to learn from."

"Do you both have the day off?"

"Aye," Jamie answered, "we do."

Liam nodded. "And do you have any knowledge of the land and how to survive it?"

The boys looked hesitant before Simon answered, "We think so."

"Can you make a fire?"

"Aye."

"How to build or find shelter?"

Jamie pursed his lips. "We can manage."

"And what you can eat and not eat from the forest?" Liam asked.

"No, we dinna ken that," Simon said, his cheeks coloring with embarrassment.

Liam nodded again, finished with his assessment. "We'll start with that, then, when we go out today."

"Will ye let us carry a weapon?" Jamie asked.

Liam raised a thick brow. "Have you ever shot a bow?"

"Well, no," Jamie started, "but—"

"Then you won't today." Liam held a hand up when Jamie protested. "There is nothing more dangerous than a hunter who doesn't know how to use his weapon."

"Listen to him, Jamie," his mother cut in when her oldest was about to protest again. "He kens what he's about."

Jamie remained silent, turning an attentive eye on Liam.

"You'll both go with me to hunt, and once we've finished there, we can work with the bow," Liam explained, beginning to eat. "And keep working until you're good enough to shoot something."

Liam waited for Jamie and Simon at the back of Gretta's eatery, holding more supplies than he would normally take hunting. He could at least get the boys to carry some.

Gretta shooed both boys out the door, each with a knife strapped to their hip. "Ye'll be safe, aye?"

"Dinna be worrit, Ma," Jamie told her, though his cheeks were flushed with pleasure over the attention.

"Come along, then," Liam commanded, nodding to Gretta before leading the boys to his usual hunting grounds.

He remained silent on the open dirt trail until he came across a tall, thin plant that looked like a miniature green tree that lacked leaves. Liam stopped the boys, kneeling next to the weed-like plant.

"Have you ever seen asparagus, lads?" Liam asked, eyes scanning the high grass for the purplish crowns.

"Dinna ken," Simon said.

Liam triumphantly broke off one of the stalks, holding it up for them to see. "This is asparagus, and you can find them wherever you see one of these. He motioned to the weed that led him to the spot.

Jamie and Simon stared in silence at the tree-like vegetable.

"That isna a weed?" Simon asked. "Jimmy down the way said it was a tree weed an' that's how all trees start."

Liam smiled patiently. "No. They're good for you too."

"...How d'ye eat 'em?" Jamie asked, looking even more dubious than his brother.

"Well, you can boil them," Liam instructed as he gathered a fair amount of the stalks, "but I prefer roasting them."

"If ye say so, Liam." Simon shrugged.

"We'll stop by one more place before we settle for lunch and wait for the deer to come to us."

Liam walked off, not waiting for them to follow. He could hear them follow behind, their feet slapping loudly on the trail. There was a small pond before reaching the forest, lined with reedmace.

"I know you have seen these before," Liam said as he pulled forward the brown seed head. "Reedmace is what it's called."

"It isna poisonous?" Jamie asked, surprised.

"You're thinking of the poison iris," Liam corrected, "that has a white fluffy head." Liam squatted, pulling one out by the roots and cutting another as far down as he could. He washed each of them off in the shallow water. He pointed to each part before speaking. "This is a shoot," he said of the spike under the stringing roots, "and the little buds can be eaten raw if you'd like—with the skin removed—but the shoot should be cooked."

"What about the rest of it?" Simon asked, looking at the plant in fascination.

"You can eat the head before it turns brown," Liam instructed as he dug his thumb through the leaves to release them, "and this white part of the stalk, but not the leaves."

Jamie watched the leaves fall to the ground. "Seems a right waste."

Liam nodded. "You can use them to weave a mat, or baskets if you're skilled enough, and pillow stuffing."

He cut off the tough top part of the stem before handing a plant to each of the boys.

"Go on and pull more up, and we'll add it to our feast," he commanded. "And then we'll be on our way."

Liam lazed at the side of the pond on a grassy hill while the boys worked. He closed his eyes, sighing with pleasure when a breeze blew a fluffy cloud over the sun, shading the area. The leaves whispered a lullaby as the wind picked up, soothing Liam. He heard the wet shuffling from Jamie and Simon washing their finds.

The sun lit his eyelids red when it emerged from behind its veil. Liam groaned his protest, turning his head to the side. When he opened his eyes, he saw Simon to his right in his same prostrate position. Looking to his left, he saw Jamie in the same position as he and Simon. A smile crept on Liam's face; his heart swelled in a different way than Margaret had ever made it feel. He returned to his original position, letting Gretta's sons rest.

After a few minutes, seeing that the sun would not retreat again, Liam cleared his throat. He rose, looking between the two young men. "Are you ready to be on our way?" Liam asked.

Jamie was the first to rise. "Will ye teach us how to track too?"

"I can show you what to look for," Liam said hesitantly, "but you learn more from experience than me telling you."

Liam helped Simon up while Jamie put the reedmace in their pack with the wild asparagus. He led the boys to one of his favorite places to hunt. It was on the outside of the forest, a deep grassy triangle jutting into the tree line. Liam easily hid among the trees while the deer munched unawares on the sweet grass.

Liam started into the forest when he saw stark marks on the dark bark.

"Old marks, made by a buck," Liam explained. "When they're fresh, the tree looks a bit green before it dries out. These are no more than a day or two; any longer, and they start to dull."

Liam set down his pack. "We'll wait here and see if a deer will come along."

Simon's face showed his disillusionment. "Ye just wait?"

"Most of the time." Liam shrugged. "We'll set up camp and wait."

Liam dragged, with Jamie's help, the two deer he shot on a handcrafted litter. They dragged it behind Gretta's eatery, faces red from pulling them the mile from the forest.

"Simon, call your mother to open the slaughter house," Liam commanded, standing up straight. He wiped his sweaty brow, letting out a heavy breath of relief. Liam fanned his shirt away from him, seeing that Jamie was doing the same.

Gretta followed behind Simon, wiping her hands clean with a ratty cloth.

"Two!" She exclaimed excitedly. "Ye got two today!"

Liam nodded. "I wouldn't have even seen the second had Jamie here not pointed her out to me."

Jamie's chest puffed as Gretta praised him profusely.

"Aye, well," he said modestly, "Liam showed us what to look for."

Liam grinned, clapping him on the shoulders. "Modesty is an admirable trait."

"Help me get these in and hung," Gretta commanded, hands on her hips, standing in the doorway. "And then clear yerselves off."

"Go on, boys," Liam urged. "I'll help your mother."

Jamie and Simon went without protest, leaving Liam alone with their mother. When they were gone, Gretta unabashedly wrapped her arm around Liam's middle. Liam smiled, kissing the top of her head. She was a tall woman. He did not have to bend far to reach it.

"I havena seen them so excited since before their da passed," Gretta commented.

"It was easy enough to do," Liam said, disentangling himself to move the deer. He tied a rope to each of his kill's back legs before dragging them into the slaughterhouse. Lam hung each in turn, waiting for Gretta to move the blood cauldron before slitting the throat of the first one.

"Will you be needing help with the slaughter?" Liam asked.

Gretta shook her head. "I'll be fine on my own if ye'll be wantin' to wash."

"I'll go home to wash, and then I have a few errands to do," Liam told her.

Gretta nodded. "Will I see ye tomorrow, then?"

"I have work early," Liam said, "but I'll be by for dinner."

She kissed him lightly before going to work on skinning the bleeding deer.

Liam went to the postmaster to see if there were any letters from Margaret after cleaning himself from his hunting trip. He had yet to receive any from her, though he had sent a few to her himself. No doubt, she was busy settling into court life, remaking the connections she had before leaving.

"Is there anything for me?" Liam asked.

"Your name?" the postmaster asked monotonously.

Liam gave him his name, shifting uncomfortably. He had been in there several times before, and there had never been any recognition from the postmaster.

He came back from the back room with a stack of letters, seals still intact. "A copper stral per," the man behind the counter said, counting up the letters. "Five coppers."

Excitement bubbled in his chest. The letters must have been lost somewhere and finally arrived. He felt bad for doubting Margaret would keep her word to stay in touch with him. Liam dug the money out of his pocket and put it on the counter, taking his letters and going home to read them. He broke all the seals and read the one with the earliest date.

He was surprised to learn she had become the king's ward—he could at least rest assured that she had been able to lie her way out of any consequence of helping him and she would be safe. Liam inhaled deeply—he would not leave his promise of staying as close as he could in case she ever needed him, but would that mean finally having the possibility of starting a family of his own here? Did he even want to have his own instead of intruding on Gretta's family as a surrogate father to her boys for as long as she'd let him?

Liam continued reading through the letters, pleased that she was doing well. Knowing her, it wouldn't take her long to go from a maid of honor to the queen to being one of her ladies. He was even more pleased to see she missed him as much as he missed her. Gretta and the boys took away the loneliness, but he would delight in her company if he were graced with it again.

Flipping to the next letter, he tutted. Theotes knew her father deserved a better burial than what Liam gave him, but he was sad he wasn't able to support Margaret through it as he had when she had first lost him. But she was strong enough to get through it.

Liam folded the last letter up. He put it on top of the pile of other letters. Margaret deserved a long letter telling her of all that had happened to him. Most of his previous letters had been small details about his life here and that he had missed his time with her and the Gollacks, and how he wished they could go back to those days.

24 Semonat 2283
Dearest Margaret,

I have settled well in Numetra. Master Thorkelin has kept me on in his smithy, and I learn more and more each day. The work is long and tedious but enjoyable. It's a wonderful thing to create something with my hands that is useful to others. I have been slowly learning the intricate work that Jossnon does on the blades and armor. He is truly a masterful smith whom I am privileged to be working under. He does work that is worthy to be on a king's side.

There is a tavern here that I frequent called the Frothing Wench. I enjoy listening to the men talk of their lives after the war. I hear many stories of their war heroes and, surprisingly, some of the men from our country. I am glad that this particular city and its citizens were not irreparably damaged by the war as many others were.

I have started to help provide for a widow and her three young sons. She owns an eatery here, and the deer bring in I relieve the burden of cost off her shoulders. I wish you had come with me–this is a town that could use the help that you brought to Marbon. Every city needs a woman like you. You brought joy to the Gollacks I didn't know they possessed, and you have made me want more from life. You can still come here and be with me. My offer stands for as long as you need it. If you don't adore court life as you predicted you would, my home is open to you. I could make you happy here.

I miss you too, Margaret. More than I thought I would. I hope that you are doing well where you are.

Love,
Liam

Liam frowned as he read over the letter. Even though she missed him, he didn't know if she would appreciate his affection in his letter to her. Margaret had been affectionate in a roundabout way in her letters. He appreciated it nonetheless. Liam sealed the letter and went back to the postmaster to have his letter sent to the Gollacks to have them send it on to Margaret. Elizabeth had addressed the letters she sent with Margaret's inside to a 'Liam Gollack' so it would not seem odd that letters would be sent between the Anatalian capital and Salatia. Elizabeth's letters had not said much other than well wishes.

Liam went to the smithy after running his errands. He heated up the forge that he saw was starting to cool. Liam immediately went to work alongside the blacksmith.

"Ye look happy today, lad," Thorkelin said.

"I received some letters from Margaret," Liam said with a smile. "She apparently been sending them for a while, and they just now got to me."

"I'm happy for ye." Jossnon grunted as he hammered.

"She's settling in well," Liam went on. "I think she's really going to enjoy herself there."

"Are ye happy about that?" Thorkelin sounded hesitant asking the question.

"I think I am," Liam said slowly.

"An' have ye told her about Gretta?" Thorkelin asked.

"I did in my letter today," Liam told him.

"Did ye say what Gretta and the boys mean to ye?" Thorkelin gave him a pointed look.

Liam remained silent, going to pump the bellows to feed the fire.

"Ye canna play both sides, Liam," came Jossnon's scolding, "it's one or the other."

18

Lord General Crompton walked the corridors, unable to sleep. He turned the corner to see Sorren exiting Lady Margaret's chambers, his hair in disarray.

Theotes.

Crompton's mouth twisted into a scowl. His suspicions from their lunch together that the king would eventually do something to her turned out to be correct. She was his latest victim.

Lady Margaret would not be so easily moved as the servants he had spirited away from the monarch's grasp. He stood, paused at the end of the hall, watching the retreating form of his cousin. Crompton almost hoped the king would turn and see him, would want to confront him over what he saw.

He hesitated for only a moment before letting himself into Lady Margaret's chambers. A small bronzed woman let out a shriek when she saw him. The bedding she held dropped as she turned to retreat into the inner chamber.

"Sarah?" Lady Margaret called, alarmed, nearly running into Sarah as she entered the antechamber.

"Lady Margaret?" Crompton called out, his hands held up to show he had no ill intent.

Lady Margaret drew her wrap closely around her, putting herself between him and the ladies maid. He could see the calm anger on her face. "Your Grace, I don't believe you've been invited into my chambers."

"I saw the king leaving." He watched her face visibly pale.

"I also don't believe that is any of your business," she acerbically countered.

Compton stepped closer to her. He was impressed she stood her ground, though he noticed she tensed. "Is there something happening between the two of you?"

Lady Margaret glared daggers. "I would like for you to leave, Your Grace."

"Lady Margaret," —Crompton took another step toward her, extending a hand toward her— "I can—"

"Sarah, please go fetch Captain Vojvo, and tell him I require his assistance," Lady Margaret interrupted, turning to the wide-eyed girl behind her.

"My lady, I shouldn't leave you alone," she timidly said.

Lady Margaret smiled at the younger woman reassuringly. "The sooner you leave, the sooner you can come back."

Sarah forewent the curtsy, scurrying out of the room without a backward glance.

"Would you care to leave now or with assistance, Your Grace?" Lady Margaret crossed her arms in front of her, pulling her shawl tighter with the movement.

"Is the king hurting you?" Crompton asked bluntly.

Her knuckles whitened around her shawl. "Once again, Your Grace, that is none of your business."

Her stubborn refusal to give him any information grated on his nerves. He knew the answer, but he needed to hear it from her to be able to help in any way. "Lady Margaret, answer my questions."

"No," she spat, moving toward the door to the corridor. "Now will you leave?"

"I will not," Crompton told her, standing firm.

"Your Grace, you are an unwelcome visitor in my chambers, demanding conversations I do not wish to have." Lady Margaret let out an exasperated sigh. "Please respect my wishes and leave."

Crompton made to leave, instead grabbing her tightly by the upper arms. He knew it was improper to touch her like this, but he knew doing it would goad her into an answer. It was too important for him to let an opportunity pass him by.

She violently struggled against his grip. "Get your hands off me!" There was panic in her voice.

He let go, standing in front of the door. He didn't need to, though—Lady Margaret had retreated almost to her bedchamber. "Is he raping you?"

She stopped abruptly, turning toward him. "I beg your pardon?"

"Is he raping you?" Crompton repeated, stepping away from the door in case Sarah returned. He didn't have time to be delicate. He would need to form a well-oiled plan if he had any chance of getting her away safely, as he had with the others.

"What would make you ask me that?" she demanded harshly, though she started to tremble.

"He's done it before," Tobias quickly told her, "to many, many women. Mostly the servants who cannot do anything in retaliation. I have moved many of them where I can to keep them away from his reach."

"Why are you telling me this?" She was still hesitant to trust him, her eyes narrowing.

"Because I want to help you." He removed a long knife from his belt.

"What are you planning on doing with that?" Lady Margaret demanded, panic seeping back into her voice. She backed up so abruptly, she ran into the wall.

He supposed he should have unlatched the sheath first. Crompton removed it, returned the blade to its sheath, and held it out to her. "Nothing nefarious, my lady. It is for you."

"For me?" She continued to eye the knife warily. "What for?"

"For protection, Lady Margaret." Crompton stepped closer to her. "I don't yet have the motive to move you from court out of his grasp. Keep it close to your person, and if you ever feel unsafe with the king...use it."

Lady Margaret hesitantly took it, her knuckles white with her grip. "I wouldn't know how to use this."

"I sincerely hope that you will not need to use it." He looked her over, his eyes going soft.

The door opened behind them, revealing Captain Vojvo, his expression murderous. "My lady, may I offer assistance with this...'guest'?"

"No, thank you, Captain. His Grace was just leaving," she told him, her face relaxing from its pinched expression.

Tobias bowed his head to her, saying before he left, "Good night, Lady Margaret. Remember what I told you."

Crompton scolded himself when the door closed. He should have been more delicate in his action. It would be hit or miss if she wanted his help now.

He prayed to Theotes she would let him.

19

Margaret sat by the window in the queen's sitting room, trying her hardest to avoid any conversation with Lillian. She did not particularly want to engage with the queen when the king had left her bed only that morning. The sky was gray with the threat of another snow, the last one having only just melted. How she wished for springtime again, where she could watch the golden plovers scurry around the lawn, looking like silly long-legged ducklings.

"She looks distracted," Lillian commented.

"I heard she's taken a lover." Duchess Cecily leaned over to the queen, not bothering to be quiet.

Margaret closed her eyes and inhaled deeply. She couldn't say anything. That would only bring their eyes further on her.

"A lover?" Lillian asked, sounding scandalized. "*Her?*"

The duchess chortled. "No one knows who it is, though I doubt anyone would actually admit to taking her to bed. She has nothing to offer."

"Even if she had it, her title isn't worth anything," agreed the queen. "Spit-shined until it looks a pretty thing."

Margaret turned her head, catching the duchess' eye. She was sure a lot of people felt that way—otherwise she would have been married off before her father ever became ill. She would have made an especially rich wife, but the courtiers of Anatalia were vain and preferred precedence to money.

Duchess Cecily smirked, holding her eyes as she continued, "She's nothing more than a farmer's daughter. No one would want her empire of dirt."

Margaret's cheeks heated, and she turned to look back out the window. The duchess wasn't much different than her. If Crompton were not were not a duke or a lord general, he would simply be a grape farmer instead of a tobacco farmer. Perhaps one day Margaret would remind her of that, but it seemed pointless now. She had already ruffled enough feathers and paid for it.

"Perhaps it's one of the guards," the duchess went on. "They have no scruples, and they would be excited to bed a noblewoman."

Lillian scoffed. "Her own guard, no doubt. Captain something or another."

"Paying him in favors instead of a salary," laughed Duchess Cecily.

Ladies Elizabeth, Aurora and Victoria watched silently, looking between Lady Margaret and the queen and Duchess Cecily, waiting for a reaction. When she caught their looks, Margaret's cheeks only heated more. She raised her hand to fiddle with her necklace, trying to calm herself.

Queen Lillian's eyes lighted on the motion. "Lady Margaret, that's a beautiful necklace," she said with a smirk. "May I see it?"

Margaret hesitated. She moved to stand, stopping when the queen raised a hand.

"Take it off, Lady Margaret," the queen commanded, "and show it to me. I do not wish to have your bosom in my face."

Her ladies in waiting tittered as Margaret removed the necklace, handing it over. Lillian examined the necklace closely.

"It was my mother's favorite," Margaret said.

"I like this very much," the queen commented, looking at Margaret pointedly.

Margaret rolled her lips between her teeth, looking at the other women in the room. They all looked at her expectantly. She wouldn't be able to refuse the unsaid request. "I would be greatly honored if you would have it, Your Majesty."

The queen smiled brightly at her. "You are too kind, Lady Margaret."

Margaret curtsied briefly before returning to her seat by the window.

Duchess Cecily leaned over to look at the necklace. "A very beautiful acquisition, Majesty."

"You think so? I'm unsure it will suit me." Lillian held it up to her neck before looking to the duchess. "It would look beautiful on you, " the queen commented, holding the necklace to the duchess and examining her closely. "Perfect. You should have it."

Duchess Cecily demurely bowed her head. "You honor me greatly, Your Majesty."

Margaret looked at them, incredulous, her mouth hanging open. All of that, and the queen wouldn't even keep her mother's necklace?

"Close your mouth, Lady Margaret," Lillian snapped. "You'll catch flies."

She snapped her mouth shut, the look of incredulity still on her face.

"You'll attend me at dinner tonight, Lady Margaret," Lillian informed Margaret as she put on her jewels.

Margaret curtsied low to the queen. "You honor me greatly, Your Majesty."

Lillian only smirked, shooting ice down Margaret's spine. She sought the eye of Duchess Cecily and saw she was also looking smug. Margaret's stomach clenched. She could only imagine what was in store for her.

"Come along, Lady Margaret," Lillian commanded, going to the door.

Margaret obediently followed the queen to the great hall. The nobles gathered for the evening meal bowed or curtsied as they passed, going to their seats when they rose. The queen settled in her seat next to the king, and Margaret arranged Lillian's skirts comfortably around the chair.

Margaret moved to stand behind the queen on her right, only to be stopped by the monarch.

"Lady Victoria will stand there," Lillian told Margaret, raising a hand to beckon her.

Furrowing her brow, Margaret stepped forward. "Where would you like me to stand, Your Majesty?"

Lillian pointed to the ground between her and her husband. "Here."

Margaret moved to the queen's left, standing behind the chairs.

"No," Lillian corrected. "Here between us."

Awkwardly, Margaret moved to the appointed spot.

"Now pick up my napkin," commanded the queen.

Margaret did so, moving to put it in the queen's lap.

"Did I tell you to put it in my lap?" snapped Lillian.

Cheeks hot, Margaret pulled the napkin back. "No, Majesty."

"Kneel," Lillian ordered.

Margaret looked at her incredulously. "I beg your pardon?"

"Are you deaf?" the queen fumed. "I gave you an order."

Margaret resisted the urge to look at the king in hopes he would refute his wife. She slowly went to her knees, looking to the queen for instruction.

"Hold the napkin so that I can reach it," Lillian irritably prompted.

Swallowing hard, Margaret held Lillian's napkin level with her hand. "How long must I stay here?"

"Until I tell you to move," snapped Lillian. "And you will not question me again."

Margaret fell silent, keeping her eyes on the napkin.

As the meal went on, Margaret's arms burned, and her back started to ache. She shifted uncomfortably, lowering her arms to her lap to rest them. Margaret raised herself on her knees slightly, hearing them pop. She grimaced at the sound.

"Did I tell you you could lower the napkin, Lady Margaret?" Lillian demanded.

Immediately, Margaret raised the napkin to its original position. "My apologies, Your Majesty."

Lillian went back to ignoring Margaret until she needed her hand cleaned. The queen simply extended her hand to Margaret and let her take the hint. Margaret thoroughly cleaned the extended appendage. Margaret subtly shifted her weight back on her heels. She stiffened when Sorren covertly ran a finger down the underside of her arm, raising goose bumps.

Lillian glared at them, deliberately flinging her hand too far. Her hand connected with Margaret's face, leaving bits of chicken and gravy on her cheek.

Margaret gasped, moving to wipe her face.

The queen snapped her fingers at Margaret. "Don't sully my napkin wiping it on your face!"

Margaret reluctantly wiped only Lillian's hand, leaving the food on her face. She was hit several more times, depositing more food. The longer the food sat there, the more Margaret's hackles raised. How could the queen be allowed to treat her like this? She snuck a glance at Sorren, but he steadfastly ignored her.

Dinner that night lasted three hours, Margaret on her knees for the entirety of it. Lillian rose after she finished her dinner. Margaret tried to stand, her legs wobbling as the blood rushed back into the numb limbs. She let out a shriek as she fell backward, her legs having buckled under the pressure.

Her face and neck turned red, flaming with her embarrassment. Several men came to help her up, but the king took the honor for himself. Sorren scooped her into his arms, picking her up effortlessly. He glared at Lillian as he passed to return Margaret to her chambers. Margaret buried her face into his chest to avoid the eye of all in the room.

"Do you think you can stand?" Sorren asked when he reached her door.

"Yes, I think so," Margaret hesitantly told him.

The king set her on her feet as she clung to him. Margaret tested her weight and found none of the earlier wobbliness remained. She pulled away from him, moving awkwardly away. He raised his brows at her expectantly.

"Would you like to come in?" Margaret reluctantly offered.

Sorren opened the door for her. "I would love to."

Margaret tried to keep the dismay from her face as she led the way. Sarah came from her bedchamber, falling into a curtsy when she saw the king. "Good evening, Your Majesty."

Sorren nodded to her, gently pushing Margaret at Sarah. "Clean your mistress and ready her for bed."

Sarah took Margaret into her bedchamber, first wiping her face clean of the mess. "What happened, my lady?"

"The queen," Margaret said, knowing that answered any further questions.

As Margaret helped Sarah undo the plethora of laces on her many layers, Sarah spoke, "You received a few letters from the Gollacks while you were with the queen."

Margaret looked back at her. "Oh?"

"Two or three, I think," Sarah told her.

"I'll read them once the king leaves," Margaret finally said.

Sarah nodded, helping her into her shift. "Would you like to invite His Majesty in?"

"No," Margaret told her. "I'll go to him. Where is my robe?"

Sarah fetched it and helped Margaret into it before she returned to the sitting room. The king had already removed his waist coat and was sitting comfortably on one of Margaret's couches. Margaret sat on the couch opposite him.

Margaret watched the king warily. "Sarah, would you pour His Majesty more wine?"

He thanked Sarah when she finished pouring. He took a drink, gazing back at Margaret over the rim of his glass.

"Will you be staying the night, Your Majesty?" Margaret asked.

Sorren raised a single brow. "Would you like me to?"

She would much prefer he leave her in peace. "I will not say no."

Draining his wine, he stood with his hand extended. Margaret took it, standing herself. She allowed him to lead her to her chambers.

Once the king was asleep, Margaret snuck into her sitting room to read her letters from the Gollacks. She found them piled on the table in the alcove. The seals were surprisingly still intact. As much as she wanted to save Liam's letter for last, she found it first.

12 Omonat 2283

Dear Margaret,

Eli recovered well from his illness, thank you for asking. Gretta thinks that it was from drinking bad water when he was playing with the other village boys. I'll need to teach him how to identify safe water.

I have started to teach Jamie and Simon how to hunt and forage so that they can provide for their mother if I ever have to leave. Simon seems like he will be the best at tracking, but Jamie is showing the most aptitude for the bow. They each have to practice when they come home from their work.

They're upset I won't let them carry a weapon on our hunting trips, but they will understand eventually. I don't want them to hurt themselves—or me–so far from a healer. Numetra isn't as fortunate to have an apothecary. The closest one is in the next town, Castenra.

Have you had any problems in the queen's ladies? Are you still having problems with "playing the game," as you put it?

I hope you are doing well.

Love,
Liam

Margaret snorted at the irony. Of course, she was having problems in the queen's ladies, but none she would tell him about. He would try to convince her to leave before she achieved what she came for. She rose and threw his letter in the fire as she did with all of them. Margaret would not chance incriminating herself further.

Grabbing the three other letters, Margaret settled to read them in a row. She furrowed her brow at the date—they must have forgotten about it for a while and sent it when Liam had written his latest letter.

Aram had apparently almost given himself heat sickness. She shook her head. Margaret wished they would take better care of themselves. She could move them to Dorcia to live a life of luxury, but she knew they would refuse. They were not the type of people to feel comfortable in luxury. She moved on to the more recent letters.

5 Omonat 2283
Margaret,

We sold two of the three litters of piglets and butchered one of the male pigs to eat this month. The paddock needed some repair. One of the males tried to escape, and did, by knocking down one of the sections of fence. He was the one we killed.

I saw the children in town today with Claudette. They all seem to be doing well. Their manners have improved considerably since the last time you saw them.

According to Suzanna, she could hear Claudette giving the new cobbler a piece of her mind all the way in her seamstress shop. I think you made the right choice in governess.

We miss you.

Aram & Elizabeth

She was pleased the children were doing well and that Claudette had the strength to deal with anything that prevented the children from getting the best—

as they deserved. Margaret took out the last letter and saw that both Aram and Elizabeth had written this time.

29 Omonat 2283
Margaret,
   I visited with Suzanna today, and she said Claudette came to the shop with the boys, and the oldest is towering over the governess. Suzanna said Jonathan is starting to grow into his looks and is sounding much more like a man.
   The children still miss you and ask when you'll be back to visit them. I know it will be a while yet before you can return, but we still wish you could come home to us. Hope all is well with you in the capital.
   We love you.
                                             Elizabeth

Dearest Margaret,
   Beth has been reading me all your letters. It sounds like you are settling well where you are, but I wonder if you are happy? You always seem to be a little sad when talking about your life now. Beth and I miss you terribly. We feel like our daughter has left to go on to bigger and better things and we can't compete.
   Won't you come home to us?
   We love and miss you always.
                                             Aram

Tears pricked her eyes. Margaret wished more than anything that she could return to them, or that she had never left. Now she didn't know if she would ever be able to return. Margaret wiped her eyes when the door to her bedchamber opened. The king emerged from the dark room, searching for Margaret in the dimly lit sitting room.

"What are you doing out here?" he demanded sleepily.

Margaret gathered the letters from the Gollacks, happy she had already burned the letter from Liam. "I was reading the letters I received today."

The king took them from her hand, sitting beside her to read them. He put up his hand to stay her protests. He spent the longest reading the last letter they had sent, turning an eye on Margaret when he finished.

"Who are these people?" Sorren asked.

Should she tell him the truth? Margaret searched his face before answering. "They're the people who took me in after my father died and I fled from your soldiers. We became a little family—Aram felt much like the father I wish I still had."

Sorren's face hardened. "And these children this Elizabeth spoke of?"

"They're orphans I found living in an abandoned building," Margaret told him, purposefully leaving out the name of the town. "I bought them a manor, clothes and food, and hired a governess to teach them."

"Do you want to see them again?" His face was an unreadable mask.

Margaret looked at him sharply, unsure of what to say. She would give anything to go back to them and see the Gollacks and the children. If he let her go there, she would stay as long as she was able. This place truly wasn't for her. "More than anything, Your Majesty."

The king examined her. "And would you return if I allowed you to leave?"

Her hesitation to answer gave him all the information he needed.

"You will remain here in Jalmar until I give you permission to do otherwise."

Margaret's heart twinged, her face falling. She should have lied and said yes. "As you command, Your Majesty," she said sullenly.

Sorren stood, holding out his hand to her. "Come to bed, my dear."

20

Liam wiped his hands on a near-black cloth, already covered with soot and grease, in an attempt to clean his hands. His shift was finished at the smithy, but he stayed to help Thorkelin close and clean everything.

"Is there anything else that I can do for you?" Liam asked, watching Jossnon hang the last of the swords.

"Get on wi' ye," Jossnon waved his hand with a smile. "I'm sure ye have a good time planned wi' Gretta."

"I do," admitted Liam.

"Away wi' ye then, an' have fun wi' the boys." Jossnon guided him to the door. "Tell 'em I said hello."

"I will," assured Liam, still hesitating to leave. "Are you sure you don't need any more help?"

"If ye dinna leave now an' go to yer woman, I'll drag ye by the ear so I dinna havta hear about it later," Jossnon told him sternly, mirth twinkling in his eyes.

Liam held his hand up in mock defense. "All right, all right. I'm going!"

Liam leaned back in his chair; it responded with a loud creak. He rubbed his stomach, groaning with his fullness. "You spoil me, Gretta," he told her.

She only smiled, taking away his plate.

Liam furrowed his brow, looking between Gretta and her boys. "Is there something wrong?"

"Go on an' get yerselves ready for bed, aye?" Gretta gave a pointed look to her children, jerking her head toward the stairs.

The pleasantly full feeling turned into one of overfullness spilling into his throat. Gretta had her back to him and would not look directly at him.

"Gretta?" he asked nervously.

She turned to him, face clouded with doubt. Gretta hesitated before pulling a chair to sit next to him. "Liam—"

"Have I done something wrong?"

She grabbed his hand and squeezed it. "Ye've done no but good for my family, Liam, an' I canna thank ye enough for it," she told him fervently.

"But?" Liam prompted.

Gretta looked down, squeezing Liam's hand again. "But it's only that I wondered... Well, I was wonderin' with the way we've been carryin' on, why ye havena made any proposals."

With the tension released from his gut, Liam let out a surprised laugh. "You're wanting a marriage proposal?"

"It's no laughin' matter." She glared at him, ripping her hand out of his grasp. "Ye already act as a husband should, providin' extra for me and teachin' the boys to be good men. It's no a large leap."

Liam grabbed her hand back and kissed her knuckles tenderly. "You're right, I'm sorry. I shouldn't have laughed."

"No, ye shouldna," agreed Gretta. "Now what d'ye have to say?"

"If you are wanting a husband, I cannot be that for you," Liam told her, watching her face fall. "This is the longest I've stayed in one place for nearly a decade."

"And?" Gretta raised her brows.

"I've made some mistakes in my life," he explained gently, "and I don't want you and the boys to live with them."

"Surely, ye canna have done annithin' sae bad ye canna have a life here," Gretta countered.

"One of the reasons I even thought to stay here is for a young woman whose life I ruined," Liam said sadly. "I brought soldiers to her home when I came begging for food, and her father was murdered as a result."

"Poor thing," Gretta cooed.

Liam nodded. "So I stay close in case she ever needs me, since I feel I am now responsible for her welfare."

"I dinna understand why ye canna take our relationship any further," Gretta said, searching his face. "I dinna mind ye wantin' to help this poor girl when she needs it."

Liam smiled at her, kissing her hand. "That means a great deal to me, but I don't want any harm or danger to come to you or the boys on my behalf as it did Margaret and her father."

"No one kens ye here, Liam," Gretta tried to reassure him.

"Do you want to take the chance?" Liam asked her. He didn't, that was for certain. He'd already ruined enough lives being around. Only the Gollacks, Margaret, and now Gretta had managed to get him to stop and be involved for the pleasure of their company. "Take the chance that Jamie, Simon, or Eli could get hurt because of me?"

"Ye've been here o'er a year, an' no one has come for ye," Gretta reminded him. "Do ye no think the danger has passed?"

"Perhaps," Liam reluctantly conceded, "but I still couldn't marry you, not when at any moment, I would have to abandon you and the boys if trouble ever came. I couldn't deny you the chance to marry someone who could support you if I left."

"Will ye tell me what ye did?" she asked.

Liam hesitated. "It's better if you don't know."

Gretta sighed. "My boys love ye, Liam. Will ye no consider livin' here to teach 'em how to be men?"

"Gretta..." Liam squeezed her hand. "I'm not sure that's a good idea."

"Take a few days to think on it," Gretta urged. "Think at least of the boys."

He paused before nodding. It was the least he could do for her. "I'll think about it, but I think perhaps I should leave for the night."

"Aye," she agreed. "That's all I can ask of ye."

Liam aggressively pumped the bellows, a blast of heat hitting him. He had not been back to see Gretta in a week. He couldn't face her until he had an answer.

An answer he came up with on his own.

"What's the matter wi' ye?" Jossnon demanded. "Ye're gettin' the forge too hot, Liam! Pay attention, lad!"

Liam took his hands from the handles. "I'm sorry, Master Thorkelin. I'm distracted today."

"Aye, I can see that. Ye've been distracted all week," Jossnon replied acerbically. "I've eyes."

Chagrin twisted Liam's face. "I'm sorry."

"What's troublin' ye?"

He sighed heavily, backing away from the hot forge. His brow was already beaded with sweat. Liam looked over the smith before sighing again. "Gretta asked why I've made no proposals to her, and when I told her I could not be a husband, she asked if I would take residence with her to teach the boys to be men," Liam explained. "I haven't seen her since she asked—I can't face her until I have an answer."

Jossnon remained silent as he thought, his face an impenetrable mask. "Is it yer Maggie that's givin' ye yer trouble?"

"She's part of it," Liam agreed. He feared that if he truly committed to Gretta and the boys that he would not want to answer Margret's call for help, even after having given his word. After all, Margret had made him forget his word to himself that he wouldn't get involved with another person for fear of harm coming to them. "The other part is my past that I want Gretta to have no part of."

"Then ye should tell her no," Jossnon advised.

Liam looked at him helplessly. "But I miss her."

"Then say yes," Jossnon told him.

Sighing heavily, Liam went to the back of the shop to get more steel to heat. When he returned, Jossnon told him he had a guest waiting in the front shop. Liam abandoned his work, going to his visitor.

Jamie fidgeted uncomfortably in front of Liam, not looking him in the face.

Liam grasped him firmly on the shoulder, a smile lighting his face. "Jamie, what are you doing here? Shouldn't you be working?"

"I asked to be let off early," Jamie said slowly. "I wanted to see ye."

Liam's heart swelled. "I've missed you and the boys, and your mother of course."

"That is what I came to talk to ye about," Jamie said. "Ma has been terribly sad since ye left."

"I didn't mean to make her sad," Liam told him.

"She told me what she asked ye," Jamie revealed.

Liam's brows rose. "Did she?"

"Aye, she did," Jamie said. "An' I wish ye would come back an' make her happy."

"I can't see her until I have my answer." Liam squeezed Jamie's shoulders. "It's unfair to the both of us."

Jamie nodded solemnly. "I understand, I only wished to tell ye that we want ye to be our da, even if only for a little while."

Shocked, he stood speechless as Jamie walked away. He had said his peace, and there was no point in sticking around. Liam returned to the back where Jossnon was working.

Jossnon raised his brows, remaining silent as he struck the heated sword.

"Jamie asked me to be his father," Liam said in a daze.

"Did he now?" Jossnon seemed surprised himself.

"I've never had someone ask me anything like that before," Liam continued. "Never in my life have I thought I would be seen as a father."

"It's an amazing thing," Jossnon told him.

Liam nodded, turning to his work.

Liam stood at the back door, fist poised to knock. He could not bring himself yet to put it to the wood. If he did, he would be committing to family, to protect them from within. To ensuring their welfare, and being responsible if one was ailing. Once he knocked on that door, there was no turning back. There would be no escape to bachelorhood, no returning to his own little room or leaving without explanation.

Closing his eyes to gather his courage to accept such a heavy responsibility, he knocked on the door.

Jamie pulled open the door, his face lighting when he saw who was there. "So ye've accepted us, then?"

"Yes," Liam said quietly. "I am yours now, and you are mine."

Jamie moved out of the way, a wide grin on his face. "Welcome home, Da."

Liam stepped over the threshold, feeling the mantle of welcome rest on him. It was the first time since he'd left his parents' home fifteen years ago that he had such a feeling. It was a long time to not have somewhere he could truly call home.

He went to the kitchen, finding Gretta making dinner for her—for *their*—family. He cleared his throat, waiting for her to turn around.

She turned at the noise, hope flooding her eyes. "Liam?"

"I'm home, Gretta," he whispered.

21

argaret sighed as she lay awake, sore from the king's visit. Bruises had already started to form on her arms and legs. Sarah entered the room, opening the curtains to let in the light.

"Find something easy for me to wear today. I don't want to wear anything too heavy," Margaret called from the bed.

"Yes, my lady," Sarah curtsied and went into the large closet, bringing her a dark blue house dress to hide the bruises.

"Thank you, Sarah."

Concern donned Sarah's face as she helped dress her. Margaret was in obvious pain, hardly able to strand straight without flinching.

"My lady, please," Sarah pleaded, "is there anything I can do for you?"

Margaret patted Sarah's hand with her own shaking one. She tried to smile. "This will pass, Sarah."

"Yes, my lady…"

Margaret smoothed the front of her dress. "We need to prepare for Annabel's arrival. We will find her a room befitting her station."

The mention of Annabel brought some excitement to Sarah's face. "She'll be here so soon?"

Annabel had sent a letter ahead of her that she would be arriving within the week, and Sarah couldn't have been more excited. Annabel took four months, after traveling, to spend with her family before coming into Margaret's service for some time. She was traveling from a small town not far from Rivack called Loford, and the lateness of the year would not impede her travel.

"Before we do anything, I need to speak to the queen." Margaret would need at least a few days to settle Annabel, and she couldn't do that with the queen tormenting her all day. "If you would, please get the captain and tell him to meet me here? I doubt it will take long with the queen."

Margaret went to Lillian's chambers, knocking lightly before she entered. She didn't have time to see if the queen was going to torment her again by making her wait outside until she entered on her own. Surprisingly, no one paid much attention to her.

Lillian was next to the fireplace with Duchess Cecily, quietly working on her needlework.

Inhaling deeply, Margaret steeled herself to talk to her. She approached, curtsying deeply. "Your Majesty?"

"What is it you want, Lady Margaret?" Lillian didn't even look up at her.

"One of the young ladies that was in my entourage for my father's funeral has written that she will be arriving soon to join my household." Margaret paused, chewing on her upper lip for a moment to calm her nerves. "I would like to ask if I could have a few days away to acquire her a room and settle her in."

At this, Lillian did look up. It was the first time she had seen the queen look excited since joining her service at the king's command. "You have my permission, Lady Margaret." She smiled. "You may leave now if you want."

It was what she wanted, but Margaret couldn't help feeling insulted at how happy the queen was she wouldn't be there. "Thank you, Your Majesty." She curtsied once more before going back to her rooms.

Margaret leaned on Captain Vojvo's arm as they went to the east wing of the palace where temporary guests, lower ranking nobles, and the ambassadors to the other countries resided at the invitation of the king. The west wing was for the royal family and the higher ranking nobles to reside. As the king's ward, Margaret was placed in the west. There were several rooms empty in the east wing. Nice enough rooms, but none would compare to the ones reserved for the high nobility. They would certainly be much nicer than the lodging Annabel would be used to.

Margaret and Sarah toured several rooms before coming to one Margaret felt was appropriate for Annabel. It was a single room with a window overlooking a small man-made lake on the palace grounds. There was simple cream colored molding at the top of the gold-and-cream walls. Next to the window was a cherry writing desk with a cushioned chair. On the wall opposite the window was a large dark cherry bureau with lighter cherry inlays of a rose bouquet design in the center. Set on the wall in between was a bed covered in white sheets with a dark gold cover. Behind the bed was the same dark gold-colored fabric in a tented canopy that could be pulled forward to shield the sleeper from the sun. At the foot of the bed was a dark colored chest Annabel could store her things in.

"I think this will be perfect for her, my lady," Sarah commented, running her hand over the bedcovers.

"I think so too," Margaret agreed, looking around the room. It would be adequate for her needs. "We'll send one of the servants to clean away the dust before Annabel arrives."

They left, Sarah trailing behind her and Captain Vojvo. As they walked back to Margaret's room, they came across a few of the men in the king's entourage. And wherever these men were, the king was not far off.

"Oh no," Margaret said quietly to herself. "No, no, no." She turned, trying to find any corridors she could escape down to avoid seeing the king. After the previous night's abuse, she hoped to avoid him for as long as possible.

"Lady Margaret!" the king boomed, a smug look on his face. "It's nice to see you up and around."

Margaret slowly turned around and curtsied low to him. "I have a young woman joining my household to introduce her to court, Your Majesty. I had to find a room to place her in."

"Did you have this approved by me, Lady Margaret?" Sorren looked her over, his eyes lingering low for a moment before they came to her face again.

"No, Your Majesty," Margaret hesitantly admitted, her anxiety growing. "I didn't think you would mind if I commandeered a room for Annabel."

"I'll allow it this time, Lady Margaret, but next time, you will need my permission in advance."

"Thank you, Your Majesty." Margaret curtsied low to him again. "You are most generous."

"I have no doubt you will find an appropriate way to thank me soon," the king said with a leer.

Lightning flew down her back, her chest tightening. Another debt to be paid. "Yes, Your Majesty."

The king passed by her, letting his hand gently pass over her hand.

Margaret closed her eyes tightly, fisting her trembling hands in her skirts. "Come along, Sarah, we need to prepare."

Captain Vojvo grabbed Margaret by her hand, placing his other hand on her back, prompting Margaret to move. He quickly escorted her back to her apartments.

She immediately went into her bedchamber, gasping for breath. Was this how her mother had felt? She sank to the ground next to her bed, gasping, gripping her skirts tightly in her fists. Margaret saw Sarah kneel in front of her, but she couldn't hear anything over the sound of her own breathing.

Vojvo knelt in front of her, gently grabbing her face in his large calloused hands. "My lady," he said first as gently as his hands, "my lady, you need to breathe slowly."

She tried. She couldn't. She could only stare at him wide-eyed, sucking in air rapidly.

"Sarah, go and get the palace healer," he commanded. "Now!"

Sarah soon left and returned with the court healer. Margaret didn't know how long had passed. All she knew was the tightness in her chest and her inability to take a deep breath.

The healer lifted her onto her bed in a single motion. "Lady Margaret, you need to calm yourself."

Margaret nodded and tried to steady her breathing. It took Sarah stroking her hair and the captain holding her hand tightly to slowly get it back to a normal rate.

"Tell me what happened, my lady."

"I-I just felt like I couldn't breathe suddenly." Margaret put her hand to her chest as if to make sure that her breathing was really back to normal. She knew it was provoked by the king's insinuation there was one more thing she owed him.

"It seems to me that you've just had a small bout of hysteria, my lady," he explained. "I want you to rest for the remainder of the day."

"I have a young woman joining my household. I cannot just rest." Margaret looked at him incredulously, speaking to him as if the concept of preparations were foreign to him.

"I'm afraid you'll have to, Lady Margaret. Don't force me into having guards stand outside your door," the healer said before leaving her apartments.

"I'll rest as much as I can," she evasively called after him.

Margaret waited for Annabel in the windowed alcove of her drawing room, tea steeping for the two of them. Upon her arrival, Margaret sent Sarah with instructions to bring Annabel to Margaret's opulent apartments when she was ready.

"My lady," Sarah interrupted gently, "Annabel is ready to see you."

Margaret smiled. "Bring her in, Sarah."

Annabel looked around in wonder. "My lady, these rooms are magnificent!" she gushed, taking it all in.

Margaret stood to greet her. "Annabel, I'm so pleased that you made it safely."

Annabel curtsied to her. "It was good to see my family before coming here."

"Please, sit," Margaret said, sitting herself.

Annabel looked around the room, amazement still on her face. "When will you be able to introduce me to prospective husbands, Lady Margaret?"

"Soon, Annabel," Margaret started. "I need to know more about you and what you're looking for."

118

"What do you need to know, Lady Margaret?"

"Everything."

"Everything?" Annabel asked, a small frown on her face.

"Absolutely everything, Annabel," Margaret said. "Have you ever been courted?"

"Yes," Annabel shyly answered.

"Good. You know how it goes, then. That will make this much easier."

Annabel answered Margaret's questions for well over an hour. She seemed to be a very naïve, but sweet, girl. She had been courted by a soldier in Loford who was under her father's command. Their courtship had ended when the young man got another woman pregnant. Annabel looked despondent when she recounted the event.

"What exactly are you hoping for, Annabel?" Margaret asked her.

"I don't want to reach too high, Lady Margaret," Annabel started timidly. "Perhaps a baron?"

Margaret chewed on her lip as she thought. "Baron William Lavon is currently looking for a wife."

"Is he handsome?" Annabel asked winsomely.

"My dear, if you're looking for a title, his face does not matter," Margaret said with a laugh.

"Oh…" Annabel's face fell.

"Surely, you knew that, Annabel."

"Well, yes, I suppose I did." Annabel looked at her hands. "When will you be able to introduce me to Baron Lavon?"

"First, you will need to be seen around court, establish yourself as a charming young girl who is learning the ways of court. Perhaps even trying to get your father a petition for one of the knight's prestigious orders."

Annabel's father, Sir Adam Lurant, was awarded his knighthood by his lord general for his exemplary duty during the war between Anatalia and Salatia. He had stepped up to take command when the leader of his squadron was overrun by enemy soldiers and killed. Sir Adam was awarded an honor for bravery at the time and, by the end of the larger battle, had his knighthood and was given command of his own squad of men. If Annabel was able to gain access for her father, then she would rise higher in her standing, and it would be much easier to marry her into the nobility.

"I don't know of any order that he would be qualified for, Lady Margaret," Annabel said, looking confused. It was obvious she did not have a mind for scheming.

"There is the Order of The Gauntlet, one of the lowest orders. He would be perfectly fitted to it, having been a soldier and a knight, and you would also gain some esteem," Margaret said. "It would put him at the same level as the younger son of a baron."

"How would I do that? Shouldn't he be here to make his rounds in the right circles?" Annabel asked.

"You can start the process, and I will speak to the king on his behalf." Margaret motioned for Sarah to come over to them. "Sarah, can you arrange for us to sit with Sir Edward and Lady Grey tonight?"

Sarah curtsied to her. "Yes, my lady."

"Sir Edward is the Knight Commander in the Order of The Gauntlet," Margaret said to Annabel as a side note. "He'll be a good place to start talking up your father."

"Yes, Lady Margaret." Annabel smiled. "I don't think it will be long before I have a husband and my father has a more respectable standing."

Margaret patted her hand. "I hope not."

Annabel wore one of her finest dresses to dinner, which Margaret admitted to herself could have been nicer. The Honorable Sir Edward was already seated when they arrived for the evening meal with court. The knight stood when he saw them approach the table.

"My Lady Margaret, how nice of you to join us tonight." Sir Edward gave her a small bow.

"It's our pleasure, Sir Edward," Margaret said with a charming smile. "This is Lady Annabel Lurant of Loford. She has joined my household to learn about court life."

Annabel curtsied to him. "It's a pleasure to make your acquaintance, Sir Edward, Lady Grey."

"Sit down, girl." Lady Grey scolded Annabel, a sour look on her face.

Annabel promptly sat, a blush dusting her cheeks, while Sir Edward pulled out Margaret's chair. Margaret sat with a flourish and gave another smile to the man who could help appoint Annabel's father to a position in his order.

"Lady Grey, how is your daughter?" Margaret asked.

Lady Grey's puckered face released at the mention of her daughter. "She is well, thank you, Lady Margaret. Elizabeth is nearly ready to go into her confinement."

"Sir Hartly is truly a lucky man with your Elizabeth at his side," Margaret said, raising her glass to the knight's wife. "You've done a wonderful job with her, Lady Grey."

Lady Grey smiled at Margaret. "I see your time away from court has not diminished your knowledge of the goings on here, my lady."

"You cannot risk not knowing everything here, Lady Grey, if you wish to survive."

Margaret had gone to her old friends and bribed them with favors to learn everything she could about what had happened since she left. She had been able to glean some gossip from the king freely but felt that was no longer an option. She would have to pay for her information in favors and gifts now. The only free gossip left to be had was from the time she spent among the queen's ladies in waiting.

"That should be your first lesson in court life, Lady Annabel," Lady Grey told her. "This life is not for the unambitious."

"Lady Grey is right," Margaret said. "The faint of heart stay away from court as much as they possibly can."

"I think I have what it takes, Lady Margaret." Though she said it was confidence, her eyes betrayed her—they were filled with worry.

"Sir Edward, Annabel's father is also a knight, Sir Adam Lurant, who fought valiantly in the Great War between Anatalia and Salatia," Margaret informed Sir Edward, changing the subject away from Annabel's possible ineptitude.

Sir Edward raised his eyebrows, looking at Annabel. "Oh? Tell me about your father, Lady Annabel."

"I was just a child when the war broke out, but my father told me wonderful stories of how he had to take command after his leader had been slain. He helped win what seemed like a hopeless battle that day, Sir Edward. Lord General Crompton himself awarded my father his knighthood as soon as the battle had been won." Pride shone bright on her face as she spoke.

"A commendable man then," Sir Edward Grey said. "You must be proud to have such a man as the head of your family."

"Very proud, sir," Annabel told him with a bright smile.

Sir Edward stood suddenly, bowing. "Your Majesty, you honor us with your presence!"

The ladies stood and curtsied low to Sorren with quiet "Your Majesty's."

"Please, ladies, sit," Sorren said, resting a hand on Margaret's shoulder after she returned to her seat. "My dear, my healer told me you had an attack this morning."

"Just a small bit of nerves preparing for the day's events, Your Majesty," Margaret said calmly. Her skin crawled where he was touching her. "It's nothing to worry over."

"I will check on you later this evening, Lady Margaret," the king said, running his fingers intimately off her shoulder as he departed.

"I hadn't realized you were so close with the king, Lady Margaret," Lady Grey said with raised brows.

"I am the king's ward, Lady Grey," Margaret informed her tersely.

"Aren't you a little old to be a ward to the king, my lady?" Sir Edward asked.

"I have no family left to negotiate my marriage for me. So His Majesty has taken pity on me and made me his ward," Margaret said. "If the king finds me fit to be titled as such, I do not see where you have room to question his decision."

"Lady Grey, how long has your daughter been married to...?" Annabel quickly interjected.

"Sir George Hartly of the Order of The Garland," Lady Grey said with pride. It was a higher order than her husband's. "They will have been married a year by the time the baby arrives."

"How wonderful she was able to bear children so quickly!" Annabel congratulated her as if it were the mother's doing for an easy conception.

Lady Grey smiled with pride. "Aren't you a charming girl?"

The remainder of the dinner passed without incident, Annabel charming Sir Edward and Lady Grey throughout the courses. Margaret escorted Annabel back to her room, a smile on her face.

"I'm very proud of you Annabel," she praised. "You did well tonight."

"Thank you, my lady," Annabel said diminutively. "Is it always that way?"

"What way?"

"A dance of compliments and snide undertones, mixed with ambition to reach further than your arms can go."

"Not always," Margaret told her. "My father hated the game as well, but he played along with the rest of us."

"What if I am not cut from the same cloth as you and cannot play these games?" Annabel's concern was all over her face.

"Then you will pray for a quick marriage and have as many babies as you can so that you can stay away from court," Margaret said with a shrug. "Or you can go back to your father's house and marry a commoner."

"I don't want to marry a commoner," Annabel said hastily.

"Then you'll stay at court until we find you a husband, and then you can avoid it."

Margaret left Annabelle with a good night and went to her own room to ready herself for bed. The king had left the dining hall with Lillian before she and Annabel departed, and she hoped that meant that he would be visiting his queen's quarters and not hers. The thought of the king entertaining himself with her made her stomach roil and her skin crawl.

"Sarah, get me out of this monstrosity of a dress," Margaret called upon entering her apartments.

"My lady," Sarah murmured, quiet as a mouse. "His Majesty is here to see you."

"Leave us. Lady Margaret will not be requiring your services for the remainder of the evening."

"Yes, Your Majesty," Sarah said, curtsying low to him before scampering off.

Margaret gave him the barest of curtsies. "Your Majesty, what is it that I can do for you?"

"Why don't we get you out of that 'monstrosity of a dress,' and then we can discuss what it is you can do for me," the king told her, holding out his hand for her to take.

Lady Margaret hesitated before placing her hand in his. She could use her compliance as a stepping stone to helping Annabel. "As you wish, Majesty."

The king led her into her bedchambers, his fingers pulling the laces of her dress at once. It was laced at the front of the dress for the surcoat and in the back for her corset.

"What did you think of Annabel?" Margaret asked when he turned her around.

"Who?" Sorren asked as he kissed her neck gently while he loosened her corset.

Margaret cringed at the touch, glad that he could not see her face. "The young woman who joined my household. I am hoping to persuade Sir Edward Grey to petition you for her father, Sir Adam, to join the Order of The Gauntlet to elevate her status." Margaret turned to face him, standing only in her chemise. "She is hoping for a noble husband."

"I see." Sorren began taking down her hair, letting it fall down her back.

Margaret knew that affection would increase her chances of him helping. She gently cupped his cheek in her hand. "Do you think his joining the order would be possible?"

Sorren kissed the inside of her wrist, pulling her close to him. "I suppose anything is possible, my dear. You helped a traitor, and your head is still attached to your neck."

Margaret's stomach dropped. "My apologies, Your Majesty, I ask too much of you."

Sorren took her to the bed and kissed her, cupping the back of her head in his hand, being more gentle than he had the previous night.

The king departed from her for a moment to look over her. "Look happier, Lady Margaret," Sorren said, grabbing her wrist tightly. "I enjoy a mistress who is honored when their king finds them desirable."

"I am pleased that I please you," Margaret said, a tight smile on her face.

The king kissed her once more. "Better."

As the king dressed, he spoke to Margaret. "Have you been drinking your tea? I do not wish any bastards borne by you."

Margaret only nodded.

"Be ready at the same time tomorrow evening," he said, kissing her once more before leaving.

Margaret arrived early to the queen's chambers. It was time for Margaret to ask for a much longer hiatus from Lillian's service. The queen was traveling to the coast to picnic by the sea, and Margaret did not want to abandon Annabel when she was still so new to the palace.

"Your Majesty?" Margaret called out timidly, poking her head into the bedchamber.

Lillian was still being dressed by Duchess Cecily and Lady Victoria. She glared at Margaret, making her want to retreat to her own rooms.

"What do you want, Lady Margaret?" Lillian snapped.

Margaret cleared her throat nervously, entering the room.

"Well?"

Margaret looked at the floor instead of the icy glare the queen leveled at her. "I was wondering if you might allow me to spend time with Annabel. I am helping her search for a husband."

"Yes," the queen agreed hurriedly. "I will summon you when you are needed again."

Her head snapped up. Margaret looked at the queen, surprised until she saw that Duchess Cecily was smirking. She would be called back. Margaret curtsied low to the queen.

"You are most kind, Your Majesty," praised Margaret.

Lillian waved her hand in dismissal. "Goodbye, Lady Margaret."

Margaret retreated to the giggles of Duchess Cecily.

Margaret did not know whether she was happier to be away from the woman whose husband she was sleeping with or that she would not be tortured by her on a daily basis. It was early yet, and Margaret did not want to wake Annabel—not when she did not have a plan for what to do with her husband search.

Margaret went to the library to clear her mind. She would prefer to take a walk, but snow had started to fall in the night. She grabbed the first book she came across, settling on one of the couches in front of the windows.

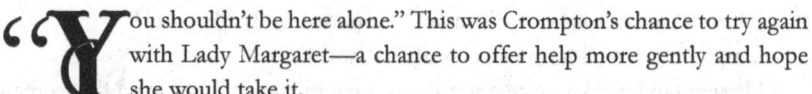

22

"You shouldn't be here alone." This was Crompton's chance to try again with Lady Margaret—a chance to offer help more gently and hope she would take it.

Lady Margaret nearly dropped her book when she jumped. She turned to look at him and frowned. "And why is that, Your Grace?"

"The king enjoys trysts in the libraries. It gives him a thrill." He had walked in on more than his fair share. Crompton was sure he enjoyed being caught in the act and no one being able to say anything about it.

"I'll be sure to take Captain Vojvo with me the next time I come," Lady Margaret assured him.

"Take a turn with me." Crompton offered his arm to her.

Lady Margaret hesitantly took it. They walked quietly for a while, neither feeling the need to speak to one another. He was preparing to break the silence when she snorted, smiling ironically.

Crompton quirked an eyebrow at her. "Something amusing?"

Her face closed at once. "I'm not sure I should tell you, after all, you are the one who betrayed him."

"And who is it you are believing I betrayed?" His brows were still raised.

Lady Margaret shrugged, finally saying, "Liam Fulton. Had you not betrayed him, he would have not made his way to my door, and I would not be the king's mistress to pay for the stay of execution for helping a traitor who is not a traitor."

Crompton stopped their leisurely stroll to look at her directly. "And how is that amusing?"

"Because he could solve all my problems were he here," she said, remaining evasive.

"How could a farmer's boy solve your problems here?" Crompton demanded. What was she going on about? He had picked Liam as a scapegoat for being nosy, but there was an added benefit of him being no loss to society when he was gone. "Other than being executed to sate the king's image."

"Do you know his full name?" Lady Margaret asked, her mouth pulling into a tight smile.

"Liam Ettien Fulton, if I remember correctly," Crompton recited, his tone unimpressed.

"His name is Liam Ettien Fulton Triburn," Lady Margaret told him lightly, despite the heaviness of the subject. "And he is the rightful king of Anatalia."

Crompton turned incredulous. "What are you saying?"

"I'm saying, Your Grace, that you now have a new strategy to rid yourself of the person we most abhor." Lady Margaret looked at him coquettishly, a small smile playing on her lips.

Maybe she would survive this yet. Crompton grinned at her. "I think I've underestimated you, Lady Margaret." He squeezed her hand on his arm, untangling himself from her.

He had work to do.

23

L iam took the last plate from the table in their private dining room. He handed it to Gretta, smiling. She returned it gently, touching his arm. He had never seen her so happy.

"All right now, up to bed wi' ye all," Gretta said to the boys, waving her hands. "It'll be a long day for the new year tomorrow."

Eli groaned. "But, Ma, Da hasna told us a story, yet!"

Not wanting to say as much, the two older boys shot Liam pleading looks. Liam made it a habit of telling the boys stories of his travels. Not being his own children, Liam's stories and wisdom were the only thing he could pass on.

"All right, then." Gretta easily gave in—she enjoyed his stories as much as the boys. "If Liam promises to keep it short."

"I'll do my best," Liam assured her.

He settled in front of the fire, a mug of ale in hand. Liam remained silent while the others gathered around him. He was unsure which story to tell them. Radovan, perhaps, was where he would take them tonight—he had learned a great deal there.

"A year after the war ended, that was in 2275," he added for Eli's sake, "I traveled to Radovan. I met a very wise man there—"

"Was he verra old?" Eli interrupted.

"Very old, indeed," he confirmed. "He had hair whiter than snow and a beard that went down to his navel."

"How did ye come to meet such a man?" Jamie asked, pulling a fidgeting Eli into his lap to keep him still.

"I was in a coffee house when I was invited to drink *doogh*—a milky drink— and smoke poppy tears with the wise Siam Salik," Liam started.

"Why would he do that?" Simon asked. "I dinna ken anyone here who would ask a stranger to drink an' smoke with 'em."

Liam patiently endured the interruptions. "He wanted to speak with me," he told them, "and he had a great deal to tell me. Siam Salik said he could see I was de *ænyuu*—a great noble—and wished to lend his wisdom for my future endeavors."

Jamie laughed, his face alight with disbelief. "He couldna been such a wise man if he thought ye were a nobleman."

"Dinna be rude to Liam," Gretta scolded, giving him a swift slap to the back of his head.

Jamie flinched, rubbing the back of his head. "Sorry, Ma."

"What did he want to tell ye?" Simon asked.

"First, he bade me smoke with him—to clear the mind, he had said—as he told me stories of his country. He—"

"Why would he do that?" Eli asked, his voice whining.

"Because he was a wise man, and I was not about to instruct him on how he liked to conduct his business," Liam told the youngest boy, a little irritably. "May I proceed?"

"Hush up," scolded Gretta before nodding to Liam to continue.

Returning her nod, Liam went on, "He told me of their great king and princes, who fought for peace. Their neighbors to the south, before they became Salatia, Mekhor, and Glessic, waged constant war against the peaceful Radovians. They would kill any delegate Radovan sent—"

"Salatia wouldna do somethin'—" Jamie started.

Liam held up a hand to stop him. "You don't get to tell someone how their history happened."

"Let Liam tell his story," scolded Gretta.

He waited to make sure no one else would speak before continuing, "As I was saying, the Salatians would kill any of the Radovian delegates they came across, even though they came bearing the flag of truce to start peace negotiations. After the fourth delegate was murdered, Radovan declared war on Salatia."

The boys remained silent, but Liam could see on Gretta's face that she had heard of this war before. It was clouded with sadness, much the same way it would when telling someone bad news.

"Radovan slaughtered nearly half the fighting men of Salatia," Liam finished. "It's what helped Anatalia divide Salatia into three countries twenty years later."

"Did he tell ye annithin' important?" Simon asked. "Ye could have looked up the history yerself."

"He did. He said to me, 'Time changes all circumstances; one day the birds are eating the ants; the next, the ants are eating the birds. Remember always: time is more powerful than you can ever be, so do good in this world while you can.'"

Liam shifted in his spot, back heated pleasantly by the fire. "He told me, when my time comes, to remember him and what he told me."

"'Tis a very nice lesson," Gretta said, "an' one we should all take to heart."

Eli looked between Liam and his mother. "I dinna ken what it means."

"It means annithing can happen at any time to anyone, so be good to people," Jamie told him.

"Ma makes sure we're always kind," Eli piped up.

"Aye, she does," Jamie confirmed, peeking his head around to look at his younger brother.

Gretta stood. "All right, boys, off to bed wi' ye."

Liam waited for the boys to leave before he moved. He stood, ambling over to Gretta. She slid her arms around his waist, looking up at him sleepily. "You look ready for bed yourself," commented Liam.

Gretta laid her head on his chest and nodded. "Aye, but I canna just yet, I need to prepare for the morning."

"Why don't you let me help you?" Liam asked.

She smiled tenderly, resting a hand on his cheek. "Ye've a long day tomorrow, love. I'll be up in a little while."

Liam cupped her face in both her hands and kissed her. "I'll see you upstairs. Don't push yourself too long tonight."

Her eyes crinkled at the side, her face glowing. "I promise."

He kissed her again before going upstairs. Liam had to resist the urge to check each of the boys' rooms to make sure they were in bed. He had fallen so easily into this new fatherhood role. Liam inhaled deeply as he sank into his bed.

This was the happiest he had been since he was with Margaret in Marbon with the Gollacks. He hoped she wouldn't end up needing him—he wasn't sure he would be able to abandon his family to help.

24

argaret strolled the hall, her arm linked with Annabel's. They watched the men in heated conversations of philosophy or playing games of chess or cards. There were many other women clustered in groups near windows, sitting on plush chaises, gossiping, or even doing what they were doing—searching for prospective husbands.

"My lady?" Annabel asked tentatively.

"Yes?" Margaret did not look at Annabel, her eyes roving admiringly over Sir Arthur Tadmen's tall frame. She smiled coyly when she saw Sir Arthur was also admiring the two of them.

"Why is it that you yourself have no suitors?"

Margaret looked at her sharply, eyes frosty. "I beg your pardon?"

Annabel's eyes widened. "I only mean, my lady, that you are one of the richest women in Anatalia. It seems you should be fighting off suitors with a stick."

Margaret's eyes softened, patting Annabel's hand on her arm. "With my father deceased and my mother missing, my claim on that fortune is tenuous at best. I am not a son, and therefore, His Majesty must grant me the title of Countess of Dorcia. Until then… Well, no man will take the chance of having a pauper wife."

"But you're a count's daughter!" Annabel protested. "That is unfair!"

"Life isn't fair, Annabel." It was a harsh lesson Margaret was learning herself. "We are here to see what you like, not talk about my prospects."

Annabel looked around the hall, her gaze lingering on several of the men. "I'm not quite sure what I would like."

Margaret made another turn about the room before she spoke again. "No? Close your eyes and picture who you would want standing in front of you right now, telling you he wishes for your hand."

Annabel closed her eyes, letting out a sigh, mostly through her nose. "I don't know…"

"Don't think about title or wealth," Margaret instructed. "If you could have anyone, who would it be?"

"I…I don't know, Lady Margaret." Annabel opened her eyes and looked at her pathetically. "I can't choose."

Margaret shrugged, pulling the other woman along the edge of the hall. "You don't know what you want. You'll learn eventually."

"Sir Arthur is quite handsome," Annabel admitted.

"Indeed he is," Margaret agreed, "and, unfortunately, spoken for."

"How is it you know all of the unavailable men, Lady Margaret?" she curiously asked.

"We are sent a list each month," Lady Margaret said with a shrug, "so that we do not have any unfortunate encounters."

Surprised, Annabel stopped walking. "Really?"

Margaret laughed, eyes dancing. "Of course not. We learn who is available and unavailable through gossip."

"Is that the only way to gain knowledge here?" Annabel frowned. "I do not like to gossip or get involved with scandals."

Margaret had some bad news for Annabel then. She shrugged before saying, "You could always ask them yourself."

"Can I not let you arrange everything and just show up on the day?" Annabel looked around the room helplessly.

Margaret frowned. How romantic. If that's what Annabel wanted, she could have stayed with her father for that sort of arrangement.

More people flooded into the hall as the morning grew later. The men and women separated, finding their friends in games or chatting. Finally. It would make it easier to speak to some of the men.

Margaret nodded to a card table that was relieved of two of its members. "They seem in need of new players."

Annabel looked over the two men shuffling the cards. "Are we allowed to play?"

Raising a brow, Margaret raised her chin defiantly. "Who will tell us no?"

The two men at the table stood when they spotted Margaret approaching. They were handsome enough and seemed to be well-groomed. They would be a good starting point for Annabel to try talking to someone.

Margaret boldly sat in one of the open seats. "It seems you two gentlemen are short players," Margaret commented in a voice lower than usual.

They sat once Annabel did; the man to Lady Margaret's right looked her over slowly. "We are short no more, if you are here."

Margaret smiled without showing her teeth, lips pushed out slightly. Her eyes crinkled as she examined him as frankly as he did her. "And with whom do we have the pleasure of playing?"

He stood, bowing over Margaret's hand. "I am Lord Thomas Ravinsmeur, son of Count Tomund Ravinsmeur, and this is Lord Gregory du Levian of the Frasiscan Levians."

Margaret lowered her lashes when Lord Thomas kissed her hand. "I am Lady Margaret Doremis, daughter of the late Count of Dorcia, and this," —she motioned toward Annabel— "is Lady Annabel Lurant, daughter of Sir Adam Lurant."

"A pleasure to meet you both." Annabel smiled at the two men.

"Indeed, a pleasure," agreed Margaret as Lord Thomas sat.

Lord Gregory looked between the two women. "Do you know how to play Kings?"

Margaret quickly answered for both of them when it looked like Annabel was going to say she did. "No. Would you teach us?" Men loved to explain things to women. It made them feel important.

Lord Gregory happily agreed. "Perhaps we should play partners?"

"We should," Lord Thomas said. "I would be honored if you would be my partner, Lady Margaret."

She lowered her lashes demurely. "It would be my pleasure, Lord Thomas."

"The goal is to have no cards left in your hand," Lord Gregory said as he dealt each person five cards, "but since we are playing partners, we both must have no cards." He set down the cards, flipping the top one over on the table. "You must match the suit of the rank, and if you cannot, then you draw another card until you can."

"That seems simple enough," Margaret said as she picked up her cards.

"The kings are wild, so you can use them for anything," Lord Gregory quickly added.

Wasn't that ironic? Margaret tried not to let her annoyance show. "Who goes first?" She looked around the table with a smile she didn't feel like holding.

"Lady Annabel does," Lord Thomas answered, nodding in her direction.

Annabel looked over her cards. She laid down one, nodding to Margaret.

Margaret laid down her own card, turning her attention to the men. "How long have you been in Anatalia, Lord Gregory?"

"Only a few months, Lady Margaret," Lord Gregory told her. "Lord Thomas and his family have been kind enough to secure me an invitation to your court."

Annabel looked over Lord Gregory. "Lady Margaret has been kind enough to do the same for me."

Margaret smiled only slightly at the mention of her kindness. "Are you staying here in the palace, Lord Thomas?"

"No," he told her after he took his turn. "We are in Ravineire House in the city."

Annabel looked at Margaret, her brows knitted in confusion.

Margaret's eyes widened only for a moment before sliding a coquettish smile on her lips. "Ravineire House?" she asked, her voice light. "The one next to Faucon House?"

"The very same, Lady Margaret," Lord Thomas confirmed. "Have you ever been there?"

"Once before," answered Margaret, "it was an extraordinary home."

"Where is this?" Annabel asked, still confused.

"It is on Molliere Street," Lord Gregory told her, looking amused, "where the richest of the rich live."

"Ahh," mused Annabel, looking at Lord Thomas in a new light.

"We used to live in Cerule House before father fell ill," Margaret interjected lightly, picking up three cards before laying one down.

"Cerule?" Lord Gregory asked, sounding surprised. "I have never heard of Cerule House."

"It was relatively new," Lord Thomas informed his friend, "but had the makings for a very prominent house."

Margaret bowed her head to him, a small smile on her face. "I'm pleased to hear we were looked on favorably."

Annabel's partner laid down his last card, an eight. "Hearts," he said for the suit to match.

Annabel grinned, laying down her last card. It was a king as well. She let out an undignified squeal. "We won!"

Laying down her cards, Margaret gave Annabel a disapproving look, her eyes narrowed. She subtly shook her head, and Annabel's grin faded.

Lord Thomas cleared his throat, turning his attention on his partner. "Lady Margaret, would you like to take a tour of Ravineire House to see how it has changed?"

"Would anyone else be welcome?" Margaret arched a brow at him. It would be convenient for her to look for a husband now, but she was unsure how the king would react to her finding one. Or if he would even let her marry while he seemed so attached to her bed.

Lord Thomas looked chagrined. "Ahh," he said rubbing the back of his neck, "it would be a private tour, I'm afraid."

She was surprised to have such a brazen offer. Luckily, Annabel did not pick up on his meaning. Perhaps she would get Annabel to be more interesting next time and tempt a potential suitor into such a proposition that could be leveraged into a courtship. Margaret turned her head slightly, away from him, her lashes lowered. "Perhaps another time."

Margaret rose gracefully, nodding to both Lord Thomas and Lord Gregory as they hastily stood, and motioned for Annabel to come stand by her side. When she did, Margaret finally spoke: "Thank you, my lords, for teaching us such a delightful game," —she linked arms with Annabel— "but unfortunately, we must be going."

"Will you and Lady Annabel be here tomorrow?" Lord Gregory asked.

Margaret shrugged minutely, a small smile dancing on her lips. "Perhaps, perhaps not."

Annabel followed Margaret before either Lords Thomas or Gregory could say any more. "Why did we leave?" Annabel demanded. "They seemed nice."

"They were," Margaret agreed, "and very rich."

"How did you manage to gain an invitation to Ravineire House?" Annabel asked curiously. "You didn't do anything extraordinary."

Margaret smiled at her, eyes dancing. "The key is to seem as though you have someone more important to be with or somewhere more important to go than with them. It piques their interest."

A small dawning of realization raced across Annabel's face, her mouth opening for a reply, but Margaret had already moved on.

A page boy caught Margaret as she meandered with Annabel to the great hall for the evening meal. "Lady Margaret!" the page called out, making her turn. "A message for you."

Margaret accepted the sealed parchment, placing a small coin in his hand in thanks.

"Who is that from?" Annabel inquired, peering over Margaret's shoulder.

She stamped down her ire before answering, "It's from His Grace, the Duke of Rivack."

Annabel's eyes widened. "Why is he sending you messages?"

"I don't know," she snapped, keeping the seal intact. She did not want Annabel to read her messages. "Go on to dinner without me."

"Are you certain?" Annabel hesitated to move.

"Yes," Margaret assured her. "Now go."

Annabel curtsied minimally with the dismissal, carrying on to the hall.

Margaret retreated to an alcove before opening the message.

My Lady Margaret,
    I have acquired an item you must see. Meet me in my chambers once you've received this message.
                      Lord General Crompton

Margaret raised a brow at the scrolling font Lord General Crompton accomplished, expecting a messier text. She sighed, making her way to his chambers, nodding to the men and women heading toward the hall. She knocked lightly on the door when she came to it.

Crompton opened the door himself, his eyes bright. "Lady Margaret, come in."

She hesitated only a moment before entering. "You said you had something I should see?"

"Yes, yes," Crompton said, almost distracted, pouring her a drink without asking. He poured his own, taking a drink before handing her her own.

Margaret sniffed tentatively at the glass. The liquid was a light amber; the smell alone burned her nose. She took a sip, and her face immediately pinched with disgust. Her throat burned as the liquid slid down, feeling inflamed as she gasped to catch her breath. Margaret imagined, had dragons been real, this was how they felt preparing to spit their flames.

Crompton let out a sharp laugh, taking the glass from her. "My apologies, my lady. I should have poured you wine."

She nodded, not trusting she would not burst into painful coughs that would reignite the fire in her throat.

Crompton handed her a glass of wine, taking another sip of his amber drink. "Please, sit, Lady Margaret."

She followed his suggestion, sitting in one of the plush chairs. "What is it that you wanted to show me, Your Grace?" she asked finally.

"Ah, yes!" Crompton set his drink down, grabbing a large tome. There was a piece of parchment sticking out near the end of the book. He handed it to her wordlessly.

Margaret ran her fingers over the spine, reading the title. *A Collective History of Anatalian Monarchs.* The title was familiar to her—it was one she had read to her father many times while in Silvica. She lifted her head to look at him, raising a brow in question.

"Open it to the marked page," he instructed.

Margaret did as she was bid, nearly dropping the book when she saw the picture on the page. She looked at the duke incredulously. "Is this real?" How had she not seen this before? They had skipped around to her father's favorite monarchs, but surely, she had read it in its entirety to him at least once.

He nodded. "Read the name, Lady Margaret."

Margaret looked at the picture again, running a finger over the face that looked so much like Liam's. "King Ettien Triburn, at his coronation in the year 2145."

"Yes." Crompton grinned at her, taking a heavy swig of his drink. He let out a hiss after he swallowed. "And Liam is his descendant, plain as day."

"He is," Margaret agreed, her eyes glued to the portrait of Liam's ancestor. "Did you find this in the Triburn Room?"

Crompton furrowed his brows. "The Triburn Room?"

She nodded. "Gareth took me there once to threaten my mother's social climbing. He said it was to show me what happened to families that get too powerful."

"Do you remember where it is?" Crompton sat forward in his seat, eyes intent.

"It's behind a bookcase in the library." Margaret took a long sip of wine, remembering that night. She wouldn't want to go back down that corridor again. "There's a trigger in one of the books. It's not far into the corridor."

Crompton watched her, plans forming behind his eyes. "I will search for what I can use in the room for proof and then travel to wherever Liam is—"

"Numetra," Margaret interrupted helpfully.

"To Numetra then, and convince him I can help him regain his throne."

"He doesn't know that he's the rightful king," Margaret told him. "I tried to tell him several times, but it never came all the way out."

Crompton nodded to the book. "Then, I'll take the book with me and tell him. I'll have proof to back up my claims."

"Would that I could go with you," Margaret said wistfully, her eyes hopeful.

"Would that you could," Crompton agreed.

Margaret put a comforting hand on Sarah's arm as she glanced frightfully at the king. Sorren watched Sarah undress Margaret from the fauteuil in the corner. He leaned back, his eyes half-lidded in thought. He had come in in a foul mood, slamming doors and shouting.

"Out," he commanded, waving his hand.

Sarah froze, staring at him, wide-eyed.

"It's all right, Sarah," Margaret murmured reassuringly, touching her arm again.

Broken from her fearful trance, Sarah curtsied to him before scurrying from the room.

Margaret continued with the laces on her own, her face contorted in concentration. She was unable to reach all the laces and turned her back to Sorren in invitation, her face questioning.

"Why?" Sorren demanded, coming to help her.

"Why, what, Your Majesty?" She looked over her shoulder at him, confusion clouding her features.

"Why are you spending so much time with Lord General Crompton?" Sorren roughly jerked the laces loose, moving her with the force of his tugs.

"Who am I to deny a duke the pleasure of my company if he so wishes?" she asked, flippant.

"You are mine," he seethed, "and you will not see him again. Are you having an affair?"

Margaret turned to look at him incredulously. "I beg your pardon?"

"I forbid you to see him ever again, Margaret," fumed the king. "Do you hear me?"

"I'm not—"

"Do you understand me?" Sorren demanded.

Margaret lowered her lashes demurely. "Yes, Your Majesty."

"Good," Sorren said, retreating to the sitting room to pour himself a drink.

Margaret joined him after adorning a robe, sitting close to the fire. The first night of Jamonat was particularly frigid. She poured herself a glass of wine, sipping it silently.

"What did he want with you?" demanded Sorren, finally breaking the silence.

"Who?" Margaret asked, pulled from her thoughts.

The king glared at her. "Crompton. Who else?"

"He only wanted to talk," Margaret told him, shrugging her shoulders slightly.

"About what?"

Margaret frowned, looking annoyed. "Forgettable things: the weather, why I haven't been with the queen. Just nothings."

"I want that to stop," declared the king. "Immediately."

"We have already agreed upon this, Your Majesty," Margaret told him tersely.

Sorren glared at her, his eyes icy. "Go to bed. I'll join you in a moment."

She wordlessly put down her wine and went to her bedroom. There was no point in arguing when Sorren was in this kind of mood. Only compliance would save her from acquiring bruises by the morning.

25

fter posting Her Ladyship's letters, Sarah browsed the street, not sure what she was looking for. This was her first occasion to be in the city with no business to attend to for Lady Margaret.

The streets were surprisingly crowded for the hour, clogged with people running their own errands. Sarah waited for a gap in the passing stream of people, flinging herself into the crowd and struggling to keep up with their fluid pace. She looked for the first opening that came up and took it.

Sarah looked around, unsure of where she was. She did not have many opportunities to explore, and she got lost easily in the endless side streets. Her brows knitted together at the sight of adults and children alike huddled together on the corners, hardly dressed and begging for drica. Wasn't this supposed to be the richest city in Aratia?

She looked for anything familiar, catching sight of the graying sky. The air was overtaken with the lack of smell that came when snow was near. When she could find nothing familiar, Sarah continued on the street she was already on.

The sound of hammering accosted her, and Sarah knew she had gone too far. She peeked her head in the door to ask whoever was working how to return to the main street. "Pardon me—"

"Lamb!" came a surprised voice, George flooding her vision.

"George!" Sarah exclaimed, equally surprised, as she took a step back. "What are you doing here?"

He laughed, wiping his hands on his leather apron. "Working. What are you doing here?"

Cheeks coloring, Sarah cleared her throat. "I was lost, and I thought I would ask for directions."

George pulled her into his shop as snow started to fall. "Are you not working today?"

"Her Ladyship is away for the day," Sarah informed him. "She was kind enough to give me time to myself."

George started to remove his apron, looking back at the other worker. When he nodded, George removed the gear completely and hung it on the wall. "I'll join you, if you don't mind?" he suggested.

Sarah looked him over slowly before admitting, "I wouldn't be able to find my way back otherwise."

He grinned, a single brow raised. "I suppose I shouldn't complain, since I wouldn't have seen you otherwise."

He offered her his arm, leading her out the door when she took it. George easily led her through the side streets until they reached the main road in the center of the city.

"Have you eaten yet?" George asked.

Shaking her head, she answered, "No."

Grinning, he pulled her into an eatery ahead of them, the Whistling Squire. Sarah waved a hand in front of her face, coughing when a patron blew smoke in her direction. None of the chairs seemed to match, the tables varying in size and shape.

"What is this place?"

George flashed her a smile. "The Whistling Squire is the best eatery in Jalmar," he told her. "And very rarely empty."

He pulled out a chair at the empty end of a long table, pushing it forward as she sat. George took the seat across from her, lifting a hand to call over the serving wench.

"A pitcher of wine," he ordered, "and two plates of your mutton pie."

Sarah started to protest, but George held up a hand to stem her complaints.

"Trust me," he said, "you'll thank me when you try it."

She reluctantly settled back, trying not to bristle at his taking control. It was presumptuous of him—she had only seen him here and there when she was in the city on errands for Lady Margaret, and only long enough to say hello and exchange pleasantries. "Hopefully I will."

George smiled despite her irritation. "Tell me about yourself, Lamb."

The serving wench returned with their wine as Sarah shrugged. "There is nothing to tell, really."

"Sure there is," George encouraged.

"I'm a lady's maid," Sarah told him slowly.

His mouth twisted. "I'm a cooper," he countered.

"I didn't know there were any in the city," Sarah admitted, taking another sip of her wine.

"We're the only ones in the city," George proudly told her. "We were here when the city was still wine country, and stayed even after it turned into the capital of Anatalia.

"How long has that been?" Sarah asked, enthralled.

"Coming close to four hundred years now," George boasted, his chest puffed proudly.

She read his body language carefully. "Is this your family business?"

He nodded. "It is. My brother Henry would have inherited, but he died in the war."

"I'm sorry for your loss," Sarah told him sincerely.

Waving his hand in dismissal, he continued on, "My two young brothers work for me, along with my youngest sister."

"Your sister works for you?" Sarah asked, brows crinkling.

"She helps keep everything clean and organized," George assured her. "She doesn't do any of the hard labor. Mary will stay until she marries, and then she'll be at her husband's home, making a life for herself."

"What will you do when she leaves?"

George shrugged. "I have a few years yet to think of a solution, but hopefully, I will have a wife to take over Mary's duties by then."

Nodding along, Sarah hardly noticed when the serving girl returned with their mutton pies.

"Enjoy," she said before leaving.

Eyes dancing, George watched Sarah take a bite of her food. She let out a pleased moan, closing her eyes.

"Did I not tell you?" he asked, his voice excited.

"You did," confirmed Sarah, shoving another bite in her mouth.

George helped Sarah into her cloak. She pulled it closer to her, taking note of the snow that had continued to fall while they were eating.

"Would you like me to escort you back to the palace?" he asked.

Sarah hesitated. "I have yet to see the market in the winter," she said slowly, looking up at him demurely.

George offered his arm. "I'd be happy to show you, Lamb."

Sarah snaked her hand through his arm, moving closer to him. "Lead the way."

Eyes twinkling, George forged forward as the snow started to fall harder. He led her to the market. A fair number of the vendors starting to pack away their things due to the weather. The only stalls that stayed in were the vendors selling winter wares.

Sarah let out a heavy breath into her free hand before also tucking into the crook of George's arm.

"Cold?"

She nodded, gripping his arm tighter. "Very."

"Do you not have gloves?"

"No." She shook her head. "An oversight by both Her Ladyship and myself."

George pulled her to a vendor, her table lined with gloves. Most were knit, but a few were made of leather, and even fewer were fur-lined. He picked up one of the fur-lined gloves, a soft, light brown leather with matching fur. The tall red-head handed them to Sarah.

"See if they fit," commanded George.

Sara slipped her small hands into the gloves, closing and opening her hands several times to test them. "They are very nice."

"How much?" George asked the woman, who was eyeing them skeptically.

"A tholar," the woman said.

George dug one from his pocket and handed it to the vendor.

Hands warm, Sarah looked up at George with a small smile. "Thank you," she breathed.

"My pleasure," he sincerely told her.

The snow started to fall in fast, fat flakes. It obscured the sky, leaving it an odd mix of gray and white.

"I should take you back," George said in her ear, oddly loud in the void the snow left.

Sarah reluctantly nodded. "I think that would be for the best."

Grabbing her freshly gloved hand, he put it on his arm. "Hold on to me so you don't fall."

Sarah gripped his arm tightly as they made their way to the palace. Snow was starting to stick to the uneven cobblestones, and Sarah was thankful for George's support. She slipped several times on the way to the palace, grateful when it finally came into view.

"Would you like me to take you to the servant's entrance?" George asked, stopping at the gate.

Servants were already out sweeping away what snow they could. It seemed like a hopeless job.

"I'll be all right," Sarah said, turning to him.

"How can I let you know I want to see you again? George asked, looking her over.

"You can send a note to the servant's hall in the palace," she said, cheeks red with the cold. "To Sarah Essler."

George lifted her hands to his lips. "You'll be hearing from me soon, Lamb."

Sarah felt herself smiling. "I look forward to it."

 **26**

Crompton looked back when the door closed behind him. He was glad he had chosen to take a candle with him. He picked up the first torch on the wall and lit it with the candle. He only had to walk a few feet before he found the doorway to the Triburn room.

He paused when he opened the door—it was filled with books and furniture. Crompton lit a few candles around the room and put the torch in the hook on the wall. He pulled back a frame against one of the walls—it was a portrait of a monarch he had never seen before. He put it back gently, going further into the room. There had to be something in there that he could use as proof.

Crompton opened a chest at random, surprised to find jewels. Should these not have been in Lillian's collection? He pulled one of the necklaces out, holding it up to the light. It would need polishing, but it was beautiful. It had three chains of diamonds that ended in a square citrine and a trio of diamonds, making the necklace come to a point. It was certainly nicer than most of Lillian's jewels, but he thought it would suit someone else better. Maybe he should give it to Lady Margaret for telling him about the room.

Digging further into the chest, a thrill went through him. Crompton pulled out a ring, holding it close to the flame. A signet ring. He slipped it into his waistcoat. He would have to leave this with Margaret—he couldn't risk bringing it to convince Liam and having something happen to it.

Crompton searched the rest of the room, not finding anything better than the signet ring and the book he already had in his possession. He blew out the candles and picked up his torch. He didn't know who could be in the library at this point, so he tried following the rest of the corridor out. He was surprised to find it led out near the barracks by the stables.

He furrowed his brows. How had he never noticed this before? He'd passed it often enough. Crompton must have assumed it was storage for the stables. He tossed his torch into the fire barrels regularly spaced through the barracks courtyard and went back to his chambers in the palace.

Pouring himself a drink, Crompton sank into his chair in front of the fire. He pulled out the ring from his waistcoat, examining it carefully. It certainly wasn't anything especially ornate—a simple gold ring inset with obsidian carved with a scrolling T. It was likely a personal ring instead of one for the monarchy, but that made it all the more valuable. He inhaled deeply—he would need a plan, and a backup plan. Crompton had too long relied on the hope that Theotes would aid him in unseating his unrighteous cousin.

All of his plans had failed, but this one could not. Crompton would first convince Liam of his heritage, then travel to the King of Salatia to show he had a viable replacement for Sorren and collect on the promised army. Once that was done, he would find a bride for Liam to give him more legitimacy. It would only be a question of whether he would find a princess within Aratia or without.

Throwing his drink back, Crompton went to his writing desk and pulled out a piece of parchment. He needed some assurance that if anything happened to him, his plan could still go on. He wrote a letter to the Salatian king, saying that anyone claiming that Liam was the rightful heir to the Anatalian Throne was speaking only the truth and his promise of an army should transfer to Liam. He signed his name, putting under it both the seals from his personal signet ring and the Triburn ring.

He folded it carefully, sealing it on the outside with his official crest as lord general of Rivack. He would give the letter and the Triburn ring to Lady Margaret for safekeeping, and to carry on his mission should he fail. She certainly wouldn't want to continue on with Sorren as king when she could have someone who wouldn't hurt her.

Crompton looked at the clock on the wall. He'd have to go to Lady Margaret now—the evening meal in the hall would start soon, and Sorren would be in his own chambers to be readied.

He changed into appropriate dinner attire, slipping the Triburn ring and letter into his waistcoat before he went to Lady Margaret's chambers. He looked to either side before knocking on her door lightly.

Lady Margaret's lady's maid—Sarah? Hannah? He wasn't sure of her name— answered the door. Her face went from dread to relief quickly. "Your Grace, is there something you need from Her Ladyship?"

"May I come in?" Crompton glanced around him to check again if anyone was around.

"Of course, Your Grace." The maid opened the door wider. "Lady Margaret is almost ready."

Crompton went in, noting Captain Vojvo in the corner by the fireplace. "This won't take long."

"If you wait here with the captain, I'll see if Lady Margaret is finished." She disappeared into the bedroom and emerged a few minutes later with her mistress.

"Your Grace," Lady Margaret said with a smile, "does this mean that your search was fruitful?"

"It was indeed." He pulled the ring and letter from his waistcoat, looking around the room. "May we speak privately?"

"I don't think—"

"Captain, it's all right." She held up her hand. "I promise you, he does have my best interests in mind."

"But—"

"We can speak in my bedroom, Your Grace." Lady Margaret gave her captain a hard look when he began to protest again, leading him into her bedroom.

Crompton waited until the door was closed before he spoke. "I found a signet ring from the Triburns."

Lady Margaret gasped. "Will you bring it to him?"

"I can't risk something happening to it." He handed her the ring and the letter, explaining his plan. "I want you to keep this safe, in case something happens to me."

She looked at the ring closely, running her thumb over the T. "I'll hide them in the same place I hide the dagger you gave me." Lady Margaret looked up at him. "When will you go?"

That would depend on how Sorren would react. "Ideally, tomorrow. I'll tell Sorren after dinner tonight that I've been hearing reports of more rebel activity at the border and would like to investigate."

A look crossed Lady Margaret's face he couldn't quite interpret before she said, "I wish you the best of luck, Your Grace."

He would need it.

 **27**

illian walked with her ladies clustered behind her, only Cecily invited to walk by her side. They walked the corridors of the palace, unable to go outside with the deep snow Marmonat brought. They often did this to see if they could catch any of the court ladies engaged in trysts. Gossip was often as valuable as gold in the lives of courtiers, and the queen was determined to be the richest of them all.

Their arms linked, Lillian and Cecily both stopped with noises of startlement when a door was flung open to their left. Lady Margaret emerged, her face flushed. The pins were coming out of her hair, fingers having been run through it indelicately.

"Lady Margaret," Lillian greeted coldly.

She started violently, whirling toward the queen. She curtsied deeply, not raising her eyes to look at the monarch. "Your Majesty, I am honored to be in your presence."

"It seems another was honored by yours," Cecily quipped, a smirk settling on her face.

Lady Margaret remained in her curtsy, leaving the slight unacknowledged.

"Stand up and look at me," Lillian commanded, exasperated.

She stood slowly but kept her eyes downcast.

"I said look at me!" Lillian fumed.

Lady Margaret met Lillian's eyes, flinching when she saw the hateful fire in them. Her cheeks flushed deeper the longer she looked at the queen. "May I go, Your Majesty?"

"You may, Lady Margaret," she dismissed curtly, "but I would advise you think over the vow you gave me when you joined my service."

"As Your Majesty wishes," Margaret said, falling into a deep curtsy once more before fleeing the presence of the queen.

Cecily squeezed her arm lightly, prompting her to lead the ladies on. It would do no good to linger and let the women in attendance of the queen see who would exit the room Lady Margaret had departed from. The herd of women moved forward with the queen when the door opened once more.

"None of you will look back," Cecily commanded, despite the queen already turning her head to gaze back over her shoulder.

Lillian's eyes caught and held her husband's, his hand poised to close the door. Her face pinched, crow's feet crinkling before she closed her eyes. The queen turned her head forward, straightening her back as she walked away from him.

 **28**

iam sat in his usual place at the bar. He didn't come often anymore, only stopping in on particularly busy days at the smithy so that he could have a pint and unwind before seeing Gretta and the boys. It'd do none of them good for him to snap at one of them from being tired when he could take twenty minutes for a drink and be by himself for a few moments.

The acoustics in the spot allowed him to hear most of the people, listening to their conversations without needing to befriend them. As he raised his tankard to his mouth, he heard a familiar voice.

"I'll need more men. This development will ensure that, if we are victorious, we will never suffer from any of the Platiri family again."

Liam chanced a look behind him. He saw Lord General Crompton sitting across from a rugged-looking man.

"There are no more men, my lord. My master has instructed me to tell you he wants to see action soon, or he will be withdrawing support from you."

"There will be action when my cousin travels with his court in the summer," Lord General Compton told the other man sharply. "It will give us the greatest opportunity to attack and take Jalmar."

What the hell was he doing here? Liam clenched his fists as he fought the urge to sprint to the door. That would just call attention to himself, and then what? Would Crompton arrest him and bring him back to Anatalia to face his execution?

He let out a slow breath.

No.

He couldn't be seen.

Couldn't risk anything happening to Gretta and the boys if there was an altercation. Liam left his mostly full tankard and a copper stral on the counter and meandered toward the exit.

He had to get home.

Liam tried to walk normally back to The Smiling Fox to avoid making any sort of commotion, but he still walked faster than his usual pace. Once the door was shut behind him, he bounded up the stairs in search of Gretta and the boys. "Gretta!"

She came out of their bedroom, her brows knitted together. "What is it? What's the matter?"

He pulled her to him, inhaling deeply. Liam heard the boys clamor behind him in their rooms to open their doors. Good. They were still there and safe. Liam pulled back from her, holding her at arm's length so he could look at her face. "Someone from my past is here."

Her eyes went wide. "What? Why?"

"I don't know." Liam looked back at the boys. They hadn't told them anything about Liam's past, and he wasn't sure they should hear now. He ushered Gretta into their bedroom. "I don't know how he would have found me or what he wants."

"Could it be that this was just a stop along the way?"

"Unlikely," Liam said. "This would be a nowhere town for him. And I overheard him talking of war, so he's planning something."

"*War?*" Gretta's brows shot up. "What were ye involved with, Liam?"

Liam hushed her. "Keep your voice down, I don't want the boys to hear." He looked back at the door but didn't see the shadows of any eavesdroppers stationed outside their bedroom. "I don't want to tell you so that he won't have anything to use against you, but I think it would be wise for me to disappear for a little while."

"Absolutely not." Gretta's face turned hard. "What ye face, we face together."

He paused, searching her face. It was stubborn, with a look that said if he left, she would come after him and drag him back. "If anyone comes looking for me, you don't know me and have never heard of me."

She nodded. "Aye, and ye can bet most here willna be givin' up names if they dinna think ye've done annithin'."

"I'll need to tell Jossnon—"

"Jamie'll tell him in the mornin' that ye're ill and will need a few days." She inhaled deeply, setting her shoulders back. "That should be long enough for him to leave, an' we'll figure it out from there if he hasna."

"By all above," Liam said, grabbing her face and kissing her, "do I love you." A slow smile slid across her face. "And I, you."

Liam let out a frustrated sigh when he looked down at his work. The orange glow had faded. He'd let the blade cool too much as he watched the door. He hadn't seen Crompton since the week before, and Gretta said no one had been in looking for him by name that she didn't recognize.

"Wha's the matter wi' ye, lad?" Thorkelin asked, shoving his heated blade into a bucket of oil. A responding hiss and flood of steam followed. He turned a skeptical eye on Liam. "Ye've been distracted ever since ye came back."

Liam sighed, putting his work aside. "I saw someone from my past the other day."

Jossnon's brows raised curiously. "Oh? An' who would that be?"

"It doesn't matter," Liam told him, getting up to put his blade back in the forge.

"If ye say so, lad," came his dubious reply, "but ye've been cagey ever since ye saw this person."

Liam made a face. "I doubt he'll stay long in any case, and things can go back to normal."

"Why dinna ye go home to Gretta? I can manage without ye," Jossnon suggested.

"Are you certain?" Liam was eager to leave the smithy and get away from all the blades that he could strike Crompton with.

"Go, lad," Jossnon commanded. "Gretta'll be happy to see ye so early."

Liam flashed him a grin before leaving the smithy. He wished it was still winter—having a cloak and hat would go a long way to hiding his face. He scanned his surroundings, letting out a relieved sigh when he made it to the back alley to go into the family entrance behind The Smiling Fox.

"Liam!"

Liam spun on his heel. Crompton.

Fuck. Fuck. *Fuck*.

He had done so well avoiding Crompton. He glanced back at the door to The Smiling Fox. Liam couldn't let Crompton anywhere near his family. He didn't want them to share the same sort of fate Margaret did, with their lives ruined because of him.

"You need to leave," Liam spat.

"Liam," Crompton started, moving toward him.

"Don't speak my name," Liam growled. "It's tainted in your mouth."

Crompton hesitated, looking around the alley. "I need to speak with you."

Liam scoffed. "The time for speaking is long over." He turned to the side, holding out his arm to point the way toward where the alley led to the main road. "Now, if you would, leave me the hell alone before I make you leave me alone."

"I will not," Crompton told him, firmly bracing himself with his feet wide. "Not until we've spoken."

Liam's face darkened, grabbing the lord general's upper arm in a vice grip. He dragged him from the alley. "I don't want to see you here again. You've ruined my life enough, and I won't let you take me from my family again."

"Liam, wait." Crompton ripped his arm from Liam's grip when they were out in the open. "I need you to—"

Liam landed a blow on the duke's cheek, causing him to stumble. "The time for conversation is over," he hissed. "You need to leave."

"I have something important you need to—"

Liam landed another blow, pushing him back even further. "No! You do not get to come here and tell me I must listen to you!"

"Liam—"

He hit Crompton hard enough to knock him to the ground. The duke landed in a puddle of muddy water, splattering his clothes with grime.

"I said do not speak my name, filth," Liam growled lowly before stalking a short distance away.

"I will return for you later," Crompton said from a safe distance. "You need to hear what I have to say."

Liam advanced, Crompton retreating out of sight. Liam let out a heavy sigh, running his hands over his face. Liam paced for a moment to clear his head.

How had Crompton even found him? It couldn't have been through Margaret, could it? No—that would mean the king would also know, and even in the smallest of towns, gossip of the nobility of every country reached their ears if it was scandalous enough. And a countess helping a traitor would be scandalous enough to spread like wildfire.

When he could breathe easier, Liam went into The Smiling Fox to find Gretta. She was back in the kitchens and smiled at him when she saw him.

"What are ye doin' here?"

"Jossnon sent me home early for being too distracted." Liam came behind her, wrapping his arms around her waist and rested his chin on her shoulder. "The man who came looking for me is gone now. He found me, and I ran him off."

Gretta dropped her spoon, turning in his arms. "Is it done, then?"

"For now." Liam kissed her forehead. "He said he would be back, but I can't be sure he'll bring trouble for himself before then."

"Aye, well, we'll deal with it then." She leaned into him. "For now, we'll go on livin' our lives together."

Liam held her close. "And I look forward to every moment of it."

29

"**E**nter," Sorren commanded when a knock sounded on his door.

Sir Germain Wouverman, the king's spymaster, bowed upon entering. "Your Majesty, if I may have a moment of your time?"

Sorren raised his brows with surprise. "Of course, Sir Germain. What brings you here?"

Wouverman struggled a moment to find the words to express what he needed to say before pulling out a thick piece of folded parchment. "Your Majesty, I'm afraid I must disappoint you."

"Out with it, man," commanded the king.

Sir Germain sighed, handing him the letter. "This is a copy of a letter we intercepted from the Lord General Crompton."

> Mr. Hackaert,
> I trust that this reaches you and Beatrice in good health. Have you found the item I requested? An item as such will be suitable for my needs, as you well know. I wish it to be a surprise, a replacement if you will, for Her Grace. The wastrel servant who sought to teach her a lesson, thinking her a voluptuary, has been suitably punished. I thank you for your kindness in helping me so eagerly.
> Lord General Crompton

Sorren read over the letter more than once, looking to Wouverman for the point of it. "I see nothing amiss. Other than a servant, apparently."

Sir Germain held his hand out for the letter. "It is in code. His Grace uses a solution to hide or keep the letters he wishes to portray the message. We have finally replicated it and can intercept his messages without their notice."

He pulled out a brown glass bottle, shaking it vigorously before brushing it over the whole page. Sorren watched in amazement as entire words faded away.

I have found a suitable replacement for the wastrel voluptuary, it read.

"Who is this 'wastrel voluptuary'?" Sorren asked, looking back at his intelligencer.

Wouverman cleared his throat uncomfortably. "We believe that it is you, Your Majesty, based on his other letters."

Sorren's cheeks colored hotly. "*Me?*"

"Yes, Your Majesty," he confirmed.

"So Crompton is trying to push me off the throne," Sorren murmured, thinking back to the words Liam Fulton had boldly said to his face. *Can you not see that Lord General Crompton is a traitor?*

"Yes, we believe so." Germain nodded. "This is the first time we have proof of our suspicions."

"Do we know where he is now?" Sorren asked, getting up to look out the window.

"He was seen traveling back from Salatia, Your Majesty," Sir Germain told him.

The king cleared his throat, clasping his hands behind his back. "You may go, Sir Germain."

The sound of his retreating feet disappeared before Sorren let out a long breath he was holding.

Something would need to be done about this, and quickly.

30

Margaret walked the city with Annabel, Captain Vojvo trailing discreetly behind. It was hot for Amonat, but she needed a day out of the palace walls. The king had been possessive since learning of her meetings with Crompton. Margaret barely had a moment to herself without a servant being seen following her or the king himself calling on her to attend him.

"What is the name of this place again?" Annabel looked around curiously as they exited the alleyway. "I didn't realize it was so far out in the city."

"Theotes's Benevolent Home for the Poor," Margaret told her.

Margaret quietly entered the building, seeing it was much improved from when she had been there last with her mother. The sickly were no longer taking every open space available, but had been separated by ailment. She looked back at Annabel, whose face held only relief, smiling at her. There were other women there, aprons pinned to the front of their dresses, watering the patients.

"We'll find the matron and see what work she has for us." Margaret was already walking through the halls, looking for the matron of the home.

They found her in the back with the laundry cauldron, stirring the load with a paddle. She leaned heavily on it to ensure the entirety of the load was touched by the cleansing lye. Her cheeks were mottled red with exertion.

"Mother Clotilde?" Margaret called out tentatively, pleased when the squat woman raised her head. It was the same woman who ran the house the last time she had been there.

"Yes, my lady?" Mother Clotilde turned her attention back to her work.

"We wish to help in the home today, if you will allow us," Margaret told her, motioning to herself and Annabel, despite the fact the matron was not looking at her.

"You may start hanging the rinsed clothing on the line there, or you may check the dry ones for need of mending," the nun told her, wiping her glistening brow.

"Thank you, Mother Clotilde." Margaret urged Annabel toward the drying line.

Margaret took her time ringing out the clothing cooling in the clean water, hanging them when they were rung sufficiently. When that was done, she went to the lines with dried clothes to fold them. She stretched her stiff back after folding her third line. She wouldn't complain—this was far better than being at the king's beck and call.

"How long must we stay here, my lady?" Annabel asked after mending her fifth shirt.

"You are more than welcome to return home, Annabel." Margaret turned a perturbed eye on her. "Captain, would you be willing to escort her?"

Captain Vojvo peeled himself off the wall by the gate and came to her side. "If you command it."

It was not a yes, but Margaret would take it. "Yes, please. I think Annabel has had enough philanthropy for the day."

Vojvo gave her a stern look. "Will you remain here until I return, my lady?"

"I'm unsure," Margaret started. Catching his glare, she changed her mind. "All right, Captain. I'll be here upon your return."

"And you won't leave in the interim?"

Margaret let out an exasperated sigh. "I promise I will stay on the premises until you return."

"Good." He nodded to her. "Come along, Lady Annabel."

She gratefully put down her mending and nearly ran to the captain's side. Margaret resisted the urge to roll her eyes. She was disappointed in Annabel—she had been excited to be charitable, though Margaret suspected she thought that meant smiling at the sick and then going home.

Margaret began to fold the clothes, happy to be on her own. She could almost imagine herself in Silvica, before all her troubles started. Her stomach was rumbling by the time that Vojvo returned. All but the damp clothes were folded and in baskets for the nuns to take at their leisure.

"Do you wish to leave?" Vojvo asked. "It's near dinner time."

Margaret nodded. "I think that I am. Would you mind terribly if we took the long way?"

"Not at all, my lady." Vojvo offered her his arm to escort her. "Annabel wishes me to tell you she will be taking dinner in her room tonight."

"Better that she does," Margaret said. "She's been wearing on my nerves lately."

"Do you wish to send her home?" Vojvo asked.

"No." Margaret sighed. "I made her a promise I would find her a husband."

They remained silent for the remainder of their journey to the palace, taking as many twists and turns they could to delay their return. Margaret and Vojvo were almost to her apartments when she caught sight of the king leaving her chambers. She pulled the captain with her as she ducked into a darkened hallway.

"My lady—"

Margaret put a hand to his mouth to quiet him, watching the king walk by without a second glance. She held her breath as she listened to his footsteps, letting it out when she could no longer hear them.

"I think I should follow Annabel's suit and take dinner in my chambers," Margaret said before she peeked her head out of the corridor. "I do not wish to see the king tonight."

Vojvo took her to her door before he spoke. "Would you like me to stay here while Sarah sends for your dinner?"

"No, I think I will be all right. The king has to make an appearance, after all," Margaret told him. "You should go and get your own dinner. I'm sure you're just as hungry as I am."

"As you wish, my lady." Vojvo bowed but did not leave until she was safely inside.

Not long after she had settled into her apartments did a knock at the door come. Sarah was not there yet, so she answered the door herself. It was a small page who wordlessly handed her a note from Lord General Crompton summoning her to see him.

Her stomach dropped. He would have news about Liam if he was back. She waited until Sarah arrived to tell her where she was going.

When the door opened to Crompton's chambers, Margaret curtsied deeply to him before she came into the room. She waited until the door was firmly closed behind her before speaking. "I must inform Your Grace that His Majesty has forbidden my seeing you again."

Crompton scoffed. "Has he now?"

"He has, indeed," she sardonically confirmed. "Is he aware of your arrival?"

"Not yet," he told her, pouring her a drink. He offered it to her before sitting again.

"How did it go?" Margaret asked, taking a large drink of the wine.

"Poorly." Crompton touched his lip.

Margaret furrowed her brow. Nothing remained on his face, though she was sure the memory of it still smarted. "What happened?"

"He hit me, for one," Compton admitted, "and for second, he refused to listen to anything I had to say."

"I cannot say I'm terribly surprised," Margaret told him over the rim of her glass. "You are the one who ruined his life, after all."

"I did, at that." He sighed. "I couldn't even mention your name before he beat me to the ground before leaving."

"I'm sorry to hear he wouldn't listen," she said honestly. "What will we do next?"

"I hope that you will go with me when I return."

Margaret balked. "Me? I don't know if the king will allow my travel."

"He doesn't need to allow you, Lady Margaret," Crompton told her. "If your trip is successful, you will have a new king. One that will most likely end up your husband."

"My husband?" Her cheeks colored brightly, though she did delight in the prospect.

"He will need one of the nobility as his wife, and as far as I can tell, you are the only one whom he knows that has a large enough fortune to fund a campaign. And one that he would consent to marrying." Crompton downed the rest of his drink. "No doubt, you would be more than happy to marry a king, Lady Margaret."

"No doubt that I would, were it the right one" she said, her thoughts far off. "And what of my responsibilities here?"

"Leave them," he said simply. "Take who you want, and send the rest to Dorcia or wherever else you think they will be useful."

Margaret rolled her lip between her teeth, her eyes clouded with thought. "The king rarely leaves me to myself for more than a few hours. Do you think you would be able to spirit me away from court without his notice?"

Crompton nodded. "I can start the preparations immediately."

Margaret gave him a bright smile. "I should be happy to see Liam again, Your Grace."

"Then you will be happy again very soon, my lady." He smiled at her. "Start preparing your things. I will let you know when we shall leave."

"Thank you, Your Grace," Margaret said as she stood.

Margaret excitedly closed the door behind her, letting out a high-pitched squeal, stamping her feet. Freedom was in sight. She went to her bedchamber, throwing open the doors to her armoire. How much should she take? Would she just commission a new wardrobe for her new position—a queen, as Lord General Crompton said?

Unable to decide, Margaret rang the bell to summon Sarah from the servant's hall. She chewed on her lip, indecisive until Sarah entered the chambers. Margaret turned to the sound of the door opening, nearly pouncing on the tiny maid.

"Sarah! We're leaving!" Margaret squealed.

"What?" Sarah asked, so confused she forgot to add, "my lady."

"Lord General Crompton is arranging for me—you and Vojvo too—to leave the capital with him to convince a friend who he really is," Margaret informed her maid excitedly.

Sarah watched her brighten with each word. "Where will we be going, my lady?"

"Salatia," Margaret said. "I need help packing."

"What would you like to take?" Sarah asked, going to the armoire.

"Definitely the blue dress I came here in," Margaret said, "and a few house dresses. I want to be comfortable while traveling."

She heard the door open and, thinking it was Captain Vojvo, ignored it.

"And I think perhaps one of the red dresses, it's my color," said Margaret, lost in thought, "or do you think it would be too easy to dirty while traveling?"

"I—"

"And where will you be traveling?" Sorren asked, making the two women jump.

"Your Majesty," Margaret cried, falling into a curtsy.

"Where will you be traveling, Lady Margaret, without my permission?" Sorren demanded.

"I thought I would travel to Marbon—Elizabeth Gollack has fallen severely ill," Margaret lied, keeping her eyes to the ground.

"And when were you planning on leaving?" inquired the king.

Margaret looked up at him. "I'm unsure when I would leave."

"It would not be any time soon," Sorren told her, "as you will not get my permission."

"Your Majesty—"

"I've been told you were seen leaving Duke Rivack's chambers today," Sorren cut her off, raising his hand.

"I—"

"If you are going to say you do not know what I am speaking of, remember how I punish people for lying to me."

Visibly swallowing, Margaret conceded. "He summoned me."

"You could have refused," Sorren told her. "Why didn't you?"

"To feel I still had control of my life," Margaret told him.

It was not untrue. She felt as though she had more control of herself when she defied the king's orders. No doubt, Margaret would do it again before Lord General Crompton was able to spirit her and her staff away.

"You will grow used to the constraints I have put on you in time," said the king sympathetically. "I will let this pass for now."

"Your Majesty is too kind, truly." Margaret swallowed against the bile in her throat. He was anything but.

"Come with me to the hall," the king commanded, offering his arm.

Margaret reluctantly took his arm. "It would be my pleasure, Your Majesty."

Margaret stood next to the king, her arm firmly locked in his. She had barely been able to leave his side to even use the privy. She could see the looks of disdain on the faces of any of the peers they came across.

"Your Majesty," Margaret whispered once they were as alone as they could be. "Your Majesty, you must let me off your arm."

"No."

"Your Majesty," she protested, "you are giving them fodder for gossip!"

"You think I care about the gossip of these peons?" he demanded.

"You should," she scolded boldly.

"Say no more of it, Lady Margaret," he commanded.

Terror struck Margaret when she saw Queen Lillian enter the hall with her entourage following behind. She swallowed hard, trying to put as much space between them as she could before the queen saw her on the king's arm.

"Stop squirming," Sorren whispered harshly.

"Your Majesty, please, the queen is here." Hurriedly said, she sounded strangled.

"And?" He raised a single brow.

"She'll find out I'm your mistress!" Margaret hissed.

Sorren shrugged, saying nothing.

Margaret flinched when the queen made eye contact with her, turning her face away to avoid her gelid stare.

31

Liam looked to Gretta next to him. She was still dead asleep—it had been a late night for the both of them. Gretta had been hurting more with the constant rain that spring brought, and he had not slept well since Crompton had shown up at random. He looked through the window, rain gently pattering against the thick glass. Sighing, he pulled himself from the bed, his tired muscles protesting. He lit the fire in their room to warm it up before she woke up. Hopefully, it would help her joints when she got out of bed.

Liam went downstairs, rubbing his hands together to fight off the chill the rain brought. He lit the fire in the kitchen and looked at the clock. The boys would be coming down soon. He did his best to make breakfast for them. He was much better with fireside food—at least, Margaret had never had any complaints.

Eli was the first to venture downstairs, rubbing his eyes while he yawned. "Where's Ma?" he asked with another big yawn.

"Your Ma is still sleeping," Liam told him, "Are you hungry?"

Eli nodded, yawning hugely.

"Let's get you something to eat then," Liam said, sitting him at the table.

The other boys came down, sitting with bleary eyes at the table. Liam scooped eggs onto the plates, face red with embarrassment. He scorched a good amount of the breakfast. He set the plates in front of the boys, sitting across from them. "I thought we might collect a few nettles for your mother—to help with her hurting," Liam suggested.

In truth, he wanted to get in nature and clear his head. It had been clogged with thoughts of Crompton and why he had been in Numetra. He should have asked questions when he had the chance, but seeing Crompton had unnerved him, and Liam wanted the man gone quickly.

"She would like that," Jamie told him. "She always hurts around this time, and in the cold."

"After you've finished eating, gather a pail and some gloves, and we'll be on our way," Liam instructed the boys.

After breakfast, he led them to a stream on the way to Castenra to the east of Numetra. The farther they were from town, the more relaxed Liam became. This was what he needed. The stream was lined with stinging nettle and would give them plenty to make the nettle beer.

"Don't touch the nettles with your bare hands—wear the gloves," Liam reminded them. "Eli, you'll stay by the pail and push the nettles down so they don't overflow."

Liam stepped over the nettles and put a small amount of water in the bottom of the pail to soak the stinging plant. He set the receptacle next to Eli and handed him a stick. "Don't touch them," Liam warned. "You don't want to have your hands stung. Just push them down with the stick."

"Aye, Da." Eli had such a serious look on his face when he nodded, Liam almost laughed.

He put on his gloves and made sure Jamie and Simon did the same before he knelt in front of the plants. "Only take the top few leaves, they are the best," Liam instructed, pulling the leaves off the top of the plant he came to first.

He gathered a pile before taking it to the pail Eli dutifully guarded. Dumping them in, Liam returned to gather more. Jamie and Simon started flicking water at each other, laughing. Liam smiled. It reminded him of the day at the river with Margaret when he had flung water at her and they had first kissed.

He sighed at the thought. He wished they were able to talk more, their letters getting more infrequent. Liam hoped she was doing as well as her letters suggested. He looked around at the boys—his boys—in case there was a possibility he couldn't come back. Not without knowing Margaret was for sure in danger.

They gathered enough to tightly fill the bucket, Eli proudly pushing down the nettles any time they started to come out. They piled their gloves on top to keep the nettles inside as they started their walk home.

"Where will we make this?" Jamie asked.

"We can make it in the slaughterhouse so your Ma doesn't see it," Liam told them. "We'll take all we need in there before we start."

Liam led the boys back to The Smiling Fox, pointing out the edible plants along the way. He'd get them proficient on their own before too long. Eli already showed some aptitude toward foraging, regularly handing him edible plants Liam had shown the boys when they were out. As they got closer to the town, he picked some dandelions to add to the mix.

"Jamie, be so kind as to get water from the well," Liam said. "I'll get the other ingredients out of the kitchen."

"What should I do?" Eli asked.

Nothing, but Liam couldn't tell him that. "Keep making sure the nettles don't come out of the bucket." He looked at Simon. "Start the fire for the cauldron, and I'll be right back."

He went into the kitchen, glancing around to see if Gretta was in there. Liam didn't want to spoil her surprise by being caught grabbing ingredients he normally wouldn't touch. He quickly gathered the remainder of the ingredients he would need for the beer.

When the cauldron was on the fire, Liam added the pail of nettles, along with a few handfuls of dandelion and a small nub of ginger he had pounded lightly. He caught the confused looks of the boys.

"It's to make it taste better," he told them.

They let it boil for almost an hour before straining the mixture into another vessel. He stirred in brown sugar until it dissolved in the faintly green liquid.

"Now we let it sit until it's near cold, and then we add the yeast," Liam told them.

"Can we go inside while we wait?" Simon whined.

"Go on, I can finish this for your Ma. You already did the hardest part," he told them.

The boys left, and Liam remained to finish the work.

Gretta was at the table with Liam and the boys for breakfast when he noticed that she was rubbing her joints to try and ease the pain.

"Jamie, go and get your Ma something to drink," Liam said with a nod toward the door.

Light dawned behind Jamie's eyes. He went to the slaughter house to grab the nettle beer he and Liam had bottled. Upon returning, Jamie set a mug and the bottle in front of her. He was unable to keep the grin from his face.

Gretta looked between the two of them. "What is this?"

"The boys made you a special drink," Liam told her. "For your pain."

Gretta's face softened from her surprise. "What did ye make?"

"Da showed us," Simon said quickly.

"It is nettle beer," Liam told her. "My father used to make it frequently for the pain in his knees."

"I helped too!" Eli interjected.

Gretta smiled at him gently, cupping his cheek. "Thank ye, all. 'Twas a verra kind thing to do for me."

Liam looked at the clock on the wall. "It's time for you boys to get to work. Don't want to be late."

"Aye, Da." Jamie kissed Gretta on the head before he left with Simon.

"And you," Liam said, looking at Eli, "need to get dressed. You're starting at the schoolhouse today."

"But—"

"Do as your da says, Eli," Gretta said, squeezing Liam's hand.

Liam couldn't help but smile. He still got a thrill every time they called him Da. At this rate, he didn't know if he would ever leave.

Liam wiped his face clean of sweat and soot, putting down his work.

"Go home, lad," Thorkelin waved his hand at him. "I ken Gretta still isna feelin' well."

He nodded. "Aye, we're going to need a healer if she doesn't start feeling better soon."

"Tell her I hope she feels better," Jossnon said as Liam left.

Liam paused at the door, catching sight of Jamie handing a pretty young girl with mousy brown hair a flower he had obviously picked. Liam saw the girl blush and raise the bloom to her nose. She inhaled deeply, dimpling at the young Jamie.

Liam smiled to himself, letting them have their private moment. He returned home, immediately bounding the stairs to check on Gretta. She was still in bed, the sheets tangled around her feet. He sat on the side of the bed, stroking the hair back from her face.

She did feel cooler than when Liam had left her that morning, her color returning. He was ready to leave when she groaned, and he returned to her side.

"Gretta?" he asked softly, not wanting to wake her if she was not ready.

She looked at him through slitted eyes. "What time is it?"

"It's near sunset," Liam told her. "I've just come home from the smithy."

"Is it that late already?" she groaned. "Where are the boys?"

"Simon and Eli are downstairs," Liam informed her, "and Jamie was with a young lady."

"A lassie?" The news seemed to bring her out of her fog.

Liam's mouth curled in amusement. "I saw him give her a flower. I think he's trying to court her."

"But he's too young!" Gretta complained, her eyes looking mildly panicked.

"He's near seventeen, Gretta," countered Liam. "He's practically a grown man."

"He's still my wee Jamie!" Gretta sat up. The more she focused on Jamie, the less she seemed to realize she was sick.

"If you're worried about him leaving, you could have them both here, and she can help you with your customers," suggested Liam. "You could use the help." Liam could see the calculation in her eyes as she thought.

"Aye," she said quietly, "aye, I could."

Amused, Liam squeezed Gretta's hand. "Are you feeling better?"

"What?" Gretta asked, pulled from her thoughts. "Oh, aye. D'ye ken the girl?"

"No, I don't know her," Liam admitted. He didn't know why, but his shoulders slumped when she looked disappointed.

"We need to invite her here," Gretta said hastily, trying to pull the cover away from her.

Liam stopped her, pulling the covers back up to her chest. "We don't even know if they are courting," Liam reminded her.

Gretta turned her head toward the hall when she heard the door close below them. "That must be wee Jamie. Will ye go to him?"

"If you'll stay here," Liam countered. "You shouldn't be out of bed yet."

"Aye, fine," Gretta reluctantly agreed.

Liam kissed her before returning downstairs. Jamie sat at the table, head in his hands when Liam entered. "What's wrong?" Liam asked.

Jamie's head flew up, staring at the older man. "Ye scairt me, Da."

"My apologies." Liam sat across from him. "Is there something on your mind?"

"Aye," Jamie nodded, his cheeks coloring. "I dinna ken what to do."

"About...?"

Ears turning red, Jamie said, "I dinna ken how to tell ye."

"How about you try to tell me like you would Eli," suggested Liam.

"There's a lady I fancy, an' I dinna ken how to tell her I fancy her," Jamie admitted. "I dinna ken if she fancies me too."

"Does she seem to want to be around you?" asked Liam.

Jamie nodded. "Aye, she comes to give me lunch every other day."

"And does she do that for any other young man you work with?"

"She doesna, no," he confirmed.

"I would say it's safe to say she fancies you, but I'll tell you honest, Jamie, you can never really tell if a lady likes you," Liam told him, thinking of Margaret. "You never really know until they agree to marry you, I think."

"Ma seems to like ye just fine," Jamie commented, his cheeks darkening.

"Aye, she does," Liam agreed, "but I've not always been so lucky. There was once a lady, Maggie, I fancied. I admired her very much, and she did all your young lady does for you for me, but she still did not want me."

"Why would she do it if she didna want ye?" Jamie asked, his brow furrowed.

Liam laughed without humor, shrugged. "Hell if I know, Jamie, but I loved her for being her."

Jamie shifted uncomfortably. "Do ye still?"

"I do," Liam honestly told him, "I will probably always love her, but that doesn't mean I don't have room to love another. Love doesn't belong to one person alone."

"Did she ken ye felt so?"

"I never explicitly told her I loved her," Liam said, "but she knew. Tell this young lady how you feel about her, and see if she reciprocates."

"What do I do if she doesna?" Jamie asked.

"You move on," Liam answered. "You move on and find another, because there will be other young women that you'll like, and if they don't feel the same way you do, you'll move on from that."

Jamie nodded slowly. "What did ye do when your lady didna return yer affection?"

"I tried to run away from my feelings for her and acquainted myself with a few other ladies." Liam's cheeks flushed. "But, in the end, I came back to her until she went somewhere I couldn't follow."

"And now ye're here with Ma," Jamie finished.

"And now I'm here with all of you," Liam corrected. "I don't just love your mother; I love you and your brothers like my own sons."

32

Crompton groaned, pulled the knife from his inner pocket, and tossed it on his desk, taking off his waistcoat after he returned to his chambers following the evening meal. His stomach was full, still unused to the overstuffed meals at court instead of his traveling rations. A knock sounded on his door as he poured himself a drink.

"Enter," he called.

A servant entered his quarters, bowing. "Your Grace, a message for you from His Majesty."

Crompton grabbed the sealed parchment from him, nodding. "Thank you, you may go."

He broke the seal, quickly reading the message inside.

Meet me in the dungeons, our usual spot. I want a mission report.
S

Tobias sighed, shrugging into his coat. He did not want to do this now. He was unprepared with what to tell Sorren. He had spent his return journey trying to find a way to help Lady Margaret and her two servants escape the king's clutches. His plan was to dress them all as servants and lead them out as his own staff for a brief sojourn at his home in Rivack, one he would not take, before returning to Numetra.

With Lady Margaret in tow, Crompton had no doubt he would succeed in getting Liam to listen. He should have made arrangements to bring her the first time. If he had, a strong enough army could have been gathered within the year, and the Anatalian throne in better hands by the end of the next. It was all Crompton had wanted for years, and he had foolishly missed his opportunity to do it correctly the first time. He had overestimated his abilities to persuade others, especially ones who hated him.

Crompton arrived at the dungeons in short order. They typically had their meetings of heavy content there so they could speak freely without worry of anyone hearing them. Anyone who could use it against them, at least. No one would believe tales from a raving prisoner, especially one who had a grudge against the king for being there. Having only just returned from his travels, Crompton was sure that Sorren wanted as fresh a report as he could of what Tobias found. He had told the king he was going to find out why there was an increase in Salatian rebels breaching their borders.

He was the first to arrive, ignoring the prisoner who reached out to grab the unfamiliar person. Crompton grimaced, stepping out of reach of the filth-streaked hands. This was his least favorite part of their dungeon rendezvous. Luckily, Sorren arrived not long after.

"Was your trip productive?" Sorren asked in an odd tone.

"Not as productive as I would have liked, Your Majesty." Crompton's mouth turned downward into a frown.

"Too bad." Sorren looked into the cell they were in front of. It was occupied by a known murderer, covered in his own filth; he had gone mad a few years prior.

"I think I may have found a solution to our problems, however," Crompton told him evasively.

"Oh? Did you find your replacement for the—how did you put it?—'the wastrel voluptuary'?" Sorren asked coldly.

Crompton blanched.

Never once in all his failed attempts had they been able to trace it back to him. He must have gotten sloppy in his confidence.

"Did you not think that I would have you watched?" Sorren looked at Crompton with gelid eyes, his arms crossed in front of him. "Especially since that soldier's trial when he declared you the traitor?"

Crompton looked around for an easy exit—there weren't any. Even if he ran, no doubt, Sorren would have already alerted the guards to stop him if he was seen. He reached for the knife hidden in an inner pocket of his waist coat. Crompton looked down to realize he had never put it back. "What do you know?"

"I am the *king!* I know *everything* that goes on in my country."

"You shouldn't be," Tobias said quietly.

"And who do you think should be king instead?" Sorren demanded. "Yourself?"

Did Sorren think he was just as power hungry? Crompton had only ever worked in the service of Anatalia and Theotes. The same things Sorren should have been doing.

"Not me. I am not meant for ruling." Crompton's lip curled in disgust. "You are not fit to rule this country. This country needs a king who is more interested in ruling than in whoring!"

"And who do you think is?" Sorren yelled back. "It certainly is not my son. He is a bumbling idiot."

"You think I would tell you?" Crompton laughed, incredulous at the gall. "Do you even know how many times I have tried to kill you or had someone else try?"

Sorren paused, looking over his cousin. "It's been at least three years you've been trying."

"More like fifteen years." Crompton laughed at himself—the unending years of failure were coming to a head in front of him. "Fifteen years I have been trying, and you keep crawling back like the cockroach you are."

He could see the betrayal spreading through the king's face before Sorren drew a knife. Crompton put distance between him and his cousin, cursing himself again for forgetting to put back his knife.

"Are you going to try to kill me now?" Crompton bent his knees to spring when he needed to.

The king assumed a similar position. "You tell me you have been attempting to kill me for fifteen years now and expect the two of us to walk out of here alive?"

"I expect I will walk out of here alive," Crompton countered.

"You say that I am not fit to rule," —Sorren edged closer— "but you are not fit to live anymore." The king darted quickly at Crompton and plunged his knife into the side of Crompton's neck.

Crompton's face pinched as Sorren pulled the knife from his neck, blood spurting out of the wound. He clawed at his neck as he sank to the ground, trying to stop the bleeding. His breath gurgled, blood slipping down his chin from the corner of his mouth.

"Goodbye, Cousin." Sorren squatted to look him in the face. "Your usefulness has ended, and now so have you."

The king walked out of the dungeon calmly, stopping once to look at his cousin clawing at his neck, watching him with cold disinterest until he stopped struggling.

"Lord General Crompton was murdered by the prisoner whose cell he's in front of," Sorren said nonchalantly to the guards upon his exit, as if the events had been an everyday occurrence. "Clean it up."

The guards scrambled to follow his orders as the king returned to his chambers.

33

argaret woke to the church bells ringing in solid, even tones, indicating someone of import had died. Theotes, she hoped it was Sorren. Margaret pulled the bell to summon Sarah to her chambers to find out what was going on. It did not take long for Sarah to arrive, her cheeks flushed from hurrying.

"Do you know what is happening?" Margaret asked, a small hope that the king had suddenly died in his sleep.

"Lord General Crompton is dead," Sarah said breathlessly. "Murdered in the dungeons by a criminal who somehow got a weapon."

"No!" Margaret covered her mouth. "I need to go to his chambers!"

"My lady?" Sarah furrowed her brow.

"To make sure there isn't anything to incriminate me," Margaret went on, slipping on her housecoat. "I have to go now."

Crompton was dead. The man who would help her raise Liam to his throne was dead. Disappointment more than sadness fell over her. He was her escape, but he had ruined Liam's life and caused both of their problems. She hadn't forgiven him for that yet.

"My lady," —Sarah reached out and tried to stop her— "what about Captain Vojvo?"

"I have no time!" Margaret called over her shoulder.

No one was in the halls, no doubt waiting for the news to come to them or still sleeping. Margaret winced as her bare feet slapped meatily against the stone floor, but she had no time to quiet her step. Crompton's chambers were unlocked, and she entered without thought. His candles burned low, casting a dim light over the room.

She looked around helplessly. Where would he put something secret? Margaret went to his travel bag, dumping its contents in search of it. Nothing but papers and coin fell out, and she threw it away from her. Margaret dropped on her stomach and looked under the bed, feeling the slats beneath to see if he had hid anything incriminating her there.

He had not.

Margaret let out a growl, slapping the floor in frustration. She rose and pulled the drawers of his desk, rifling through its contents to no avail. She tried to shove the contents back the way she found him, not wanting someone to think he had been pilfered.

Of course he wouldn't keep anything here. He wasn't an idiot.

She looked around the room one last time before returning to her own, her cheeks red from her run.

Sarah rose immediately. "Did you find anything?"

"No," Margaret said breathlessly, "I couldn't find anything."

"Come back to bed, my lady," Sarah tried to tell her, opening the door to her bedchamber.

"I need to send a letter!" Margaret suddenly said, scrambling to get the parchment and pen. Her mind was reeling with a million swirling thoughts. She sat to address the issue to Liam.

> 20 Amonat 2284
> Liam,
>   Lord General Crompton has been murdered in the dungeons tonight.
> You have a modicum of justice.
> > Love,
> > Margaret

Margaret kept it short, not wanting to be cold. A man was dead, after all. "Make sure this goes out."

Sarah nodded, tucking the note into her apron. "Yes, my lady. I'll have it out at first light."

Margaret nodded, her mind racing. "I should send a note of condolence to His Majesty as well."

"Would you like me to wait while you write it, my lady?"

"Yes," Margaret said, "yes, that would be good."

She paused for a moment, thinking what to say. Margaret certainly could not tell him she was sorry that her last chance of escape had perished.

> Your Majesty,
>   I am deeply saddened to hear the news that Lord General Crompton
> has passed. Please accept my condolences.
> > Lady Margaret

Margaret once again handed the note to Sarah for delivery. "Deliver these with all due haste, Sarah."

Margaret woke in the morning to the king sitting in the plush chair next to her bed. She sat up with a gasp, pulling the sheets up to her neck. "Your Majesty, what are you doing here?"

"I wanted to be here," he said as if that explained everything, sinking further into the chair. There were dark circles under his eyes, looking as though he had not slept at all the previous night.

"Have you slept, Majesty?" Margaret asked, scrutinizing his appearance.

"No."

Margaret hesitated before holding her hand out to him. "Is it because of the Lord General's death?"

The king took her hand, sitting on the bed next to her. "Yes."

Margaret was unsure of what to say. "It's a...very upsetting time." She squeezed his hand.

"I killed him, you know." Sorren watched her face intently.

"W-what?" Margaret asked, her eyes wide, trying to pull her hand out of his.

"He was trying to take my throne, Margaret." He held onto her hand tightly. He was looking at her intently. "I don't like when people try to take things that are mine."

Fear clenched Margaret's stomach, her mouth drying. "I'm sorry that it came to that," she said carefully.

"Do you understand, Margaret?" Sorren continued holding her hand in a crushing grip.

"Y-Yes, Your Majesty," Margaret said quietly. She understood explicitly. She was his, and he would kill anyone who tried to take that away from him, just like he had with the queen's lover.

Margaret sat dazed in her bed after the king left her chambers. She looked up when Sarah walked in, staring at her blankly.

Sarah stopped short. "My lady? Is there something wrong?"

"I'm doomed." Margaret flopped back onto her bed, looking up at the ceiling.

Sarah pushed back her covers. "My lady, you are not doomed."

Margaret covered her face with her hands. "The king all but threatened me. I can't ever leave!"

"I don't understand, my lady." Sarah shook her head, her brow furrowing.

"He killed Lord General Crompton," she said in a harsh whisper, "for trying to overthrow him. I-I was going to help him, and I think His Majesty suspects it. He won't ever let me go, Sarah."

"There must be a way," Sarah tried to console her.

Margaret ran her hands over her face. "I don't know if there is."

She didn't know how the queen dealt with the king without wanting to fling herself over a ledge. Margaret wondered if anyone else knew how controlling he was, anyone else she could depend on to help her. She could not confide in Lillian herself, though she had no doubt the queen would help her escape if only to get her out of the king's grasp. But then they would both be punished.

Margaret could not understand why Lillian would ever want to stay close to Sorren, or would even care if he left her bed once she had her heir. Margaret certainly wouldn't—if she were ever married to Sorren, she would welcome the reprieve a mistress brought. There was no way Lillian could not know Sorren had affairs. He did not care who saw him with whomever was on his arm.

Standing, Margaret went to her vanity, picking up her brush. "Do you know anything of what will happen with His Grace?"

"He has been put in Saint Asesia's Cathedral for viewing until the funeral." Sarah took the brush from her hand.

Margaret opened a ceramic jar on her vanity as Sarah brushed her hair free of tangles, putting cream on her hands. "Have you heard when the funeral will be held?"

"I have not, my lady," Sarah told her regrettably.

Margaret closed her eyes to enjoy Sarah's ministrations. "Alert me as soon as you hear anything."

Sarah remained silent, picking up a particularly tangled section of hair.

"Have you heard anything from Annabel yet?"

"No, my lady," Sarah said as she finished Margaret's hair. "She is still asleep, most likely."

Margaret nodded. "She does sleep more than any other person I know."

Snorting in agreement, Sarah helped Margaret into her house coat. "Your breakfast is in the sitting room, my lady."

"Thank you, Sarah," Margaret murmured as she passed through the door "Will you tell Annabel I would like to see her at her earliest convenience?"

Sarah laid a napkin in Margaret's lap. "As you wish, my lady."

Margaret pulled Annabel into the crowded throne room. All the nobles were summoned for an announcement. She could barely move away from the door, the room full almost to bursting. Annabel stayed close to Margaret, nearly running into her when someone else came into the room. Confused murmurs ran through the nobles the longer they waited, but Margaret knew why they were here.

Sorren was announced and headed to the front of the room. Many of those in the room attempted to bow to him, but they were packed too closely to do it justice.

Sorren raised his hand in acknowledgment. "Thank you all for coming," he started. "Many of you know why you are here, but for those of you who do not: it is with a heavy heart that I announce the death of His Grace, Duke of Rivack, Lord General Tobias Crompton. He was killed by a crazed criminal while walking the dungeons last night."

Louder murmurs erupted between the nobles, concerned looks exchanged by more than a few. Margaret watched them, her shoulders heavy with the knowledge of what had really happened. If only they knew the truth.

Sorren held his hand up for silence. "The prisoner will be executed tomorrow by hanging in the courtyard, open to anyone who wishes to attend. His Grace is in Saint Asesia's Cathedral until the time of his funeral in six days' time."

Margaret watched as the crowd parted for the king when he decided to exit through the door the nobles had entered from. She pulled Annabel to the side, bowing her head deeply to him as he passed.

"Will we attend the execution?" Annabel asked in Margaret's ear.

Margaret did not answer until they were in the hall. "Have you ever seen someone die, Annabel?"

"No, my lady," answered Annabel.

"It is not a pleasant thing," Margaret told her, thinking of her father, "but if you wish to attend, I will not prevent you from doing so."

"I don't think I have decided yet," Annabel said quietly.

Margaret nodded. "Is there anything you would like to do today?"

"It seems too somber of a day for much activity, my lady," answered Annabel.

"I agree," confirmed Margaret. "We'll luncheon in my chambers and perhaps, afterward, take a walk in the garden to see the Amonat blooms."

Annabel nodded along silently as they returned to Margaret's chambers.

It seemed Margaret's idea of spending time in the garden had not been an original one. Several groups of ladies, and even some lords to accompany them, filled the gardens. There were several flowers already in full bloom for her and Annabel to admire.

By the time Margret reached the end of the first garden, a page stopped at Margaret's elbow, bowing to her. "My lady," he said, holding out a sealed letter.

"Thank you," she said, taking the letter and opening it quickly.

I require your presence in your chambers.

S

Margaret sighed inwardly. "My apologies, Annabel, I have been summoned for a meeting."

"Shall I go with you?" asked the young woman.

"I'm afraid that it is a private meeting," Margaret answered firmly. "You may continue on here or find something else to do. Let Sarah know if you are going out into the city."

With that, Margaret left Annabel to her own devices and returned to her chambers. Sorren was already waiting for her when she arrived.

"What took you so long?" demanded Sorren.

Margaret took a breath before she answered. "I had to come all the way from the gardens."

Sorren looked her over, taking note of her flushed cheeks. "Sit."

Margaret sat across from him, eyeing Sorren warily.

"Will you attend the execution tomorrow?" asked Sorren.

"I had not planned on seeing an innocent man hang, no," Margaret said, happily including the barb.

"He is not an innocent man," Sorren snapped. "I have said it, and it is so."

Margaret's hackles raised. "He is innocent of the crime you accused him of," she said testily, refusing to back down. "You cannot rewrite history simply because you wish it."

"I am the king, Lady Margaret," he reminded her. "I can do what I want, and say what I want, and get rid of whomever I want."

Looking still defiant, Margaret asked, "Is that why you murdered Lord General Crompton?"

"He was a traitor." Sorren spoke easily as though they were talking of the weather. "And actively tried to replace and kill me."

Margaret remained silent. She was actively trying to replace him too. Or, at least, she had been until Crompton was killed. Now she didn't know what she was going to do. She couldn't leave, and she suspected her mail would be watched closely from now on.

As if guessing her thoughts, he spoke again. "I hope you understand what this means, Margaret."

"I do," she said quietly.

Sorren poured himself a drink, tossing it back. "I want you to attend the execution with me."

"Kings don't attend executions." Margaret looked at him, surprised. Monarchs never attended executions—they didn't want to invite the thought of their deaths.

"I am making an exception, since he killed my beloved cousin."

Margaret resisted the urge to roll her eyes. "As you wish."

Sorren stood, heading to her bedchamber. "Come."

She allowed her sigh to be audible this time, going to him.

The execution started precisely at two in the afternoon. Clouds floated in front of the sun, casting a shadow over the scaffolding. Margaret stood with the king on a separate platform, along with the Dowager Duchess Cecily. The dowager's eyes were rimmed red and puffy.

Margaret knew it would be cathartic for the new widow to see her husband's alleged murderer executed. If only Margaret could tell the dowager who really had ended her husband's life. Maybe eventually she would be able to, once she was out from under Sorren's thumb.

Margaret scoffed to herself. That would only happen when he was dead, and would happen no time soon.

A murmur rumbled through the gathered crowd as the prisoner was escorted to the scaffold. His face was covered with dirt, his bright blue eyes crazed. The prisoner's hair stuck out in all directions. He looked around frantically, searching for an escape. He tried once but was quickly pulled back by the guards.

The dowager flinched when he screamed, flailing against the iron grips of his captors. The prisoner was pulled onto the platform. He doubled as the guards pulled him toward the noose, trying to resist its advance.

"No!" he screamed, filling the courtyard with his panic.

He continued to scream as a hood was shoved over his head, the noose slipped over it. The executioner tightened it as he spoke a prayer over the panicked prisoner, waiting until the prisoner stood still before pulling the lever that released the floor beneath him.

Margaret turned her head, closing her eyes tightly. She would have covered her ears if she could. The noose had not been tied properly, and the prisoner was emitting strangled noises.

After a long moment, Sorren waved his hand to signal the guards. They grabbed the prisoner's spasmodic legs, pulling him down until he no longer undulated against them.

Turning her head when Margaret heard the dowager duchess let out a relieved breath, she herself felt relief when she saw the prisoner hung limply. He was taken down and tossed into the back of a cart. The crowd started to disperse before anyone on Margaret's platform moved.

"And history is written," Sorren said quietly to Margaret before he parted company.

A chill ran down her spine as she watched him walk away.

It would end up being either him or her, but only one of them would make it out of this before it was all over.

 **34**

Vojvo stayed behind in his room while Lady Margaret attended the execution. Someone knocked hurriedly on the door until Vojvo answered. He yanked it open, prepared to yell at whomever disturbed him. His mouth hung open, his protest dying on his lips when he saw the frantic Sarah.

"Has something happened?" he asked instead.

Sarah looked around to see if anyone else was in the corridor. "Inside."

Marius let her in, closing the door behind her. "Tell me what has happened."

"We need to leave," Sarah hurriedly said, "Lady Margaret is in danger."

Vojvo turned on her, his brows raised. Why wasn't she talking? "Speak of what you know. Now!"

Sarah shifted uncomfortably. "Lady Margaret was plotting with His Grace. A plot that got him killed."

Grabbing Sarah's shoulders, Vojvo resisted the urge to shake her. "What plot?"

"I don't know," Sarah answered, looking at him wide eyed. "Her Ladyship only said His Grace was going to spirit us away so she could help convince whomever it was to join them."

"Join them for what?" demanded Vojvo.

Sarah searched his face. "To overthrow the king."

"What?"

"His Majesty is who killed His Grace," Sarah continued, "not who they're executing."

"Does His Majesty know of Lady Margaret's involvement?" He finally released Sarah.

"She thinks he suspects her. He would have shoved her out a window if he did," Sarah answered sardonically.

Vojvo did not appreciate her humor, and gave her a look that told her as much. She had the grace to look chagrined. His mind raced as he paced the room.

"When will Her Ladyship return?" asked Vojvo, still pacing.

"Not until after the evening meal," Sarah told him.

Vojvo nodded, stopping in front of Sarah. "I will speak with her tonight."

Vojvo waited for his mistress outside her door. She returned from the night's dinner, thankfully on her own. Her face was flushed with wine, eyes glazed.

He opened the door for her before she reached him. "My lady, may I speak with you?"

"Of course, Captain," she conceded, her words slurring slightly.

He waited until she was through before entering the room. "Sarah has told me what happened," Vojvo said without preamble.

Lady Margaret snorted, wobbling toward the decanter of wine and goblets, pouring herself a goblet nearly to the brim. "Did she?" she asked before putting it to her lips.

Half was gone before Vojvo spoke again. "She did." He took away her glass before she could fill it again. "I think we should leave."

"And how do you propose we do that?" she demanded.

Grabbing another goblet, she turned her back to him as Vojvo tried to take it away from her. She poured another full glass. Lady Margaret defiantly drank it, turning in a circle as Vojvo tried to take away her new glass again.

"We can flee in the night—go to Dorcia," Vojvo suggested.

Lady Margaret looked at him, wide-eyed, her mouth open. "Flee in the night like a common criminal?"

"What other choice do we have, Margaret?" Vojvo demanded.

"We don't have a choice, Marius! That is the point of this trouble!" Lady Margaret fumed. "I do not have any options. He all but threatened to murder me right along with His Grace!"

"I cannot accept that," Vojvo yelled, face red.

"You must," she said—almost hopeless—collapsing onto the couch, her face flushed red with wine. "We have no escape, Captain."

"There must be another way," Vojvo said, almost despondent, as his hope started to wane with her defeat. "There must be."

Lady Margaret poured another glass of wine, offering it to him.

He held his hand up in response, sitting on the other couch, his eyes sad. "I should have protected you from this."

"You could not have saved me," Lady Margaret said, taking a large gulp of wine. "I put this into motion long before we even knew the other existed."

Vojvo took the wine from her again. "You'll make yourself sick," he warned, finishing the glass for her.

Sighing, Lady Margaret sat back against the couch. "I don't hold you responsible, you know."

"I do," he countered. "You hired me to protect you, and I have failed you at every turn."

"You haven't failed me," Lady Margaret told him. "I have failed you, and myself."

"I suppose we can agree we've both failed." Vojvo sighed.

Lady Margaret nodded slowly, staring at the table as her face fell in dejected resignation.

35

Margaret woke to the smell of breakfast, rubbing her eyes sleepily. Light poured through the small divide in the curtains, making Margaret squint against the brightness. She wanted to hide her face in her pillows, but Sarah entered the room, opening the remainder of the curtains.

"My lady?" Sarah asked gently. "Are you awake?"

"Unfortunately," grumbled Margaret.

"Today is His Grace's funeral," Sarah reminded her.

Margaret sighed heavily, sitting up. "I know. I could hardly sleep, dreaming of the king murdering the duke."

Sarah made a sympathetic noise in the back of her throat. "Better him than you, my lady."

Margaret hated to admit that she agreed with Sarah's sentiments. She pulled the covers back, getting out of bed. "I will be with the queen and the dowager duchess today for the funeral. I already sent word to Her Majesty that I would like to join her, and the queen conceded."

"Are you sure you want to?" Sarah asked, helping her into her robe.

Nodding, Margaret went to her vanity and began applying her creams on her face and hands. "I feel somewhat responsible. I was the one who mentioned someone he could put on the throne, and because Lord General Crompton went after him, the king killed him."

"His Grace was his own man," Sarah defended her. "You did not make him do anything he didn't want to."

Margaret sighed. "I know, Sarah."

"My lady…" Sarah started hesitantly, bringing her her morning tea still steaming from the pot. "Now that His Grace is no longer a buffer between you and His Majesty, perhaps you should find another way to protect yourself."

"What do you mean?" Margaret furrowed her brow.

"You've said the king has threatened you already if you stepped out of line." Sarah pulled the tea away from Margaret's reach. "Perhaps you should give yourself some assurance."

Bile rose in Margaret's throat at her implication. She pulled the tea back to her. "If ever I got pregnant with his child, that child would be ruinous to Anatalia. I would rather he kill me."

"Yes, my lady." Sarah curtsied to her, leaving Margaret to finish her tea in peace.

Margaret shuddered. What a thought. It would possibly bring her protection, but there was no guarantee of it, and she didn't want to have any part in birthing his horrible spawn.

Once she was readied for the funeral, Margaret went to Lillian's chambers. Margaret was dressed in a dark gray gown with pearl gray stitchwork. It was a diminutive ball gown, the outer skirt lined with scrollwork while the inner skirt was patterned with evenly spaced martlets. She had a modest neckline that was lined with the same scrollwork on her skirts.

Margaret knocked on the door lightly and was let in by one of the ladies of the privy chamber. They were all dressed in gray, waiting with the dowager duchess and the queen. Margaret curtsied to Lillian, taking a seat in the remaining chair farthest away from the prominent women.

A knight knocked on the door and opened it without invitation. He bowed deeply to the room, waiting for the queen to speak.

"Rise, Sir Nial," Lillian said, bored.

"Your Majesty," he greeted reverently, "Your Grace, I am here to escort you to Lord General Crompton's funeral."

Tears welled in Cecily's eyes, but she bravely held them in. She was the first to stand, and Lillian followed behind her. Sir Nial offered his arm to the dowager, moving only when she did. Several knights loitered in the corridor, standing straighter when the women entered the hallway. Each lady in the dowager duchess's entourage had an escort, and they were led to Saint Asesia's Cathedral.

Annabel would have loved to see this—the knights looked fine in their ceremonial robes—but Margaret was glad she wasn't with her. There was enough to worry about for the day without having to worry about Annabel as well. She could line the streets with the others, but the cathedral was only for those of importance.

Margaret sat not far away from the dowager—she didn't know how Cecily was managing. With the way they had behaved toward one another, Margaret assumed they were not close, but she had never seen someone mourn as heavily as the dowager. Cecily wore the darkest gray possible on every part of her body, finishing off her look with a gray lace veil that reached the floor. She began wailing when she saw her deceased husband, the mourning sound echoing throughout the cathedral.

With no choice but to ignore her crying, the funeral started. The first speaker stood at the altar that held the duke. He cleared his throat, looking uncomfortable. He spoke at great length of the accomplishments as Rivack's Lord General. Many people in the crowd nodded at the familiarity of the stories.

The funeral lasted well over two hours, several people speaking at length to the character of the Duke of Rivack. The last speaker was the king, who played the part of mourner with exceptional skill.

"We have lost a great asset to this country," Sorren started. "A man who fought so diligently for our great nation and helped keep the Salatians at bay. There is nothing that saddens me more than the knowledge that this great man was senselessly murdered due to the carelessness of a few."

There were many nods in the crowd, agreeing with the king's sentiments. Only Margaret knew he didn't mean a single word he said. He was Crompton's murderer, and only the two of them—Sarah and Vojvo, too—were aware of that fact.

"He will be deeply missed by all, and Anatalia will never be the same without him," the king finished.

Margaret tried not to scoff. She was glad she did not have to suffer through his lies for longer than necessary—she assumed that he did not have many kind words to say about his cousin. Margaret wanted to stay with the funeral party in the event Lillian would need her assistance, though she doubted it would be called upon—the queen had made no attempt to recall Margaret back to her service since her request to spend time with Annabel.

The pallbearers came forward once the king finished speaking. Sorren himself joined them, taking his place at the head of the casket. As they passed, Dowager Duchess Cecily fell in line to follow her late husband. The queen and the remainder of the duchess's entourage followed after, Margaret taking up the rear. The casket was placed on a horse-drawn funeral caisson, already blanketed with flowers. The pallbearers mounted black stallions, their coats shining brightly, and surrounded the caisson. A riderless horse, with boots turned backward, followed behind at an even pace.

The streets were lined with mourners, all throwing flowers at the funeral parade. Margaret marveled at the amount of people who made the journey for Lord General Crompton's funeral. They walked the winding road to the palace, where he was to be entombed in the catacombs beneath. Once the parade reached the entrance to the catacombs, only the pallbearers and Duchess Cecily were permitted to enter.

Margaret settled to wait with the other ladies for the funeral party's return, her back to the entrance of the catacombs.

Lillian turned to Margaret with a glare. "You may go now, Lady Margaret."

"But—"

"You are dismissed, Lady Margaret," Lillian snapped. "I don't want to see you again until I summon you."

Margaret swallowed hard. "As you wish, Your Majesty." She curtsied, leaving to the sound of whispers.

A month after Lord General Crompton's funeral, Lillian finally recalled Margaret to her service. Margaret avoided eye contact with Lillian and Sorren as much as possible, not daring to let the guilt her eyes held reveal her secrets.

Sorren entered the queen's sitting room, causing the ladies to promptly rise and curtsy. "Lady Margaret will join me in the garden to discuss a matter regarding her young acquaintance Annabel."

Lillian raised her eyebrows high.

"As you wish." She turned a gelid eye on Margaret. "You may go, Lady Margaret."

Margaret curtsied low to her, keeping her eyes downcast. "Thank you, Your Majesty."

The king held out his arm for Margaret to take when she joined him.

"Your Majesty, this is certainly a surprise," Margaret said, walking with him to the maze.

"I wanted to see you," Sorren admitted.

"You couldn't have waited until tonight?" Margaret felt her hackles raise. He was going to get them caught, and Margaret did not have much to fall back on to save her reputation if anyone found out. "You'll make the queen even more suspicious of me!"

"I will deal with the queen." Sorren shrugged off her concern. "Are you drinking your tea?"

"Yes." Margaret had surprisingly enjoyed the taste with a bit of honey and milk.

"Good," the king said, pulling her into an alcove in the maze.

"Your Majesty!" Margaret exclaimed.

"Hush," the king told her before his lips were on hers. He sat on the bench in the alcove and pulled her onto his lap. She had learned over the past year to return his kisses with enthusiasm—real or otherwise—lest she have bruises on her arms as a reminder.

Margaret wrapped her arms around his neck, breaking their kiss. "Your Majesty, please. Not in the open like this."

Sorren gave her a boyish grin. "I have guards at all the entrances to the garden to keep others out." He promptly buried his face in her neck.

Margaret gasped when she heard a guardsman clear his throat behind her. She tried to stand, but the king kept her firmly in place. "Majesty, please," she whispered quietly to him.

"I specifically said we were not to be disturbed, Orland," the king said heatedly. "What is it?"

"Her Majesty wishes to enter the gardens. She says she is feeling chilled and wishes to warm herself in the sun," Orland said.

"Restrict her to a small portion of the garden, and keep her far away from here."

"Yes, Your Majesty." The guardsman bowed his way out of the alcove.

Margaret was happy when they were finished. "Majesty, please, next time, let it not be in such a public place," she pleaded.

Sorren gently stroked her cheek. "As you wish, my dear. Next time, we will be where Lillian cannot disturb us."

Margaret squeezed his arm. "Thank you."

"I will take you back to Her Majesty," Sorren said as Margaret straightened her skirts.

Margaret's anxiety grew the closer they came to finding the queen. After this, there was no doubt in her mind the queen would know she was the king's mistress. She walked as slowly as she possibly could alongside the king to avoid seeing the look in the queen's eyes.

"My dearest, I'm here to return Lady Margaret to you," Sorren said as the ladies curtsied to him.

"And what is it you had to discuss that was so private you felt it necessary to close off the gardens?" the queen demanded, an accusing look going to Margaret.

"That is a private matter, but if you must know, I am awarding her companion Annabel's father with a place among the knights in the Order of the Gauntlet."

Margaret tried to keep the surprise from her face. "His Majesty has decided to help ease my time of trying to find Annabel a husband in a most gracious manner."

"How gracious, indeed," the queen said tartly, obviously not mollified with their answers.

"I will leave you to whatever it is you ladies do here," Sorren said before leaving Margaret to face the full judgment of the queen.

Lillian gave Margaret a withering glare and sat closely with the dowager duchess, whispering to her.

Margaret sat awkwardly off to the side of the rest of the ladies. She could feel the icy stares of the other women as she refused to look at them. Her shame would have shone clearly on her face if she had.

"Lady Margaret, won't you stay behind and attend me while the ladies go and bring refreshments?" the queen asked.

"Of course, Your Majesty," Margaret said, her stomach churning. "Nothing would bring me greater pleasure."

"Good." Lillian dismissed the rest of the ladies with a flick of her hand.

Margaret moved closer to the queen, as would be expected of her. "How may I serve you?"

"You can stop your affair with my husband, Lady Margaret," Lillian spat, hate in her eyes. "His Majesty will not divorce me for a harlot trying to raise her position."

Margaret paled. "Surely, Your Majesty, I don't know what it is you are talking about."

"You know exactly what I'm talking about, Lady Margaret," Lillian hissed at her. "He has taken mistresses before, and I am always the one he returns to!"

Margaret looked at her hands resting in her lap. She was in an impossible situation. She was not a willing participant in the king's affair. Margaret could not tell her queen that the only reason that Margaret was allowing the king to defile her as often as he pleased was to keep her from being executed.

"Your Majesty, I have no knowledge of what you're talking about," Margaret said more firmly.

"Lady Margaret, you do know what I'm talking about," she yelled, standing in her frustration. "How dare you tell me otherwise?"

Margaret stood as well, watching Lillian anxiously. "Your Majesty, please, really I don't know—"

Lillian cut her off with a slap. "Lady Margaret, you are my husband's mistress, and I will not have you sitting in my company day after day, knowing that my husband is bedding you whenever and wherever he pleases!"

Margaret's cheeks flushed hotly. "Your Majesty, are you dismissing me from your service?"

"Are you daft? Yes, I am dismissing you!" Lillian yelled, sitting as if overcome with exhaustion, shading her eyes with a hand over her brow. "Get out of my sight."

Margaret curtsied quickly and scurried away. She touched her cheek, still hot with embarrassment. She was terrified the news would spread throughout the court and she would be shunned by the men and women alike. The queen was a vengeful woman, but Margaret was not sure if she would embarrass herself by telling everyone.

"Sarah?" Margaret called out when she reached her apartments.

"My lady?" Sarah looked perplexed that her mistress was back so early.

"The queen dismissed me from her ladies," Margaret told her in a whispery voice, covering her mouth with a shaking hand as the horror of what was happening set in. "She knows."

"What?" Sarah breathed, aghast.

Margaret sat with a plop on the white couch in the center of the room. "The king made it all but obvious this afternoon."

"What's going to happen now?" There was dread in Sarah's voice.

"I don't know," Margaret said hopelessly. "I don't know what will happen if the queen tells someone."

 **36**

arah returned from the city streets of Jalmar, where she was running errands for her mistress. She had stopped by the post as requested for Lady Margaret, though she was surprised that there was a letter from the Gollacks. She dutifully brought back the assorted items she had been sent to get. She was astonished—and thrilled—she had lasted this long in the service of Lady Margaret. Sarah was not, in her opinion, a particularly skilled lady's maid.

Sarah curtsied before she presented the letter to her mistress. "Will there be anything else, my lady?"

"No, Sarah, thank you," Lady Margaret said.

Sarah went to clear off the table from her breakfast. She watched as Lady Margaret tore open the particularly fat letter and discarded the outer portion for a smaller letter within. A bright smile donned her mistress's face as she read the letter.

"It's from Liam," Lady Margaret commented when she caught Sarah looking. "He's finally sent me a letter in return."

"I'm happy for you, my lady," Sarah said with a smile.

She had not understood the fuss that went along with the man who had sent the letter. Her own country of Mekhor had not participated in the war against Salatia and tried to stay neutral in any talks that the country participated in during the end of the war.

A blush settled on Lady Margaret's cheeks when she finished the letter.

Sarah finished her chores and stood in front of the countess. "May I have the rest of the afternoon off, my lady?"

"Of course, Sarah," she said with a smile. "Will you be going out?"

"Yes, my lady," Sarah said.

"Be safe," was all she said before turning to write her letter.

Sarah went to her room in the servant's hall and changed her clothes. She had seen George out in the city, and he had invited her to dinner that evening. He told her he would show up whether she could be released from her duties to dine with him or not.

Sarah let her hair down from the tight bun she wore during her work day. She smudged kohl on her eyes after changing into a simple dress. She wasted no time in making her way to the city for dinner. She did not want to leave time for her mistress to change her mind and request her presence to ready her for dinner.

Sarah searched the crowd for the tall redhead. She saw the gaunt man, freckles covering his pale face and large lips that seemed to protrude out due to his sunken cheeks.

"George!" Sarah called so he knew she had come.

A large smile split George's face when he saw. "Hello, Lamb," he cooed at her.

Sarah gave him a shy smile. "Lady Margaret has given me the night off."

"Good," George said. "That means that I get to spend as much time with you as I wish."

Sarah blushed again. "Shall we proceed to dinner?"

"If you'd like," George said. "Or we could walk the market first if you aren't hungry yet."

"I wouldn't mind the walk."

George grabbed her hand. "The market it is, my lamb."

Sarah almost took her hand from his, but allowed him to lead her quickly through the clusters of people. They darted in and out of the people at a dizzying pace.

"Slow down!" Sarah called out.

George only slowed when he got them to where he wanted to go. There were fewer people there, and crushed flowers littered the cobblestone street. "This is my favorite part of the market."

"Why's that?" Sarah asked curiously.

"At the end of the day, all the flowers are given away or set to dry." George grabbed a bouquet of flowers for Sarah and handed it to her. "For you, my lamb."

Sarah blushed, smelling the flowers. "Thank you," she said sweetly.

George grinned at her, grabbing her hand once more as he walked her through the market. "Where are you from, Sarah?"

"Mekhor," Sarah responded quietly.

George's brow crinkled. "You don't look like you're from Mekhor,"

"My mother was Frasiscan."

"How is it that you've become the lady's maid for Anatalian nobility?" George's eyebrows were raised while he questioned her.

"I traveled to Anatalia for a new start, and I happened upon Lady Margaret as she was interviewing for the position, and she hired me," Sarah told him as they walked together.

"Why did you leave Mekhor?"

"Does it matter?" Sarah demanded.

"No, Lamb, it doesn't," George soothed. "You're just bein' tight-lipped about the whole thing."

"I just needed a new start," Sarah said quietly.

George let the subject drop, walking her to a tavern. "Are you hungry?"

"Famished," came her vehement reply.

George led her to the Whistling Squire. Sarah smiled at him over her shoulder, sitting when he pulled her chair out for her. She was glad to see that he had manners.

George ordered for both of them and got them a pitcher of wine to start with. He poured for her first before attending to his cup. He held up his cup to toast her. "To a wonderful evening so far."

"A wonderful evening so far indeed." Sarah clinked her glass to his.

George took a long drink from his cup, pouring himself more when he finished. "How long are you plannin' to stay in the capital?"

"As long as Lady Margaret remains here," Sarah told him. "I enjoy very much being her lady's maid. It's full of intrigue and never a dull moment."

"I'd ask you what kind of intrigue, but I doubt you'd tell me," George said.

"You're right, I would not," Sarah told him with a level gaze. "I am very loyal to Lady Margaret."

"That is good." George took another sip of his drink, watching her over the rim of his glass. "It is good to be loyal to someone."

"Are you loyal to anyone?" Sarah asked.

"I was," George said. "I was loyal to my brother until he died in the war. And now I've no elder to be loyal to but myself."

"I'm very sorry to hear that," Sarah said as she finished her glass of wine.

George immediately poured her another, shrugging. "It is the way of the world, my lamb."

Sarah found out more about George the more he drank. He was the second oldest of eight and had seen three of his sisters married, one of his brothers die in the war, and the other three children, one girl and two boys, working his cooper shop. There was a sadness on his face when he talked about his family. Sarah gently touched his hand to show her support.

"Enough about me." George cleared his throat. "I know nothin' about you, my lamb."

"Why do you keep calling me 'my lamb'?" Sarah didn't mind him calling her that, but she wanted to know why.

"It's what my Mam called all the pretty girls that came into her shop," George said, making Sarah blush.

"I see," Sarah said. "Then, you're more than welcome to keep calling me that."

"I planned on it," George told her with a grin.

Sarah was glad when the food finally came to their table. There was too much wine on her stomach, and she did not want to have an unfortunate headache in morning readying Lady Margaret. On the plates were lamb chops with smashed potatoes that had been smothered with gravy. Plated in a messy pile next to the potatoes was spinach drenched with cream. She inhaled deeply, smelling the garlic, and let out a low moan. "This looks delicious."

"You're in for a treat," George said excitedly, not waiting for her to start before digging into his food.

Sarah tentatively tried the lamb, closing her eyes as the smoky flavor flooded her mouth. She held up the meat on her fork. "How is it that I've never heard about this before?"

"I imagine that you haven't talked to many people out in the city to find out about it," George said. "You seem like a secretive girl who doesn't talk to many people."

Sarah pushed her lips out in a small pout. He was right, she was secretive and didn't talk to many people. As it was, Lady Margaret knew the most about her, and that wasn't much. "What do you want to know?"

"Why did you leave Mekhor?"

"I was the kitchen maid to Lord Baas Nakato of the Udo province. Another maid blamed me for a theft of one of the lady's rings," Sarah said, a scowl on her face. "I hardly ever saw the upstairs and stuck to the kitchens."

"You could have stayed there if they couldn't prove it, Lamb," George told her.

"Lady Adaeze threatened to have me branded for thievery and thrown out if I did not leave on my own," Sarah growled. "I did not want to tarnish my name, especially as I did not commit the crime."

"You wanted to stay an honorable woman," sympathized George. "There's nothin' wrong with that."

"So I came to Anatalia to get away from the rumors that would ruin my chances of having a proper job."

"Well, you'll be free of rumor here," George assured her. "Is that why you've been so secretive?"

"Yes," Sarah said.

In truth, it had been easier to tell him that she had been labeled by her household as a thief than she thought it would be. As soon as the rumor had been started by the other maid, it had run rampant through the rest of the servants. Sarah did not want to be labeled as such in her new life here with Lady Margaret.

"Why didn't go to your family in Frasisca?" George asked.

"My mother's family disowned her when she married my father. She was already pregnant with me when she married him." Sarah shrugged. "She never heard from them again."

"Where are your parents now?"

Sarah sighed, sitting back in her seat. "The last I heard, my father was working as a bar keep, and my mother was a maid at an inn."

George frowned at the nonchalance with which she answered.

"They were not the greatest of parents, George," Sarah said when she saw his look. "They sold me when I was eight in order to make money for them instead of protecting me from the world, and I've only seen them once since."

George raised his eyebrows at her admission. "That sounds an unhappy childhood."

"It was, and I'm happy to be out of Mekhor and here doing work that I enjoy."

"I'm happy that you're here too," George told her.

Sarah only smiled, taking a sip of her wine.

Once they were done with dinner, George walked her back. Sarah leaned on his arm, her stomach full. "Why is it you'll not meet me at the palace?"

George patted her hand before gesturing to the homeless settling in front of closed shops for the night. "Because this is what the palace has done."

Sarah watched a mother pull her children close under her shawl as she leaned back against the shop wall. "Surely, there are downtrodden everywhere."

"The Platiri taxes for their extravagance has made more and more homeless as the years go on." George's eyes were hard. "Ten years ago even, you'd only see one or two beggars in the city, and now? Look at all of them."

Sarah's shoulders dropped the more people on the street they saw. "What's being done to help them?"

"More taxes." George shrugged. "And more parties."

How had no one helped them get back on their feet instead of letting them stay on the street? She had seen some of the dinners the royals had hosted for the whole of the nobility—they were lavish, and the food went to the servants in the morning, but even then, there was an overabundance of it, and it spoiled.

"But what can be done?"

George sighed. "Plenty. Just one of those dinners at the palace could get half of these people off the street and somewhere they can be useful. But they won't, because the people like us don't matter to them."

"That can't be tr—"

"Lamb, I promise you it is," George said. "Even your lady does nothing for them."

Sarah bristled. "Lady Margaret is a good person."

"I'm sure she is," George said with a shrug. "But she has the ear of the king and does nothing for anyone but herself. None of them do."

Sarah was relieved when the palace came into view. "I should get back to Lady Margaret to see if she needs help dressing for dinner."

George turned to her, kissing her hand. "I hope to see you again soon, Lamb."

She smiled. "I hope so too," she said, though she wasn't sure she meant it.

37

"**D**a!" was called as soon as Liam walked in the door.

He smiled, letting out a happy sigh. "Jamie."

"Ellie came to see me today," Jamie said. "I did as ye bid an' told her how I feel."

Liam clapped him on the shoulder. "How did that go?"

"She felt the same." Jamie grinned widely. "We're courtin' now."

"Your mother will be happy." He put his tools down. "You should bring Ellie here to meet her. She's been excited since I told her I saw you with a young lady."

"Ye told her?"

Liam nodded. "Your mother and I don't have any secrets."

"I'm surprised she hasna been pesterin' me about the whole thing," Jamie said.

"She knows you'll tell her when you're ready." Liam clapped him on the shoulder again, pulling Jamie under his arm. "Why don't you tell me how it went?"

Jamie's cheeks colored as another grin split his face. "When she came to the fields to bring me lunch again, I asked if she was attached to anyone. When she said no, I asked if she'd like to be attached to me, for I liked her verra much."

"And obviously, she said yes."

"Aye," Jamie confirmed. "Verra enthusiastically—she nearly gave some of the other workers an attack."

Liam laughed. "I suppose she's been waiting some time for you to ask."

"She said she was starting to think me daft after the first few meals she brought didna result in my asking."

Liam laughed harder. "Generally, when a woman brings you food, it means she likes you."

Jamie shrugged, his cheeks coloring. "I thought she was bein' nice."

"Well, now you know for sure," Liam said. "Make sure to tell your mother before the day gets away from you."

Liam turned when the door to the private portion of their home opened. Jamie stood in the doorway, looking around nervously.

"Ma?" he tentatively called.

"She's in the slaughterhouse," Liam answered.

Jamie moved further into the room, revealing Ellie. She was a lithe girl, her skin darkened into a deep tan and her hair bleached by the sun. "I'd like ye to meet Eleanor Kaneh."

Liam rose from the table, coming to face the nervous young lady. "It's a pleasure to meet you, Miss Kaneh. I have heard wonderful things of you."

Ellie blushed a rosy pink, looking back to Jamie. "Thank ye, sir, it's nice to meet ye as well."

Liam smiled at her encouragingly. "I'll go get your mother, Jamie. Why don't you get out a pitcher of wine?"

Jami launched into action. "Aye, that would be good."

Holding in his amusement, Liam exited the kitchen to retrieve Gretta.

"And ye think I am the worrit one." He heard Ellie's voice wobble with suppressed laughter. "Ye look as though ye mean to piss yerself the moment ye see yer Mam."

Liam tried not to laugh as he went to the slaughterhouse. He opened the door just a hair to see where she was. "Gretta?"

"Behind the door, love."

He tried to open the door as little as possible so he wouldn't hit her with it as he snuck through. "Jamie's young lady is here."

Gretta gasped, almost touching her face with her bloodied hands before she pulled them away with a grimace. "I'll be ready in a minute."

Liam kissed her on the cheek. "She's got a fire to her—I heard her telling Jamie he looked ready to piss himself on my way out," Liam said, laughing. "I think you'll like her."

Gretta grinned, waving her hands at him to shoo him away. "Away wi' ye. The faster I'm done, the faster I can meet her."

Liam went back to the kitchen. He found Jamie with Ellie in his arms, ready to kiss her. He cleared his throat, making Jamie jump. "Your mother will be in in a moment, Jamie."

Heat radiated from Jamie's face. "Da, when did ye come in?"

Liam smirked, saying nothing.

"Da?" Ellie asked, looking between Liam and Jamie. "Yer Mam remarried?"

"Ahh, no," Jamie explained awkwardly, "we call him Da on the fact he decided to be our da for a time."

Shifting uncomfortably, Liam's face broke into a relieved smile when he saw Gretta. "Here's your mother now."

Gretta straightened her skirts and ran her hands over her hair to smooth it. She came to stand beside Liam, looking first at Jamie and then Eleanor. Liam could see Gretta's slow examination of the young lady, intentionally criticizing her. He turned his attention to the young couple and found them shifting uncomfortably.

"Aren't ye goin' to introduce me to yer lady?" Gretta asked, raising a sardonic brow.

Jamie cleared his throat, stepping forward to stand between the two women without blocking either of their views. "Ma, this is Eleanor Kaneh. Ellie, my Ma, Gretta McWard."

Ellie nodded, giving Gretta a shy smile. "A pleasure to meet ye."

To break the silence, Liam cleared his throat. "Jamie, did you get the drinks?"

"Aye," came his reply, more enthused than he intended. "They're at the table."

Liam led Gretta to the table and pulled a chair out for her. He was pleased to see that Jamie emulated his performance. Liam slid a full cup to Gretta, giving her a knowing look. She was more nervous than Ellie and Jamie combined.

Gretta took a long drink before she spoke again. "Have ye met Miss Kaneh's parents yet?"

"Just her father, briefly," said Jamie, his face seeming relieved.

"I forgot to tell ye," Ellie said, chagrined. "Mam invited ye to dine with us when it's convenient for ye."

"Choose the day, and I'll be there," Jamie told her.

Ellie smiled, looking at him almost adoringly. "I'll tell Mam to plan on ye comin' on Thursday then. It's yer slow day."

Liam covertly snuck a glance at Gretta. She was covering her smile with her mug. "Are ye stayin' with us for dinner tonight, Ellie?" she asked.

"If ye'll allow me, Mrs. Mcward," answered Eleanor.

Nodding, Gretta stood. "If ye'd like to join me in the kitchen for a moment, Liam?"

He looked between the couple and Gretta a few times before Liam stood and followed Gretta into the kitchen.

She waited until they were alone before she spoke. "What d'ye think of her?" asked Gretta.

Liam shrugged. "She seems a lovely girl."

"Aye, she does," Gretta agreed. "D'ye think she'll be well-suited for wee Jamie?"

"You know Jamie far better than I do." Liam rested a reassuring hand on her waist. "You'll know by the end of the night whether she'll be well-suited for him or not."

Gretta nodded again. "Aye, ye're right."

"I know," Liam told her. "Why don't you pull out dinner, and I'll call Simon and Eli down."

Gretta nodded, letting out a nervous sigh. "Aye, thank ye Liam."

Liam brought the boys downstairs and sat as Gretta put the roast on the table. "Will ye pray for us, Liam?" Gretta asked, looking at him with raised brows.

"Uh...yes...?" What was she doing? They had never prayed in the household before. He wasn't even sure he knew where the church was. Worse, Liam didn't know the prayers typical of Olam—only Theotes. "Our E-Eternal Olam—"

Jamie cleared his throat. "Mayhap—just this once, Ma—we dinna have to pray."

Liam shot Jamie a grateful look. "Perhaps Jamie is right. We don't want to make Miss Kaneh uncomfortable."

"I dinna mind," Ellie said shyly, "though I canna say we're much the prayin' type."

Gretta opened her mouth to speak, but Liam cut her off quickly. "That's settled then. We'll skip tonight and start our meal." He stood, carving the roast and doling out portions, starting with Gretta and finishing with himself.

Gretta turned her eyes to Ellie. "Will ye no tell us about yerself?"

Panic flitted across the young girl's face, her eyes going wide. "I'm a person."

Liam coughed, nearly choking on a piece of carrot. He glanced at Jamie, who was holding back laughter behind his napkin. And Ellie was the one who thought Jamie looked like he'd piss himself.

"Aye, that ye are," Gretta said before turning to Simon. "How was your day?"

"Fine, Ma," Simon said. "The same as always."

Ellie slumped back against her chair, letting out a slow breath.

Liam let out a sigh when he lay back in bed. "That could have gone better."

"I thought ye said she had a fire." Gretta lay next to him, resting her head on his chest. "She seems a shy lass to me."

"She seemed more spirited before she was with all of us." Liam wrapped his arm around Gretta, pulling her closer. "She was probably nervous to meet you."

"Aye, yer prob'ly right." Gretta curled her fingers around Liam's waist, her breath fanning against his chest. "What did ye think of her?"

"She seems sweet—and Jamie is head over heels for her." He smiled, thinking of how Jamie looked at Ellie. "And I think she feels the same."

"I wish I could stop him growin' up fast." Gretta sighed. "I canna say I'm quite ready for him to be off on his own, a married man."

Liam kissed the top of her head. "You've got time yet. They won't be getting married tomorrow." He blew out the candle next to him. "Now let's go to sleep. Morning already comes too early."

38

Margaret tried to quell her nerves as they waited for Annabel's first suitor to arrive. She had not been able to spend as much time mingling among the eligible bachelors to find a suitable husband for Annabel as she would have liked, but she had managed a chance encounter with the Baron Lavon as she was returning from the market a few days prior. Unfortunately for them, both Lords Gregory and Thomas had returned to Glessic in her absence from the hall gatherings.

Annabel paced around Margaret's antechamber, rubbing the pads of her first three fingers together as they waited for him to arrive. "What if he doesn't like me?"

"Then, he's a fool and not worthy of your time," Margaret said. "Now sit down. You'll run a track through the floor at that pace."

In truth, Margaret was just as nervous as Annabel was.

Annabel sat across from Margaret. She inhaled deeply, smoothing out her skirts. "Is it always this nerve-racking?"

Margaret gave her a gentle smile. "Always."

Sarah entered the room. "My lady, Baron Lavon is here."

Annabel stood quickly, an excited look on her face.

"Sit down, Annabel—and look occupied!" Margaret snapped.

Annabel sat with a plop, picking up the book in front of her on the table.

Margaret stood when Baron Lavon came near and smiled. "My lord, welcome."

The baron bowed and kissed her hand. "My lady, it was an honor to receive your invitation." His eyes were intent on his face. "You look lovely today."

Margaret kept the smile on her face, turning to motion at Annabel. "Baron Lavon, may I introduce you to Lady Annabel Lurant of Loford? She has joined my household to learn about court life and find a husband here in the capital."

"A pleasure, I'm sure," the baron said in a bored voice.

Annabel stood and curtsied to him. "My lord, Lady Margaret has told me so much about you."

"I'm sure she has."

Annabel stared at him awkwardly, waiting for him to say something else.

The baron raised his eyebrows, looking at Lady Margaret. "Does the country bumpkin know how to speak, or is she here to gawp at her betters?"

Margaret watched as Annabel blushed brightly. "My lord, that was unkind. Lady Annabel is a very nice young woman, whom I'm sure you'd like very much if you got to know her."

Realization dawned on his face. "Is this why you invited me here? For her?" the baron demanded. "Does this mule of a girl even know how to read or write, being of such low birth?"

Annabel's eyes filled with tears. "Excuse me, my lady, I'm feeling quite unwell at the moment," she said as she rushed from the room.

Margaret glared at Baron Lavon. "Out!"

The baron gave her a mocking bow before leaving.

Annabel was in her room when Margaret reached it. "Annabel?" Margaret called out gently from outside the door.

Annabel opened the door, her face red and blotchy from crying. She quickly wiped her face of the recently fallen tears. "I'm sorry, Lady Margaret. I couldn't stay there."

"The baron was atrocious, Annabel," Margaret told her. "I had no idea he would behave so poorly."

Annabel opened her door wider to let Margaret in. "I know you didn't, Lady Margaret."

Margaret sat in one of the chairs in the room. "We'll find you another prospective husband soon enough."

"What if the next one is the same?" Annabel asked anxiously.

"I'll make sure to learn more about him before I introduce you, Annabel," Margaret promised. "I will not put you through another fiasco."

"Thank you, Lady Margaret," Annabel breathed. "I just want someone who will be kind to me."

"And we'll find you just that," Margaret said. "Have you heard any news from your father as to when he'll be here for the knighting ceremony?"

Annabel's face brightened at the mention of her father. "He'll be here a week early to familiarize himself with Sir Edward Grey and the other members of the order."

"Wonderful," Margaret said with a bright smile. "I'll start looking for rooms for your father to stay in."

"Thank you, Lady Margaret." Annabel gushed.

Margaret smiled at her. "Would you like to accompany me tomorrow to find them? Tonight I will ask the king's permission."

"I would love to," Annabel said. "I've never had a tour of the palace."

"Wonderful, I'll be here early," Margaret said, turning to leave.

"My lady?" Annabel asked quietly. "Why aren't you in the queen's service any longer?"

Margaret put on a tight smile. "A difference in opinion, Annabel. The queen can be very high-minded at times about things."

"Yes, Lady Margaret," Annabel said quickly.

Margaret left the room, going to her own apartments. She needed to get a list of the eligible bachelors who were currently at court. She would even be willing to introduce Annabel to bachelors of the foreign countries. The men of Glessic were known for being particularly handsome, and to frequent the Anatalian court in search of wives.

Margaret found a small piece of parchment. It was better to ask the king now for permission before he started drinking for the night at dinner.

"Sarah?" Margaret called as she wrote her note.

I need to see you.

M

Sarah came into the room. "Yes, my lady?"

"Please find someone to give this to His Majesty."

Sarah took the note and curtsied. "Yes, my lady."

"Come back quickly," Margaret commanded as she left the room.

Sarah returned to Margaret's apartments, her cheeks red and slightly out of breath. "The king has received your note, my lady, and immediately excused himself."

There was a hurried knock at the door.

"Please get that, Sarah," Margaret said as she pulled out her hair. The king liked her long tresses flowing down her back.

"His Majesty is here to see you, my lady," Sarah said as the king unnecessarily plowed past her to get to Margaret.

"Leave us," the king told Sarah, wrapping his arms around Margaret.

"Yes, Your Majesty," Sarah curtsied low before leaving.

Sorren kissed Margaret heatedly, fingers in her hair. "You needed to see me?"

"I would like your permission to find and ready a room for Annabel's father," Margaret told him. "I would like to take her around tomorrow to help me pick one."

"That is what you called me out on a meeting of the nobles for?" Sorren demanded, balling his fist in her hair.

Margaret let out a small cry. "Your Majesty, you're hurting me."

"I am not here to come at your beck and call," Sorren told her with a dark look, tightening his grip on her hair.

"My lord, I did not think you would leave a meeting for my note!" Margaret cried out again when he pulled her head back.

Sorren let go of her hair with a shove. "Lady Margaret, do not ever summon me again," he growled.

"Yes, Your Majesty," Margaret said meekly. "Do I have your permission?"

"Yes," he said, exasperated. "You have my permission." Sorren left the room, slamming the door behind him.

Margaret woke that morning to the king's arm wrapped around her waist. He was pressed tightly against her back, his breath fanning her neck. She looked at her forearms—dark bruises formed from the king's displeasure. He had been angrier than he had let on about her summons.

Sarah entered quietly, readying the room for their breakfast. "Your Majesty, my lady, your breakfast is ready."

Margaret rubbed the king's arm to wake him. "Majesty?"

Sorren groaned, pulling her in tighter. He kissed her shoulder and neck several times. "Yes, my dear?"

"Our breakfast is getting cold," Margaret said gently.

Sorren disentangled himself from her, turning her face to kiss her. "Good morning."

"Good morning, Your Majesty," Margaret said with a smile. She looked over at Sarah. "Sarah, I'll ready the king this morning. You can have a few hours to yourself."

"Thank you, my lady," Sarah said, muttering 'Your Majesty' before leaving.

Sorren stroked Margaret's cheek tenderly. "You'll ready me?"

"I don't think you want others at court seeing your valet coming into my room this early in the morning," Margaret told him plainly. "Very few people know about our affair as of now, and I would like for it to stay that way. I must marry some time."

Sorren furrowed his brow. "You'll marry when I say you marry."

Margaret's mouth formed a thin line. She hoped he would get bored of her sooner rather than later so that she could marry and go back to Dorcia. "Your breakfast is getting cold, Your Majesty."

Sorren ate voraciously while Margaret dressed herself. After she was done, she helped the king dress.

"Are you picking out rooms today?" he asked while she tied the front of his shirt.

"I am," Margaret told him. "After you leave, I'll fetch Lady Annabel, and we'll start our search."

"Give him something nice," Sorren said offhandedly.

"Lady Annabel will be pleased about that," Margaret said with a smile.

Sorren grabbed her face gently, kissing her tenderly. "I will see you tonight."

Margaret curtsied to him as he left. She went to get Annabel after the king was out of sight. She gently knocked on Annabel's door. "Annabel? Are you awake?"

Annabel opened the door looking tired. "Yes, Lady Margaret?"

"Are you ready to search for your father's room?" Margaret asked brightly. "The process takes all day to pick one."

"Yes, my lady." Annabel yawned sleepily.

Margaret linked her arm with Annabel, a bright smile on her face. "The king has given me permission to give your father a very nice room."

"He'll be very pleased," Annabel told her. "He's been very excited."

"That's wonderful to hear," Margaret said. "I'll have Sir Edward write to your father to let him know what's expected of him."

Annabel was impressed with all of the rooms they looked at that day. The room they chose was much more spacious than Annabel's, the walls a pale yellow color with white trim and crown molding. There was a small room off to the side meant to store the guest's belongings. Against that wall was a four-poster bed made of dark cherry wood, topped with a large cherry panel. The bedding was a cream color with a twisted pinch in each square section of the covering and three decorative pillows of cream, yellow, and burgundy that matched the color scheme of the room.

In front of the bed was a small fainting couch of burgundy and gold. At the far end of the room, there were three floor-length bay windows covered with burgundy and gold curtains, opened to let in the light. Next to the windows there were portraits of King Sorren and Queen Lillian that Margaret thought very accurately depicted the monarchs. Facing the room there were two plush burgundy armchairs with a small table between them. In the center of the room, there was a small chandelier that hung from the ceiling with four sconces that were to be lit in the evening hour. There were several tables around the room that held candles to keep the resident from being in the dark.

"Lady Margaret, this room is perfect for him," Annabel gushed. "He'll love it."

"I'll have Sarah tell the servants to make sure the room is clean for him when he arrives," Margaret said to her young charge. "Now what do you say about going to the hall and seeing if there are any other young men you might find interesting?"

Annabel hesitated, chewing on her bottom lip. "What if there's another like Baron Lavon?"

Margaret tried to smile comfortingly. "I think if you're there from the start, we can avoid another incident like that." She linked arms with Annabel. "Shall we?"

A slow smile spreading on her face, Annabel nodded. "We shall."

39

Sarah took her free morning to see George. She had not previously minded the small amount of time that she had off of work—not until she had met George. The cooper had made her laugh and blush, things she had not freely done since her parents had sold her into Lord Baas' service. She searched for him now, looking first in the flower market.

The vendors were finishing setting up their booths for the day, the colors bursting through the streets. Sarah smiled at the myriad of blooms, finding that after visiting with George, this portion had also become her favorite part. Sarah inhaled deeply as she walked through the flowers, picking up a few bouquets for Lady Margaret's chambers, having the bill sent to her. Lady Margaret would not mind—she and the king both enjoyed having fresh flowers in the rooms.

"Sarah?" George asked from behind her. "What are you doing here?"

Sarah turned to smile at him. "Lady Margaret gave me the morning off."

"That was kind of her." George grinned, wrapping his arm around her.

"Yes it was," Sarah said with a blush, putting some distance between them.

He furrowed his brow. "What's the matter, Lamb?"

"I don't want to give anyone the wrong idea about us," Sarah said shyly.

"That we are courtin'?" George asked with raised brows. "I thought that's what we're doin', Sarah."

"Are we?" This was news to Sarah. She had assumed that they were just friends who had a strong physical attraction for each other.

"If we aren't, I'd like to be," George said, pulling her back into his arms gently. "Would you like to be?"

Sarah blushed, biting her bottom lip. "I would like to be."

"Good." His wide grin was back before he gently kissed her.

Sarah pulled away from him with a blush. "Were you on your way to work?"

"Aye," confirmed George, "I was planning on sending you a bouquet today."

Sarah raised a brow, her smile deepening. "Were you?"

"I suppose now that you are here, you can pick out your own." George shrugged.

"Why not send them tomorrow?" asked Sarah.

"As you'd like, Lamb," George conceded, offering his arm. "Would you like an escort back to the palace?"

Sarah took it, leaning close to him. "Not just yet."

Smiling, George kissed the top of her head. "Will you come to my shop then?"

"For a little while," Sarah told him.

George led her through the winding backstreets to reach his shop, Clark Coopery. He held the door open for her, a wave of heat hitting them.

"Is something burning?" Sarah asked, panic edging into her voice.

"That's just Gordon charring the inside of the barrel," assured George.

"Why?"

"Flavor," George said. "We're the only ones who do it."

Sarah looked impressed. "Do you sell to the palace?"

George's face darkened slightly. "We only sell to the vineyards now."

Raising a brow, Sarah asked, "Why not?"

"I refuse to do business with anyone as corrupt as the Platiri family," George said heatedly.

"But you could make so much more money," Sarah said. "You could expand, open another shop."

"Money is worthless when you earn it doing something you know is wrong," George told her. "And supporting the Platiri family is wrong."

Sarah nodded, knowing better than he how terrible the Platiri king was. She wished Lady Margaret would flee in the night like the captain had suggested, or something other than accept her circumstances. But Sarah couldn't make Lady Margaret's decisions for her—and she certainly didn't have the responsibility that rested on her mistress's shoulders. Sarah might have stayed too if it meant getting her title and lands to ensure the prosperity of thousands of others.

"Besides, had I been so high and mighty sellin' to the palace, I doubt I'd have ever met you," George said with a grin. "And that's well worth the gold I'm not makin'."

Sarah's face heated as she tried not to smile silly. "I can't say I'm disappointed in that."

40

I t was the last week of Junmonat when Annabel's father arrived at the palace. Annabel, Margaret, and Sir Edward Grey were waiting for him in the courtyard.

"Papa!" Annabel yelled out when she saw him, running to greet the knight on his mount.

With a vigor that surprised Margaret, Sir Adam swung down from his horse to wrap his arms around his daughter. It was much the same way Margaret would have greeted her own father.

"Sir Adam, it's a pleasure to finally meet you," she said with a bow of her head.

Sir Adam bowed to her. "My lady, my daughter looks to be in good spirits."

"I've certainly tried to keep her that way," Margaret said. "I'm sure your arrival has much to do with it."

"Let us show you to your room, Papa," Annabel said excitedly.

After formal pleasantries between the two knights, Annabel and Margaret led Sir Adam to his room. "How was your journey?" Margaret asked cordially.

"Pleasantly uneventful," Sir Adam said. "I'm just happy to be reunited with my daughter."

Margaret smiled as Sir Adam wrapped his arm around Annabel's shoulder. "You'll have a few days of rest before the ceremonies begin, and then we'll have a two day feast in celebration of this honor."

"Right to business, aren't you, Lady Margaret?"

"You must be all business if you want to succeed here, Sir Adam." Margaret stopped in front of a door. "This is your room. I'll leave you and Annabel to reacquaint yourselves."

"Thank you, my lady," Sir Adam and Annabel said in turn.

The ceremony was short. The majority of the knightly orders were in attendance, as well as the lord generals of the realm—Margaret was surprised to see so many, but she was informed that any chance they got to have a lavish meal and stay in the palace, they would come.

Sir Adam wore a ceremonial robe worn by all the knights inducted into the Order of the Gauntlet. The red velvet robe was lined with ermine, with a matching trim. The back held the sigil of the order embroidered in golden thread, a gauntleted hand holding a sword at the ready.

As his only family in attendance, Annabel escorted her father down the center of the throne room where the ceremony was held, dressed in a gown Margaret commissioned for her. The hem was trimmed in the same ermine as the robe, the scarlet gown embroidered with golden flourishes to mirror the colors of the knight's order. It was a splendid sight to see the two of them walking down the aisle together. Margaret was pleased to see her handiwork running smoothly.

King Sorren and Queen Lillian sat on their thrones to hear the oaths of the knight inductee. Sir Edward presided over the ceremony, citing the new codes and duties he would expect the new elevated knight to perform as part of the order. At the end of the oaths Sir Adam made to Sir Edward and the order, Sir Edward anointed Sir Adam with holy oil in the form of a six-pointed star on the newest member of the order's forehead, and slathered the oil down Sir Adam's sword arm. Sir Adam was handed the only sword that he would be able to use from that point on, the handle gilded with a gold chainmail motif.

After Sir Adam was handed his sword, he was guided to kneel in front of the king and queen of Anatalia to swear separate oaths to the monarchs. To the king, Sir Adam swore his renewed fealty and to protect, without bias, whatever part of the realm he was in and to care for the women and children left helpless by war or other disasters. Sir Adam was required to kneel with his sword resting in his outstretched hands. "To His Majesty, I pledge my fealty to you and your house, and to serve you and your sons and for my sons to serve your son's sons."

King Sorren stood once the oath was finished and handed him one of the golden gauntlets that Sir Adam was to wear for ceremonial purposes. "I accept your oath and your fealty, Sir Knight," the king said before returning to his throne.

Sir Adam turned his attention to Queen Lillian. "To Her Majesty, I pledge on my honor to serve you to my utmost ability and to give my life in the protection of yours."

Queen Lillian went to Sir Adam, the matching golden gauntlet in her hand. "Sir Knight, I accept your oath and pray that it need never be fulfilled. Rise, Sir Knight, and sheathe your sword," the queen commanded, putting the golden gauntlets on his hands once his sword was in its scabbard, kissing both of his cheeks.

Sir Adam bowed to her, kissing her hand. "What is your first command to me, my queen?"

"Go, Sir Knight, and from this day on, protect our great realm," the queen said.

"As my queen commands," Sir Adam called, walking out of the throne room to the applause of the crowd that filled the hall.

Annabel beamed with pride, following after the royal procession to congratulate her father. She kissed both of his cheeks. "Papa, you look so wonderful!"

Sir Adam grinned at her. "Thank you, my darling."

Margaret smiled at the pair. "Congratulations, Sir Adam. The ceremony was beautiful."

Sir Adam bowed to her. "Thank you, Lady Margaret, for all your help."

"It was a pleasure, Sir Adam," Margaret said with a small nod. "Will you lead us into the feast?"

"Absolutely, my lady." He escorted Annabel on his arm to the head table, where the king and queen were already seated. It was a great honor for Sir Adam and Annabel to sit at the same table as the royal family.

Margaret sat at a table with Sir Edward that was placed next to the head table. "Sir Edward, is Lady Grey feeling unwell?"

Sir Edward beamed at her. "Our daughter has gone into her confinement, and Lady Grey has gone to join her."

Lady Margaret smiled. "I'm so pleased for you."

The feast lasted for several hours. There were thirty courses served that night, with twenty different wines imported from all over Aratia and even Tyradrica. After the dinner, there was dancing.

The king rose from his seat, going to Margaret. "Lady Margaret, will you honor me with a dance?"

"Of course, Your Majesty." Margaret placed her hand in his, following him to the center of the room.

As they danced, Margaret caught sight of the queen and Sir Adam dancing as well. Lillian whispered to him, glancing at Margaret as she did. She felt ice run down her spine when Sir Adam turned with the queen to glare at her.

The second day of feasting started earlier than the previous day's. Margaret stood with Annabel in the great hall, speaking with a Glessican nobleman. The nobleman was a tall man with rich dark eyes and sun-kissed skin. Annabel blushed every time she looked at him, and he edged closer to her every chance he got.

"My lord," Annabel started. "Where is it that you are staying?"

"I've acquired a home in the city for when I'm at the Anatalian court," Lord Stavos Costas told her, his voice heavily accented.

"Since you're so close, perhaps you could both go for a walk in the gardens tomorrow," Margaret suggested.

"I would love to if Lady Annabel is willing to join me." Lord Stavos directed a charming smile at Annabel.

Annabel blushed prettily. "I would be delighted."

Margaret gently touched Annabel's arm. "Your father is about to lead in the feast."

Stavos offered his arm to Annabel to escort her to her table, Margaret leading the way to the table closest to the head table. At tonight's feast, Sir Adam as well as Sir Edward were placed at the head table with the royal family. Sir Adam sat next to the queen, the both of them watching Margaret and Annabel.

Margaret shuddered. The way he looked at her…it was like he knew what she was doing with the king. She tried not to put too much thought into it; he'd been pleasant enough to her in conversation. It could just be his way of looking at people he didn't know well.

The feast that night was more grand, with more people in attendance, the courses and wine doubled. Sixty courses made the previous night's food seem bland by comparison. There were forty different wines, ten coming from each Frasisca, Glessic, Mekhor and Anatalia. The Anatalian monarchs spared no expense when it came to entertaining their court and feasting days. Margaret spent a portion of the feast circulating with Annabel to show her to the eligible bachelors looking for a quick marriage.

Lord Stavos came up to the two ladies. "Lady Annabel, will you honor me with a dance?"

"I believe I will, Lord Stavos," Annabel said with a blush.

Margaret watched the pair dance for several dances, Annabel blushing frequently and Stavos looking delighted that she was with him. Margaret's charge whispered to the Glessican nobleman, and he returned her to Margaret.

"My lady, I noticed that you are without a partner this evening," Lord Stavos commented. "Would you care to join me for a dance?"

"I would, thank you, Lord Stavos." Margaret took his hand, letting him lead her to the other dancers. "Annabel seems to be quite taken with you my lord."

"I'm quite taken with her myself, Lady Margaret," Stavos confided.

She smiled brightly, leaning in slightly. "I'm pleased to hear it."

Margaret turned when she heard a chair sharply scrape against the marble floor. Sir Adam was barreling toward her, his face darkly clouded.

"Are you going to sleep with him also to ensure he marries my daughter, just like you slept with the king for my knighthood?" Sir Adam screamed at her.

The color drained from Margaret's face, and she began to tremble. "Sir Adam—"

"Hold your tongue, sir, when speaking to a lady," Lord Stavos defended her.

"Don't you defend this harlot!" Sir Adam yelled, throwing his golden gauntlets at Margaret's feet. "Keep them, Lady Margaret. You earned them, not me!"

Lord Stavos placed himself between Margaret and the angry knight. "Go sit, sir. You've had too much of the wine tonight."

Sir Adam pointed a shaking finger at Margaret. "I will not have my daughter parading around with a whore," he screamed at her before finally storming out of the hall.

The room grew silent with all eyes on Margaret. She glanced around to look for Annabel, instead seeing the queen barely concealing her delighted smile.

"My lady, are you all right?" Lord Stavos asked her in a hushed tone.

"Yes," she said simply. Holding her head high, she walked out of the hall to nothing but the sound of her own heels clicking on the marble floor, all eyes watching her leave the room.

Margaret quickly went to her apartments. She waited until she was in her room before she let out any noise. She closed her door, leaning against it, covering her mouth and letting out a small sob. Margaret went into her bedroom, throwing herself on the bed, feeling her sobs overtake her.

"My lady?" Sarah called out, distressed at the sight of her sobbing mistress. "My lady, what's wrong?"

"They know, Sarah!" Margaret sobbed. "They all know!"

"Who knows, my lady?" Sarah asked. "What do they know?"

Margaret sat up, wiping her face clear of tears only to have them be quickly replaced by fresh ones. "Sir Adam found out that I've been with the king and yelled it at me in front of the entire court, and he's going to take Annabel away. He yelled, 'I don't want my daughter parading around with a whore!'" Margaret felt another sob escape through the hand she had covered her mouth with.

Sarah covered her own mouth with both her hands. "Oh, my lady…"

"What am I going to do?" Margaret asked Sarah through tears.

"You'll think of something." Sarah led her to her vanity and started taking down her hair, gently combing it out.

Margaret was only starting to relax when a timid knock sounded on the door. "Sarah, would you please answer the door?"

Sarah opened the door. "Lady Annabel," Sarah said in a surprised tone.

"May I please see Lady Margaret?" Annabel asked.

Sarah showed her into Margaret's bedroom, where she still sat at her vanity, wiping her tears. "My lady, Lady Annabel is here to see you."

Margaret felt the color creep into her cheeks. "Annabel, what are you doing here?"

"My father and I are leaving tonight." Annabel said. "Is it true? What my father said?"

"Which part, Annabel? He yelled a lot of things at me," Margaret said tartly.

"That you whored yourself to get my father in the Order of the Gauntlet," Annabel spat out.

"Lady Annabel!" Sarah cried out, her face aghast.

Margaret held her hand up to quiet Sarah. "The king used it as an excuse with the queen to cover our affair, yes."

Annabel covered her face. "How could you do this to us? Now we'll always be associated with the name of a whore!"

Margaret stood, anger boiling. "How could I do this to *you*? How could I raise your father's income, standing in society, and your ability for a better marriage? You're right, how dare I."

"By having an affair with the king!" Annabel pointed out with a raised voice.

"Get out," Margaret told her coldly.

It angered her that Annabel could only hear her father's words and not see all Margaret had tried to do for her and her family. She did not want to bother herself with someone such as that in her household any longer.

"Go home and marry a commoner," Margaret sneered. "That's all you have the aptitude for."

Annabel let out an indignant huff before storming out, slamming the door behind her.

Margaret ran her hand over her face, sitting wearily. "Sarah, please don't let anyone else in tonight."

"Of course, my lady," Sarah said, and returned to brushing out her hair. "That was very rude of Lady Annabel."

"She's had a very big shock," Margaret commented. "There was potential for her, but she is not cut out for life here."

Sarah turned quickly when she heard Margaret's bedroom door open, ready to reprimand anyone who dared to enter. She curtsied deeply when she saw that it was the king. "Your Majesty."

Margaret stood slowly. "Please, Your Majesty, I would like to be left alone after tonight's ordeal."

"Leave us," the king commanded.

"Yes, Your Majesty," Sarah said meekly. She set down the hair brush and gave Margaret an apologetic look.

"Sit," Sorren said to Margaret, grabbing the brush.

Margaret did as she was told. "I'm sorry for tonight. I have no idea how he found out."

"The queen is trying to run you out of court." Sorren gently ran the brush through her hair.

"Why would she do that?" Margaret looked at him through the mirror. "You've had other mistresses before me."

"I've kept you the longest," Sorren said quietly, "and it's making her anxious."

Margaret searched his face in the mirror. "What's going to happen to restore my reputation?"

"The queen has had her own indiscretions in the past that can be renewed for the public eye," the king said. "She'll make a mistake soon enough."

"Perhaps if I had my title officially restored, I could return to Dorcia until this is forgotten," Margaret told him, turning around to face him. "Or, at the very least, not the main subject of gossip."

Sorren cupped her cheek gently. "Why don't we get you into bed, my dear? You look exhausted."

Margaret nodded, knowing that he was avoiding her subtle inquiry to when she would be able to officially claim Dorcia as her own since she was not a male heir.

The king undressed Margaret to her chemise and helped her into her bed before undressing himself and joining her. He held her close, stroking her long hair. "This will all blow over soon, my dear."

"What if it doesn't?" A fresh wave of tears rolled down her cheeks. Margaret felt the king pull her tightly against his side, wiping away her tears.

"It will go away. I'll make sure of it." Sorren kissed her forehead.

The gesture strangely comforted Margaret, despite the fact that this man had forced her into being his mistress. She had accepted her servitude to him and even come to enjoy the conversations they had once she had paid the night's installment of her debt.

"Go to sleep, my dear," the king said. "This will all look better in the morning."

41

Liam made his way to the Frothing Wench to enjoy a drink after a long day at the smithy. A rarer occurrence now—he usually went straight home to Gretta. At this hour, most of the patrons were the farmers who did not want to be at home with their wives, and the drunks who littered the town. Liam liked to sip his dark ale in silence while he listened to the other men forget their troubles.

Many of the men there had been to war with him, albeit on the opposing side, and told old stories of their time in the field. Many of the stories told were of mighty battles and the legendary men who had come from their home country, and very rarely, some were told of Liam's compatriots who had been legendary in battle. Even more were of friends lost beside them. Liam listened to one particularly gruesome-looking farmer who had delighted too much, in Liam's opinion, of killing his Anatalian countrymen.

"An' the boy fell on his knees in front of me, the scum, an' begged me for his life," the farmer said with a disgusting gleam in his eyes. "I let my answer sink in before I cut off 'is head."

A few of the men had raised their glasses to him, others had looked uncomfortable in his delight. It was no secret that, even more than a decade after the war, there was a strong hate between the Salatian and Anatalian peoples. The Anatalian soldiers were told to be as ruthless as their ancestors had been in their wars.

"One less Anatalian scum t' kill us in our beds, I say!" the farmer boisterously called out, his ale sloshing out of his tankard when he lifted it. "I only wish I had gotten more of 'em before they left."

"Hear, hear!" A few of his fellow soldiers cried out.

Liam took a long drink of his ale. He did not like the hate festering between the two countries. He was glad that no one here knew he was born on Anatalian soil—how he had managed to keep it a secret all this time, he wasn't entirely sure, but he wouldn't help them figure it out. He finished his ale and set a few coins on the bar, standing to leave.

"What's the matter, boy?" the farmer asked. "Canna handle a little war talk?"

Liam looked at the drunk man, sickened by his taste for blood. "I don't revel in the men that I had to kill," he said as he began to walk away.

"Ye was prolly one of the ones at the back of the lines, too cowardly t' fight for yer country."

Liam stopped in his tracks at the accusation. He had only ever stayed at the front lines with his men. He had tried his hardest to never leave one of his fellow soldiers fighting when it was time to retreat from their attacks.

"What did you say to me?" Liam asked, his voice quiet as a whisper.

"Ye heard me!" the drunk farmer bellowed. "Ye was prolly a coward, and still are a coward, an' that's why ye canna stomach the war talk!"

At once, Liam was in front of him, his fist in the farmer's stomach. The drunk leaned into Liam, the breath knocked out of him from the blow.

"I am not a coward, and you had best remember that, or next time, you won't walk away so easily," Liam growled lowly at him.

Liam shoved him back onto his compatriots. The others in the bar looked at him with wide eyes—Liam had never lifted a hand to anyone in the two years he'd been there. He walked away as the farmer sucked in air as if he would never have another chance.

Thorkelin worked silently beside Liam, save for the pounding of their hammers. Liam occasionally caught him glancing over at him. If Thorkelin expected him to break the silence that had settled between them, he would be disappointed. He knew the news of last night had traveled the town already—he had received strange looks on his way into the forge that morning.

"Do ye want to talk about somethin'?" Jossnon finally asked.

"No." Liam didn't look at him.

"I heard about what happened at the Frothing Wench the other night," Jossnon said offhandedly.

"Oh?" Liam said lightly. "And what is it that you're supposed to have heard?"

"That ye beat a farmer for havin' brought up the war."

"He was not beaten—I only hit him once—and he tried to accuse me of being craven," Liam said hotly, finally looking at the blacksmith.

"And were ye?" Jossnon asked.

"Was I a coward? No." Liam gripped his hammer tightly, tempted to throw it off to the side. The farmer's accusation goaded him more than he cared to admit.

"Then why did ye hit 'im?"

"Because he took too much pleasure in killing people he didn't know, and him calling me a coward was the last straw," Liam said irritably.

"He's an old war veteran who had nothin' left but his naggin' wife and his stories. He enjoys 'is stories, Liam, there's nothin' wrong with that. Ye saw how the Anatalian soldiers slaughtered our people—ye were there," said Thorkelin, his accent thickening with his passion.

"I saw how everyone was slaughtered in that battle, no matter what side they fought for," Liam told him.

Thorkelin snorted exasperatedly, throwing his hands in the air. "Those animals are the ones who brought the war to our doorstep, Liam!"

Liam's face hardened, his mouth set in a thin line. Just because they were better trained and better equipped didn't mean they were animals. "And what would you say if I were to tell you I was one of those animals?"

Jossnon Thorkelin looked at him with his mouth open and eyes a strange combination of wide and squinted. "Are ye?"

What the hell had he done that for? Years of secrecy broken in a moment, and all because someone had called him a coward? He was endangering his life with Gretta and the boys—if Jossnon reacted poorly, the rest of them would. He would have to leave and start over again.

"Yes, I am," Liam said, adding passionately, "and hearing about his delight in killing my countrymen was sickening. I took no pleasure in what we had to do for our country."

"If yer Anatalian, then why are ye here in Salatia, workin' in my forge?" Thorkelin asked in a suspicious tone. He gripped his hammer in front of him, knuckles going white.

Liam supposed he should have expected that, but it still hurt, seeing his friend and mentor ready to turn on him. "Because Anatalia has betrayed me while I remained loyal," Liam said quietly.

"Just who exactly are ye?" Jossnon demanded impatiently, picking up his hammer.

Liam fell silent, looking at his friend. He had only ever told him the name Liam and was never pressed for a surname. It hadn't seemed important to either of them to know it.

"Who are ye, Liam?" Jossnon demanded.

Liam noted that color was starting to rise on Jossnon's face. "You wouldn't let me stay here if you knew who I was."

"Lad, just tell me, and we'll see how I feel after," Thorkelin tried to reason with him.

Liam looked at him desperately, still remaining silent.

He put down the hammer, crossing his arms over his chest. "Go on, lad, tell me," Jossnon coaxed.

Liam hesitated before giving Jossnon what he wanted. "Liam Fulton."

"The Hero of Chenalieu?" Jossnon asked, incredulous.

Liam's face scrunched in confusion. Hero of Chenalieu? Is that what people in Salatia had been calling him? "I am not a hero," Liam said, trying not to sound exasperated. "I was wrongly accused of helping your general."

"Ye're the reason we won Chenalieu." Thorkelin said. "The reason we didna lose the war right then."

"Lord General Crompton," he spat the name out in disgust, "is the reason you won Chenalieu, and he betrayed me, my men, and our country to do it. You know why?" Liam asked the older man, his voice escalating. He didn't wait for the older man to reply. "Because he wanted nothing more than for his own ambitions to succeed."

Thorkelin raised his brows. "But ye were convicted of the crime. We all heard about it here; we was all so happy when we heard ye escaped." Thorkelin clapped him on the shoulder with a chuckle. "To think, I got a hero workin' fer me!"

"Wrongly convicted, Master Thorkelin," Liam reminded him.

"And what does yer Maggie think of all this?"

"She was at my trial, and she's one of the few who believe I'm innocent." Liam thrust a sword back into the hot coals to reheat. "And she's not 'my Maggie,'" he added tartly.

"She is yer Maggie, Liam," Thorkelin said. "Because she holds a place in yer thoughts."

The next few days, Thorkelin grew progressively surlier each time he saw Liam. When Liam walked into the blacksmith's shop, there was a scowl on his face.

"Something wrong, Master Thorkelin?"

"Ye were at the Battle of Chenalieu," Thorkelin muttered.

"You were happy about that just a few days ago," Liam reminded him.

"Ye were on the side that killed my boy, the side that drove my wife from my arms an' into an early grave," Thorkelin said darkly.

"I wouldn't have hurt a child, Master Thorkelin," Liam defended himself.

"How do ye ken ye hadn't accidentally killed 'im, or yer men didn't do it?" Jossnon demanded.

"Jossnon, it could have been one of them, or it could have been one of the hundreds of other countrymen I was fighting with," Liam said, trying to placate him. "I am sorry that it happened in a battle I know I was at."

Thorkelin muttered to himself, throwing himself into his work, reheating the forge. Liam knew he would go back to his normal self soon. Thorkelin didn't speak to Liam for the rest of their working day.

Liam turned to the smith once his work was finished. "Master Thorkelin, let me buy you a drink at the Frothing Wench."

"I could use a drink, lad," Thorkelin said grudgingly. "Yer buyin'?"

"I'm buying," Liam confirmed.

"Good," the blacksmith said as he quenched a blade. "Let's go."

The Frothing Wench was already starting to fill up, the day's work done for most of the men.

Liam sat at the bar with Jossnon. "Get whatever you want."

Jossnon ordered his drink, looking around the bar. "Do you come here often?"

"I did before Gretta and the boys," Liam told him, picking up the drink that was automatically given to him. "I like to listen to what people are talking about around here."

"Tha's the man," the drunk farmer Liam had hit shouted when he saw him. "Tha's the man who tried t' kill me!"

Liam raised his brows, standing. The story the farmer was telling had obviously been exaggerated more and more by the day. "I did not try to kill you."

"Ye did!" The farmer accused.

Jossnon Thorkelin stood, his face as thunderous as a storm cloud. "Ye better watch who ye're talkin' to, Robert."

Robert seemed surprised that Jossnon would even talk to him. "Who I'm talkin' to? I'm talkin' to a coward!"

"Yer talkin' to the Hero of Chenalieu, an' I won't have ye disrespectin' him in my presence," Jossnon said heatedly. "He's the only reason some of ye survived that battle."

"Him?" Robert demanded, pointing at Liam. "*He's* the Hero of Chenalieu?"

"That's right," Thorkelin said. "Liam Fulton in the flesh."

Liam was surprised at the visceral reaction to his name. Whispers went through the men, some trying to shove their way through the crowd to have a look at him. "I'll not have you call me a coward again."

"Nor will I," Thorkelin said.

"The ale is on the house, Liam," said Elias behind him, breaking the tension between the two groups.

"Thank you," Liam said to the bartender, turning his back on the group that had gathered behind Robert the farmer.

When Jossnon and Liam left the Frothing Wench, the night was clear, and a weight was lifted from the both of them. It seemed he wouldn't be run out of town for being Anatalian.

"I'll see ye tomorrow, lad," Thorkelin said before turning the opposite way to go home.

It was a few days before Gretta started to look at him strangely. She knew. It was obvious in the way she was acting.

"Do the boys know?" Liam asked, making her jump.

"Jamie was the one who told me," admitted Gretta.

"This doesn't change anything," Liam told her. "My feelings for you and the boys are still the same."

Gretta nodded silently.

"Does this change your feelings for me?" Liam asked. "Do you want me to leave?"

"No!" Gretta rushed to say, stepping back when she noticed she had come closer.

"Are you scared of me now?" Liam's shoulders fell. He couldn't bear it if she were scared of him.

Gretta looked at him briefly before looking away. "Ye're Anatalian," she answered as if his nationality explained everything.

"I'm a person, Gretta," he told her, a little irritably, "no matter where I came from—I'm a person."

"I ken well what ye are, Liam!" Gretta snapped.

"But?"

"But I canna forget what the Anatalians did to our country," Gretta told him. "Why wouldna ye tell me ye were from there?"

"I told you it was for your safety, but it was for mine too," he said. "I didn't want to be run out of Numetra."

"They willna run ye out. Ye're the Hero of Chenalieu." Gretta finally looked at him, her eyes sad. "Did ye want to be there?"

"I wanted to serve my country," Liam told her quietly, "even if that meant having to go to war and fight men serving their country."

"Will ye go back?"

"I don't know," Liam answered honestly. "There's always that possibility, but until then, I'm here with you."

"I'll let ye stay—I want ye to stay, the boys love you—on one condition," Gretta said.

"What is that?" Liam raised his brows.

"Ye tell me everything."

"Done," Liam easily agreed.

Liam sat silently at the table, nursing a stein of ale. Gretta stared at him expectantly, her own drink untouched. He looked at her and felt his stomach clench in nervous excitement.

Finally, Liam asked, "Where do you want me to start?"

She inhaled deeply, looking nervous herself. She sat farther away from him than usual. "At the beginning, if ye please."

Sighing, Liam took another deep drink. "All right then. At the beginning."

Gretta quickly grabbed her drink, holding it close as though it were her safety line. "Aye, the beginning," she confirmed.

"I grew up in the Duke of Rivack's land, where my father managed a small section of a vineyard—"

"Is that how ye ken how to make that beer for me?" Gretta interrupted.

"Yes," Liam answered before continuing, "I wanted to travel, so I joined the Anatalian ranks. I was there for three years before the war started, and I was sent to Salatia to fight with the Lord General Crompton."

Liam paused, looking into his cup. When he found it was empty, he returned it to the table. "During one of the ceasefires, I found Lord General Crompton with Lord General Baur—"

"Baur?" Gretta demanded, her face slack with shock.

Liam continued without answering her. "They were discussing Anatalian troop movements, and then Lord General Baur gave Crompton money for his trouble."

"But Lord General Baur is a hero! He would have never done such a thing!" Gretta countered.

"I thought the same of Lord General Crompton." Liam rested a hand on hers to quiet her. "I got caught spying on them, and I was blamed for Crompton's crimes. I was taken to Jalmar to be imprisoned. I was forced to run alongside the horses. If I couldn't keep up, I was dragged, and if I was dragged, I was beaten—"

"Are those the scars on yer back?" Gretta asked.

Liam nodded. "Yes," he said softly, "I would have died if it weren't for a kindhearted healer named Woolsey. I was imprisoned for three years before my trial. I would have been executed immediately if we had not won the war."

Gretta made a sympathetic noise but said nothing.

"I was found guilty at my trial," Liam told her, as though it weren't obvious. "My execution was set for a week later when the executioner would return—I was to be drawn and quartered. I escaped the day it was scheduled and never looked back. I traveled Aratia for seven years before I met Margaret."

"The Margaret whose father ye got killed?"

"The very same." Liam rose to pour himself another drink.

Gretta watched him down a full serving before he poured another. "What happened?" she asked when he sat again.

"Do you want to know the whole truth?" Liam asked, looking hesitant.

"Aye," she said after a long pause.

Liam inhaled deeply before plunging into the second half of the story. "I came across Margaret in the country—Lady Margaret, Countess of Dorcia, actually—caring for her infirm father. I was so hungry. I hadn't eaten in days, and I knocked on her door even though I knew I shouldn't have. I had just seen a soldier patrol not far away from her home.

"She opened the door and graciously offered me a cooked meal and new clothes on the condition that I bathed first. By the time I finished eating, soldiers had come to her door, saying they had seen me in the area. She knew who I was then—I didn't know at the time that she did—but she still told them they must have been mistaken, that she didn't know what they were talking about."

Liam fell silent. He took a drink before he spoke again. "She knew the soldier who entered the home. They had courted once, and she refused his marriage proposal when her father fell ill. I knew him too—he was the one who ordered and dolled out my beatings. They fought in her father's room, and when I saw him hit her, I came out from hiding. We fought, and Nicholas misjudged his momentum and killed Margaret's father."

"Poor girl," Gretta cooed.

Nodding, Liam went on, "Nicholas gloated over her while she mourned, and I killed him. Or, at least, that was the intention. I took Margaret away before we could confirm. We traveled to Marbon near the Frasisca River to stay with a couple I knew would help her—"

"Why would ye no take her back to Dorcia?" Gretta's brow creased.

"Because I didn't know if Nicholas lived long enough to tell anyone Margaret had helped me. The king had made it treason to aid me in any way, and I didn't want her anywhere near where they could find her and hurt her."

220

Gretta nodded. "A smart choice."

"I agree," Liam said with a smile before he picked up the story. "I hated her with every fiber of my being after traveling with her. I thought she was spoiled and annoying, and I would leave her with Aram and Elizabeth Gollack, and she would just find her own way with them."

"Did ye?" Gretta asked. "Leave her there?"

"No," Liam said. "I caught the winter fever, and Margaret refused to allow the Gollacks to come close to me in case they caught it. She bullied the healer to make my medicine that night, and—I was unconscious and found out later—she stayed with me for an entire two weeks, night and day, giving me my medication until I woke up. Margaret barely left long enough to care for herself. She even almost killed herself in a blizzard, bringing me back more medicine from the healer."

"She sounds a verra carin' lady," Gretta told him slowly.

"She is," Liam told her, falling silent.

Gretta watched him stare at his cup. "Did somethin' happen between ye two?"

"No," Liam said, sounding almost disappointed. "A kiss here and there, but nothing serious."

"Are...are ye certain?" Gretta hesitantly asked.

"I stayed with the Gollacks for months longer than I should have to be around her. I loved her, but I never explicitly told her. I couldn't. She would never have returned my affection. She was a noble, and I was not." Liam gave her a sheepish grin. "I asked her to run away with me to anywhere I could keep her safe, and she refused me on several occasions."

Worry clouded Gretta's eyes. "D'ye still love her?"

Liam took her hand in his, kissing it gently. "I do," he told her quietly, "I always will, but I love you and the boys too. There should be no doubt in your mind that I love you."

She smiled halfheartedly. "I ken ye do, Liam."

"I promised Margaret I would make sure she was all right wherever she was," Liam finished his story. "I intend to keep that promise."

Gretta looked over his face slowly. "I won't keep ye from keepin' your word."

Liam smiled at her. "Thank you, Gretta. Do you feel better about me now? I'm still the same person I was before you found out I was Anatalian."

"Aye, I do," she said. "I'm sorry I treated ye poorly."

Liam gently grabbed her hand and kissed it. "I'll forgive you of anything, Gretta. I love you."

42

argaret went to the great hall to mingle with the other nobles for the first time since Sir Adam had denounced her as a whore two months before in Jumonat. Anxiety raced through her chest as she walked toward the double doors. The king had been particularly attentive to her needs but would never answer her question when it came to her marriage or her title.

Margaret needed to start mingling with other men of the court—someone with some semblance of power to help her out from under Sorren's thumb. She needed a marriage soon, and Sorren would be the last person to arrange one for her now. If she knew anything about men, it was that they did not like other men around their toys. Maybe if she found herself a powerful suitor, it would allow her to manipulate Sorren into giving her things she wanted.

Margaret smiled at her idea. If Sorren was growing attached to her, she was going to use it to her advantage. She entered the great hall, where the other courtiers gathered, first making her hellos to her friends and then sought out to make new acquaintances, despite the stares and whispers every woman in the room directed her way.

Duke Rowan Fradure would be her first attempt. He was a cousin of the king and recently a widower. He had just returned from his period of mourning, though he had not taken the typical year that was proper. He had come back after only three months to return to court life. Clairance Fradure had died during childbirth with their second son. The babe had refused to turn during the three days of labor. In the end, both mother and child had died of exhaustion. After his loss, the duke refused to have his first son, Samuel, away from him. The little lord stayed close to his father's leg, looking around the court.

Margaret smiled at the young boy as she approached them. She could see the king watching her closely, looking to see what she would do. She gave a small curtsy to the duke. "Your Grace, I am very sorry to hear about your wife."

Duke Fradure nodded. "Thank you, Lady Margaret."

Margaret smiled again at the young lord and crouched to his level. "My lord."

Samuel looked at her solemnly and gave her a stiff, practiced bow. "My lady."

It wasn't her most favorite of ideas, but if she could get the duke's son to like her, she would have a better chance of wooing the duke to her side. "Have you ever seen the gardens here?"

Samuel simply shook his head.

Margaret looked up at his father with a coy smile. "Perhaps your father will allow me to show them to you?"

Samuel looked up at the duke expectantly. "Can she, Father?"

Rowan looked Margaret over slowly. "Only if she will allow me to accompany her."

Margaret stood, offering her hand to Samuel. "I would be delighted if you would."

Rowan offered his arm to Margaret. "Shall we?" He smiled when Samuel took her proffered hand.

"I believe we shall." Margaret placed her hand in the crook of his arm. She wanted to look at the king to see his reaction but knew it would goad him more if she did not.

In Aumonat, the garden was a luscious green spotted with jewel tones of pink, red, and white with intermittent purples, blues, and yellows. Margaret relaxed the further they moved into the garden. It made her feel like she was stepping back into her life at Silvica, surrounded by the smell of fresh air and dirt.

Margaret could see Captain Vojvo following them at a discreet distance. Good. The king could have no argument of impropriety when she returned. She watched as the young boy ran ahead of them, going from one rose bush to the next, smelling the blooms that he could reach.

"You have a very handsome son, Your Grace."

Rowan only smiled lightly at her.

Margaret grew awkward with the silence. He was quieter than she thought. Rowan seemed perfectly content to simply walk. Unfortunately for him, Margaret could not stand the silence after returning to the noise and gossip of court. "How old is your boy, Your Grace?"

He watched Samuel move between the shrubs. "Samuel will be five next month."

"Does he have many friends here?" Margaret noted that Samuel seemed to be content on his own as well.

"Not many. He seems to be very selective of whom he wants around him." Rowan patted her hand on his arm. "I'm surprised that he didn't shy away from you."

"He just seemed so solemn there in the hall, and I thought the both of you could use some fresh air." Margaret looked up at him, examining his face. She found him an attractive man. He was not taller than Liam but incredibly tall next to her short frame.

"Samuel doesn't like to be around so many people. I felt that we both needed to get away from the house his mother died in, no matter his anxieties." There was a sadness in his voice that made Margaret feel his loss.

Samuel abruptly fell, his foot caught on a root. Margaret involuntarily gasped. She picked up her skirts and rushed to the fallen boy. Tears welled in the young boy's eyes, but he refused to let them fall.

Margaret knelt and gently kissed his scraped hands. "Are you all right, Samuel?"

The little lord's lip quivered, but he nodded. Rowan helped the both of them stand, and Margaret shook out her skirts to remove any debris that had gotten on them when she knelt.

"Would you like to see my favorite flower?" Margaret asked the young boy.

Samuel nodded and slipped his hand into hers. He walked close to her side as she searched the gardens.

Rowan gently took her hand and placed it back on his arm. "You are remarkable with him," Rowan said quietly to her.

Margaret smiled at him brightly. "I adore children. The ones in Silvica used to run up to me and give me little gifts of flowers that they had found in the fields."

"They must have been drawn by your kindness," Rowan told her, returning a charming smile of his own.

Margaret blushed prettily and pointed to a flower close to Samuel that had a cluster of red flowers on a single stem with a yellow streak in the center of its bottom lip. There were others colored in yellows, whites, pinks, purples, and some peaches mixed in the patch of earth dedicated to the flower.

"Do you see that flower there?" Margaret asked Samuel. "It's called a dragon flower, and it has a mouth that opens if you press on it." She laughed when she saw the look of amazement on his face. "Go pick some!"

Samuel let go of her hand to gather the blooms. Margaret sat on the grass under a shady tree, Rowan joining as she spread out her skirts. Samuel came back to her with an arm full of the flowers and, without hesitation, sat on her lap. Margaret unabashedly wrapped her arms around him to examine the blooms.

"Remember how I told you they have mouths that open?" She smiled when Samuel nodded excitedly. "Hold up your hand."

Samuel complied easily, his eyes widening when Margaret placed a dragon flower with an open mouth on one of his fingers. Samuel let out a pleasured cry, holding his hand out to show Rowan. "Look, Father! It's eating my finger!"

Rowan ruffled his hair and smiled, making his face look ten years younger. "So it is."

By the time the three of them returned to the grand hall, Margaret's hair was littered with dragon flowers and pink hellebore. Samuel had enjoyed placing the flowers in her hair while she talked with his father. She had enjoyed learning more about the duke and his son and couldn't care less that the court was examining her odd appearance.

Rowan ducked his head to speak quietly to her. "Everyone is staring at you now."

Margaret looked at him slyly. "They all think that I'm husband hunting to dispel any rumors of my affair."

The duke raised his brow at her frankness. "And are you?"

"Maybe." Margaret smiled when Samuel flared out his fingers she had placed dragon flowers on. She knew she should feel guilty for putting them in the line of fire, but she had no choice. It was this or her title, and she couldn't let Sorren dally on it any longer.

"I see." There was a disapproving tone in Rowan's voice. He must not have heard about her affair with the king yet, having only recently arrived back at court.

Sorren was suddenly at Margaret's side. "I see you've bedecked my ward with flowers."

"My son thought she would look like a princess with all the flowers in her hair." Rowan bowed to the king but did not allow Margaret's hand to fall from his arm.

"I have something that certainly will make her look the part." Sorren looked her over and waved his hand, and a servant appeared with a small case. "My dear Lady Margaret, may I present you with this necklace?"

Margaret gasped when the wooden box was opened. Inside rested a diamond necklace with a large teardrop diamond in the center. The diamonds glimmered in the light and held her captive as she stared at them. The chain was made entirely of one-carat diamonds, twenty-three of them all told. The center teardrop diamond was at least fifteen carats by itself. "Your Majesty, that is too much for me to accept!"

"Nonsense." Sorren had the necklace on her in seconds. "It would make me very happy to see you wear this."

Margaret's face briefly conveyed her dismay. The court would think that the extravagant gift was a public declaration of her being his mistress. "Your Majesty, this is really too much."

Sorren only looked her over critically before leaving.

Margaret wore only the necklace when the king arrived. He came to her chambers at the same time he had since their affair started. Margaret reluctantly nestled into the king's side, not waiting to gain any fresh bruises as a result of his anger.

"Is there something wrong?" Margaret gently traced out circles with her finger on his chest.

Sorren grabbed her hand tightly. "What were you doing with the Duke Fradure for so long today? You had dirt all over your dress."

Margaret frowned. "You're hurting my hand."

His grip tightened. "What were you doing with him?"

Margaret flinched. "I only talked with him in the garden. His son was with us the entire time, putting those flowers in my hair. My captain was even there."

"I don't want you spending time with him."

Margaret sat up on her arm. "Why does it matter if I spend time with him? I'm supposed to be looking for a husband, aren't I?" Margaret scowled at him. "And what we do here is only a transaction, not an act of affection."

Sorren pulled her onto his chest. "It matters because I don't like it, and I will find a husband for you. One who won't be disappointed when I continue your punishment."

Margaret attempted to sit up but was stopped by the king grabbing the hair at the back of her head tightly.

"Do you understand me?" he demanded. The look Sorren gave her was frightening.

"Yes, Majesty," Margaret said meekly, relieved when the king let go of her hair.

Margaret woke the next morning to an empty bed and dark bruises on her upper arms. She frowned at the hand shaped bruises and slid out of the plush bed, weary from the lack of sleep. Margaret had not been able to get comfortable after the king had fallen asleep, unable to sleep until late into the night. Margaret called Sarah to help her ready for the day.

"My lady, are you all right?" Sarah asked, examining her arms.

"I'll be fine," Margaret said. "Please find me something light, but dark. I don't want anyone to see the bruises."

"Of course, my lady." Sarah went to her wardrobe, bringing back a dark blue silk dress. "Will this suit you, my lady?"

"Perfect. Thank you, Sarah." Margaret held her arms out to be changed.

Margaret went to the great hall to watch the proceedings for the day. Sorren, already sitting on his throne, listened to the petitioners. She wandered through the crowd, pausing here and there. The courtiers would move away so she was once again standing alone. It seems that her indiscretions would not be easily forgotten. Margaret spotted Rowan and Samuel in the crowd, Samuel fidgeting in his boredom. She went to stand by them, pleased that Rowan did not move away from her like all the rest.

Rowan smiled at her when he noticed she was next to him. "My lady," he said quietly with a small nod.

"Your Grace," she said with a smile. Adding to Samuel, "My lord."

Margaret quietly stood next to the two, starting to get as bored as Samuel looked. She leaned over to covertly whisper to Rowan, "Would you like to have tea in the gardens with me?"

Rowan gave her a sidelong look. "I would like that very much, my lady."

Margaret nodded subtly. "Meet me in an hour? I'll arrange everything."

He nodded silently, his eyes forward.

Margaret nodded in return, waiting a few more minutes before she left to go to her chambers. "Sarah?"

Sarah came out of the bedroom, a pillowcase in hand. "Yes, my lady?"

"I want to have tea in the gardens with His Grace," she told her lady's maid. "Would you go to the kitchens and arrange for some sweets and tea to be made up in a basket and also have a canopy and chairs placed?"

"Of course, my lady," Sarah said with a curtsy. "When are you wanting to have this ready by?"

"In an hour—plenty of time for everything to be done. The king will be listening to petitioners all day, so he won't be looking for me." Margaret was happy she would be able to have an afternoon to herself without the prying eyes of the king.

"I'll make arrangements immediately," Sarah told her before she left the room.

Captain Vojvo quietly entered Margaret's chambers. He found her by the bay windows, reading a book. "I'm surprised you aren't listening to the petitions, my lady."

Margaret looked up at him with a small smile. "I'll be having tea in the gardens with His Grace in about an hour."

"How nice," Vojvo commented dryly. "And you've arranged a proper chaperone I assume?"

Margaret had the grace to look chagrined.

"Oh, you haven't, have you?" Marius asked, a teasing glint in his eyes. "Should I forbid you from going, then?"

Margaret gave him a bland look. "Captain," she said boredly, "we both know you can't forbid me from doing something."

Captain Vojvo raised his brows at her. "You don't want any more rumors, do you?"

"Perhaps you can be my chaperone, then?"

"Why, Lady Margaret, truly you flatter me," the captain said with mirth still in his eyes. "It brings me the greatest pleasure to keep your meddling out of prying eyes."

Margaret rolled her eyes, though there was a small smile on her face as she returned to her reading. She waited for three quarters of an hour before she went to the gardens with the captain. She sat and enjoyed the fresh air and the gentle scents of the flowers wafting toward her. Closing her eyes, she waited for the duke and Samuel to arrive. Not long after the tea had arrived, Rowan did also.

"My lady, thank you for inviting me," Rowan said upon his arrival, eyeing Vojvo warily.

Margaret smiled at him. "My pleasure," she said, looking for his son. "Where is Samuel?"

"He was tired. He is napping in his room," Rowan said as he sat. "I hope you don't mind that you only have me for conversation."

"Not at all," Margaret assured him, pouring the tea herself, adding cream and sugar to their tastes.

They sat silently for a moment, enjoying the quietness of the royal gardens. "Do you come here often, my lady?"

"I like to come here and remember my father from when we lived in the country," she told him. "It's very comforting."

"I'm sure," Rowan said, picking up a sweet. "And how often do you come here?"

"At least three times a week," Margaret admitted. "After leaving the queen's service, I have ample time to myself."

"Perhaps I will have to follow your example and forget my worries away from the pomp," Rowan said.

"Perhaps you should," she said with her lashes lowered.

"Would you allow me to accompany you on your next visit?"

"I would enjoy that very much, Your Grace." It would be nice to once more have someone to talk with other than Sarah, Vojvo, and Sorren.

"Good," Rowan said with a small grin before turning the conversation to something benign. "Have you been back at court long?"

"Two years now." Margaret was surprised it had already been that long. It did not seem to her that things had raced by, her months in seclusion after the scandalous reveal of her affair creeping by like a snail.

They idly chatted until their tea and treats were gone, settling into a comfortable silence. Margaret snuck a glance at Rowan. He seemed content to sit in the silence and enjoy their surroundings.

Margaret stood, not wanting to prolong the silence into awkwardness. Rowan immediately followed suit and faced her. "Thank you for such a pleasant time, Your Grace," she said.

Rowan picked up her hand and gently kissed her knuckles. "I hope that we can do this again sometime soon, my lady."

"Yes," Margaret agreed. "Yes we must find a time soon."

43

"I'm to do what?" Shock slackened Liam's face.

Jamie shifted uncomfortably. "Ye're to negotiate the marriage contract. Ma wants ye to."

"I've never negotiated a marriage contract," Liam countered, continuing quickly when he saw Jamie ready to argue again, "nor have I ever participated in a ceremony like your mother has."

"But ye will have more sway than Ma," Jamie protested.

"Why?" Liam pushed his empty plate farther from him and crossed his arms in front of him, leaning back against the kitchen chair.

Face pinkening, Jamie hunched his shoulders sheepishly. "Ye're the Hero of Chenalieu, and Mr. Kaneh greatly admires ye."

Liam raised a brow. It seemed everyone but him would benefit from Crompton's betrayal. "Oh?"

"Aye, he does." Jamie nervously picked pieces of his roll out, tossing them onto the table. "Will ye do it, Da?"

Sighing, Liam asked, "When will this negotiation be?"

"In two days."

"Do you have a ring for her?"

Jamie's face deepened in color. "No as of yet."

Liam raised both his brows this time. "And does she have one for you?"

After a long pause, Jamie said, "No."

"Come to the forge on your way to work," Liam said with a sigh. "And tell Ellie to come see me this afternoon."

"Aye, I will," Jamie said as he rose to change. "I'll meet ye there?"

Liam nodded. "I'll see you there."

He found Gretta in the public dining room and kissed her goodbye for the day. Liam traveled down the street to the Heated Forge and strapped on his leather apron. How did he always manage to get himself into situations he was unqualified for? It was like a plague that followed him everywhere.

"Joss, do we have any spare wedding rings?" asked Liam when he saw him.

Thorkelin nearly dropped his tools, his face surprised. "Are ye thinkin' of marryin' Gretta finally?"

"Ahh, no," Liam said sheepishly. "It's for young Jamie and Ellie Kaneh."

"Are they gettin' married?" Jossnon asked. "Aren't they a little young?"

Liam nodded. "I think they are, but Gretta has no objections. I am supposed to negotiate the marriage contract for Jamie."

"That's quite the responsibility." Jossnon looked impressed.

Liam's mouth quirked. "I'm not sure I will be much good. I've never participated in one of any form."

"Ye'll need to do most of the talkin', aye?" Jossnon instructed. "And if ye dinna think he is bein' fair, ye counter with another offer."

"Sounds simple enough," conceded Liam.

"Da, are ye in the back?" Jamie called.

"Come on back," Liam returned, asking Jossnon again, "Do we have bands?"

"Aye, lad," Jossnon said, handing him a key, "in the safe."

Liam grabbed the bag with jewels and bands, returning to see Jossnon offering Jamie a congratulation. Liam found a clean surface and dumped the bag, separating the loose jewels from the bands. Most were silver, and others were gold of various colors. There were even a few with jewels already attached.

"Come here, please," Liam called to Jamie.

Jamie separated from the conversation with Jossnon, coming to stand next to Liam. "Are these the rings?"

"Silver or gold?" asked Liam.

Jamie examined the rings closely, looking to Liam for help. When none was offered, Jamie answered, "Silver."

Liam nodded, taking away the gold rings. "Try them on until one fits, and that will be your ring."

Jamie silently tried rings until he found one that fit comfortably. He stared at it on his hand before starting out of his trance and looking to Liam. "What about her ring?"

Holding his hand out for Jamie's ring, Liam spoke. "She'll try the rings to find the right size, and we'll make sure the one you pick for her will fit. You can choose if you want her to have a jewel put on it or if you want it plain to match yours."

Jamie gave Liam his ring, looking over the jewels. "What would ye pick for Ma?"

Liam caught the amused smirk on Jossnon's face as he heated metal. He was sure Jossnon was enjoying this, knowing how uncomfortable it made Liam. "I wouldn't. Your mother would say it would get in the way."

Jamie's face fell. "That's no help."

Liam shrugged, unsympathetic. Jamie would have to get used to making decisions on his own soon enough if he thought he was old enough to marry and be in charge of his own home and family. "You know Ellie far better than I do."

"Aye, well," Jamie murmured with a shrug. "Can she no pick one out herself?"

"She can," Liam said offhandedly, "but it seems something you'd like to be a surprise for her."

Jamie fell silent, looking as though he were waging a mental battle. "Da…"

Liam looked at him sharply. "Yes?"

Jamie shifted awkwardly from foot to foot. "What would ye have picked for Maggie?"

The hammering behind Jamie stopped abruptly. Liam looked at Jossnon, surprised, before looking back at Jamie. "Margaret and Ellie are very different ladies, Jamie."

"I dinna ken what to do, Da," whined Jamie. "I want her to have somethin' nice."

Liam sighed. The hammering still had not resumed. He barely glanced at the jewels—he didn't need to—and picked one of the sapphires. "She would have liked this one," he said quietly. "She would have said she felt regal wearing it."

Jamie nodded thoughtfully, looking at the sapphire. "Aye, well…leave the jewels out when she looks and see if she admires any?"

"I'll tell you all about it tonight," Liam assured him, waving as he left.

Jossnon waited until he was sure Jamie was gone before speaking. "Ye told the lad about yer Maggie?"

"He was asking how to tell if a young woman liked him, and I gave him Margaret as an example," Liam defended himself. "I couldn't well tell him about the ladies he has no business visiting."

"Aye, ye're right," Jossnon agreed.

Liam slipped Jamie's ring into his apron before putting away the bag.

Jossnon patted Liam on the arm, pointing to Ellie waiting in the front room, basket still in hand. She nervously waved to Liam when he looked at her. He wiped his hands free of grease before going to greet her.

"Miss Kaneh, you're here early," Liam commented.

She smiled timidly. "Jamie said ye had somethin' important for me."

"You need to be fitted for a ring," Liam told her. "Wait here, I'll bring them out to you."

When he returned, Ellie set her basket down, clasping her hands in front of her. Liam motioned for her to join him at the counter and laid out the jewels and the silver bands.

"Try on rings until you find one that fits," Liam instructed. "Jamie did the same thing this morning."

She tried on the rings silently, completely ignoring the jewels. Ellie paused, fiddling with a ring that didn't fit.

"Is there something wrong?" Liam asked her, his brows furrowing.

"D'ye think I might call ye Da too?" Ellie pulled her lips in between her teeth, looking worried he might say no. "Jamie loves ye so, and I would like it if I could share it with him."

Liam grabbed a ring he thought would fit her, replacing it with the one she fiddled with. He was unsure himself, but said, "I would like that."

She smiled brightly, slipping on the ring. She admired it on her hand. It fit perfectly. "Thank ye...Da."

Liam smiled, holding his hand out for the ring. "Will you be coming with your father to the negotiation?"

"No." She shook her head, her red curls bouncing off her cheeks. "He wants it just to be ye, him, and Jamie."

"And where will the negotiations be?" Liam asked. Jamie had been scant on the details.

"At my father's house," Ellie informed him. "In two days."

"Thank you," Liam said, leading Ellie to the door. "Will you be with us for dinner tonight?"

Ellie shook her head. "Not tonight."

Liam gently squeezed her arm near her elbow. "Then I'll see you when I see you."

"Goodbye, Da." Ellie smiled.

Liam watched her walk away. It would be a new thing for him to gain a daughter. Even in the few moments she had called him Da, he felt the strong pull to protect her. Was this how Margaret felt with her orphans? He inhaled deeply before letting it out. He thought Margaret would approve of the way things were going for him.

Jamie and Liam walked side by side to the Kaneh house. It was outside of Numetra, closer to the forest than Liam had expected.

"Are you nervous?" Liam asked as his own stomach clenched.

"Aye, are ye?" Jamie countered.

Liam looked over at him quickly. "Very."

Jamie knocked on the door, returning to Liam's side as they waited for it to open. When it did, Mr. Kaneh filled the doorway. Jamie would have stepped back had Liam not put a firm hand on his back.

"We are—I am—here to ask for yer daughter's hand in marriage," Jamie said formally.

"Come in," Mr. Kaneh said, vacating the door.

Liam nudged Jamie forward, following after him. Mr. Kaneh motioned toward the table, two seats on one side and one on the other.

"Please sit, Mr. Fulton, Mr. McWard," Ellie's father offered.

They did as they were bid, and Mr. Kaneh followed suit. He waved for his wife to come and pour the drinks.

"A pleasure to meet you finally, Mr. Kaneh," Liam said, taking a drink.

"I assure ye," Mr. Kaneh said with an excited smile, "the pleasure is all mine." Liam smiled slightly. "Shall we start the negotiations right away?"

"Aye, I suppose we should," Mr. Kaneh agreed. "We'll start with the bride price."

"The bride price?" Liam questioned. "Not the dowry?"

"Aye, we'll talk dowry after," Mr. Kaneh confirmed, sitting back in his seat.

Liam tried not to let his anxiety show. He cleared his throat, leaning back to match Mr. Kaneh's calm demeanor. "How many children do you have, Mr. Kaneh?"

"Three. Two lads and the lassie," he answered.

Liam pursed his lips. "So you'll gain two daughters. I have an offer, a generous offer, on the condition that Miss Kaneh receive both the bride price—"

"What?" demanded Mr. Kaneh.

"And Mr. McWard will not be allowed access to any of it, unless she allows it," Liam finished. "It will pass, if she does not spend it, to her children."

Jamie and Mr. Kaneh were looking at Liam with unveiled surprise. Liam raised a brow at them.

"Is this how ye do thing in Anatalia?" Mr. Kaneh asked.

"It is how I do things, Mr. Kaneh, to ensure Miss Kaneh will be well taken care of. As long as she remains wed to Mr. McWard, she will co-inherit the Smiling Fox, and her monetary compensation will be twenty gold stral."

"Twenty gold stral?" Mr. Kaneh nearly rose from his seat as his voice climbed in volume. "I canna match even half that for her dowry!"

"If you do not agree to my condition, you will only receive ten gold stral and the assurance of her inheriting the Smiling Fox with Mr. McWard."

Mr. Kaneh took a long drink from his cup. "I'll accept yer condition," he said after a long moment. "We can afford to send Ellie with only five gold stral for her dowry."

Liam briefly looked at Jamie before answering. "These are acceptable terms."

Mr. Kaneh stood first, holding his hand out to Jamie. "Ye have my blessing, Mr. McWard."

Jamie shook his hand firmly, his face serious. "Thank ye, Mr. Kaneh."

Liam shook his hand next. "A pleasure negotiating with you, Mr. Kaneh."

"Ye'll make my Ellie a very happy lassie, Mr. Fulton," her father told him. "And a verra rich bride."

Smiling, Liam shrugged slightly. "I hope so. She asked if she could call me Da like the boys do."

Mr. Kaneh gave him a knowing look. "Bein' called Da gives ye a powerful need to do anything for them."

"It does," agreed Liam. "We will see you for the wedding, Mr. Kaneh."

Jamie led them away, barely containing his excitement. "Twenty gold stral, Da?"

Liam nodded, staying silent as he and Jamie walked home.

"How can ye and Ma afford so much?" asked Jamie.

"We've been saving everything extra since you started talking about courting, and the Smiling Fox has been doing much better lately," Liam told him. "But remember, that is Ellie's money unless she decides to share it with you."

"Aye, I'll remember, Da."

44

argaret sighed as she sat in a small alcove in the maze with her most recent letter from Liam, once again accompanied by Captain Vojvo. It was unorthodox for her to have a male chaperone, but she doubted she would be able to find a female willing to get within ten feet of her—particularly when it came to any sort of courtship. They thought it would ruin their own reputations. Sarah was too busy with her duties to accompany her everywhere, and the captain did not care what was said about him. Anyone who challenged him could face him in a battle of strength, and the matter would be settled.

She delightedly cracked the seal on the letter Liam had sent, finally taking the time to read it.

15 Junmonat 2284
Dearest Margaret,

The people of Numetra have found out who I am—that I am an Anatalian. They call me the "Hero of Chenalieu," though I don't know why. It was Crompton who betrayed us and helped their General, not me. It is at least better than them hating me. Thank you for your letter about his demise. It has cheered me greatly.

Gretta now knows everything. It was her stipulation for allowing me to stay with her. She seemed to think I was suddenly a different person because I was not a Salatian like she thought. I told her all about you and what was between us, and how we met, and my trial and escape.

Jamie and Ellie will be married on the fifth of Omonat. Gretta said it would take that long to receive all the food she wants to prepare for the wedding feast. I was asked to negotiate the bride price, and I managed to have it given solely to Ellie rather than her family. I don't want her to struggle like Gretta did when she was widowed.

Ellie asked if she could call me Da, like the boys do. I'm unsure how to feel about it, but I told her she could. I never thought I would have so many people thinking of me as a father. It's a strange feeling, but a nice one.

I will write again after the wedding to tell you how it went.

Love,
Liam

Margaret lifted a hand to her mouth. She was happy that they did not publicly shun or torture him for being Anatalian, but calling him a hero? She was just as confused as Liam. She read the letter again and couldn't help but feel jealous of the life he was starting there. He had offered so many times to take her with him, and this could have been their life instead. She wouldn't be forced into an affair she did not want, playing games she did not—

"Lady Margaret?"

Margaret gasped and quickly concealed the letter, looking up to see Rowan. "Your Grace, what a pleasant surprise!"

"Am I interrupting?" He raised a brow at her odd behavior.

"No, no," Margaret assured him with a smile. "I'm just reading a letter from an old friend. Please, sit!"

Rowan sat next to her, close in the tight quarters of the alcove. It was not made to accommodate the ever-growing circumference of the ladies' skirts. He let out an awkward chuckle at the uncomfortable closeness before he relented and wrapped his arm around her to create a more comfortable space. "Have you been well?"

"Very well, thank you." Margaret felt slightly awkward. They hadn't spoken since their tea in the garden last month, only passing by each other with nods and smiles. Sorren had found out about their tea and reminded her once again of what happened to those who tried to take what was his, so she had stayed away. "And you, Your Grace?"

"Very well."

"And Samuel?" Margaret asked.

"Also well. He's made a few friends among the children here," Rowan told her with a smile. "He's doing far better than I had hoped he would."

Margaret smiled at him. "I'm pleased to hear it."

Rowan nodded, falling back into an awkward silence.

Margaret chewed on her bottom lip, looking the other way.

"Lady Margaret…" Rowan said quietly. "Lady Margaret, I'm not very good at trying to romance women after my wife, Clairance. I didn't think I'd ever need to try and woo anyone again."

Margaret turned to him sharply, a light blush dusting her cheeks. "You're trying to woo me?"

"And failing miserably if you can't see my interest in you," Rowan told her, his mouth falling into a frown.

Margaret smiled at him timidly. "I think that I would like to be wooed by you, Your Grace."

Rowan smiled at her reassuringly, picking her hand up and kissing it. "Have you any other prospects?"

"Not as of yet. His Majesty has said that he will find me a husband, but I am unsure of his commitment to doing so," Margaret told him. He wasn't, and she knew it. Sorren only wanted her to be available to him whenever he was bored. "Surely, one of his own family would easily be on his list of potential suitors."

"Surely," Rowan agreed before standing. He held his hand out to her. "Would you like to take a turn about the gardens?"

Margaret tucked the forgotten letter into her waist before taking his hand. "I would love to."

Rowan pulled her to her feet, tucking her hand into the crook of his arm, taking her through the gardens. They talked at length about benign subjects, getting to know each other's interests and dislikes.

"It's getting late." Margaret looked to the dusky sky, sighing. "And we both must change for dinner."

"Will you allow me to escort you to your chambers?"

Margaret squeezed his arm, a small smile forming. "Of course."

Rowan took her back to her apartments, garnering many looks as they passed. He stopped at her door and bent over her hand. "I will see you at dinner, Lady Margaret."

Margaret smiled and waited until he walked away to go into her chambers. "Sarah, pick something exquisite for dinner. I am being courted!"

Sarah came to Margaret with an excited gasp, forgetting the formalities between them and grabbing her hands. "Who is courting you?"

"His Grace, the Duke of Fradure!" Margaret gushed just as excitedly. "I finally have a chance to leave court and get away from His Majesty."

Letting out a girlish squeal, Sarah disappeared to find Margaret a dress. "You will be the most radiant woman at dinner tonight!"

Margaret was dressed in a full red satin gown that tightly cinched in her waist—it was not a gown she could eat in, but one to be displayed in. The gown only had one shoulder on it, and it was a sheer red with rubies sewn on it in a vine pattern. The bust was covered with black lace that still let the crimson color show through. Sarah put Margaret's hair up in curls, a single curled strand falling on her cheek. Her jewelry was simple and her eye makeup smoky.

"This is perfect," Margaret breathed, looking herself over.

Margaret went to the dining hall, walking in confidently for the first time since her fall from grace. She was pleased to see that many of the men had stopped to look appreciatively at her while she walked to her table, sitting with a flourish. Margaret looked at Rowan sitting next to the king with lowered lashes, pleased to see that his cheeks were starting to color. She hoped a relationship would be able to blossom without the king's interference.

Rowan came to Margaret as the music started, pulling her up for a dance. "I could hardly wait for this," he breathed quietly in her ear.

A blush on her face, Margaret smiled at him. "Oh?"

"Did you purposefully dress so that I could not keep my eyes off of you?" Rowan pulled her close as they danced.

"Would you be happy if I did?" Margaret asked coyly.

"I would be." Rowan looked over her face intently. "And I am."

"Good." Margaret smiled at him coquettishly.

The pair danced the night away, enjoying only each other's company. There was a comfortable air between them after Rowan's confession earlier that afternoon. Margaret laid her head on Rowan's shoulder as she began to tire. Rowan tightened his arms around Margaret.

"Would you allow me to escort you back to your apartments?" Rowan asked as her eyes began to droop.

She nodded, trying to stifle a yawn. "Yes, that would be much appreciated."

Rowan placed her hand on his arm before he took her out of the hall. He walked her back to her apartments at a comfortable pace. "I immensely enjoyed spending time with you this evening."

Margaret smiled tiredly. "I could tell. You barely let me sit once the dancing started."

Rowan gave her a wry smile. "I didn't want someone else to snatch you up."

Margaret stopped at her door, looking up at him. "Thank you for the wonderful evening."

"It was my pleasure, Lady Margaret."

"Please, just call me Margaret."

"If you'll agree to only call me Rowan," he countered.

"I think we've come to an agreement, then, Rowan." Margaret rested her hand on his arm, gently squeezing it. "I will see you tomorrow?"

"With certainty, Margaret." Rowan picked up her hand and kissed her knuckles. "Good night."

"Good night," she returned before going into her room. Margaret went into her bedroom, falling onto her plush bed. "Sarah!"

Sarah came into the room. "My lady?"

Margaret inhaled deeply. "Please help me get out of all of this."

"Did His Grace enjoy himself?" Sarah asked in reference to her special appearance.

"He did," Margaret told her with a grin. "You did a wonderful job."

Sarah helped her off the bed. "I'm pleased to hear it."

Sarah started to unlace her gown, stopping when they heard the door open, going to see what it was. "Your Majesty!" she said loudly enough for Margaret to hear.

Sorren waved his hand in dismissal as he walked into Margaret's bedroom. "Lady Margaret," he said, pulling her to him. "You looked beautiful this evening."

"Thank you, Your Majesty," Margaret said with a smile.

"You know how much I love you in red," he said into her neck.

"I do."

"My cousin seemed very interested in you this evening," the king commented, finishing what Sarah had started.

"Yes he was." Margaret tried not to sound too excited, knowing it would upset the king.

Sorren paused and gripped her arm tightly. "Did you enjoy his attentions?"

"And if I did?" Margaret asked defiantly. She had enjoyed feeling like she was wanted by someone as a prospective wife and not simply for pleasure. It had broken a dam in her, and she could not repair it.

Sorren's face turned stony. "Did you?"

"So what if I did? I need a husband!" Margaret yelled at him, trying to pull out of his grasp.

Sorren glared at her coldly. "Remember what I do to the people who try to take what's mine, Margaret."

"How can I not? You've so generously reminded me at every turn!" Margaret snapped. She could hardly take it anymore. "I need a husband to give me a title, or you need to give me my title, Majesty. It has been more than a *year* of this" —she gestured between the two of them— "and I am no closer to it or being able to ensure my people have what they need."

Sorren stepped back, surprised by her outburst. "Margaret—"

"No!" She threw up her hands. "You have already said you would continue once I have a husband, so to what end are you keeping me trapped and without prospects?"

"Lady Marg—"

"Sometimes I wish I had told you no so this would have been over long ago," Margaret spat, balling her hands in her skirts. Tears started to well in her eyes, and she angrily wiped them away. "I cannot take much more of this, even for the people of Dorcia—even for my title and my father's legacy."

Sorren grabbed her shoulders, holding her at arm's length. "Lady Margaret, I think you are overtired. You are saying the most nonsensical things," he said hurriedly before she could interrupt him again. "I will leave you to go to bed."

Margaret blinked at him in confusion, the corners of her mouth falling downward. "Goodnight, Your Majesty."

"Goodnight," he returned before quickly leaving the room.

Margaret furrowed her brow. What had just happened?

45

Sorren wandered the gardens in hopes of finding Margaret. She was not in her chambers, and she was not in the hall he had just left. The only place remaining within the grounds was the gardens. Sorren went toward the sound of chatting and giggling, stopping short when he saw his cousin with his arms tightly around Margaret. Rowan leaned down to kiss Margaret, and she was excitedly waiting to receive it.

It was something she had never done for him, at least not where she had meant it.

"Lady Margaret," Sorren said sharply, making her pull away with a gasp before Rowan could kiss her.

"Your Majesty," Margaret said curtsying to him.

Rowan bowed next to her, an annoyed look on his face.

"Should you be out here without an escort?" the king asked, eyeing Rowan. "Especially with a man?"

Margaret's cheeks colored brightly. "I…"

"I'm sorry, Your Majesty," Rowan swooped in for her, "I surprised Mar—Lady Margaret by being out here. This incident is my fault."

"It certainly is," Sorren chided. "Shouldn't you still be mourning your wife, not imposing on poor, vulnerable women?"

Rowan's mouth went into a thin line. "Yes, Your Majesty."

"Well?" Sorren raised his eyebrows.

Rowan hesitated, sneaking a glance at Margaret. "I'll see you at dinner," he said quietly before leaving.

Margaret backed away from Sorren, a cautious look on her face. "Your Majesty…"

"Did I not tell you what I do to people who try to steal what's mine?" Sorren demanded, stepping closer to her, though the words felt hollow in his throat. She had been right—he did remind her every chance he had. "You will stay away from His Grace."

"But, Majesty," Margaret pleaded, "I must find a husband soon before I lose any hope of children. You don't want any from me, and I want a legitimate child that can inherit my father's lands."

Sorren looked over her pleading face. He swallowed hard—he had not been able to let go of her words wishing she had chosen an execution instead of continuing on how they had.

"Lady Margaret," he said quietly, "I don't want you alone with His Grace again. Your captain will not leave your side whenever you are with him."

"As you wish," she said, her expression perturbed. "May I go?"

The king nodded, watching her walk away. Maybe he should start giving her some concessions—Rowan was the obedient sort, and he could easily control the younger man with his lands and inheritance for his young son.

Her title was nothing to him, only something to hold over her; it would have made Jerone happy to see his daughter inherit. He had asked enough times about it. Sorren supposed it was the least he could do for his dead friend, considering he'd slept with both his wife and his daughter.

He sighed.

Concessions would be better than finding out she had flung herself from her window in the middle of the night to escape him.

46

Liam woke to his stomach rumbling. He groaned, turning to wrap an arm around Gretta, finding the bed empty. He was confused before he remembered today was Jamie's wedding day, and Gretta would be up early to prepare. Liam yawned, rubbing a hand over his face, his stomach growling again. The smell of fresh bread reached his nose, prompting him to get out of bed. Liam threw on clothes before going downstairs, nearly running into several women.

"Gretta?" he called out, alarm lining his voice. "What's going on?"

She fought her way through the gaggle of women, swatting one away with a rag when she wouldn't move. "Did we wake ye, Liam?"

"No," Liam assured her, "my stomach did."

Gretta smiled, amusement dancing in her eyes. "Are ye hungry, then?"

"Famished."

"Ye'll have to eat in the dining room," Gretta said. "There's no room left in the kitchen."

Liam rested a hand on each of her shoulders to slow her down.

Before Liam could say anything, Gretta spoke again, "Is there somethin' the matter with ye?" she asked.

He kissed her, taking his time in ending it. "Good morning."

"Good morning," she dreamily repeated, smiling.

"I'll go wait in the dining room," Liam told her. "Is Jamie awake yet?"

"Not yet. Ye can wake him after ye eat and help him ready himself."

Liam kissed her again, retreating into the dining room.

After he ate, Liam went upstairs to find Jamie. He was still in his bed, staring at the ceiling. Jamie looked at Liam when he stepped into the room.

"I dinna think I slept at all," Jamie admitted without prompting.

Motioning for Jamie to move over, Liam sat on the edge of the bed. "You're nervous?"

"Aye," he confirmed. "And excited."

"Your mother wants me to help you get ready."

Jamie snorted. "She doesna think I can ready myself?"

"No. She knows what it's like to be nervous on her wedding day," Liam told him. "You don't want to have a cut face when you see your bride for the first time, do you?"

"No," Jamie admitted.

"All right, then." Liam patted his leg succinctly. "Up and eat something, Son. You'll need your strength for the day."

Jamie nodded, pulling his knees up to move around Liam.

"Come find me when you're finished, and don't let those women downstairs bully you into letting them stuff every food known to man down your gullet! You'll end up vomiting all over the place," Liam called after Jamie as he left the room.

Liam took the opportunity to bathe and shave while Jamie was downstairs. As happy as he was for Jamie, Liam was a little jealous. Liam didn't know if he would ever be able to settle permanently. As nice as it was to live with Gretta and the boys, it was the closest he would probably ever come to marriage.

"Sit," commanded Liam, mixing the shaving cream with a shaving brush.

Jamie sat in the chair by the window, inhaling deeply. "I can shave myself, ye ken."

"You can shave yourself tomorrow," Liam told him. "Your hands are shaking."

Sighing, Jamie sat back. "Have ye seen Ellie yet?"

Liam brushed on the shaving cream as he spoke, "Not yet. I probably won't see her until you do."

Jamie sighed nervously again, closing his eyes and tilting his head back for Liam to start under his chin.

"Stay still," Liam instructed, pulling out his straight razor and sharpening it briefly before putting it to Jamie's cheek.

Jamie started to speak, but Liam interrupted him before he could. "And don't speak. I can't shave you while you're talking."

Gretta knocked on the door, coming in with freshly laundered britches, vest, and shirt. "Are ye ready to be dressed, Jamie?"

"He will be in a moment," Liam told her. "Leave them here, and you can ready yourself. How long do we have?"

"An hour," Gretta said. "Ye'll need to hurry."

Liam finished shaving Jamie, cleaning his supplies. "Do you need any help dressing?"

"I think I can do it myself," Jamie confirmed, an amused look on his face.

Liam followed directly behind Jamie as he walked in front of the crowd of people attending the wedding for him. They journeyed outside of the town to the large weeping willow everyone in the small town of Numetra married at. Olam's wizened face had been carved into it to bless every union.

Jamie stood in front of the yellow spray of leaves, waiting for Ellie's party to join them. Liam and Gretta stood to the side, in front of the invited guests, Eli's hand in Gretta's. Simon stood next to his brother as his witness, whispering to Jamie as he shifted nervously.

A man in a blue robe and mask of grayed wood arrived, standing in front of the marriage tree. Liam was sure the face carved into the wood was important, but he couldn't have said who. All he knew was that it wasn't Olam, as his face was very different on the willow behind them.

When a look of wonderment crossed Jamie's face, Liam turned to see Ellie leading her family and guests. She wore a new dress with a flower crown atop her head, two blue ribbons trailing behind her. She stood across from Jamie, another girl Liam had never seen before standing at her side in a similar outfit.

Liam felt Gretta slip her hand into his when Jamie held out a hand to Ellie, his face alight with excitement. Ellie grabbed it, giving him a nervous smile.

"Thank ye all for comin'," Jamie said loud enough for everyone to hear. "We'll be sayin' our words, an' then we'll go to the Smilin' Fox."

Silence fell over the crowd as they waited for the priest to start the ceremony.

Liam's brow furrowed as the priest spoke in a tongue he didn't understand. He looked around the crowd—everyone nodded along, smiles on their faces. It seemed they knew what was said. Shrugging, he squeezed Gretta's hand. He didn't need to know what was being said to know what was happening.

When the priest looked at Jamie, he nodded hurriedly. He turned to Ellie with a wide smile, grabbing both of her hands firmly in his. "Eleanor Kaneh, I receive ye as mine, so that ye may become my wife, and I yer husband."

Ellie smiled nervously, her knuckles turning white as she gripped his hands. "James McWard, I receive ye as mine, so that ye may become my husband, and I yer wife."

Liam looked down at Gretta. Her face was glowing, and she smiled with crinkled eyes when she looked up at him. Gretta would have made a beautiful bride when she married her first husband. It wasn't long ago that he had pictured himself marrying Margaret, but now he wasn't so sure he would leap at the chance.

Liam stepped forward and handed them their rings, and they exchanged them silently.

Jamie pulled Ellie close and kissed her to seal their contract. They pulled away from each other, blushing when the crowd clapped.

Gretta waited until the clapping stopped before announcing, "To the Smiling Fox!"

47

Margaret had grown to enjoy going to court once more. Her stomach would tighten excitedly when she wondered if Duke Fradure was there or not. She felt guilty each night that the king came to her, thinking about the time she had spent with the duke and his son. Samuel had grown close to Margaret, sometimes wanting to be closer to her than his father.

Rowan smiled when Samuel ran to greet Margaret as she entered the room.

Margaret knelt to receive his greeting, wrapping her arms around him and holding him close to her. She had not followed the king's order to stay away from Rowan, but she had made sure that they stayed in the grand hall so that they could be seen and never alone as he had commanded her in the gardens. Margaret led Samuel back to his father, a bright smile coming to her face.

Rowan watched her affectionately, kissing her knuckles when she got close to him. "Dearest Margaret."

Margaret smiled at him again. "Rowan, I'm glad you're here."

"I am too," he said to her.

Margaret still had nobles looking at her with knowing eyes. The gossip had run rampant about her, but it was starting to die out due to her courtship with the duke. Rowan ignored any rumor that reached his ear, not believing Margaret capable of such an act, and she did not correct him. Sorren had questioned her intently on whether she had become the duke's lover, as he had not shied away from her.

Rowan circulated the room with Margaret on his arm until the king stopped them. "Your Grace, may I borrow Lady Margaret for a moment?"

Rowan hesitantly let go of Margaret. "As you wish, Your Majesty."

Margaret went with the king. "What is happening, Your Majesty?"

"You'll see, my dear," the king told her with a boyish grin. They stood at the front of the hall, the king clearing his throat. "My lords and ladies, in honor of her father who has been gone two years now, I would like to present to you the Countess of Dorcia. As a gift for her appointment, I am extending her lands to encase the town my dear friend Jerone so dearly loved, Silvica."

Margaret gasped, looking at him. She could hardly believe the words that came out of his mouth. What had finally changed his mind? "Your Majesty, that is too much!"

"Think nothing of it, Countess," the king said.

Margaret curtsied low to him before rejoining Rowan, her face beaming, even though the gathered courtiers were staring at her and whispering—surely, spreading more rumors of a continuing affair. "This is such wonderful news!"

Rowan tucked her hand into the crook of his arm as they started walking again. "I'm very happy for you," he said with a smile. "Your lands now extend into mine. Or what used to be mine, rather."

"I would like to take a tour of my new lands soon to show my people my face," Margaret told Rowan. "I don't see how His Majesty could say no to a tour."

"I think that's a wonderful idea, and perhaps you would also take the time to take a tour of my own lands?" Rowan asked her, quickly adding, "With Samuel and me, of course."

Margaret's cheeks started to color. "I would like that very much."

Rowan kissed her hand. "We'll set a date and explore our part of the country."

That night, Margaret was particularly affectionate with the king. "What made you change your mind concerning my lands and title?" Margaret asked, tucked under his arm, her head resting on his shoulder. To be honest, she wasn't quite sure she cared. She was just relieved to have her title and lands officially be hers.

"There needs to be someone with real authority managing the land, and not just your business that nobody manages," Sorren said, stroking her hair.

Margaret sat up on her forearm, a grin on her face. "Whatever the reason, I'm very happy that you did."

The king gently touched her cheek with one finger, looking at her tenderly. "Good," he said, "I like making you happy."

The new countess smiled brightly at him. "If that's the case, I wonder if I might go on a tour of my lands now that I have my title."

Sorren shifted to look at her directly. "I'll give you my permission so long as you promise that you'll return to court."

"I promise." Margaret decided to leave out the fact Rowan would be going with her. That would be the duke's business to ask permission or not.

Margaret had nearly forgotten about Charles with his lack of communication until the king mentioned him. With everything that had happened since her father's funeral, all of her time was occupied. Margaret readied herself that morning, wearing a black and cream-colored dress. The neckline was a modest one, the bodice made of cream-colored fabric, the light colored fabric going all the way down the front of the dress to the floor. The rest of her dress was black, cinching together at her waist with the ties crossing over in a diamond pattern. The sleeves were tight on her arms, opening up at her wrists to form a small train, revealing an interior of the cream fabric.

Margaret decided to leisurely walk to Charles's home in the city with Captain Vojvo.

"You seem happy, my lady," Vojvo commented.

"I am," Margaret told him. "I am going on a tour with His Grace, and I can finally be free of the king for a time."

"That will certainly make us both happy," Vojvo agreed intently.

"We'll be leaving in two weeks so that we can hopefully reach my family home before the winter," Margaret told him.

Vojvo brightened. "Will you need me to pick out a large guard or a small one, my lady?"

"A small one, I think," Margaret said slowly, a ponderous look on her face. "Duke Fradure will surely bring his own guard as well."

"Very good, my lady." The captain looked years younger with the smile donning his face.

Margaret did not have the tightening in her stomach as she had the previous times she had gone to the Luthers' home in the city. Margaret's feelings had waned for the man she once thought was the only one who could make her happy. The butler opened the door to the house, a somber-looking man with dark hair littered with white streaks. "The Countess of Dorcia for Mr. Luther, please."

"Right this way, my lady," the butler droned, extending his arm out toward the drawing room.

Margaret looked at the captain. "Would you wait here, please?"

"Yes, my lady," Vojvo said, stepping down to stand guard at the door.

Margaret went into the drawing room, sitting on the pink couch to wait for Charles. The room had not changed since the last time she had been in it. She was glad that Charlotte was not there to stare at her in silent contempt.

Charles looked surprised to see Margaret sitting in his drawing room when he entered. "Lady Margaret, what are you doing here?"

Margaret stood, clasping her hands in front of her. "You wouldn't answer any of my letters or summons," she said with a hint of irritation. "The news I have is too important for you to ignore me any longer."

"What news is that, Lady Margaret?" Charles shifted uncomfortably. Clearly, it still did not sit well with him that she had kissed him at her father's funeral.

"Not only have I been officially granted my title by His Majesty, but I have been granted the lands to include Silvica and extending to touch the borders of the other provinces."

"What does this have to do with me and the business?" Charles asked shortly.

Margaret frowned at him. How had she ever thought such a petulant man to be the greatest thing Theotes could send her way? "Charles, are you still upset over my kissing you? It was over a year ago!"

Charles gave her a hard look. "Lady Margaret, it was inappropriate for you to behave that way, and it seems I'm not the only one you've been inappropriate with."

"I beg your pardon?" Margaret could feel her hackles raise.

"You seem to have a problem with appropriate behavior with married men."

"Are you speaking of His Majesty?" Margaret asked coldly.

"Yes," Charles said, raising his voice. "The king you've been having an affair with."

"Rumor," Margaret said. "Rumor started by the queen and her ladies because I have a close friendship with the king, blown out of proportion by Sir Adam."

Charles did not seem placated by Margaret's explanation. "Again, Lady Margaret, what does this news have to do with me and the business?"

"I want you to expand the business with the new lands, Charles. You've refused to help me understand the business any further after our kiss, so either do this, or I will find someone to replace you," Margaret said firmly. "You will be including me from now on in your decision-making, and I want regular reports on how the business is faring."

Charles raised his eyebrows at the threat of being replaced by another executor. "As you wish, Lady Margaret."

Margaret smoothed the front of her dress. "I will be leaving for a tour of my lands soon, but I expect a summary of all that's been happening when I return."

"Yes, Lady Margaret," the older man said stiffly, his face red. "Will there be anything else?"

"No, that will be all for now, Charles," Margaret dismissed irritably.

Charles frigidly bowed to her, leaving the room without another word.

Margaret sighed, leaving the house without the butler to escort her.

"How did everything go, my lady?" Vojvo asked, peeling himself from the wall upon her exit.

"Strained." Margaret's mouth formed a thin line. "He has yet to get over the kiss I gave him."

"Might I make a suggestion, my lady?" When Margaret nodded, he continued, "I know he was your father's man, but he will only see you in that moment from now on. Perhaps it is time to pay him a sizable retirement and look for a replacement and have someone more reliable at your side."

Margaret sighed heavily. He was right, but she wasn't sure she could bring herself to do it yet. "I might need to if he doesn't do as he's bid upon my return."

"Very good, my lady," he said. "Shall we return to the palace? Or do you need to purchase luggage for your travel?"

"Oh, yes." Margaret grinned. "We'll need lots of luggage."

 # 48

S arah went to find George in the city. She would be leaving with Lady Margaret tomorrow. With the extension of her property, Lady Margaret would have to inform the tenants of their change of landlords, and it was a duty the king could not stop her from doing. Sarah wanted to tell George that she would be gone for an undetermined amount of time before they left.

She snuck up behind the tall redhead and wrapped her arms around his waist. Grinning, George turned around. "Lamb, what are you doing here?"

"I wanted to see you," Sarah told him, keeping her arms firmly in place. "Lady Margaret is going on a tour of her lands soon, and I with her."

George frowned at the name. "Is she the same Lady Margaret we've all been hearing so much about? The one havin' an affair with the king?"

Sarah pulled back from him slightly, hesitating. "She is."

"I don't know if I like you bein' involved with someone like that, Sarah," George told her sternly.

"You don't like me being involved with someone like that?" she asked incredulously.

George nodded as if there was nothing wrong with his statement. "Yes."

"And what do you actually know about Lady Margaret?" Sarah demanded, growing angry.

"That she's been sleepin' with the king since she came back to court," George said with a shrug.

"Since I have known Lady Margaret, she has started an orphanage in lands that aren't her own just because she saw the need, continues to give them well over what they need so that it can be saved for dowries for the young ladies, ensures that, in her lands, any family who is struggling is given a stipend each month until they get on their feet, and helps people that no one else will, including someone it was illegal to help because she saw his need." Sarah took a deep breath and held up her hand to stay George's protests, continuing on unhindered, "And what does she get for her troubles? Forced into an affair with the king so her people won't suffer with her lands taken over by His Majesty."

George opened his mouth to reply only to be cut off again.

"I don't know of anyone better to be involved with," Sarah finished her argument, giving a look to George that dared him to contradict her.

"I concede, lamb!" George told her quickly before she got it in her mind to chastise him some more.

"Good," Sarah said with a satisfied look on her face. "Now that we have that settled, we can have a nice time."

Shaking his head, George wrapped his arms around Sarah's shoulders and pulled her to his chest. "What am I goin' to do with you, Lamb?"

"Enjoy my company," she said into his shirt, "and not suffocate me."

George relented in his grip only slightly, letting her move her face. "Do you have time to eat dinner with me?"

"Lady Margaret gave me the evening off to do just that," Sarah said with a smile.

Sarah went with him to the Whistling Squire to have a last meal before returning to the palace. As always, she let George order for her. He had a gift for knowing exactly what she wanted without her having to tell him. She smiled as she watched him, enjoying how well he knew her.

"I'm going to miss you while I'm gone," she said when the barmaid left.

"I'm going to miss you too," George told her, holding out his hand to her, wrapping his large fingers around her hand when she accepted his offer.

"I don't know how long we'll be away," Sarah told him as she squeezed his hand.

"I'll be here, waitin' for you to come back."

Sarah smiled brightly at him. "I'm very happy to hear that."

"Perhaps when you come back, Lady Margaret will consider lettin' you marry," he gave the proposal nonchalantly, but his eyes were settled intently on her face.

"Oh?" Sarah's cheeks heated, her eyes alight with excitement.

"To me, of course," George added quickly. "If you wanted to."

Sarah grinned at him. "Of course I would want to."

"That makes me very happy, Lamb." He stood with a large grin on his face, yelling out to the barmaid. "Wine for me—and my fiancée!"

A cheer went up through the inn at the announcement, the barmaid bringing them their wine.

Sarah returned to Lady Margaret's chambers, her cheeks flushed and eyes bright. "My lady?" she called out quietly.

Lady Margaret came out of her bedchambers, her dress halfway on. "Sarah? Is there something wrong?"

"No, my lady," Sarah told her, going to help her mistress with her dress. "I have some news, and you are my only family to share it with."

"What is it?" Lady Margaret asked with her eyebrows raised.

"I am engaged to be married, my lady," Sarah told her brightly. "To George."

"That is wonderful news, Sarah!" she exclaimed, pulling Sarah into a tight hug.

"You have no objections?" Sarah asked, worry coming to her face.

"Of course I have no objections," Lady Margaret told her, still smiling. "I'm happy for the two of you."

Sarah let out a relieved sigh. "And you would let me stay on, even if I married?"

"Of course, I don't see why I shouldn't." Lady Margaret furrowed her brow. "I wouldn't want anyone else here with me."

49

"Margaret?"

Margaret came out of her bedchamber with an armful of dresses in hand. "Rowan!" Margaret dropped the dresses and went to him.

Rowan wrapped his arms around her. "Are you almost ready?"

She smiled up at him. "Almost. One more hour, and I'll be ready...maybe."

"Maybe?" Rowan raised his brows, an amused smile twisting his lips. "You know we're on a schedule."

"I know." Margaret pouted at him, her bottom lip pushed forward only slightly. "This is my first pilgrimage of lands...I don't know what to bring."

Rowan smiled tenderly at her, looking over her face. "One hour, my dear, and then we're leaving—with or without all you're intending to pack."

Margaret scrunched her nose but flitted away to finish packing nonetheless. "Sarah, hurry!" she commanded as she dragged dresses to the chests.

"I'll see you in one hour," Rowan called from her door before leaving.

Margaret looked around the room hopelessly. There was so much to do before they left. She packed hurriedly, going over the day as she worked. She had left a note for the king earlier that morning to inform him she would be leaving that afternoon. She hoped she could avoid seeing him until she left, with Rowan as a barrier.

She packed as much as she could before Sarah took over, waving her away. Apparently, she was doing it wrong. Margaret went to the chairs by the bay windows to wait until Rowan returned. She was looking forward to spending months away from the king coming to her rooms or taking her out of conversations for the pleasure of her company.

Margaret stood when her door was opened without invitation.

"Maggie!" Samuel yelled, running to her, arms outstretched.

Margaret smiled and knelt for his hug. "My little darling," she said, holding him close. Margaret looked up at Rowan with a smile on her face.

"Are you all packed?" Rowan asked.

"That you will have to ask Sarah about. She took over," Margaret told him.

Sarah came out of Margaret's bedchambers. "My lady, everything you need is packed. Would you like to go over what's left to see if there's anything I missed?"

When Rowan helped Margaret stand, she said, "Yes, thank you, Sarah." She offered her hand to Samuel.

Samuel took it and followed her into her bedchambers. He looked around curiously. Margaret picked him up to go through the clothes that she had left, asking his opinion on each one of them. She ended up packing three more dresses for their trip.

Rowan wrapped his arm around her. "I love how wonderful you are with him."

"Are we all ready to leave?" Margaret turned so she was out of his arm, smiling at him. "My guard is waiting for orders, and I know the captain is anxious to be on the road again."

"Of course," Rowan said. "We'll have servants bring down the rest of your things, and the three of us will say our goodbyes." Rowan kissed her knuckles. "Don't keep me waiting."

"I won't," Margaret promised as Rowan left with Samuel. She couldn't if she tried. There was no one she wanted to say any parting words to.

Margaret went to the courtyard, where the loaded wagons and Captain Vojvo waited.

"My lady," Vojvo said to her and bowed.

"Captain." Margaret looked around the wagons where her things were being loaded. "Is everything running smoothly?"

"Absolutely, my lady," Vojvo told her. "Everything will be on the wagons shortly, and the party can make its way to Dorcia."

Margaret inhaled deeply, excitement building in her. She couldn't wait to go home. Couldn't wait to escape this place.

Vojvo cleared his throat and bowed. "Your Majesty."

Turning slowly, she tried to hide her dismay. "Your Majesty. Have we not already said our goodbyes?"

"Step away," Sorren said, waving his hand at Vojvo.

Vojvo glanced at Margaret before nodding and walking to the other side of the carriage.

Margaret clasped her hands tightly in front of her. "How can I help Your Majesty?"

Sorren stepped closer to her, grabbing her arm tightly. "I wanted to remind you that you are required to return." He leaned in to make sure he looked directly into her eyes. "If you don't, I will drag you back, kicking and screaming, by your hair if I have to."

She swallowed hard, her stomach curling. "Yes, Your Majesty."

"Good." He let go of her, walking away without another word.

Margaret let out a shuddering breath. She couldn't get away fast enough.

Rowan joined Margaret and Sarah in the courtyard. He smiled when Samuel went to Margaret and put his hand in hers. "May I help you in the carriage, Margaret?"

Margaret helped Samuel into the carriage and placed her hand in Rowan's to help her in. Samuel switched sides to sit with Margaret, and Rowan was forced to sit opposite Margaret.

"Are you ready?"

Margaret looked out the window, the king's warning still fresh in her ear. "Very."

CONTINUE THE STORY!

THE ANATALIAN
KING

BOOKS2READ.COM/ANATALIANKING

About The Author

Rebecca Mikkelson has been writing fantasy stories since her early teens for fun and was thrilled to turn her dream into a reality when she was published for the first time in an anthology. She currently lives in Maryland with her husband and three cats.

In her free time, Rebecca likes to cross stitch to relax when her cats aren't hogging the embroidery floss. She also enjoys reading a wide variety of books, ranging from non-fiction biographies of historical figures and families to high fantasy.

As well as being an author, Rebecca works as the editor-in-chief at Authors 4 Authors Publishing, which she helped start in 2018.

Follow her online:

RebeccaMikkelson.com
TikTok: **@zebookverm**
Twitter: **@zebookverm**
Instagram/Threads: **@authorRebeccaMikkelson**
Facebook: **@RebeccaMikkelsonAuthor**

Authors 4 Authors Publishing

A publishing company for authors, run by authors, blending the best of traditional and independent publishing

We specialize in speculative fiction: science fiction, fantasy, paranormal, and romance. Get lost in another world!

Check out our collection at https://books2read.com/rl/a4a or visit Authors4AuthorsPublishing.com/books

For updates, scan the QR code or visit our website to join our semi-monthly newsletter!

Want more historical fantasy? We recommend:

One Thousand and One Days
by Renee Frey

Sutaita, daughter of the Sultan's vizier, planned on a life of quiet study. But when she learns she and her sister must be the next two brides for the bloodthirsty Sultan Shahryar al'Mamun, Sutaita decides to change their fortune. Staying alive by telling stories every night, she must buy enough time to solve the mysteries surrounding the Sultan's edict. In this retelling of the Arabian Nights frame story, can Sutaita slip past the walls around the Sultan's heart and soul? Or will she end up like so many brides before—with her head on a chopping block?

books2read.com/1001Days